Praise for Jodi Ellen Malpas

"Super steamy, emotionally intense."

—*Library Journal* on *With This Man*

"The raw emotion and vulnerability is breathtaking."

—*RT Book Reviews* on *With This Man*

"A brave, cutting-edge romance...This is a worthwhile read."

—*Library Journal* on *The Forbidden*

"Unpredictable and addictive."

—*Booklist* on *The Forbidden*

"*The Forbidden* proves that Jodi Ellen Malpas is not only one of the romance genre's most talented authors, but also one of the bravest. In this raw and honest portrayal of forbidden love, Jodi delivers a sexy and passionate love story with characters to root for."

—Shelly Bell, author of *At His Mercy*

"*The Forbidden* is a gut-wrenching tale full of passion, angst, and heart! Not to be missed!"

—*Harlequin Junkie*

"Every kiss, every sexy scene, every word between this pair owned a piece of my soul. I could read this book a hundred times and still react as if it was the first time. *The Protector* is a top 2016 fave for me."

—Audrey Carlan, #1 bestselling author of the Calendar Girl series

GENTLEMAN
SINNER

Also by Jodi Ellen Malpas

This Man Series

This Man

Beneath This Man

This Man Confessed

All I Am: Drew's Story (a novella)

With This Man

One Night Trilogy

One Night: Promised

One Night: Denied

One Night: Unveiled

Standalones

The Protector

The Forbidden

GENTLEMAN
SINNER

JODI ELLEN MALPAS

FOREVER

New York   Boston

Copyright © 2019 by Jodi Ellen Malpas

Cover design and photography by Elizabeth Turner Stokes
Cover copyright © 2019 by Hachette Book Group, Inc.

Forever
Hachette Book Group
1290 Avenue of the Americas, New York, NY 10104
read-forever.com
twitter.com/readforeverpub

First Edition: February 2019

Forever is an imprint of Grand Central Publishing. The Forever name and logo are trademarks of Hachette Book Group, Inc.

The publisher is not responsible for websites (or their content) that are not owned by the publisher.

The Hachette Speakers Bureau provides a wide range of authors for speaking events. To find out more, go to www.hachettespeakersbureau.com or call (866) 376-6591.

Library of Congress Control Number: 2018958422

ISBNs: 978-1-5387-4524-3 (trade paperback), 978-1-5387-4523-6 (ebook)

Printed in the United States of America

LSC-C

10 9 8 7 6 5 4 3 2 1

For Andy—my champion from day one

GENTLEMAN
SINNER

CHAPTER 1

I grapple with the fingers clawed around my neck, fighting to pry them away. The strength behind their hold defies reason, and it's beginning to make me sweat. My windpipe is being crushed, making me gasp for breath. Fucking hell, he's going to strangle me to death. Flashbacks bombard me—his face, his voice loaded with evil intent.

I'm in a hospital, I remind myself. I'm safe in a hospital. The reminder is hard to believe when you're choking to death. With no other option left, I lunge for the red emergency button above his bed, smashing my fist into it before trying again to pry his fingers away from my neck.

"Izzy!" I hear my name being shouted, and suddenly more hands are around my throat, helping me. "Frank, let her go," Susan warns, as stern as usual. "Some help would be good, Pam!"

Pam appears, too, forcing Frank back to the bed by his shoulders. I nearly land on my arse when I'm released from the old man's clutches, his long fingernails dragging across the delicate flesh of my neck as he's forced away. Staggering back, I gasp for oxygen, drinking it down urgently as I leave Susan and Pam to calm Frank down.

My hands smooth over the side of my neck, the sting making me hiss a little. "Shit," I breathe, checking the tips of my fingers for blood. There's none, but, Jesus, it stings like hell. Frank has a few pointless shouts before relenting to the small army of nurses and flopping back on his bed, huffing and moaning about being held prisoner.

"Now, now, Frank," Susan placates him, sounding all jolly. "That wasn't very nice, was it?" She pats the covers around his legs. "Izzy was only trying to help you."

"Sheila will be wondering where I am," Frank barks, pointing a bent finger at Susan before turning it on me. "You Nazis! You can't keep me here!"

Pam gives me a concerned look, and I shake my head, telling her I'm fine, before I straighten myself out and move in to help Susan.

"Let's get you well and you can go home," I say soothingly. I pour him some water and hand him the cup, being super vigilant for any sign he might attempt to wring my neck again. He snorts but takes the water and sips it, his hand shaking. The poor man. He won't be getting well, and he won't be going home. Sheila, his wife of five decades, has been dead for fifteen years, God love him. His daughter can't look after him anymore, and he can no longer live alone. It's not safe, which leaves him in hospital until alternative arrangements can be made. Whenever that might be.

I straighten and take the blood pressure monitor, rolling it away. Susan, the ward sister, falls into stride next to me, checking her watch. "You've been pushed and pulled about this week, Izzy," she muses, giving me a sideways smile. "Let's have a look."

I wave my hand flippantly, brushing her off. "It's nothing."

"I'll be the judge of that," she scolds, pulling me to a stop and pushing my shoulder-length wavy black hair away from my neck. "I thought you asked Pam to cut his nails."

I wince, not wanting to get my colleague into trouble. "I did?"

Susan rolls her eyes at my feigned ignorance. "C'mon. It's the end of your shift. Let's get handover done so you can go home." She turns and marches to her office, her round bottom swaying, and I follow as I feel at my sore skin, damning myself for not getting through this shift unscathed. It just means more paperwork.

After half an hour of handovers and completing forms, I make my way to the maternity unit to see Jess before heading home. I spot her through the glass of the double doors, and her face lights up as she makes her way down the corridor to let me in. Her blond curls are pulled back into a tidy bun, with a few wayward strands poking out here and there, indicating that she's well into her shift. She pushes the door open and ushers me inside, and the sound of wailing babies hits me from every direction. "Jesus, there's some serious lung exercises going on tonight," I say on a laugh. My best friend nods her agreement and wipes her hands down the front of her dress. She's a midwife, and a great one. We met at college and have shared a flat since we were eighteen. She is literally my only family.

"There must be a full moon," Jess says, her eyes landing on my neck. "Wow, that's a bad one."

I reach up and feel again, wincing, my fingers slipping across the antiseptic cream. "Frank made a bid for freedom."

"Damn, girl, you should have followed my lead. Babies can't strangle you."

"No, but women in labor can."

"That's why we have birthing partners." She winks, and I chuckle, buttoning up my coat, ready to face the cold.

"What time are you done?" I ask.

"Six in the morning."

My face bunches in sympathy. The red-eye shift. "Don't wake me when you come in." I dip and kiss her cheek, just as an almighty bellow rings through the air, a woman in labor screaming to high heaven. "I'm never having children." I shudder, backing away to the door.

"Yeah, me either," Jess confirms. "Hey, only a week to go!"

The mention of our upcoming trip makes me grin like a fool. "Vegas, baby," I call, hearing more screams. They flatten both of our smiles and remind us that we have a few more shifts to go before we can get *really* excited. "There's a vagina awaiting your presence."

Jess sighs and wanders off. "I've seen enough vaginas to last me a lifetime, but I plan on counteracting them with nothing but cock in Vegas." She looks over her shoulder, all coy, and a laugh rumbles up from my tummy, erupting and drowning out the pleas for drugs coming from the room down the corridor. "Time to push, sweetheart!" she sings, all enthusiastic to her patient as she disappears. I smile and let myself out of the maternity unit.

After collecting a takeaway tea from the café, I break into the cool winter evening and start the long walk home. The fresh air instantly starts to soothe my tired body after my long shift. Walking to and from work isn't just done out of necessity. On my way to the hospital, the brisk half-hour walk does a grand job of waking me up, readying me for my shift. On my way home, the lazy stroll helps me clear my mind and wind me down. Besides, I couldn't afford a car even if it made sense to have one. Which it doesn't. The drive would probably take twice as long as the walk, and parking at the Royal London is nearly impossible.

As I sip my tea, I check my phone, faltering a split second when I see a missed call from an unknown number. I clear the screen and round a corner, trying not to let my imagination run away with me. It's probably just a sales call, I tell myself. Or one of those irritating marketing surveys. It couldn't possibly be him after all this time. Ten years since I ran. It's been ten years since I escaped him.

I stuff my hands into the pockets of my mac, bringing my

shoulders up to my ears to keep the chill at bay, and march briskly on my way, pushing the memories away, but never the heartache. It's particularly chilly tonight, but I smile, thinking Vegas will be hot, hot, hot. My first holiday in years. I can't wa—

A loud noise from behind startles me, and I stop to glance back, wary, before scanning the street for other pedestrians. There are none, just the dim glow of the streetlights in the darkness. Warehouses on the other side of the street have stood empty for as long as I can remember, and the row of houses on the same side as me are mostly boarded up. Jess nagged me constantly when she found out I took this little shortcut, to the point I told her that I wouldn't go this way anymore. But I've done it for years, and it shaves a good ten minutes off my journey. There's usually someone taking the same route. But not tonight.

The hairs on the back of my neck rise as another crash echoes around me. It prompts my feet back into action, and I start an urgent walk away from the sounds, constantly looking over my shoulder. My apprehension lessens the closer I come to the end of the street, toward the main road, but then a low, pain-filled whimper pulls me to an abrupt stop. I turn around, hearing the sound of a car screeching off in the opposite direction. And as soon as the loud noise of the engine fades, more whimpers. Instinct kicks in and takes me back down the street, despite my uneasiness. Someone's hurt. I can't just walk away. Maybe it's the nurse in me. Or maybe it's simple human nature.

I break into a jog, trying to keep my footsteps as quiet as possible so I can listen for where the noise is coming from. I catch another low cry. It's a woman. I pick up speed, reaching the entrance to an alleyway. I can't see a damn thing. "Hello?" I call, pulling my phone from my bag.

"Please help me," a woman begs, distress evident in her voice. "Please."

"I'm here. Just a second." I faff with my phone, searching for the light feature, flicking it on and shining it down the black alleyway. A woman comes into view, propped up against a brick wall. "Oh my God, are you okay?" I rush toward her, using my phone to guide me, until I'm crouched by her side, assessing her. She looks dazed, and as I shine the light in her eyes, I conclude very quickly that she's concussed. I scan her slight frame, searching her body for injuries. Her clothes instantly make me wonder if she's a hooker. Sadly, I see them at the hospital all the time.

"What's your name?" I ask, pushing her hair from her face and finding a tidy cut over her eyebrow. My teeth grate, and she doesn't answer, her head heavy and rolling. "Can you hear me?" I ask, dropping to my knees and putting down my bag. She still doesn't respond, so I work fast but carefully, getting her into the recovery position. "I'm getting help," I tell her, dialing for an ambulance.

But before the call connects, two hands grab me from behind and yank me back, shoving me aside with a pissed-off grunt. I yelp, shocked, and my phone topples and smashes against the ground. My only light is now gone, leaving me blind and panicked. I scramble back on my arse, my feet sliding across the dirty cobbles of the alley. Fear rips through me so fast it takes my heart rate from steady to wild in a beat. It's a familiar fear, and that only amplifies my panic.

I can't see a thing, but I can smell, and my nose is assaulted by the stale stench of old sweat and alcohol as flashbacks attack me, beating down the high walls that I fight to keep intact. A low whimper reminds me of the woman who is barely conscious next to me, and I reach for her, trying to find her fingers so I can squeeze some reassurance into her.

The sharpest of pains bolts through my hand when it's callously kicked away, and I cry out, bringing it to my chest protectively and sucking back my tears. I've just walked straight into danger. What was I thinking? How could I be so stupid? But part of me can't be sorry for venturing down here, for trying to help. At the very least, I hope I've halved the blows the woman next to me will be subjected to. After all, I can take them. It'll be nothing I haven't felt before. I close my eyes and see the monster who tormented me, and then his hand as it flies through the air toward my cheek.

Thwack!

I wince, my face bursting into flames when a hand, one that's not from my memories, connects with my cheek. But I beat back my tears, locating the grit I called on many years ago but haven't needed since, the strength and fortitude to just survive. I shut my mind down and wait for the next hit, breathing in more calm.

"You should have kept walking, bitch." His foul odor is starting to get down my throat, making me heave, and my body jerks forward when he grabs the front of my coat, yanking me up, breathing all over me. I open my eyes, not only to remind myself that I don't know this man, but because his face is close and I might get a glimpse in the darkness. Teeth—dirty, rotten, jagged teeth are the first thing I see, chapped lips grinning around them. "Tryin' to help the poor slag, huh?"

I look up and see pure, filthy evil in his eyes, his pupils dilated. I've seen eyes like these before. They're eyes full of cruel intentions. I keep my mouth shut, knowing I shouldn't fuel the situation, but when his grubby hand reaches for my thigh and strokes up toward my stomach, and then to my breast, I whimper, my fear reaching new heights. I can take a few slaps, but that. No. No, I can't go there again. I'll fight him with all I have. "Please no."

"Hmmm," he hums, his nasty grin widening. "Think I'll have a taste, since you seem so—" He's cut off dead in his tracks when the roar of an engine saturates the air, and the alleyway is suddenly illuminated by headlights. I squint, blinded by the sudden brightness, and blink back some of the glare, working to gain some focus, my heart beating wildly. I can feel his grip on me loosen. "Fuck," he curses, his voice now shaky rather than menacing. I hear a car door slam. I hear pounding footsteps. And then my attacker is suddenly catapulting backward with a startled yell, jerking me sharply as his hands are ripped away from my coat. The sound of him hitting the bricks of the wall opposite makes me flinch, and when my vision clears, I recoil, seeing the back of a rather large man towering over the trembling body of the scum who was about to...

I shake my head violently, not prepared to allow my mind to go there. Whoever has just shown up seems as menacing, though definitely better dressed. He's wearing a suit, his blond hair wavy and falling to his ears. The headlights bathing the alley give me a perfect view as he drags the arsehole who just cuffed my face up the wall by his sweater. I'm held rapt by the widening of his eyes, the evidence of narcotics lessening by the second, being replaced with fear.

"No, please," my attacker cries, pushing himself further against the wall.

The suited stranger says nothing, just holds him by his throat against the wall, making the man's eyes bulge. I can't move. Dare not, either. But when a faint whimper sinks into my ears, I look down at the woman beside me. She's restless, her bare legs kicking out, her head rolling. My natural instinct has me on the ground next to her in a heartbeat, with no consideration for strange suited, *large* men and drugged-up arseholes.

I shush her gently and move in close, feeling so sorry for her when she turns her face into me and nuzzles into my neck, like she's hiding. Like she's looking for protection. I don't know why, but I sense it's here now. "It's okay," I whisper, rubbing her bare arm, feeling how cold she is. I quickly check her pulse and then remove my coat, fighting to get it around her shoulders, focusing on her and not what could be a pretty nasty scene a few feet away. I have no tolerance for men who knock women around. But I also can't bear violence.

My attention remains on the woman until the sound of a car door shutting pierces the air. The spaced, even beats of shoes hitting the ground fill my ears, almost ominous in their approach. The suited guy is still across the way holding my panicked attacker against the wall, which tells me the footsteps are someone else's. I wrap my arm around the woman's shoulders and cast my eyes to the right until they find the car, which I note through my shock is a Bentley. And then my view is suddenly hindered by a pair of trouser-covered legs. Long legs. Thick legs. Strong legs. My eyes slowly start to creep upward, over thighs, a suit-jacket-covered torso, a neck...

Until I get to a face.

His piercing blue eyes force me to blink back the shine.

I swallow, inhale, and hold my breath as he looms over me.

He might be wearing a suit, but his strength isn't concealed. He's a muscular beast of a man. My mouth falls a little lax on my exhale, my mind unable to comprehend such formidable power. He looks frightening, yet those cobalt eyes hold a softness within them as he stares down at me, his brown hair limp and falling across his forehead. "Who are you?" His deep, rough voice penetrates my skin.

I remain mute, just staring, my mind working hard to try to tell me whether I should be scared.

"Who. Are. You?" he demands, sounding menacing.

"I was walking home from work," I rush to explain. "And heard..." My words fade when I realize I don't know the name of the woman in my arms.

"Penny," he prompts, nodding toward the woman. "Her name is Penny."

I swallow nervously, unable to stop my eyes from scanning the pile of muscle and power standing over me. He knows this woman? "I heard Penny. She sounded distressed."

His head cocks in question. "And you came to help?"

I frown a little. "Yes."

His stare starts to burn my skin, so intense it makes me want to look away before I turn to dust. He is positively terrifying, yet some primal instinct tells me I'm in no danger. And neither is Penny. The other man, however, most definitely is.

The guy standing over me flicks his gaze to his associate briefly before it lands on Penny for a second, obviously checking her, and then settles back on me. The deep warmth that rests under my skin makes me feel uneasy. He's a handsome man. I can see it past the harshness of his expression—his bristly jaw tight, his huge body tense. But, God, anyone would have to be certifiably nuts to mess with him. I can't help taking in as much of him as I can, and there's a lot of him. It's all inappropriately impressive. I wonder where my fear and terror have gone. It's him. His presence, his voice. The second he showed up, I was no longer scared, and that's just plain weird, since he's freakishly big and actually quite frightening. But his eyes contradict his terrifying persona.

And then I find myself settling even more when I see the most minuscule curve at the edge of his straight lips. It's not an evil smile; I'm all too familiar with those. It's an amused smile, revealing a dimple that's too cute for him.

Looking back to his associate, he nods, a silent instruction, and the guy holding the pimp in a choke hold starts pushing him on, forcing his arm up his back and kicking his feet to get him moving, ignoring the pleas for mercy. "What are you going to do to him?" I blurt, watching as he's shoved down the alleyway to constant screams of panic—panic that intensifies when a truck pulls up. He's thrown into the back, the door shuts calmly, and the truck is pulling away a second later.

I turn my attention back to the giant before me, finding he's not moved one inch. He doesn't answer me. "Here." He offers me his hand.

I clamp my lips together and hold my breath, instinctively bracing for contact. It's beyond me, but when I reach forward and he swoops in to claim my hand, I feel an immediate boom in my chest. He gives me an almost dirty look, one laced with annoyance, as his hand squeezes around mine. I'm on my feet in a second, feeling light-headed. Intoxicated. Totally unstable. What the fucking hell is that?

He quickly pulls his hand free, and I take a few steps back as he watches me putting distance between us, looking deep in thought. "What?" I ask, if only to break the suddenly uncomfortable silence.

"Your hands are so warm," he says quietly, looking down at them. "And it's so cold tonight."

"Did I burn you?" I ask on a nervous laugh, and he frowns, once again ignoring my question as he turns toward the other suited man, who's back and collecting Penny up from the ground, cradling her in his arms and carrying her to the Bentley.

"Get her back to the Playground," the guy before me orders brusquely.

"She's concussed," I blurt. I have no idea what the Playground is, but I realize that it's not a hospital.

He moves forward a step, almost threateningly. I don't move, finding the strength I need to stand my ground, and he's surprised, judging by the slight tilt of his head. "Concussed? How do you know that?"

"I'm a nurse," I explain. "She needs to go to a hospital."

"You're a nurse?"

I nod, and intrigue springs into his eyes. "She needs medical attention. I was calling for an ambulance before he..." My intended words disappear. I can't finish.

His lips twist, abhorrence rampant in his expression, taking a fraction of his good looks away. The sight, though actually very scary, fills me with reassurance, even more than his formidable presence. "No hospital," he declares, leaving no room for argument, stepping forward again.

No hospital? That's crazy. I don't care how big he is, or how frightening he appears. That woman needs treatment. "I'm afraid I have to insist," I say firmly, breaking free of his iron stare to see his associate lowering Penny carefully into the back seat of the Bentley. "I don't mind accompanying her if your presence will be a problem or spark unwanted questions." I'm not stupid. I don't know this man, but everything is telling me that people prying into the circumstances of Penny's injuries wouldn't be gratefully received. Or people prying into *him*, for that matter.

"What makes you think that?" His voice is deep and low. It's rough but silky, threatening but soothing, and his cobalt eyes seem to dance as I stare at him. He's getting a little thrill from my approach. He likes me challenging his authority.

"Instinct."

His lips quirk a touch, that dimple forming again, his eyebrows rising in amusement. His humor irritates me now, and I muster up some fortitude and step forward, showing him my determination. The look of shock on his face fascinates me. He's surprised that I'm standing up to him. Frankly, I am, too. "She needs a hospital."

His dimple deepens. "What's your name, girl?"

"Izzy." I don't hesitate to tell him, and I have no clue why. "Izzy White."

"Izzy White. I'm Theo. Theo Kane." I fall victim to his eyes again, staring in wonder. There's a certain prettiness beyond the hardness of his face, making him appear younger than I initially thought, yet his presence is that of a far more mature man.

He steps forward, offering his hand. I stare at it and roll my shoulders to rid myself of the tremor of apprehension. "Take it, Izzy."

I do, immediately, and he tugs me forward, my front coming dangerously close to his. He gulps, his hand beginning to shake, and he pulls away but doesn't release his grip, like he's having a fight with himself over whether or not to let me go. I look up at him in question, seeing that battle in his eyes. This close, I get to truly appreciate his height, my level vision falling just below his throat. Jesus, he's a mountain.

Constricting his hand around mine, he takes another tiny step forward, almost as if he's approaching me with caution. His persona and behavior could be interpreted as intimidating, but I feel nothing but intrigue. He's studying me closely. The sharp stubble of his jaw is perfectly even, his lips parted just a fraction. "You have soft hands," he murmurs quietly. "Warm and soft. I like the feel of them."

Oh my God.

I look away, completely stunned. "She needs professional care," I say mindlessly, feeling his grip flex around mine. I try to pull away, but he laughs in the face of my strength, keeping a firm hold of me. "I strongly urge you to take her to the hospital. It's the best place for her."

"You don't think I can care for her?"

"Forgive me, but you don't look like the type to have any medical knowledge."

"But you do," he replies gently, seeming to take no offense, his hand shifting a little in mine, roaming and feeling through my fingers. "So you'll come with me."

"What?" I blurt, my eyes darting upward. Is he crazy?

"Your concern for Penny is touching," he goes on. It's now him trying to pull free from *my* grasp, but nerves have suddenly made my grip tighten. His jaw stiffens, and he yanks himself free with a hiss. My arm drops to my side as I stare up at a face that is hovering on the line between irresistible and dangerous. "I'll ensure everything you need is waiting for you when we arrive."

"I'm not a doctor," I point out. "I'm a nurse. My medical knowledge isn't as broad as a doctor's."

"I have faith in you." Theo gestures toward the big, impressive Bentley, watching as I follow his extended arm. "Don't be afraid. I won't hurt you, Izzy," he says on a mere whisper, turning those big hands over and showing me his palms. "That I promise you."

I have no reason to believe him, and despite sensing that he's no danger to me, I know I should be wise. And it wouldn't be wise for me to get in that car with these two huge men. I shake my head and step back. "Please, won't you just take her to a hospital?"

On a sigh, he reaches back under his suit jacket, pulling something out. "I can't do that." He holds something out to me, and I look down to see what.

A gun.

"Oh my God," I murmur, clumsily stepping back, my composure long gone. "Okay, I'll come." I hold up my hands.

"Hey, calm down," he says, way too gently, considering he has a gun aimed at me. What does he expect? But then reason finds me, and I peek at the weapon in his hand. He's not holding it. It's simply lying in his palm. "It's for you." He steps forward and takes my hand, putting the gun in my grip. "An insurance policy."

The weight surprises me, and I look up at him, confused. "What?"

"If you feel like you're in danger, go right on ahead and shoot me." He smiles that cute smile again, and I'm forced to look away. "I'm sorry for scaring you."

With his apology, I immediately fall under the spell of the contradicting softness and hardness of his stare. He won't hurt me. Or Penny. I know the signs of a man who throws his weight around. I bet Theo throws his weight around all right, but not with women.

I swallow and straighten my shoulders, handing back his gun. "I don't think I'll need this."

He cocks his head in interest as he accepts. "Why?"

"Because I have my own," I joke and roll my eyes, and he gives me that roguish smile again. Damn that smile. It shouldn't suit him. "Where do you live?" I ask, wondering who Penny is to him.

"You don't need to worry about an address." He slips his hand onto my shoulder, and I jump under his hold, fire racing through my veins. It's making my head spin. "You'll come with me, and I'll have my driver take you home once you've seen to Penny." His grip flexes, his big hand practically blanketing my entire shoulder. The odd warmth that melts deeply into me as I move toward the car is confounding, and I can't think past the whoosh of blood pumping in my ears. Who the hell is this giant?

CHAPTER 2

I tell myself Penny's well-being is the only reason I'm currently sunken into a plush leather seat heading God only knows where, but I'm lying. Theo has reduced me to an idiot. I must be stark raving mad. He tried to give me a gun to shoot him if I deemed it necessary. A bloody gun! But he also showed up and stopped that slimeball from . . .

A cold shiver travels through me as I gently pull up Penny's eyelid to check her pupils before assessing the gash on her eyebrow. It's stopped bleeding but will definitely require a few stitches. I feel momentarily guilty for being thankful for having Penny to focus on, because he's still watching me, and it's making my heart boom relentlessly.

"You're nervous again." Theo breaks into my thoughts with his cool statement, and my hands stutter in their motions. Yes, I'm nervous, but not for the reasons I should be. "Do you really think I'll hurt you? Wasn't my offer to arm you enough reassurance?"

"You won't hurt me," I confirm without hesitation, forcing myself away from Penny and resting back in my seat. His long legs are bent at the knees, his big torso reclined, relaxed, and his thick arm is resting neatly on the ledge beside his seat. It's dark, but he's as clear to me as he would be at the height of day. He commands attention. Demands respect. Screams power. Jesus, he's as intimidating as a man could possibly be. I shift in my seat, wanting to glance away but unable to break the lock of our stares. "And I trust my instinct," I add on a swallowed breath.

Theo shifts a little, too, bringing his index finger to his lips and thoughtfully brushing the length of it across his cupid's bow. "And what is your instinct telling you, Izzy?"

"That hurting women isn't your style." I leave out everything that I think *could* be his style. It might take me a while, and I don't think insulting this man would be a wise move.

"Your instinct is right. I won't tolerate violence when it comes to women."

My shoulders must visibly drop in relief, because his head cocks, and I'm suddenly aware that I've unwittingly given him a little piece of who I am. "That's good," I say quietly.

"And where does this instinct in you come from?"

I tense in my seat, looking away from him to gather myself. And when I return my attention to him, he's smiling a little. This smile is a sympathetic one, and it carves away a fraction of the hardness that cuts his handsome face, making him even more handsome. He's so damn handsome.

Theo must sense there will be no answer from me, so he looks over to Penny, his soft smile falling. The hardness of his features returns. "She's the daughter of an old friend," he says quietly, and I follow his gaze to the unconscious woman beside me. Her blond hair is matted with blood around her ear, her face washed out and pale. "She went off the rails when her dad died. Disappeared. I've been trying to find her." His chest puffs out a little on a cold laugh. "Twenty-one years old and selling her body." He hums, sounding thoughtful, and maybe a little sad. It brings my attention back to him, just as he brings his back to me.

"I'm sorry," I offer, seeing genuine sorrow past the steel exterior of the muscle-ridden man. "Were you close to her father?"

"You could say that." He clears his throat and looks out the window, a sign that the conversation ends there. "Home."

I have to force the gasp of surprise back down my throat. Huge iron gates are creaking open, slowly revealing a mansion of epic proportions. The structure is glowing subtly in the distance, lit up by floodlights dotted around the grounds. "Holy shit," I breathe, losing the battle to hold back my astonishment. "You live here?" I could probably fit our whole apartment under the canopied driveway on the front of the house.

"I live here, I work here..." The door opens, courtesy of an old man with silver hair and round metal-rimmed spectacles, who is clearly waiting for our arrival. "...play here."

I dart a wide-eyed look to Theo, finding him studying me again. This time, I have to look away. *Play?* The door on the other side of the car opens, and another man leans in and takes Penny in his arms carefully—the other huge unit of a man from the alley. His blond hair falls over his eyes as he reaches for her, his smooth jaw tight, the nostrils of his straight nose flaring. He's not quite as big as Theo, but he still looks like a force to be reckoned with, if a little prettier.

"After you." Theo gestures for me to get out, and I do, my neck craning as I unbend my body, looking around. The huge double doors before me are wide open and the concrete pillars on either side, flanking the grand entrance, are guarded by another two big men. Suited men, both mean-looking, who nod as we pass. I try not to look too awed when we enter, as I take in the grandeur of Theo's home. A double staircase curves up both sides of the extensive entrance hall, stretching to a galleried landing that circles the space, a massive chandelier suspended from the high ceiling, the crystals dripping down nearly meeting the floor where I'm standing.

The man holding Penny starts taking the stairs up the left side, and I swing around when I hear the doors behind me close, finding the two big men who were guarding them now on the inside with us. Then a lady appears holding a tray that has a tumbler of dark liquid positioned dead center. She comes to a stop a good six feet away from Theo, the tray held out, presented to him, forcing Theo to approach in order to reach his drink.

"Do you always get such an elaborate welcome home?" I ask with a nervous laugh.

He smiles, shrugging off his jacket and handing it to the lady before taking the glass and raising it to his lips. The loss of his jacket makes my breath catch in my throat, the white material of his shirt licking every inch of his huge torso—a torso that I can see is sharp, hard, and defined. I look up, my eyes following the path of his glass to his lips. I step back and reach in my bag, needing to escape the hold of those eyes before they render me incapable of anything except trying to comprehend his sheer presence. "I have very attentive staff," he says, placing his empty on the tray. "Would you like a drink?"

"I'm fine, thank you." I rummage through my bag to find my phone, not that I know what I'll do once I lay my hands on it. I have no one to call, since Jess is still at work. I just need something to distract myself. My hands freeze in their searching, and the sound of a smashing phone in my head reminds me that my mobile is no more. I could laugh. I'm in a strange house, with lots of strange, *large* men, and I have no phone. *Smart move, Izzy. Really smart.*

"Lost something?" Theo asks, sliding his hands into his pockets.

I straighten up and raise my chin. "Yes, my gun."

His eyes sparkle, and he holds up his hands in surrender.

I sigh on a disbelieving shake of my head. "I should see to Penny and go."

"Of course." He kicks his feet into action and passes me. "I'll show you the way."

Breathing some steadiness into myself, I start to follow, focusing on anything around me except the towering frame of the man a few steps ahead—the elaborate art hanging on the walls, the striped carpet with gold stair bars in the crook of each step, the intricately corniced ceiling.

His back.

His arse.

His thighs.

I bite my lip...and trip up a step. "Shit." My face plummets forward, heading for the backs of those thighs.

"Careful." Theo swivels and catches me, his arse hitting a step as he holds my hips. I'm kneeling on the step below him, his long legs spread wide. His hold tightens along with his jaw. I feel stifling hot, my eyes locked on his chest before me. "Are you okay?" he asks, a certain strain in his voice.

"Your stripy carpet makes me dizzy," I mumble like a fool, lying through my teeth. It's him that makes me dizzy. Just him. His hard handsomeness, his voice, his physique. His touch.

"Maybe I should carry you," he suggests, but there's no hint of a teasing edge. He's deadly serious, and though it's an utterly ridiculous suggestion, I can't help but wonder just how amazing it would feel to be completely encased in Theo. How safe it would be. "Would you like me to?"

I laugh, since nothing else comes to me. "Don't be silly," I scoff, going to push his hands away from my waist, but he shifts and scrambles to his feet like lightning, almost in a panic. I stare up at him, stunned, as I pull myself to my feet. He glances down at his hands for a moment, then back to me, confusion in his eyes. A few awkward seconds tick by, his gaze passing from his hands to various parts of my body. *What the hell?*

"You've had quite a scare," he mutters, shaking his head and turning. "There's nothing silly about my offer."

I've insulted him. He offered to help me, and I laughed in his face. "I didn't mean to offend you," I call, remaining on the step halfway up the stairs. "I'm sorry." I don't know why I feel the urge to apologize, but I can't ignore it.

Theo veers to the left. "I don't get offended, Izzy. This way."

I frown, my feet taking the steps carefully. That's strange, because he seems *highly* offended.

Once I've caught up with him, I make a conscious decision to keep my mouth shut, tend to Penny, then get the hell out of here. And judging by Theo's sudden coldness and the fact that he's now refusing to look at me, he might be thinking along the same lines. He turns the handle on a door. He pushes it open. And then he stands a few meters back, opening up the way. And stares at me. A cold stare.

I sigh, weirdly upset that I've upset him. He's a big man. A very big man. *Don't tell me he has feelings under all those muscles.*

First, I spot Penny tucked up in a huge wooden bed, then next to her a trolley kitted out with every piece of medical equipment a nurse could need. I have no clue how he sourced it all, and so quickly, and I'm not about to ask. Get done and get out. No questions, no conversing. I shouldn't even be here, and neither should Penny. She should be in a hospital.

I get to work, hearing the door close behind me, and look back to find I'm alone. I'm grateful. He upsets my balance. I march over to the bed and quickly check her vitals, finding she's no better than the last time I checked in the car, but, more importantly, she's no worse. Pulling the covers back, I see she's been stripped down to her knickers. Her nakedness reveals more injuries, and my face screws up in disgust at the sight of the scattered bruises, some fresh, some with a yellow tinge that suggest old wounds. The poor woman looks like she got a good beating on a regular basis.

I swallow. She's safe now.

After washing the cut on Penny's brow bone, I close it with a few stitches and do my best to clean her up and get her comfortable. Her pulse is steady and her breathing even, and the dilation of her pupils now seems normal.

Releasing her wrist, I look over my shoulder when I hear a quiet sound. Theo is standing by the door, just watching me. How long has he been there? "I didn't hear you return. Is there something you want?"

"No."

I wander around the side of Penny's bed, if only for something to do. "Then why are you here?"

"I like watching you work."

I look at him, mystified. "Why?"

His big shoulders rise on a shrug, and something tells me that's all the answer I'll get. "I'll leave you to it," he says, backing away, eyes on me, and reaching for the door handle. He slips out, and there's a mild groan from Penny and a brief flick of her eyelids.

"Hey," I say gently. "Can you hear me? Can you tell me your name?" I ask, wanting to check for any signs of memory loss before I go.

"Penelope," she mumbles, and I smile, tucking her in tightly. "But people call me Penny."

"I think you're going to be just fine, Penny. Are you in pain?"

She shakes her head and rolls over a little, snuggling down. "No pain."

"That's good." I look to the closed door where Theo just disappeared, contemplating my intention. I've experienced danger before. I know the signs, and while Theo displays many signs of being dangerous, I don't sense he's a danger to Penny. But I have to be sure. It's what I've been trained to do, and I shouldn't forget that, no matter how much Theo unbalances me. I rest my bum on the edge of the bed and take Penny's hand. "Is there anything I can do to help you, Penny? Anyone I can call?" Maybe her mother, or a friend.

"Theo. Get Theo."

I find myself looking at the door again, picturing his big back walking away. "You're at Theo's house."

"Then I'm safe," she mumbles sleepily. She's dozed off again. Just like that. Her words warm me. She settled as soon as she knew where she was and who she was with. Theo eases her. His presence comforts her. Where was that kind of man when I needed him?

I can't dwell on it too much. I'm here and I'm alive. And, miraculously, I'm mentally stable.

I get my bag and coat and leave Penny to rest, set on finding one of the big dudes who roam the mansion and telling him what to keep an eye out for, and, finally, asking if one of them can take me home. Opening the door quietly, I step out and shut it with equal care.

"Miss?"

I turn to find the older man with round glasses and silver hair who greeted us when we arrived. "She's fine."

"That's a relief. Mr. Kane will be pleased." He holds his hand out. "I'm Jefferson, the butler."

He has a butler? I mentally roll my eyes and take his hand with a smile. "I'm Izzy, the nurse."

He chuckles, his warm brown eyes glimmering with amusement behind his round spectacles. "Pleasure to meet you."

"And you, Jefferson. The wound on Penny's eye needs to be cleaned twice a day. She's responsive, but if she shows signs of any deterioration—dizziness, headaches, confusion, or memory loss—then you should get her to a hospital without delay." I pull my bag onto my shoulder as he nods his understanding. "Mr. Kane said that there would be someone to take me home, if that's still okay?" I prompt politely.

"Oh yes," he chimes. "But first I believe Mr. Kane would like to see you." He turns and wanders off down the corridor, leaving me in a sudden state of apprehension, unmoving and unwilling to. I don't want or need to see Theo again.

"If it's all the same, I really must get home." I sound as desperate as I feel, not that it has much impact on the old man still walking away from me. I know he heard me. "Jefferson," I call, going after him, hitting the curved stairs with urgency and being sure to watch my feet on the stripy carpet.

"I'm sure he won't take up a great deal of your time, since you've donated so much already."

I grit my teeth, following him down to the lobby, where we're met by the lady who delivered Theo's drink and took his jacket. She smiles. "Can I bring you a drink?"

"No, thank you. I'll be going shortly." I should have asked for some water because I'm suddenly parched by the prospect of seeing Theo again.

"Very well." She goes on her way, leaving Jefferson gesturing toward a huge door to the right. "It's just through here."

"What is?"

"Mr. Kane's private office." He indicates with a slight cock of his head that I should lead on. I look across to the double doors, nervous as hell and fidgety. "Knock once," he says.

Knock once. Not twice or three times? As I slowly make my way over, my heart starts thumping, getting louder with each step I take.

"And keep your distance, miss," Jefferson adds, his voice now quiet. I swing around, seeing his back disappear through an arch across the hall. Keep my distance? Is he warning me? I look back at the door, my nerves accelerating. It takes a stupid amount of time for me to raise enough courage to knock—*once.*

"Come in." Theo's deep voice resonates through the wood and spreads across my skin. It's full of authority. Rough and sexy. I close my eyes and get a hold of my wayward thoughts, taking the doorknob and breathing in. Pushing my way into his office, I keep my eyes low as I close the door behind me.

"Izzy." He says my name in a breathy whisper, and my body rolls with something that mystifies me, though I refuse to allow myself time to try to figure out what it is, because I sure as hell know that I'm not going to be comfortable with my conclusion.

Say what I need to say and leave, and make sure I don't look at him while I follow my plan. "She's okay." I swallow, trying to moisten my dry mouth. "Beaten, but okay. I've given Jefferson instructions and told him of the symptoms you need to keep an eye out for."

"I'm glad, thank you. But what about you?"

I frown down at the deep red carpet. "What about me?"

"Are *you* okay?" he asks, his voice still low but getting louder. He's coming closer.

I step back, retreating without thought. "I really need to go." I'm not at all comfortable with the reactions I'm having to this man, least of all because I've already seen he carries a gun, and I watched one of his men virtually strangle someone before my eyes, before having him hauled off to... where? Where did they take him? And, more importantly, what did they do to him? Is he dead? I flinch, trying not to go there. I shake my wondering away. It shouldn't matter to me, anyway. What matters is that this man is a perfect stranger, and a dark one at that. There are so many signs that are screaming at me that he's bad news. Yet there's a sense of ease that is unfamiliar to me, and I'm not at all comfortable with how much I like it. He saved Penny tonight. Took her away from the danger. There was no man to save me when I needed it. No strapping beast of a male to rain holy hell on my tormentor.

I don't realize that I've taken more than one backward step until my back hits the door. The contact startles me, and I look up without thought, finding Theo only a meter away. He could reach me with his hand if he were to extend it. "Who are you?" The question tumbles past my lips before I can stop it.

He ignores me, his eyes dropping to my neck. His hand lifts and reaches up. I press myself into the wood, silently begging him not to touch me. His fingers skim the black waves around my neck for a fleeting moment before he pushes them away, tilting his head. "What's this?" he asks, his fingertip meeting my flesh and tracing down one of the scratch marks. I freeze, forcing air from my mouth as he makes a point of feeling every line on my neck. My skin flames, my heart galloping uncontrollably. I can't speak, and after a few tense but pleasurable seconds of him grazing my neck with his touch, he goes on. "Who did this to you?"

"A patient," I say quietly, convincing my hand to lift and replace his at my neck—not that I'm trying to hide the marks, more trying to free myself of his touch so I can move away from him. He's not holding me in place. Not physically. Yet when he's touching me, I find myself incapable of movement. But a microsecond before my hand reaches his to detach it, he jerks away, saving me the trouble.

He steps back, a slight scowl on his face. "A patient?"

"He's old. Senile." I find myself rushing to explain, not liking his reaction. There's no softness anywhere to be found now. "Perks of the job," I joke, feeling the need to break the tension. He doesn't laugh, doesn't even crack a smile. Yikes, he looks furious. "I should be going now." I thumb over my shoulder blindly.

Theo flinches, shaking his head mildly. "Certainly." He reaches into his pocket and pulls out a card, handing it to me. "I'll have a car waiting for you outside. Callum will take you home. This is my card, should you need to contact me."

My eyes drop to the black card held lightly between his fingers, with red type in one single line across the middle. His name. And a mobile number. "Why would I need to contact you?" I ask, not bothering to point out that I can't, because my phone is in a million pieces down an alleyway, and I'm not likely to be able to replace it until I'm paid on Friday. But that's irrelevant. I should never contact him again. He's definitely a man who should be avoided.

He comes forward and slips the card into the top of my bag. "Don't ever walk home alone in the dark again," he warns, glancing away for a second. It's only a second, but his craned neck reveals a sliver of ink peeking up over the collar of his shirt. Black ink, shaded subtly at the edges. I find myself straining to get a better look, silently begging for him to turn his neck farther and reveal more of the art. But he doesn't, looking back at me instead.

"Are you asking me or telling me?" I say.

"I'm telling you. No woman should roam the streets of London at night alone."

It's been a long time since I've had anyone to worry about me, to care for my well-being. Well, Jess worries all the time. But it's different when the worry is from family. The fact that a huge, mean-looking mountain of a man like this is concerned about a perfect stranger like me softens my heart to him. "I can take care of myself," I say anyway, prompting him to glare at me.

"You shouldn't need to."

"I really do need to," I assure him, catching sight of his tattoo again, more undistinguishable shadows and lines. Before I embarrass myself and reach up to pull the collar of his shirt down, I quickly scoot past him, frowning when he quickly moves from my path, putting a good few feet between us.

"Why?" he asks. "Why do you *really* need to?"

I realize I've unintentionally given him another hint of something I didn't want him to know. Something I don't want anyone to know. "Because I don't have a huge man like you to spring out of nowhere and save me." I flip him a cheeky smile, and his lips quirk through his small frown. He loses so much hardness from his face when he's amused. It's riveting.

He clears his throat, as if he's just realized that, too, and wants to uphold this iron front. The hardness returns. "Don't walk anywhere alone," he reiterates, his intense stare burning away my smile.

"Fine," I say for the sake of it, taking the door handle and quickly exiting his office, falling against the door and taking a few deep breaths.

"Miss Izzy?" A hand rests on my arm, and I jump a mile into the air with a silly squeak. "Oh dear, I didn't mean to startle you." Jefferson's hand recoils, and his old eyes behind his specs run a quick check over me, frowning. "Are you okay?"

"Yes," I breathe, pushing myself away from the door. "I'm sorry." I rub the sleeve of my coat, my head beginning to pound, and I smile tightly at Theo's friendly butler. "I'm ready to go home now."

"Callum is waiting for you outside. It was lovely to meet you."

"And you, Jefferson." I make tracks to the giant doors that will get me out of this pressure box, finding a Mercedes idling under the canopied driveway. Callum, the blond guy who was in the alley with Theo, is holding the door open for me, his face expressionless. I notice for the first time that his eyes are deep brown, warm, but he still seems cold. And inconvenienced. As I approach, he takes a step away from the car, giving me way more space than I need, and I give him a small, nervous smile as I slide into the back, a smile that's not returned.

As we drive away, I look over my shoulder through the back window, a bit bewildered by the turn of events that my regular evening has taken. The house is still illuminated, glowing up from the ground, and then it suddenly falls into darkness, disappearing from sight. I turn in my seat, resting back, and close my eyes. I've never sensed so much danger in my life. And yet, the most disturbing part is how enthralled I was.

What's Theo Kane's story? Who is he?

CHAPTER 3

"What are you doing up?" I ask Jess as she plods sleepily into the kitchen, rubbing her eyes. It's eight in the morning. She must have only gotten in from work an hour ago. She plops onto a chair, and I immediately get to making her a coffee.

"I had a shower when I got in. I should never have a shower when I get in from the red-eye shift." She gratefully accepts the coffee I hand her and takes a hungry sip. "Sleep well?" she asks.

I don't mean to hesitate, but the beat of silence doesn't go unnoticed, and she looks at me questioningly. It was a standard question that's usually answered in a standard way: so-so. I never sleep particularly well, often restless and constantly telling myself that I'm safe, that he will never find me. But last night was a different kind of restlessness. When I finally made it into bed at nearly midnight, I found it impossible to clear my mind and stop thinking about Theo Kane.

"Izzy?" Jess presses, setting down her mug.

"Something really strange happened on the way home." I take a seat opposite her, needing to get it all off my chest.

"What?"

"I was attacked."

She coughs and splutters all over the table. "Oh my God. Are you okay?" I can see her immediately start to assess my face and chest. "Where? Are you hurt? Who was it?" Her urgent questions come one after the other, knocking me back a little in my chair. "Shit, Izzy, were you taking that fucking shortcut again?"

I shrug sheepishly, and she lands a furious glare on me. "I'm fine," I assure her, ignoring the fact that it could have been a very different story had Theo Kane and his entourage not shown up.

"Damn it, I'm mad at you. What happened?"

"Someone intervened."

Her mouth snaps shut as I begin to chew on my lip, my hands gripping my mug tighter. "Intervened? Like saved you?"

"Not just me. There was a woman I stopped to help. She'd been beaten up."

"Oh my God."

"She's fine. Just a bit battered. I thought whoever was responsible had fled, but when I tried to help her I was attacked. He came out of nowhere." I shudder again, dreading to think what could have happened. "But he was interrupted by...some men."

Her eyebrows rise, interested. "Plural?"

I nod. "Two of them, but one was..." I pause, thinking how best to word Theo's status. "The boss."

"The boss?"

I nod again. "Important. I don't know. He was massive. Well, they were both big, but him exceptionally so."

Jess leans forward over the table. "Massive?"

I'm nodding again.

"Massive fat, or massive solid?"

"Fit," I confirm. "And very tall."

"Handsome?"

"Deadly." I think I mean that in more ways than one.

Her lips purse. "And what did he do?"

"Took me back to his house."

Her eyes widen.

"Or mansion," I add.

"Mansion?"

"That was massive, too."

She's concealing a grin now. "I wonder what else would be massive."

"Jess!"

"I'm just wondering," she argues, defensive. "Who was he?"

I get up from the table and rinse out my mug, then place it on the drainer by the sink. "I have no idea." I reflect a moment, remembering Theo evade that question when I'd wheezily asked it.

"I do," Jess says. "A rich, hot man with a big house and, potentially, a big cock."

My shoulders drop. She's obsessed with cock, probably because of all the vaginas that are thrust in her face daily. I head to the bathroom to get showered and ready for my shift, and, of course, Jess is in hot pursuit, hungry for more information. "What did you do at his house?" she asks, sitting on the loo as I turn on the shower.

"Took care of the girl who was attacked. Twenty-one and a prostitute. Her father died. I think Theo was close to him." While feeding Jess's curiosity, I'm also feeding my own. And I shouldn't. Curiosity is a dangerous thing, especially when Theo Kane is the subject. I should never have mentioned it at all. Forget about it. That's what I should do.

"Theo? His name's Theo?"

"Theo Kane." I strip down and jump in the shower, not in the least bit bothered that Jess is sitting on the toilet watching me, now seemingly wide awake. I can see her mind racing. I inwardly laugh. And she hasn't even met him. Didn't see his mansion. Or have a gun offered to her. She has no idea.

"Were there—"

"No." I cut her right off.

"You don't even know what I was going to say," she protests.

I wipe away the condensation and give her a look through the glass. I know damn well what she was going to ask, and the answer will always be no. There were no sparks. There were no looks. There were no electric shocks each and every time he touched me. There was no loss of breath or lustful thoughts. I should never go there. "Nothing," I reiterate finally.

"Well, that's disappointing." She grumbles, losing complete interest in the conversation, which is exactly why I made the wise decision not to feed her intrigue any more. Now I just need to work on starving my own.

* * *

"Who keeps taking my thermometer?" I mutter under my breath, rootling through the basket on the trolley. Damn it, how many times do people need to be told?

"Here." Susan passes me a spare with a knowing look, tapping her watch, a reminder that my shift is almost done, not that I stand much chance of getting out of here for at least another hour. I have handover to do, as well as observations on all the patients. Just one more shift tomorrow, I tell myself, seeing the biggest mojito awaiting my arrival in Vegas.

I return my attention to my patient. "Let's see how hot you are today, Mable," I say cheekily, spiking a wicked cackle from the dear old lady.

"Flaming," she says on a laugh. "Hey, when are you going to Dallas?"

"I'm going to Vegas, and I leave on Saturday."

"Oohhh, I bet you'll be getting yourself some American scrumpet."

I laugh as I note her temperature and check her charts. "How's your pain, Mable? On a scale of one to ten."

"Five," she answers quickly, making me smile. Always a five. The poor woman took a tumble and broke her hip, and not once has she complained about it. She's as sharp as a pin at the ripe old age of ninety-two. "American men," she muses, looking off into the distance, a fond smile on her face. "I remember the excitement when a ship full of American sailors docked during the war. Me and the girls put extra lipstick on *that* night before we danced down to the pub."

"You floozy," I tease, wagging a finger at her. "And was the extra lippy worth it?" I dip to release her full catheter bag.

She chucks me a devilish smirk. "I was quite a catch, you know. When I was a girl and my bosoms weren't tickling my knees." She gives the catheter bag in my hand a quick look of disdain, and I feel immediately guilty for reminding her that she's no longer a young woman. Now she's an old lady with memories of a time gone by. "But then I met my Ronald. Ooh, that man did things to me that no other man ever had."

"Like what?" I ask, fascinated by the twinkle in her eye and the sudden rouge of her cheeks.

"Like give me butterflies in my tummy and too many heart-stopping moments for me to remember." She sighs, sinking into her pillow. "He looked at me like a man *should* look at a woman."

"How's that?" I smile as I straighten her sheets with my spare hand.

"Like he was struggling to keep his hands off me. Like he wanted to ravish me from top to toe." She pats my hand with a chuckle. "One day, my love. You'll meet him one day."

I frown. "Who, Ronald?"

She laughs loudly, wincing a teeny bit from her sudden movement, though she doesn't yelp or curse. Just settles back down without a fuss. "No, silly girl. Ronald went to play in God's green garden seven years ago. I mean your life changer."

"My life changer?"

"The man who will flip your world up on its head and you won't care one iota." She laughs. "Just you wait. A pretty thing like you won't be on the shelf for long."

"Who said I'm on the shelf?" I ask, maybe a little delayed, but still. I've had interest, just no time *or* desire. And no world flipping, as she calls it.

"Oh, my love." She looks embarrassed for a moment. "Forgive me, but if there's a long-term man in your life, then I'm afraid you might be wasting your time on him. There's no twinkle in your eye." She pats my cheek.

"There is no long-term man," I admit. "*No* man, in fact."

"So you *are* on the shelf."

"You make it sound like I'm there to be taken by whoever comes along and likes the look of me."

"That's the long and short of it," Mable says frankly with a shrug. "If a man wants you badly enough, he'll take you."

"What if I don't want to be taken by him?"

She smiles, like she's privy to something that I'm not. "I think Dot needs some help." She nods across the way, and I see Dot struggling to sit up in her bed, grabbing the table to help, but it rolls away.

"Wait there, Dot," I call, gathering up my things. "You're not a gymnast. See you later, Mable." I head across the bay.

"I need a piss," Dot snaps curtly.

"Then I'll have someone bring you the commode, okay?"

"Make it quick."

"Yes, ma'am," I quip under my breath, getting her comfy before making my way to the nurses' station. I grab a health care assistant on my way and ask her nicely to help Dot and empty

Mable's bag of pee, before racing through the rest of my section, checking everyone's obs before I hand over.

I feel utterly wiped out by the time I'm done. After giving the next duty nurse the rundown, I grab my coat and swing it over my shoulders before scooping up my bag and waving my goodbyes.

As I pass Mable's bed, she wolf-whistles, making me grin and twirl midstride. "Why, thank you." I laugh, spotting one of my patients struggling to sit up in bed. "Hey, Deirdre, what are you up to?" I hurry over to her.

"My damn back is aching. It's these pillows. They're too soft."

"Then let me fix that for you." I spend a few moments plumping her pillows and wedging a rolled-up blanket behind them to make her more comfortable. "Try that," I say, easing her back down to the bed. "Better?"

"Oh, yes, much." Deirdre sighs and squeezes my hand. "You're an angel, Izzy."

I return her gesture before placing her hand back on the bed. "You need anything else before I go?"

"A new body."

I smile, though it's sad. "You sleep well tonight, okay? And I'll see you tomorrow."

"Okay, dear. Have a good evening."

I tuck her in and wander away, looking over my shoulder and smiling in satisfaction when I see her snoozing comfortably. She'll rest easy now. And I believe I will, too, when I make it home.

Returning my attention forward, my heart stops, my smile drops, and my pace slows. And I'm pretty damn sure my world just flipped up on its head.

"Izzy," Theo greets me softly, looking as sharp as he did the last time I saw him. His straight face takes me in, his eyes running up and down my body. I suddenly feel self-conscious, and I reach up to pat my hair down. Good grief, I bet I look a fright. *Damn it!*

Then I quickly ask myself why I'm bothered by how drab I must be looking after my shift and what Theo must think of that. Why do I care? I don't know, but I do. Annoyingly, I *really* care.

Today he's alone, no other big guy to be seen. "Your hair's perfect," he says dryly, and my hands freeze atop my head, my cheeks flaming. "But it's nice to know you care."

He has me pinned, so I don't insult him by denying it. "Is Penny all right?" I ask, wondering if she needs my medical assistance again.

"She's fine."

"Then what are you doing here?" I feel eyes on me, not just Theo's, and turn to find Mable probably enduring agony so she can get a better look at my surprise visitor. I roll my eyes and she grins, giving me a thumbs-up.

"I like watching you work," Theo says, bringing me back to face him, leaving Mable ogling from behind.

"What?"

He glances over at Deirdre. "Looking after people. It's nice to see you doing that."

"It's my job," I reply, holding back my laugh. He looks so serious.

Nodding mildly, Theo turns back toward me. "You haven't called."

"I haven't needed to."

"I was hoping you *would* need to." His quick response knocks me back a little. "And then I thought that maybe it's because you don't have a phone."

"How do—"

"One of my men found the broken pieces."

"Oh," I breathe. One of his men? He thought? He's been thinking about me? Hoping I'd call? He's being perfectly polite, yet a little brusque. I don't mention the fact that I still have his number, regardless of the small matter that I don't have a phone. It would only highlight that I could have called him, and something tells me that *that's* what's bothering him. He wanted me to call. And I didn't.

"So Penny's okay, then?" I ask, uncomfortable with the silence that's fallen.

"On her feet," he answers but says no more, telling me Penny isn't the topic of conversation he had in mind. Penny isn't why he's here. "I've come to take you home." Stepping to the side, he swoops his arm out for me to lead on. "My car's waiting."

I smile a little, though it's nervous. "I don't need a chaperone home, Theo."

"I say you do."

"And I should listen to you?" What's he going to do? Pull a gun on me?

"You should definitely listen to me." There's slight menace in his words that doesn't faze me in the slightest. He might be deadly handsome, but intimidation seeps from every inch of his towering frame. For some reason I haven't yet figured out, all of that comes second to the insane attraction I have for him *and* his dangerous allure.

"Why should I listen to you?" I ask evenly, looking up at him through my lashes.

"Because only those who are unwise do not."

"I think I would be very wise *not* to listen to you." I watch as his handsome face twists a little in growing frustration. Theo isn't the kind of man who is refused. He's dark and he's dangerous. He's a no-go zone for a sensible, regular girl like me. So why is he thinking about me, let alone actually tracking me down to my place of work?

"Your bravery intrigued me at first," he says. "Now I think it annoys me more."

I look down at his hands, letting my thoughts wander to places they shouldn't go. "I'm not scared of you," I say mindlessly, as if to enforce what he already knows, biting down on my lip.

"I know." He sighs. "You keep telling me. So why won't you let me take you home?"

"Because I'm afraid that you might expect more, and I'm even more scared that I'll give it to you." I look up at him, face straight, with no regret for saying what I'm thinking. And when our stares lock, his cobalt eyes wide, his head cocked in question, I know my fear is warranted.

"Why are you afraid of that?" he asks, low and intrigued.

"I'm busy. With work. I have a career to focus on. I'm not interested in someone like..." I drift off, realizing I was heading toward an insult.

"Someone like...?"

"I don't know." I might not be scared, but I also shouldn't insult him. Because that would be plain rude.

He smiles a little, amused. "Someone scary like me?"

I laugh a little. "I already told you, Theo. You don't scare me."

"And I quite like that notion. It's new. Refreshing."

"Because everyone is scared of you?"

"Well, yeah."

"Why?"

"Come to dinner with me."

My shoulders drop a little. "Didn't you hear anything I just said?"

"Oh, I heard, Izzy. And I don't believe a word of it." He moves behind me and presses his front into my back. He sucks in air on contact, and I breathe in heavily. *Oh goodness me.* I don't flinch. Not one bit, but past our audible breaths, I hear an old lady gasp. It reminds me of where I am, with Theo currently pressed into me, unearthing a torrent of...

Shit. It's lust and want and desire, and it's making me powerless to move away from him. His mouth falls to my ear. I close my eyes and breathe in. "You're safe with me," he says, as if knowing those words will work to his advantage. "Let's go." He slips a hand around my waist and steps forward, forcing me into walking. Or staggering. I guess I'm staggering, though it's hard to tell when Theo is practically carrying me. Oh my God, he's practically carrying me out of the ward, and I have a horrid feeling that it hasn't gone unnoticed, not by Mable and not by my colleagues.

I don't look back when an opportunity to check for a peanut gallery arises, letting Theo haul me right on out of there. *Safe.* It's like he's privy to how enticing that little word is to me. Like he's using it as a weapon.

"Theo," I complain, wriggling a little but freezing the second he comes to an abrupt halt and hisses under his breath.

"Don't do that, Izzy," he warns. "For the love of God, please don't do that."

I clamp my teeth together to the point of cracking them, trying to ignore the feeling of something stiff compressed into my bum. "I'm sorry."

"Yeah, that's not ideal, either," he mumbles, clearing his throat.

I frown. "What?"

"Nothing." He sighs, maintaining his firm hold of me. "Just give me a second."

"I'll let you take me home, just put me down," I beg, not bothering to try to pry myself free. It would be a fruitless endeavor, and I can't risk feeling that hardness again, and, worst of all, liking it. "People are staring." People would be staring whether Theo had me held against his chest or not. The sheer size of him attracts too much attention. I'm more than surprised when I suddenly feel the ground beneath my feet with no further need to plead. "Thank you," I say graciously, faffing with my coat and bag. I should just let him take me home. It will be easier and less stressful—as long as I avoid eye contact and keep a safe distance between us. "Where's your car?"

He clears his throat, seeming a little flustered himself. It's quite an amusing sight. This big beast of a man, all hot and bothered. Over me? Pointing down the corridor, he stands tall, apparently together now. "Out front."

I'm off quickly, Theo's long strides keeping up with ease. When we reach his car, Callum is holding the door open. His face is unreadable as he nods at me, and once again he moves back, giving me far too much space to get in. I slide into the seat and rest my bag on my lap, getting comfy while Theo joins me. Or as comfy as I can be in the presence of Theo Kane. Especially now that we seem to have . . . have what? What have we done? I shrink into my seat. I should maybe dedicate a bit of time to considering what *I* have done. And what I've done is confess my fear. I've told him, pretty clearly, that if he was to make a pass, I probably wouldn't deny him. I'm an idiot. Why would I do that?

As we pull out of the hospital car park, I stare out the window, wishing I could turn back time to the night I found Penny in that alley. If I knew then what I know now, I would have carried on my way. I wouldn't have gone back to help her. I wouldn't have let Theo take me to his mansion. I wouldn't . . .

I stop right there. I'm kidding myself. There's no way I could walk away from a woman in need. I don't know much about Theo Kane, but what I do know is pretty alarming. And I'm furious for wanting to know a lot more. Like *everything*.

"You seem tired," he says, reminding me that I probably look like a bag of shit. I'm once again bothered by it, and my hand goes to my hair and tucks my black waves behind my ears.

"A ten-hour shift will do that," I murmur to the window, keeping to my plan, not looking at him and staying *way* on the other side of the back seat so there's no risk of touching him, either. It's a good plan, but for it to work, Theo needs to abide by the rules, too. Except I haven't told him the rules.

I feel something brush lightly across the side of my thigh. My body temperature starts to climb, and I whip my leg away. "Tired but still stunning." Another brush of my leg.

Oh my goodness, I wish he would stop. I mentally calculate how many more minutes in this car I need to endure with him before I'm home. Seven, if the traffic is good. It's gone ten at night. I should be safe. He's pulling no punches now. It's frightening, but beneath the steel front I'm working hard to keep in place, I'm relieved and delighted that he's giving me a little peek into his mind. I was attracted to him the moment I looked at him. I didn't want to be. I picked him to pieces, weighed up the hulk of a man before me and concluded he was bad, *bad* news, but it didn't even dent the allure, no matter how much I willed it to. He's too magnetic. Too captivating.

It's frustrating.

It's exciting.

It's...I bite my lip and cross one leg over the other, squeezing the pulse away. He feels dangerous yet safe. It's completely contradictory. He looks dangerous, acts it, and he definitely felt it when he was pressed into my back. My thighs tighten, and I fight to rid my mind of those wayward thoughts. I can't seem to control my head when he's close, so I better make damn sure I control my body.

I hear a light laugh—a laugh that's smooth and laced with knowing. "Tell me," he says under his breath, "what are you imagining now?"

I'm so glad I'm facing away from him, because it means he can't see how wide my eyes go. "Actually, I'm imagining my bed and how good it's going to feel when I sink into the sheets." It all just comes sailing right on out.

"Sounds good," he muses.

"It will be."

"My bed would be comfier."

My plan and my rules go to shit. I swing to face him. I haven't seen his bed, and I don't plan to. Though I expect it's massive— it'd have to be to accommodate his huge body—and extremely comfy. "I very much doubt it."

"Then we should test it." He looks serious, yet there's a playful edge there.

"Test it?"

"Yes."

"And how would that work?" I ask.

"You want a diagram?"

"Oh, that's cute." I laugh.

He shrugs. "It'll put the debate to rest."

I open my mouth to tell him exactly where he can put his debate, but snap it shut again when something comes to me. He's goading me. This big, powerful man is pressing the buttons of a little nurse girl. For what? Why? "What do you want from me, Theo? Sex?" Being to the point is the only way forward. "Just a good screw?"

"I assure you, I have no shortage there."

I expect he's right, and I have no reason for that statement to hurt, but it still stings like a bitch. I bet they're all dolly birds, too—glamorous and well-dressed. Unlike me, currently stinking of antiseptic and looking like I'm an hour away from being carted off to the morgue.

"Then why?" I counter.

He grabs my jaw, squeezing my cheeks. "What's your story, Izzy White?"

It clicks. His motives are suddenly too clear, and it hurts like hell. Penny, his showing up out of the blue, all the women in his bed. The fact that I divulged a few too many hints of my dark past. He wants to save me. Like he did Penny. I wrench my face from his grip. I don't need saving. I fucking saved myself. "Are you on some kind of mercy mission?" I ask, undeniable resentment lacing my question. "A big, scary man out to save all the weak, vulnerable females he stumbles upon?"

He blinks, and for a second I think it might be because I've injured his ego. But then I sense anger, his hard face etched with lines of fury. It only fuels my own rage. What does he expect me to do? Fall to my knees in gratitude that he's bulldozed into my life and waved his sword? Rip my clothes off and offer my body in return for protection?

"You don't seem very weak and vulnerable to me," he grates. "But in answer to your question, no. I'm not out to save you. I'm . . ." He fades off and swallows hard. Reclaiming my jaw, he applies a pressure that's almost too much. "I'm here because I can't get this fucking face out of my head. I want you to come to dinner with me."

I stare at him in stunned silence, now at a loss for words. According to him, only the unwise say no to Theo Kane. But being unwise would be to dip my toe in Theo's world. Being unwise would be to explore the reactions he evokes from me. Being unwise would be to allow the sense of safety he offers to distract me from my mission to keep *myself* safe. And what's he going to do when I say no, anyway? Put that gun to my head? I laugh under my breath. Bring it on. I've lived half my life with an imaginary gun held at my temple.

I reach up, intending to yank his hand away from my face, but Theo drops his hold first and shoots back in his seat, as far on the other side of the car as he can get. His eyes are wide, his face tight. "Go," he orders. "Go before I do something you clearly don't want me to do." The car stops at a red light. He looks away.

"Like what?" I know he doesn't mean he might hurt me. "Kiss me? And what makes you think I would let you?"

"You wouldn't have a choice, and not because I would force you." His hands meet the seat in front of him, his fingers clawing into the leather. He's restraining himself. "Go, Izzy."

I'm out of the car quickly, my feet hitting the pavement in time with my thumping heart. The bright lights and buzz of London are a mere blur and white noise around me as I hurry down the street toward my apartment, his words whooshing in my ears.

Casting a look over my shoulder, I see his car still sitting at the light, though it's now green and the sound of impatient horns adds to the fuzz of noise around me. The Bentley eventually starts to crawl along, sticking close to the curb fifty or so feet back. Even his car looks threatening, creeping along behind me. My pace quickens, and I round the corner, seeing my apartment up ahead. The sight offers me no comfort. A quick glimpse over my shoulder tells me Theo's driver has followed me into my street, still crawling at a snail's pace, the fiasco of annoyed cars behind not prompting him to put his foot down or pull over. Because Theo will be telling him what to do, and only the unwise say no to Theo Kane.

"Damn you," I murmur, reaching the steps that lead up to my front door. His Bentley rolls to a stop, but no one gets out. The blacked-out window of the back prevents me from seeing Theo inside, but I know he's looking at me, probably even more pissed off, and if he continues to stare, I think he might burn a hole through the glass. I look to Callum in the front—no tinted windows there hindering my view—finding him sitting still, hands on the wheel, focused forward.

I reach for the handrail that leads up the stairs to my front door, keeping my eyes on the car as I take backward steps up, waiting for him to get out. But he doesn't.

The front door opens behind me. "Izzy, what the hell are you doing?" Jess asks, coming down the steps to join me. I flick her a quick look, finding a Mars bar at her lips, her eyes now on the posh Bentley still stationary by the curb. "Who's that?" she asks.

"Him," I breathe, feeling all kinds of unstable and unsteady. The car starts to slowly pull away, leaving me and Jess following its path down the road until it takes a corner and disappears. My legs give out, taking my arse down to one of the concrete steps. "Oh my God," I gasp, shock kicking in.

"Fucking hell." Jess joins me on the step, her hand coming to my knee. "The guy from the alley? With the mansion? What happened?"

"He turned up at work. Insisted on bringing me home."

"Then how come you were walking?" she asks. "I saw you from the kitchen window when I was getting some wine."

"I got out at the light," I explain, bringing my hand up to my chest and glancing down the street. "After he told me to go or he'd do something he'd regret."

She withdraws, uncertain. "What?"

"Not like that," I rush to explain. "Like kiss me. He wanted to kiss me, and he said I would never be able to stop him. And he didn't mean because he's built like a brick shithouse and I am not."

"Oh, wow," Jess whispers. "But you said there was nothing."

I clench my eyes closed and exhale my confession. "I lied."

"But why?"

"Because I'm scared by it," I admit with an apologetic smile. Jess isn't hacked-off like I expect. She looks in shock herself. "He's dangerous," I say. "I shouldn't be attracted to that." My eyes drop. "But he saved me from that arsehole who . . ."

Jess's hand reaches for mine and grips hard. She knows where I was going with that. "Don't," she warns. "Don't give that bastard a second thought."

I shake my head, frustrated. "I'm trying not to." I look at her and smile sadly. "Theo would rip him to shreds without a moment's hesitation or regret. That's how it should be. A man should protect a woman. Not hurt her. And a woman should feel safe with a man, not afraid. I'm not scared of Theo, Jess. He isn't dangerous in the sense that I think he would physically hurt me. He's dangerous because I feel so safe with him." I've never felt safe before. Not truly. I like it. And I don't want to.

My friend gives me an understanding smile, curling an arm around my shoulder and pulling me into her. "The fact that he's dangerously handsome, rich, and built like a gladiator helps, too, I suppose."

"And that," I agree quietly, resting my head on her shoulder, my mind running away with me. Theo had no intention of getting out of that car and coming after me. He was simply making sure I got home safely.

CHAPTER 4

There's someone at the door," Jess calls from her bedroom, forcing me to vacate my cozy bed. I'd heard the knock but hoped Jess would answer so I could continue to ponder just how comfy my bed is. Very comfy, actually.

"I've got it," I grumble, whipping the sheets back and dragging myself to the edge as I look at the clock. Eight o'clock. Who the hell is banging on the door at this time of the morning? I grab my T-shirt and wrestle it on as I hurry down the corridor to the door, swinging it open to find a young lad in a courier uniform.

"Morning," he chirps, holding out a small box to me as he ogles my bare legs.

"Morning," I grunt in return, taking the parcel from his limp grip and helping myself to the clipboard in his other hand. I scribble across the paper and shove it into his chest, backing away and shutting the door on his cheesy smile.

I make my way to the kitchen to fetch coffee, hearing Jess somewhere behind me. "Who was that?" she asks, towel drying her hair.

"Delivery." I slide the parcel onto the worktop and start making coffees, putting an extra heaped teaspoon of coffee granules in my mug.

"What time you starting?" She flops down into a chair at the table and accepts the cup I hand her.

"Two." Collecting the box, I join her. "Last shift." I give her a toothy smile that's returned, extra toothy. "I need to pack, find my passport, get some dollars." I start to rip open the package.

"You haven't done that yet?" she asks incredulously. "Izzy!"

"I've been working my arse off," I argue, not meaning to suggest that Jess hasn't. I give her an apologetic smile when she gapes at me. "Or I'm just not as organized as you." I backtrack a little, blindly pulling the box open. The truth is, I needed to wait until today to exchange some money. It's payday, and I've been skint for the past week. I have no excuse for not packing *or* finding my passport. "Oh, and I need to get a new phone."

"You do?" Jess's forehead becomes a sea of lines. "Then what's that?" She nods down at the box in my hand, and I follow her stare, peeking down at the now unwrapped package. An iPhone box stares back at me, and I lift the lid to find *my* iPhone. Not a scratch or dent in sight.

"What the hell?" I mumble, turning it over in my hand. "I left it in the alley in a million pieces." It bleeps loudly, and I jump in my chair, my phone jumping, too, right out of my hand. "Shit." I fumble to catch it and fail, and it tumbles to the kitchen floor, landing with a crash.

"Oh my God, you're the clumsiest person I know." Jess laughs.

I look at the phone on the ground at my feet, facedown. "I didn't send it to be repaired," I say, confused. "But here it is, fixed and shiny like new. And it's turned on, Jess." My eyes narrow. "And a message came through."

"Oh," she breathes, the penny finally dropping. "Him?"

"Who else?" I ask, my mind going off on a tangent, my nervous hands starting to twist the bottom of my T-shirt. But what about last night? He was so mad. And then he had Callum crawl along behind me in his big, flashy car to make sure I got home safely. The man is a big fat contradiction.

Jess's eyes are bright and excited as she dips and collects the phone from the floor. "The screen is cracked." She hands it to me across the table while my heart works its way up to a vibration in my chest. My shaky hands accept my iPhone, and she nods, encouraging me to look. I take a long breath and close my eyes, seeing Theo as clear as day in my darkness. His face; his body; his sharp, bristly jaw. I hear his words, threatening but encouraging. I shiver and open the message.

> Callum will pick you up at seven this evening. I'm taking you for dinner.
> You will be gracious and accept.

My shakes go up a notch, making the phone tremble in my hold, and Jess is beside me in a split second, pulling her chair closer and taking the phone from my trembling hand, replacing it with my coffee. "Okay, let's talk about this," she says, resting her forearms on the table, like she's set for a board meeting. "What's putting you off?"

"I told you last night." I neglect to mention that I expect he's not exactly a law-abiding citizen.

"You're worried you'll get attached and it won't work out?"

I shrug. "Guess so."

"But wouldn't it be nice to have sex with a man because you really want to, and not because you simply want to prove to yourself that you can?"

She's hit the nail on the head. Sex has always been purely a means to prove I'm not scarred for life by the bastard who tormented me. It doesn't mean I enjoy it. It doesn't mean I want it. My dalliances are almost robotic for me, and always without attachment. I'm not ruined. I'm just...a little broken.

Jess stands and pats my shoulder, smiling softly. "Please, Izzy, just do it. He's obviously into you." She wanders off, leaving me at the table. "I've never seen you in a tangle over a man before. Don't be afraid of feeling safe. You deserve to be."

I watch her until she disappears out of the kitchen as I turn the phone in my hand repeatedly, searching for all the reasons why I shouldn't go to dinner with Theo. They're nowhere to be found. They've abandoned me.

* * *

I wasn't quite with it for my entire shift, my focus and concentration shot. Susan pulled me aside at the end of the day, concerned I was coming down with something. She insisted on taking my temperature and, of course, it was normal. I told her I was fine, just a little tired after back-to-back hard-core shifts, and she accepted, offering to do handover so I could get away on time and get a good night's sleep. I was immensely grateful, since I've still not packed and have a list as long as my arm of things to do before leaving for Vegas. Including texting Theo back to politely decline his offer. Or demand. Whichever. My phone has been burning a hole in my bag all day.

After collecting my bag and coat, I stop off at Mable's bed to say goodbye, hoping she doesn't bring up the mammoth man who turned up yesterday to take me home. She was off being x-rayed earlier and hasn't had the opportunity to grill me since.

Her eyes shine like diamonds when I round the corner into her bay. "Here she is," she singsongs, pushing her palms into the mattress on either side of her waist to push herself up, hissing and spitting.

"Mable, stop moving," I scold, passing her the control device for the bed. "Use this."

She takes it from my hand and shoves it back to the bed, ignoring me. Because she has a more important matter on her mind. "So, the hunk who was here yesterday."

"The fracture isn't healing, then?" I say, my way of telling her not to go there.

"No, it's not." She waves a hand dismissively through the air. "The hunk."

I screw up my face in defeat. I've been looking after this woman for two weeks, and I know her well enough now to know she won't let this go. She's a stubborn old bird. "What about him?"

She gives me an impish grin. "You been telling me porky-pies, my love?"

"No."

"You said there's no man in your life."

"There isn't."

"Then who was the delicious hunk?"

"Theo."

She cocks her head, eyeing me suspiciously. "Come on, Izzy. Give an old, crippled lady *something*."

"So you want to be crippled now, huh?"

"Tell me." She pats the mattress.

"I don't really know him," I say, ignoring her offer to take a seat on her bed and opting for the chair instead. Besides, it's against the rules to sit on a patient's bed.

"You wanna change that?"

"I'm not sure." Just as I answer, Susan rounds the corner, though I can't see her face or body, only her curvy legs. Because nearly her entire form is hidden behind a huge bouquet of flowers.

Her head pokes out from the side. "These were left for you at the desk," she says, thrusting them at me.

I have to sit back in the chair to fit them on my lap, the aroma of bright red roses filling my nose. "For me?"

"Yes," she confirms, reaching for the antibacterial spray and squirting some in her palms. "No flowers on the ward."

"I'm sorry, I wasn't expecting any." I pull the card free, shuffling the roses to the side to read it.

See you at seven.

I swallow. Hard. I can't decide whether I'm flattered or annoyed by his gesture. I remember his ticking jaw as he told me to get out of his car. He was desperate to get rid of me then. What's changed? Once again, Theo Kane is throwing mixed signals. And that soon has me concluding that I'm annoyed. How does he expect me to re-act to this huge, beautiful spray of flowers? Call him and gush down the line? Swoon? I don't know where I stand with him, and having worked my arse off to stabilize myself in recent years, to find my feet and get on with my life, I don't need a man messing with that.

"I'll get these out of here," I say to Susan, who's standing over me, arms crossed over her ample chest.

"Well?" She nods at the card as I get up.

"Yes, well?" Mable backs her up eagerly. "Are they from the hunk?"

"Yes, they're from the hunk," I confirm, passing the two women. "See you in a week."

"Don't have too much fun," Susan calls after me.

"What?" Mable asks, disgusted. "Don't listen to her, Izzy. Be bad but careful!"

I laugh as I head out of the ward, reveling in the knowledge that I won't be back for a whole week. I retrieve my phone from my bag and pull up Theo's message, tapping in a reply and quickly sending it.

I was gracious.

I just didn't accept.

* * *

My to-do list is growing by the minute, things coming to me as I search for my passport and case. "Sun cream," I blurt to the drawer that I'm currently rummaging through, looking for the document I need to get me out of London and into Vegas. "Got ya." I grab my passport and throw it on my bed before rushing to the kitchen and adding sun cream to my long list. "Swimsuit," I shout.

"You don't have any?" Jess asks, relaxing at the table with a glass of wine, fully packed and organized.

"I haven't been on holiday for over ten years."

"I have loads of bikinis. Feel free to borrow."

I give her a look that Jess reads well, guilt swooping in and invading her pretty face. "Don't look at me like that," I warn, and she forces her face into a smile. "It's cool."

"I think you should wear a bikini and own it," Jess says, pushing my wine across the table.

"I'll be stared at for all the wrong reasons." Taking a sip of my wine, I find my hand on my midriff, circling the spot where the only physical reminder of him remains. I shudder, and Jess doesn't miss it.

"I might buy a new swimsuit myself." She stands and comes to me, kissing my forehead while I smile. "There's some amazing designs this season."

Her gesture is sweet but not necessary. "Shut up," I say, gently pushing her away.

She goes with ease, skipping out of the kitchen, leaving me thinking about what else needs to be added to my list in an attempt at diverting my mind from more unpleasant thoughts.

"Izzy," I hear her call, and I drag myself up, heading for her room. But I don't make it there, stalling in the hallway when I see her standing at the door. "It's for you," she says, biting her bottom lip and pulling it open to its widest, revealing a man standing on the doorstep.

My relief is profound when I note it's not Theo. It's Callum, and he'll be much easier to refuse. I walk forward and replace Jess in the doorway, spotting a Mercedes parked out front. "Hi," I say, all smiley and polite, holding on to the edge of the door.

"Miss White." Callum nods, his expressionless gaze running down my frame, probably wondering why I'm in my work uniform. His dark brown eyes scowl a little. "Mr. Kane is expecting you."

"He shouldn't be. I texted him to let him know that I couldn't make it." I congratulate myself for maintaining my politeness and sure tone. "I'm sorry you've had a wasted journey."

Theo's driver smiles tightly. It's in impatience, and it doesn't soften his features one tiny bit. "It won't be wasted if you come."

I make sure I don't break our eye contact, because that would be displaying weakness. I'm not weak. I'm strong, as Callum will soon realize. "Like I said, I'm sorry you've had a wasted journey."

His lips pucker on a light, suppressed laugh as he backs away. "Have it your way." He nods, forced, and walks away, sliding into his car and pulling off quickly.

Have it my way? Yes, I will. I close the door with a satisfied nod and find Jess behind me. "What?" Her lips are pressed together.

"And that was?"

"Theo's driver . . . I think."

Her face says it all. "Lord Almighty."

I make my way back to the kitchen, Jess hot on my heels. "Your knickers just burst into flames, didn't they?" I chuckle.

"I don't know why you won't just go for dinner with him."

"We're going to Vegas tomorrow," I remind her, as if she could have forgotten about the trip that's been in the making for a year and bled us both dry of savings. "I'll save my energy for that."

"Fine by me," she sings, discarding her wine and reaching for both my hands. I give them to her, and she starts to dance us around the kitchen. "Vegas, baby!"

I burst into fits of giggles, being twirled in circles with Jess's cheesy grin beaming at me. I was already excited, but now I'm dizzy with it. Literally. "Stop!" I laugh, closing my eyes.

And she does. Abruptly. Then I hear the hard rap at the door. My smiles and laughter shrivel up, but I remain dizzy. "Ignore it," I demand, my hands still clutching Jess's. "He'll go away eventually."

"You know, I really don't think he will," Jess replies, sounding worried *and* intrigued.

"He'll have to. I'm not answering." I shut the kitchen door, blocking out the echo of his follow-up knock.

"So we're going to hide in here all night?" Jess asks with a furrowed forehead.

"If we have to."

"Seriously?"

I laugh. "Yes, very seriously." I fetch more wine and wave it at her face. "We have supplies. Let's just drink. No work tomorrow," I remind her.

"Just tell him no if you're that determined. Simple."

"He won't listen," I grate, taking the bottle to my lips and glugging a bit down. "The phone, the flowers, turning up at work. He's immune to the word no. No one says no to Theo Kane." More wine.

I must remain strong. For the first time in a *very* long time, I feel like I'm making progress. They're small steps, but they're small steps in the right direction. I know where I'm heading.

When I look at Theo Kane, I don't know where I'd be heading if I were to get involved with him, and that's a good enough reason to steer clear. I like where I'm at in my life. I like who I am. And that's an achievement, because I hated myself for such a long time. I'm finally breaking free of the fear that's controlled me.

"I'm fine on my own," I tell her. "I'm *happy* on my own." *I'm in control on my own.* When I'm with Theo, I don't feel in control in the slightest.

Jess sighs, her shoulders dropping. "Pass me that bottle." She makes grabby hands at me, and I willingly hand it over, pleased she understands.

Another knock at the door. "So what are we going to do as soon as we arrive?" I ask, ignoring it.

"Drink." Jess takes another glug before handing the bottle back to me. I accept gratefully and take it to my lips. She looks over her shoulder to the closed kitchen door as more knocks sound.

"And on the second night?" I rush on, needing to distract her.

"I don't know. Bellagio's?"

"Great!" I swig again and give her the bottle. "And the third night I was thinking a nice meal and a little gamble." I'm literally yelling now.

"Right," she says slowly, and then she sighs. "This is ridiculous." She slams the bottle down and pulls the kitchen door open.

"Jess, no!"

"I'll tell him no if you won't." She marches on her way with determination.

"Jess!" I'm running forward a few steps and retreating again, back and forth, unsure of what to do. Hide. I should hide. "Tell him I'm out!" *Damn it!* I rush after her, hoping to make it to the door before she does so I can stop her from opening it.

"Fuck me!"

I hear Jess's startled curse as I screech to a halt behind her, finding she's already pulled the front door open and her head is slowly tilting back to find Theo's face. I can't see my friend, but I'm guessing her jaw is lax.

The sight of him, tall and oddly refined behind his intimidating front, makes me feel like I've just been smacked in the head with a baseball bat. He's a vision. His top lip quirks as he looks past Jess, abandoning my dazed friend in favor of me. And again I'm tucking my hair behind my ears, my gaze dropping. One day I won't look like a bedraggled mess when he appears from nowhere. "I texted to tell you I wouldn't be having dinner with you." I jump in before he can ask why I'm not ready.

"And I assumed it must have been a slip of your fingers on the keys."

"What . . ." I do a quick mental calculation. "All seven words?"

"Eight," he counters, getting my attention again. He watches me carefully. "If you include the kiss that you tagged on the end."

My cheeks heat under his watchful eyes, and Jess swings around with an accusing look. "A kiss?"

My lips remain locked tightly shut, not willing to explain myself. Though it doesn't stop me from justifying it in my head. I added it as a gesture, that's all. To soften the blow.

"Yes, a kiss," Theo confirms. "It said, '*Thank you, but I can't make dinner.*'" He reels off my message from memory. "And then there was definitely a kiss." He raises his eyebrows, pouting a little. "Don't take that kiss away from me, Izzy. It'll break my heart."

I want to smile, but that would be feeding his playfulness. And I shouldn't do that, no matter how thrilling it is to bounce off his light banter. I'm still figuring out what to say next when Jess opens the door wide and gestures for him to come in. He dips a little to clear the frame and avoid hitting his head. What is she doing?

I point a steely glare at her that she totally ignores, the cow.

Fuck, I'm hot. My hand comes up to fan my face without thought, triggering another knowing smile from Theo. He looks lovely when he smiles, and I sense he doesn't do it often. His smiles are warm and tempting.

Tempting.

He's that already, even when he's straight-faced and ominous. With a cute curve of his lips, he's plain irresistible. That dimple is adorable and definitely misplaced.

The narrow hallway becomes far too crowded when he enters, and I flatten myself against the wall to avoid making contact with him. I'm going to kill Jess. Slowly.

"It was nice to meet you," she chimes, trotting off, leaving me and Theo more or less wedged in the space. I breathe in to widen the small gap between our torsos when he stops right in front of me.

"Your friend is quite hospitable," he says, lingering before me. "Maybe you should take note."

My eyes narrow. "And maybe she might be easier to bed than me. Why don't you try your luck?" I want to regret my spiteful retort, if only because I've insulted Jess, but I can't. He's pissed me off now, chasing away any temptation that I was fighting off.

Though it all comes steaming back when Theo takes my jaw in his big hand and brings his face close to mine, even if his handsome features are twisting in disdain. My lungs squeeze as I fight for breath. He looks truly threatening now. Yet I'm not scared.

Why am I not scared of him?

"That was uncalled for," he whispers menacingly but softly, keeping me in place with his grip, but more with his eyes.

I clench my back teeth, not cowering nor backing down. "You want me to apologize?"

His grip loosens, going from holding to feeling, his palm encasing the entire side of my face. "I'll forsake an apology in exchange for dinner."

I shake my head no, exhausted by the strength needed to continue refusing him. Everything inside me is telling me to just go. "It's still no," I affirm. "With all due respect, Mr. Kane, I'm really not interested in getting involved with a man. Especially not a man who carries a gun. But thanks for the offer." I smile sweetly, and I can tell he's struggling to hold back his own amusement.

"But you're forgetting something, Miss White," he says roughly, and I tilt my head, prompting him to remind me. "If I want something, I have it."

"You buy it?" I ask, referring to my fixed phone and flowers.

"Yes."

"What if it can't be bought?"

"Then I take it."

"And what if *it* fights?"

His lips part, his gaze dropping to my mouth as he moves in and traps me against the wall. Our bodies meld into each other. I feel his chest inflate on a deep suck of air. He looks awed, happy, his head shaking mildly as if not believing how good it feels to touch me. It feels so good. He brings his mouth close to my ear. "Then it makes the victory so much sweeter when I win," he whispers, his hand sliding to the back of my neck and gripping gently, applying a little pressure to turn my head and bring my mouth closer to his. My breath diminishes as his lips skim over mine, and I whimper, the sensation of his mouth, the feel of his tongue tracing across my flesh, and the heat of his breath reeling me in that final stretch. He tastes divine.

Clamping his teeth lightly over my bottom lip, he retreats slowly until it pops free. My palms meet the wall behind me and press into the plaster, anything to hold on to except him. "You don't feel or sound like you would fight very hard, Izzy." He peels his body from mine and pulls the door open, watching me disintegrate against the wall. "Think about dinner." He walks out, and my fingers come to my lips, feeling gently where his mouth was a moment ago.

"Oh...fucking...hell..." Why did I let him do that? I look to the doorway of the kitchen as if searching for the answer there, but I find Jess instead, looking as bamboozled as I am. "See?" I laugh, shaken to my absolute core. "He won't take no for an answer."

"You don't need to be saying no to him." Jess looks to the closed door, her cheeks puffing out. "Shit, Izzy. You need to be letting him do what the hell he pleases with you, because it sure as shit looks like it would be quite an experience."

"I know." I'm done with denying it. I said I wouldn't pass it up if he made a pass, but he didn't give me a chance to. He left me hanging. And I'm devastated. "You need to get me to Vegas pronto." I need to get as far away from Theo Kane as possible before I cave and let him possess me. Because that's exactly what will happen. He'll possess me. One brief kiss and I'm all over the place. Anything more and I fear I'll be signing my soul over to him.

Or the devil.

CHAPTER 5

We really have gone all out. Premium economy on our flight was lush, even if it has swallowed up most of my savings. I'm not going to beat myself up about it. I've never had savings to splurge so recklessly, and I've worked my fingers to the bone to tick this biggie off my bucket list.

Jess and I are smiling like a pair of prats as we tug our cases out of the airport. "Holy shit," I blurt, being smacked in the face with heat.

Jess retrieves her floppy hat from her bag and shoves it on her head. "Don't breathe through your nose."

I see my name on an iPad screen being held by a suited man and wave for his attention. "Why?" I look behind me as I pull my case over to him, finding Jess pinching her nose.

"You might singe your nasal hair."

I burst out laughing, handing my case to our driver when he smiles and gestures for it. "Welcome to Vegas, ladies."

"Thanks!" we sing in unison, following him onward. He takes us to a shiny black Escalade and gets us comfy before loading our cases.

Jess makes a dive for the bottled water positioned between our seats and drinks it down ravenously. "Oh, that's so good."

"Hard Rock?" the driver asks as he hops in, quickly pulling out of the car park.

"Please," I confirm, giving Jess excited eyes, which she returns before diving into her bag and pulling out her makeup. She starts to freshen up, and though I roll my eyes, I accept her compact powder when she hands it to me. No work uniform for five whole days. I need to make the most of it.

The drive to our hotel is surprisingly quick, and I reluctantly vacate the cool car and step into the near-on unbearable heat again.

WHEN THIS HOUSE IS ROCKING, DON'T BOTHER
KNOCKING . . . COME ON IN!

"Okay!" Jess shouts after she's read the sign over the entrance of the Hard Rock Hotel. "I can't believe we're here."

I follow her in, and we both come to a stop as we're hit by cool air. Bright lights glow at every turn, and a fuck-off big Harley is on display. "Oh wow," I breathe.

"Check in, dump our cases, and drink." Jess makes a dash for the insanely long reception desk, and I'm relieved to find only a few people in the queue after it feels like I've done nothing but queue since we left home. We're armed with our key card ten minutes later, and up in our room ten minutes after that.

I dive on the bed and sigh. "We need to keep going or our body clocks will be buggered."

Jess frowns and spins toward the long drapes keeping the room dark. "What's that noise?"

I look toward the drawn curtain, where the vibrating beats of music sound beyond. "It's coming from out there."

Jess is over like a shot, yanking open the curtains, then the terrace doors beyond them. Music blares in, loud and pumping. Calvin Harris, if I'm not mistaken. "Fuck. Izzy, look!"

I take in the scene before us. A pool, all tropical-looking, with bodies everywhere drinking and dancing. "It's two p.m.," I murmur.

"Yes, but it's ten p.m. at home." She starts dancing around the room, singing at the top of her voice as I scan the ground below, and then the skyline. I can't believe we're here, and it couldn't have come at a better time in my life. A time-out. Room to breathe. Here, I will let my hair down and enjoy my first girlie holiday. I don't want to waste a moment of it. Especially not on thinking.

* * *

We land at the circular bar in Hard Rock half an hour later, fresh and ready for our first night. "Surprise us," Jess tells the barman, her blond curls free and loose. It's nice to see her hair down for once, instead of coiled up tightly into a bun as it always is for work.

"My kinda ladies." The barman goes straight for a bottle under the counter and starts to pour.

I pull my insanely short black dress down my thighs as I try to take in the huge space. "I'm mesmerized," I say, spotting a card table surrounded by rowdy men and a few women scattered in between.

"Do you think they're hookers?" Jess asks. I ponder her question for a few moments, looking the women up and down before I cast my eyes to my front. They look no different from me, dressed up to the nines at only two-thirty p.m.

"Here, ladies," the barman says, and we turn to find two long, clear highballs on the bar. "Some advice for you, girls." He slides a small plastic plate across the bar with our bill on it.

I sign the piece of white paper to our room, ignoring the insane cost of two drinks. "What's that?"

"Happy hour is six to seven." He smiles, obviously catching my poorly concealed gawk at the dollar signs. "Two for one," he adds, leaving us with our drinks.

I swoop mine up and turn on my stool, slurping back the mystery concoction and immediately wincing. "Fucking hell."

Jess starts coughing. "Jesus. No measly measures here."

"It's good once you get past the initial shock." I shudder and slip down from my stool when I spot some straws on the bar. I need to stir this thing. I hear my phone ring and look back as I pluck two straws from the holder, seeing Jess help herself and answer.

And when her eyes widen, I have a horrible feeling I know who is on the line. And then she nods and confirms my fear, prompting me to start shaking my head frantically.

"No, it's Jess," she says, cringing. "She's not available right now." I start nodding as I hurry back to my stool, drawing a line across my neck with a fingertip. "Uh, yeah." Jess frowns. "How'd you know?" She's quiet for a bit, and I slip my straw into my glass, taking a long draw without stirring it. The vodka hits the back of my throat, and I start to cough and splutter all over the bar. "Of course." She smacks my thigh, her lips pursed—her way of telling me to shut the hell up. "Vegas, if you must know," she says, rather snootily. "And you're interrupting, so I'll bid you farewell." Clicking off the call, she passes me my phone and I place it coolly on the bar, refusing to entertain my friend's interested face *or* my wild wondering.

She plucks the other straw from my hand, slips it into her glass, stirs, and then wraps her lips around it, watching me as she drinks. My eyes narrow on her. "Why'd you tell him we're here?"

My irritation goes way over her head. "The international tone kind of gave us away."

"Still, you shouldn't have answered."

"How was I supposed to know it would be him?"

"Who else would it be?" I ask on a laugh. "The only people who call me are you and work. You're here, and I'm on leave from work."

Her sudden straight lips make me look away, my attention now on my drink. I know who else she thought it could be. Every time my damn phone rings with an unknown number, my heart kicks with fear. It's stupid. There's no way he could track me down. I'm miles away, and now going by a different name.

"I just thought if there was any slight chance it was him, he'd hear an unfamiliar voice and conclude he has the wrong number. I'm sorry."

I smile a small smile, returning my attention to Jess's sorry expression. "This trip isn't getting off to the best start, huh?"

"Then let's fix that." She pushes my drink to my lips, and I take a slurp as demanded. "Theo is delicious in a rough, persistent kind of way, though."

"Stop trying to convince me he's a good idea." I'm a second away from telling Jess everything I know, including the fact that Theo carries a gun. Then let's see if she's so adamant that I should entertain his advances.

"I think you're being too dismissive. You don't even know him."

"I know enough."

"Or maybe you *don't* know enough," she replies, and I shoot her a surprised look. "I'm just saying, try to look at the positives rather than the negatives. He might surprise you. You'll never know unless you open your mind."

But by opening my mind, I'll be opening my heart and making myself vulnerable. I'm done with being vulnerable.

* * *

I have no idea how much later it is; there are no clocks or windows in this place, but we're huddled over a tall table cuddling two more of those mystery concoctions, laughing like we've never laughed before. We've thrived in each other's company, watched the comings and goings, and placed bets on the status of every woman we've seen—hooker, wife, girlfriend, gold digger, or singleton like us.

I elbow Jess in the side when two men break away from a crowd and make their way over, smiling. "Oh, hello," Jess says, turning on her stool to welcome them. Both are good-looking— one Latino, the other black—and both are clutching bottles of beer.

"British?" the black guy asks, pointing his bottle at each of us in turn. His ebony skin is flawless, his physique defined, his head shaved and smooth. I'd estimate he's in his mid-twenties.

"American?" I counter with a smile, diving in feet first.

He laughs and points to his mate, who's about the same age and also fit but a little shorter. "This is Kyle. I'm Denny."

I offer my hand. "Izzy. This is Jess." I cock my head toward my friend, finding she's smiling suggestively at Kyle.

"Damn, girl, I love your accent," Denny says.

"You do?"

"Yeah, keep talkin' to me."

I giggle despite myself, feeling his grip flex around mine. "Join us?" I ask.

"Awesome." He slides onto a stool smoothly, followed by Kyle.

"See?" Jess claps her hands, delighted. "In America, everything is 'awesome.'"

"So what do you guys say?" Kyle asks, amused.

"Fucking great! That's what we say, but I much prefer 'awesome.'"

Jess's eyes meet Kyle's and, God be damned, they gaze at each other like neither has seen someone of the opposite sex before.

"I prefer 'fuckin' great.'" Kyle clinks his bottle with the side of Jess's glass before taking a sip, keeping his dark eyes on her blues. We've been in Vegas for . . . I don't know how long. Hours. We're drunk, we've met some fun guys, and so far we're having a bloody blast.

Laughs roll as we spend the next few hours comparing slang phrases and curse words with our new friends. The drinks flow, though I ensure we buy our own, and the night passes so fast, I hate the notion that the whole five days might speed by this quickly.

"Wanker," Jess slurs, leaning on the table for support. "Wank-urrrrr."

"Wa . . ."—Kyle's chin juts out—"ker . . ."

"Try 'tosser,'" I say with a laugh.

"What's a tosser?" Denny throws me a look of confusion, the smooth black skin of his forehead showing creases for the first time.

"It's a wanker."

"Like 'jerk'?"

"Yes!"

"Awesome." Denny smiles, throwing his arm around my shoulder and pulling me in. I don't bat an eyelid, letting him drape himself all over me.

"You, my dear gentleman," Kyle starts in his best English accent as he points to Denny, "are a bladdy tosser."

"Bloody," I howl, my stomach starting to hurt from laughing so much. "That was the worst English accent I've heard."

"Then you need to be teaching us, darlin'." Denny grins. "What are your plans while you're here?"

I look to Jess, who shrugs. "I'm open to suggestions."

Kyle beams from ear to ear, peeking down before getting her in a headlock. She goes willingly, giving me a coy, knowing smile. "Good to hear you're thinking with an open mind."

She nudges him playfully. "Smart arse."

"Ass!" he yells. "If you're going to be my friend, sweet thing, you have to say it like me. Ass." He ruffles her hair. "There's a pool party here tomorrow. Up for it?"

"Yep!" we sing in unison, raising our glasses to toast the plan for tomorrow. I'm so glad I bought that new swimsuit.

* * *

They were total gents, walking us back to our room, with no suggestion or hint that they expected to come in. Kyle was rewarded with a full-on snog from Jess, whereas I simply pecked Denny's cheek and thanked him for a fun evening. Letting my hair down is still in the cards. Just not on the first night. He was cool with that, singing all the curse words he'd learned as he weaved his way down the corridor.

We fell into bed and giggled like teenagers about our first night in Vegas and eventually fell asleep at... I don't know what time. But I was smiling.

* * *

"Damn." Jess's eyes nearly fall out of her head when I appear from the bathroom in my new swimsuit. "Your boobs look immense."

I start to rearrange the cups around my cleavage, wondering if I'm brave enough. My stomach is concealed, just how I like it, but my boobs are on display, the plunging neckline fierce. "Too much?"

"Wow!" Jess purrs, grabbing a camisole and slipping it on over her black bikini, which has gold hoops holding it together between her boobs and on her hips. "Turn around." I do as ordered, not that there's much to see, as my swimsuit is completely backless. "I love it," Jess declares.

I pull my tousled black waves into a knot, but immediately release it when Jess shakes her head. "Down?"

"Yes, you've got that beach-tousled thing going on. It's hot. Come on."

We head down to the pool, and after collecting two towels, we venture into the crazy scene. I feel somewhat intimidated by the throngs of gorgeous women as we weave through the crowds, looking for somewhere to settle.

"Bed, ladies?" A man asks, indicating a double sunbed with a cozy mattress atop it. "Two-fifty with a free drink thrown in."

"Two hundred and fifty dollars?" I blurt, ignoring the jab in my side from Jess. "To lay on a bed?"

"Or you can take a cabana for two thousand." He points across the way to some huts.

"How much is it to lay on the ground?" I ask.

"We'll take the bed," Jess jumps in, throwing me an evil look. "Thanks." She gets her purse and counts out a pile of notes.

"Are you mad?" I whisper-hiss in her ear.

"Cool it." She brushes off my concern. "We're on holiday."

"Vacation," I mutter, spreading my towel on my side of the bed. "The drinks better be awesome."

Jess falls apart laughing as she slips her shades on and joins me in removing our cover-ups. I don't feel self-conscious. There are women with bits of material the size of pound coins covering their nipples. We settle and accept the drinks brought to us, and I slurp back my first dose of alcohol of the day, feeling surprisingly healthy considering the amount we indulged in last night. "God, this is the life." Jess drops to her back, her foot tapping in time to the beat of Michael Calfan's "Treasured Soul," while I spend some time taking it all in. The sun is blazing, happiness and fun surround us, and I have the biggest smile on my face. Yes, this really is the life. At least, it is for the next five days.

I sigh and drop to my back, but bolt up again when something across the pool catches my eye. And before I can stop it, my cup slips from my grasp and every sound and movement around me stops. "No," I whisper.

Jess is up like a shot, sitting on the edge of the bed. "Izzy, what the fuck?" She starts frantically brushing down her front, and when I look at her blankly, I find her soaking wet, her sunglasses askew and ice cubes scattered in her lap.

"I'm sorry," I mumble, pushing myself up to my feet and frantically searching the other side of the pool. Where *he* was. I turn on the spot, my tongue becoming sticky in my mouth from dryness. Nothing.

"What's the matter with you?" Jess asks, looking down at her front incredulously. "Damn it!"

"I saw him," I say mindlessly, wondering if my mind is playing games with me. He's been in my thoughts, I won't deny it, but I've done a damn fine job of pushing him away whenever he's creeped forward.

"Saw who?"

"Theo." I don't hesitate to tell her, hoping she'll join me in my search as I scan the pool area. I must have imagined it. Surely I imagined it. *Please tell me I imagined it!* I pull the waiter to a stop as he passes. "Another two, please. Extra strong." I need a drink. I know I haven't had much sleep, but . . . seeing things?

Jess circles on the spot, too, her eyes narrowed as she scans the area around us. "That's impossible."

No, it isn't. "Oh my goodness," I whisper as Jess follows my line of sight and blurts an expletive, obviously seeing what I'm seeing. I reach out and grab her arm to steady myself as he appears from across the pool, his eyes trained on me.

"Shit, he *is* here." She swings around and grabs me, pulling me down to the bed. I feel like I'm hyperventilating, my breaths becoming too short.

"I'm dizzy," I say, letting my head drop into my hands. "Jess, what is he doing here?"

"I don't fucking know. He's your stalker, not mine." She directs the straw in her drink to my mouth. "Have some."

I slurp down the icy liquid hungrily, willing myself to wake up soon. In Vegas? I want to consider the fact that I'm mistaken, that tiredness has morphed another man into Theo, but all these feelings, the instability, the breathlessness, the intrigue, it's all indicative of one man alone.

I don't need Jess to tell me when he reaches us. All the hairs on the back of my neck rise, and a prickling feeling pitter-patters down my spine. I close my eyes and pointlessly pray for someone to help me, and when I open them, a pair of dress shoes are in my downcast vision. Dress shoes? By a pool? My stupid observation is forgotten when warmth spreads across my back from the sensation of his palm resting there. I don't flinch. Nothing. I'm numb. Shock, I think.

"Izzy, are you okay?" Theo crouches in front of me, taking a wrist with his spare hand. If I weren't suffering from disbelief, I'd laugh. *Am I okay?* He's showed up on the other side of the world, and he's asking if I'm okay? "Izzy, look at me."

Jess doesn't breathe a word, yet she's holding the cup of alcohol at my lips like a loyal friend. I latch onto the straw and slurp, but it's quickly removed.

"I'm not sure alcohol is wise when she's having a funny turn," Theo chastises.

"Excuse me?" Jess retorts indignantly, and I cheer her on in my head, hoping she'll chase him away with her viper tongue. "She's having a funny turn because *you're* here."

Theo is here. In fucking Vegas. What, when, who, and why the fuck? Suddenly maddened by it all, I toss my head up and my hair back, and stand. Theo is on his feet even quicker, and now a few steps away from me. It's a fight and a half to remain steady, even more so as my eyes take in every inch of him—beige chinos and a white casual shirt tucked in, collar open. More of the tattoo on his neck is visible because of the few unfastened buttons. Black shadows, all linked, and I find my eyes root there.

Until he coughs and nudges me back to life. "What in the name of God are you wearing?" he blurts, his wide eyes fixed on my chest. I see in his face a deadly beauty that could quite possibly be the death of *me*. The sun is creating a halo around his head, making it glow magnificently. Like a god's.

My anger of a moment ago deserts me, rendering me a wobbly woman, and I feel myself tilting forward, coming closer to Theo, my hand shooting up to save me before I face-plant in his chest.

"Is she drunk?" he asks, catching my hands in one of his and laying them on his chest. He's evidently concerned as he holds them in place, his other hand slipping around my waist. I might be in a state of deep shock, but he's vibrating against me, and I haven't the brain power to consider whether that's anger or because of our contact.

"No, she's disturbed." Jess laughs. "What are you doing here?"

"She looks drunk," Theo mutters, ignoring Jess's question and hauling me into his chest. I crash against him ... and melt into the sharp planes of his muscles. It feels too good. "Izzy," Theo growls, annoyed. "For God's sake, will you look at me?" He grabs my jaw and pulls my blank face up to him. I'm totally out of it. Maybe it's shock. Maybe it's fright. Or maybe those drinks were stronger than I realized. I can't be sure.

I battle to find a little composure. "What...Why...How did...?" I stammer, unable to ignore how good he feels against me.

His face softens, and relief definitely flows across his features. "Are you okay?"

Is he joking? The gravity of it all seems to steamroll forward, and I engage my muscles to push myself off of his chest. Once again, he moves me before I can move myself, taking my wrists and separating our bodies, stepping back. I frown at him, wondering how the hell he knows every move I'm going to make before I make it. He slips his shades on, stealing away the sight of his intense cobalt eyes, and I glance at Jess. There's apprehension and maybe even a little hidden awe splashed across her face. "You came to Vegas to find me?" I ask Theo incredulously.

"Actually, no, I came to Vegas because I have some business to see to."

"What?"

"You heard me."

"What business?" What does he do, anyway?

"It's none of *your* business."

"Excuse me?" I'm insulted, and it's obvious. "You turn up here out of the blue, and you're telling me it's not—"

"Hey! It's the British girls!" The greeting doesn't have time to register in my mind. Someone grabs me around the waist from behind and I startle, flying forward away from the touch, my heart jumping into my throat. "Shit, didn't mean to scare you," Denny says, holding his hands up in apology when I turn his way.

"I'm sorry," I murmur, embarrassed, as Jess reaches for me and rubs my arm gently, seeing how mortified I am. I shake my head in despair as Denny and Kyle gleam at us, their bare chests slick with tanning oil, their board shorts low on their hips. When neither Jess nor I returns their smiles, they spend a few moments assessing the scene, both taken aback when they notice Theo, who's moved a few steps away. "Whoa." Denny laughs, seeing the mountain of man before him and realizing he's with us. I mentally rewind. No, Theo's not with us. He's gate-crashing.

I smile awkwardly, looking to my friend for help. She shrugs. She's lost, too. Theo moves in closer to me, definitely possessive. I don't know if I should be angered or appreciative. But I do know that I need to break this uncomfortable atmosphere. "I'll be back in a minute," I tell Jess as the waiter arrives with our drinks.

She takes them but shakes her head discreetly, flicking a look at Theo, who has now removed his shades and has a death stare rooted on the two American guys we met last night. Denny's hand lifts, reaching for Theo's bicep. "Hey, man," he says, but his intended friendly gesture of a light smack to Theo's arm is dodged stealthily, Theo virtually bending backward to avoid it. Denny's eyes widen at the fast move, and he steps back. And Theo's death stare intensifies. "Sorry, man," Denny says, nervous as shit. "Just a friendly hello."

"Then say it," Theo growls. "Don't touch me."

I recoil at his rudeness, as does everyone else in the group. This is horrible. I dip to get in Theo's field of vision. "Can we talk?"

"Yes," he grates and indicates some tables and chairs set back from the pool. "I'll get drinks." He starts to head off, but pulls to a stop, giving each of my friends a moment of his eyes before looking at me. "And please, cover yourself up." He carries on his way.

Jess's mouth drops and hits the rim of her plastic beaker. "Is he serious?"

I ignore her rhetorical question and slip my caftan over my head, not because I'm obeying him, but because I feel exposed enough without being half-naked in his presence. "See you in a sec." I walk away from Jess, hearing whispered questions as I go. I have a serious mental pep talk going on in my head, but as I get closer to the table at the far back that Theo has chosen for our *talk*, the sound of my determined, sensible voice gets drowned out by his growing closeness. I'm in trouble. So much fucking trouble.

I slip on my sunglasses, hoping they will help offer some protection from his burning cobalt eyes, and take a seat on the opposite side of the table. He slides a glass across the table to me. "Water?" I ask.

"Yes."

On an inhale, I stop a waiter as he passes. "A vodka tonic, please," I say confidently, returning my attention to Theo. "He's paying." His jaw is beyond tight, his eyes burning holes in me. "Be careful." I smile sweetly. "You'll burn this cover-up off with that filthy look, and we can't have that, can we?"

He reaches for my sunglasses, dragging them gently away from my face. I pull in a small hitch of breath, freezing in my chair, my sass shot down. "I want to see your eyes so I know what you're thinking past this brave front." He lays them gently on the table and places his own pair of shades down next to them.

"Business?" I ask sardonically.

"Yes, business. Why didn't you tell me you were going on holiday?"

"It's none of your *business*." I'm polite but straight, though bubbling on the inside with annoyance. "You're just a man who asked me out for dinner. That's it. I don't owe you an explanation for my plans."

"I am not *just* a man, Izzy."

"You are to me," I retort, knowing resistance is the best way forward, even though Theo's flash of hurt actually bothers me. My vodka lands on the table, and I grasp it with both hands as Theo shoves a note at the waiter, not even looking at him. "I'm on holiday with a friend," I say. "It's been in the making for years, so I would be grateful if you didn't ruin it."

"It'll only be ruined if you let it be ruined."

I peek up through my lashes. "What do you mean?"

He sits forward in his chair, coming closer. The seriousness on his face is a cause for concern. "I mean, I'll promise not to bother you again. I'll let you have your girlie break. But you have to promise me dinner."

I laugh at his cheekiness. "You'll *let* me have my girlie holiday?"

He nods, not seeing the hilarity of his statement.

"Why thanks, stranger."

"Have dinner with me."

"No."

"I've come a long way. The least you can do is give me dinner in return."

Business my arse. "I didn't ask you to come here. I didn't ask you to pursue me like some weirdo. Jesus, Theo. Don't you see how stalkerish this is?"

His teeth sink into his bottom lip in contemplation as he studies me. "Stop playing games, Izzy. My patience is already stretched."

My jaw locks in an attempt to stop it from dropping in disbelief. "I'll have dinner with you." I stand, disgusted by his behavior, now just wanting to get away before that disgust transforms into something else that's far less easy to cope with. Like lust. Like desire. Just like Theo's approach to me, my feelings are contradictory. One second, I'm wary of him, the next I'm mentally stripping his clothes off. "I'll call you when I'm home." I pass him but get no farther than two steps. His hand shoots toward me, stopping me in my tracks, though he doesn't actually make contact. I look down at it hovering a few inches from my wrist, and then look up to Theo.

"I need to touch you," he whispers, slowly reaching for me and seizing my wrist, wrapping his big fingers completely around it.

I concentrate on taking deep breaths. His touch. Oh, God, his touch. It's like an intense, deep warmth that starts in one spot before spreading in every direction across my skin like cracking glass. Need? He *needs* to touch me?

Theo watches his hand on my arm, his face thoughtful, with a definite hint of intrigue. "Tonight at eight," he says, his polite order leaving me no choice but to look at him. He's gazing up at me, waiting, his blue eyes shining with...hope?

"Here?" I ask. "You want me to have dinner with you here in Vegas?"

"I'm staying at the Bellagio. Call me when you arrive, and I'll have Callum meet you at reception." He stands and moves in closer, dipping and kissing my cheek tenderly as his palm strokes over the curve of my arse. Tingles flutter across my skin, tickling me deliciously. It makes me panic, and I engage the muscles in my arms to lift and push him away. My hands come up, but they don't connect with his torso. Theo catches my wrists, stopping me from touching him once again, predicting my move. "Don't let me down, Izzy."

He turns and is strolling away from me before I can even think to object. I immediately have to sit down again to collect myself. The lingering feel of his soft bristle on my face and his breath spreading across my cheek resonates as I watch his long, thick legs take steady strides. He moves with effortless grace for such a huge man, weaving through the crowds without even a brush of contact to a single person.

My heart is going loopy, my fingers clawed into the arms of the chair. It takes a good ten minutes of pulling myself together in my seat before I chance standing, lifting myself slowly to ensure my stability. He does this to me. He tosses me into ineptness, and no matter how hard I try to cling to my clear and stable frame of mind, I'm destined to fail each time. Theo has a hold of me and he hasn't even really had a hold of me. Not a proper hold. Where will I be then, if my mind is already consumed by the *thought* of him all over me, making love to me, his mouth touching every inch of my body? It's the most vivid fantasy I've ever had. And the most dangerous. What's worse, I know it will be as mind-blowing as I'm imagining it to be—so intense and overwhelming. I don't even know him...yet I feel like I do.

I look down at my wrist, lost in my thoughts. He told me he needed to touch me. I like it when Theo touches me. I hate it, but I like it. I sigh, so confused by it all, and especially confused by the man who is the source of my muddle. Everyone around me seems intimidated by Theo Kane, and I can't figure out why I'm not. Not in that way. For the first time in my life, I am desperate to be intimate with a man for no other reason than...to just be intimate. My need to prove myself that I'm not broken isn't featuring in my thoughts at all.

"Shit, Izzy," I breathe as I collect my drink and head back over to our sun lounger, spotting Jess at the bar with Denny and Kyle, laughing and slurping. I catch her eye, and as she makes a move to break away from the boys, I hold up my hand in indication that I'll come to her. *One sec*, I mouth, and she nods, returning to her drink.

I sit on the edge of the bed and pull out my phone, loading up Google and quickly typing in his name. It takes a few seconds to give me the results, and when it does, there's nothing connected to the strapping, handsome man who's infiltrated my girlie holiday. Not. One. Thing.

I frown and spin the phone in my hand, thinking. *Everyone* appears on Google somewhere these days. Okay, so I don't, but that's because I've made a point not to put myself on *any* social media platform that could lead to Google results. Only someone hiding something wouldn't appear online. So what's he hiding?

"Izzy!" Jess calls, snapping me from my silent pondering and waving me over. I smile and throw my phone back in my bag, standing and pulling off my caftan and slinging it on the lounger. He told me to cover up and I did, but not because he told me to. It's been a long time since I feared repercussions from a man. Theo Kane won't change that.

CHAPTER 6

We hung out with the boys for the rest of the day, Jess getting progressively closer—literally—to Kyle, while Denny was happy to laugh and mess around with me after he'd picked my brain about who Theo was and whether he should be worried. I'd laughed it off, but he must have sensed my conflict because he didn't make a pass or push his luck the whole time we chatted and laughed in the sun. I was grateful. So were the few girls sunbathing nearby who Denny gave the eye a few times. The fact that I wasn't bothered spoke volumes. I couldn't think beyond Theo's summons to dinner and whether I would be going, but I kept my frustrating debate to myself. When Jess had asked what went down with him, I'd given her a condensed version of the truth, and I neglected to mention Theo's dinner request. We've saved forever and waited just as long to have this holiday. I feel bad enough that Theo has showed up and interrupted it. I won't give Jess reason to believe it will be ruined beyond that. No dinner.

No.

Dinner.

I make a conscious effort not to get totally wasted, sipping sensibly for the rest of the day. I need to keep my wits about me. Jess, however, doesn't take it so easy. She's well and truly pissed as we wander through the casino floor, heading for the elevators that'll take us up to our room. It's six thirty p.m., and the atmosphere around us is pumping.

"I had the best day," Jess slurs, punching the call button for the elevator. "Let's shower and head out."

I laugh as we enter the lift. "You sure you don't need a power nap?" I'm hoping it's a resounding yes, because I'm feeling sluggish after a hard day sunbathing, socializing, and pretending I'm not in internal turmoil.

"Hell no." The doors close and carry us up to the twelfth floor. "If I sit down, I won't get up again. Power through." She raises her arm to cheer herself on, and then staggers back. I catch her just before she hits the wall.

"We'll head out at midnight." I try to reason with her. If we go out now, I'll be carrying her home by eleven. "Denny said things only get going then, anyway. Have a nap."

"No." She's adamant, leading the way when the doors open, zigzagging down the corridor. "No one sleeps in Vegas."

I smile with an exasperated shake of my head and take the key card from her fumbling fingers when she fails after three attempts to get it in the slot. "There." I push the door open and let her go first before following her in. "I'm going to jump straight in the shower," I call.

"I'm going to find the Red Bull."

I close the bathroom door behind me and turn the temperature dial of the shower to cool, quickly stripping down and hopping in. I groan, letting the water rain all over me for a few relaxing moments before I wash my hair, shave, and scrub.

I jump out and grab a towel. "All yours," I say as I leave the bathroom, coming to a stop at the sight of Jess sprawled on the bed. My shoulders drop, and I heave a deep sigh. She's unconscious and snoring lightly. "No one sleeps in Vegas," I say to myself, pulling in my towel and settling on my bed, annoyed that I'm now more than awake after my shower. I flick on the television and scroll through the channels a few times, hoping tiredness will return soon and I can join Jess for a few hours' sleep before we head out.

Fifteen minutes later, I'm still wide awake and getting quite pissed off about it. "Jess." I shake her and get a few snorts in return. "Wake up."

Nothing. She's out for the count.

I growl to myself and flip onto my front, burying my face in the pillow. This isn't good. I have nothing to focus on except the images in my head. Of him. "Damn it," I mutter, glancing at the clock. Seven o'clock. I roll over and stare up at the ceiling, my thoughts speeding into overdrive.

Just do it, I tell myself. *Open your mind.* I have two choices. Meet him, or stay here and drive myself mad thinking about him. I sit up abruptly, my eyes darting around the dim room. This is crazy, but no matter how hard I try to push him away, the bottom line is, I *want* to see him. For my sins, I want to see Theo Kane. Test him. Try to figure him out. Explore the insanely deep effect we seem to have on each other.

I jump up before I can change my mind, and fly to the wardrobe, flicking through the hangers of clothes. After too much deliberation, I settle on a cream—probably too tight—cap-sleeved dress and some muted gold sandals. Keeping my foundation light, my green eyes heavy with smudged gray eyeliner, and my lips bare, I scrunch my waves into a tousled mess and run fingers coated in serum though the ends, giving it extra shine. I stand back from the mirror, chewing my lip, nervous as shit. But I have to do this. I'm going around in circles and Theo is following closely behind. Bite the bullet. Dip a toe. See what happens.

I scribble a note for Jess in case she wakes up, telling her to call me when she rouses from the dead, and leave it on the bedside before heading for the door. I'll be two hours, tops. Hopefully she won't wake within that time and I can sneak back in. She'll never know I went anywhere, eliminating my need to explain my reasoning for going.

I spend the entire cab ride to the Bellagio going over that reasoning, shaking like a leaf, butterflies erupting in my tummy and going wild. I wander into the lobby, gazing around at the marble interior in awe. Trying to absorb the palatial foyer, I hover near reception, keeping a lookout for Theo's driver. The area is busy, a constant stream of people coming in and out, gambling machines dinging and players cheering.

"Miss White?"

I turn to find Callum behind me. He's his usual suited, ominous self, his blond hair looking lighter today, maybe from the sun. "Hi."

"I'll take you to Mr. Kane." He points across the way, and I look, seeing he's indicating toward the elevators.

"Where is he?" I thought I'd be put in a car and taken to a restaurant, or maybe just walked to one in the hotel.

"If you'll come this way." He takes the lead when I fail to, getting a few steps ahead before stopping and looking back at me where I'm rooted to the marble, beginning to worry. "Miss White?"

"You're taking me to his room, aren't you?"

He looks at me with definite unease. He thinks I'm going to refuse and be difficult, and I can see he's bracing himself for it. "Mr. Kane has a suite."

"A suite?"

"Yes, a suite. Not a room, but many rooms."

If I didn't know him better, I'd say he was laughing at me.

Many rooms, including a bedroom. "I see." I fiddle with my purse, glancing at the elevator again.

"You're having dinner with him in his private suite."

I ignore the fact that he's just *told* me what I'm doing and look at him cautiously. "Private?"

He nods, joining his hands in front of his big body. "Ready?"

I raise my chin and straighten my back. "Yes." I pass him, flicking him a curious look when he steps back, even though I'm making a point to keep a comfortable distance from him. I come to a stop at the collection of elevators. "Is there a written rule that says you have to be a huge motherfucker to work for Theo?" I ask as I step into a lift and peek up at him.

There's a definite curved lip threatening to break out as he presses the button to Theo's floor. "We're more friends than work associates."

"You are?" I ask, surprised. "I thought you were his driver. Or his bodyguard."

"I'm both of those, too." He looks down at me. "But more the latter."

I tilt my head in question. "Why? Does someone want to hurt him?" I'm digging for information, and I'm not the least bit ashamed.

Callum looks like he could laugh. I guess it is quite funny. I doubt there's a man alive who could hurt Theo. "Not exactly," he says, sweeping his hand out when the doors open.

I step out and look left and right, waiting for Callum to give me some kind of indication of which way I should be going. "Not exactly?" I ask as we head left down the corridor.

"No," he answers flatly, passing me. My interest in that particular topic vanishes when I clock the double doors at the end. The muscles of my legs become weaker as I follow Callum until he comes to a stop. He opens the door and moves away, again putting a big space between us and clearing the way for me. And again, I flick him a curious look as I enter. He does that a lot. I've seen him move away from Theo, and he always gives me way more space than I need. Does he have a phobia? I can't help but wonder if he thinks I'm infectious or something.

My steps slow as I'm hit with opulence of ridiculous proportions. And the atmosphere. I'm not imagining it. Theo's presence is hanging heavy in the air, and I haven't even laid eyes on him yet. My weak legs give a little, my hand reaching for a nearby table that's decorated with an elaborate flower arrangement.

"The lounge is this way." Callum walks off, and I have to take a few moments to pull myself together before I follow him. When we arrive in the extensive seating area, the atmosphere thickens further, telling me Theo is nearer now. I scan the space, noticing another door on the opposite side of the room. A door to where? "Take a seat," Callum instructs, and I do, quickly, needing to sit down and work on breathing steadily. "Mr. Kane will be with you in a moment." He leaves, closing the door behind him.

Mr. Kane? Seriously. They're supposed to be friends. I place my hands in my lap, willing my heart to slow before I pass out. And I find myself laughing out loud at the thought of Theo walking in and finding me facedown on the floor. I stand, fidgety, and then I sit back down and cross one leg over the other. Then I swap legs, unable to get comfy. I sit forward, then to the side, ruffing up my hair and smacking my lips together.

Where is he? I stare at the door, getting progressively more restless while I wait. He demands I be here, and then leaves me waiting? What makes him think his time is more valuable than mine? Suddenly irritated, I stand and pull my dress down, set on going to find Callum to tell him that I'm out of here, but as I turn to collect my purse from the couch, something across the room catches my eye.

And there goes my world again, turning up on its head. He's leaning against the doorframe—big and gorgeous, and with a dimpled smile. His gray trousers have to be custom tailored for those long legs, and a navy shirt fits perfectly across his chest, his sleeves rolled up to reveal some pretty spectacular forearms.

I force my eyes up, feeling my breathing going to shit. "You've been there the whole time, haven't you?" I ask, feeling a little stupid that he's just watched me fidget and faff all over the sofa. And I actually laughed out loud. To myself. I want to curl into a ball of embarrassment and hide.

He pushes away from the doorframe and strolls over to me, his eyes dancing playfully. I swear, the closer he gets, the harder the pressure of the air seems to squeeze, pushing every thought from my mind, except for those of him. Just him. "I enjoy watching you."

Yes, apparently. "Watching me squirm nervously all over your posh couch?" A blush colors my cheeks, and I drop my gaze to the carpet.

"Mostly I wished I wasn't admiring the back of you, though it was still extremely enjoyable." His finger comes up slowly and rests under my chin, lifting my head. The explosion of desire within me nearly puts me on my arse. I've never felt anything like it. I don't enjoy a man's touch. I don't welcome it. I usually simply endure it. Yet Theo . . . ? He smiles knowingly. "But this." His eyes roam all over my face, eventually dropping to my parted lips. "This is a vision of perfect beauty."

I feel my cheeks heat even more. "Thank you." I have no idea what to say, nor where such reverent words have come from. The softness of them defies the hardness of his appearance.

"May I kiss you?"

I don't even need to think about it. Just the fact that he's asked eases me. "Yes."

He drops his mouth to mine, stripping me of breath, and when he takes my hands and places them on his shoulders, pulling me in, I mold against him, surrendering to his inexorable tongue, meeting his soft circular motions, proving he is right. I won't fight him. I'm intoxicated, being lifted to heights I've imagined time and again as he claims my mouth with a gentle but persistent force. He tastes out of this world, smells fresh and clean, and as I feared, I'm putty in his hands, accepting and drunk on pleasure. His lips move across mine like a well-rehearsed, slow, sensual dance. My tummy twists and knots, my mind scattering. The sheer size of him holding me in place only adds to the gratification coursing through me.

Safe. I've never felt so safe before, and that alone is an alien sensation that I might find hard to let go of. Add the crazy ecstasy of his talented mouth, and I'm destined to be held a slave by Theo Kane for as long as he commands it.

His kiss slows, his hand massaging the back of my head as he groans low in his throat. "I meant to save that for dessert," he whispers, the soft tone of his words and the vibration of his mouth against mine accelerating the pulse between my shaky thighs. He pulls away and drags the pad of his thumb across my bottom lip roughly, watching. "That alone was worth the trip out here."

I'm floored, not quite able to comprehend how I'm feeling. *Utterly consumed* doesn't seem powerful enough. "Business didn't go as planned?" I ask dryly.

His smile is still small, but full of amusement. "Business is going *exactly* as I planned." His hand slides from the base of my neck, over my shoulder and down my arm until he finds my hand.

Goose bumps erupt over every inch of my skin as I anticipate what the night could bring, laughing lightly under my breath. "So I'm business?"

"No, Izzy, you are definitely pleasure," he says, holding my hand and taking us through to the dining room, where a table is set for two and a waiter stands to the side, awaiting our arrival. Theo pulls a chair out for me and helps me down before taking up the seat opposite. A plate is placed before me by the waiter, but when he reaches Theo's side of the table, he stands back a good few paces and holds the plate out rather than placing it down, like he's scared to get too close. I frown as Theo reaches for the plate and sets it down himself before he pours me a glass of white wine. What was that?

He indicates for me to start eating, so I slowly collect my knife and fork, watching him closely as I poke at the scallops. I'm too nervous to eat, especially after that smoldering kiss. I already feel like I want more, and I'm not sure I should want a man like Theo as much as I do.

"You're nervous," he states, not accusing, just observant. And rightly so. "Tell me why, Izzy."

I look up at him, my head tilting. "You've turned up in Vegas, Theo. Out of the blue. I hardly know you."

"Then let's get to know each other, Izzy White." He sits back in his chair, wine in hand, watching me. "How was your day?"

I follow his lead and try to relax back in my chair. "Full of unexpected surprises. Yours?"

"It's improving by the hour." He gives me a wolfish smile. "By the end of it, I have a feeling I'm going to have a skip in my step."

I laugh out loud, the reaction unstoppable. How is it possible that he can ease me so instantly? He's a master at the art of relaxing me. In this moment, I don't find his straightforwardness concerning, more...endearing. "Can a big man like you skip?"

"Want to help me find out?"

I shake my head and drop my eyes to the table for a moment, if only to relieve them from the blaze in his stare. "Tell me about yourself," I say quietly.

"What do you want to know?"

"I don't know. Anything would be good. All I have on you right now is that you like popping up in dark alleyways and rescuing strangers."

He laughs, light and low. It makes my smile impossible to hold back. "I don't spend all my time popping up in dark alleyways."

"Then what do you do?"

"I love eating." He motions to the table, where both our starters remain untouched. "I love working out, too, but my new favorite pastime is stalking you." He flips me a devilish wink, and once again I'm laughing.

"For a big dude, you're quite cute."

"For a little female, you're quite fierce." He toasts the air. "And second to your natural beauty, that's my favorite thing about you."

Damn it, don't blush. I take refuge in my wine, keeping my smile in check before it splits my face. "You're extremely bold," I say over the rim of my glass.

"There aren't many things in this world that I desire, Izzy. It's a short list, and therefore I have plenty of time to dedicate to each item on it. You are now at the very top."

"And the other things?"

"Peace. Happiness. Love."

I swallow, taken aback by his frank answer. "Don't you have those things in your life now?" He seems quite content with who he is.

He shakes his head. "What do you want out of life, Izzy?"

"Just love would do," I answer honestly, surprising myself. "With love, happiness and peace should come naturally."

"I like that theory." He smiles softly, regarding me closely across the table. "And if I may be bold once more?"

"Can I stop you?"

"Probably not."

"Then go ahead and be bold."

The gratification seeping from his body is undeniable, and I can't help but feel satisfied that I am the cause. "I have an unstoppable urge to take you to bed."

"We agreed on dinner."

"Which you haven't eaten," he counters, motioning to our untouched plates. "So will you let me take you to bed?"

He's asking again. It's a far cry from his original tactics of demanding, as if he's realized I don't take too kindly to demands and has decided to change his game plan. Should I tell him it's working?

I sigh, my hand resting on the base of my wineglass. "What do you want from me, Theo?"

"You're a bit slow if you haven't figured it out yet."

"Then I must be slow, because I haven't the first idea why a man of your obvious status"—I wave my hand around the dining room of his suite in the frigging *Bellagio*—"would be so interested in a normal, regular nurse like me."

"There's nothing normal or regular about you," he argues, firm but soft, leaning forward in his chair. My statement has irritated him. I'm certain anyone else would be threatened by his stance, but I'm not at all. It's as if I'm immune to his physical presence where fear or intimidation are concerned. It doesn't make any sense to me, but that's how it is. It should probably be a problem, but I have a bigger issue instead, and it's dominating everything right now. I'm drawn to him. Most people seem to put as much distance between themselves and Theo as possible. I, however, have a confusing urge to close that distance. I want to be near to him. He has a magnetic pull, luring me closer, and I'm helpless to its power. Given everything I have been through, it's even more fucked up. And then I have to ask myself . . .

Am I really as strong as I think I am? Because I'm not just

attracted to Theo Kane. Not just intrigued by him. I'm charmed by his protective instinct toward women. I might tell myself I don't need it. But you don't have to need something to want it. *Right, Izzy?*

"Then what is there about me?" I ask him, my voice annoyingly shaky.

He withdraws a little, like he's sensed he might be being a bit scary. "I can't stop thinking about you, and there's a reason for that. I need to understand."

"So I'm here for you to try to unravel why you're attracted to a lowly nurse like me. Is that it?" I stand from my chair, a little mad.

"No." His fist hits the table with a deafening thwack, yet I don't move a muscle, don't flinch or become guarded by the hint of violence. It doesn't touch me. Theo looks up at me with wide eyes, worried again that he's frightened me, and when he realizes that he hasn't, he breathes out, slumping back in his chair.

He shakes his head, somewhere between amusement, awe, and shock. "I see you're wary of me, and I don't want you to be."

"Then maybe you should stop thumping tables," I retort, and he smiles.

"You and I both know my physical presence isn't what I'm talking about. You're scared of how I make you feel. You're fighting your natural reaction to me. But you shouldn't."

"Why?"

"Because I'm not interested in hurting you. I'm not pursuing you just because I want to bed you. If I wanted a mindless fuck, I'd find one with ease."

"Wow." I all but cough.

"It's the truth. I'll never be anything but honest with you, Izzy. I'm a man of my word, trust me."

"But I hardly know you, Theo. And you hardly know me."

"I know you're beautiful. I know you're attracted to me. I know you make me smile, and I know you give me hope. You're strong and kind. You stopped to help Penny that night, and there was nothing in it for you. You could have walked on by and not given it a thought ever again. But you didn't. And not even *I* scared you off. I see fear in you, Izzy, but it is fear of another kind."

I feel a lump swell in my throat, and all the reasons I pursued a career in nursing thunder to the front of my mind. I sniff back the onslaught of emotions, mad that he's drawn them from me. Becoming a nurse and working in a hospital was the natural thing for me to do, since it was the only place I ever felt safe. "I'm a nurse. It's my job to help people."

"It's your job to ensure your own safety first," Theo says gently. It cuts deep, every bit of pain I ever felt seeming to return and hurt me all over again. "Above everything else," he goes on, "that should be your priority."

My jaw tightens, and infuriating tears stab at the backs of my eyes. "I would never leave a woman at the mercy of a violent man."

He withdraws a little. He's read between the lines, and I immediately regret giving him more than I meant to. And I hate him for forcing the matter. I stopped. I helped Penny. That's it. He needs to stop picking it to pieces.

I refuse to look away from him as he rises from his chair, seeming to take forever to reach his full height. "Why do I believe there's something more to it than professional instinct?"

"Because there is," I reply without hesitation, fixing my lips into a straight line, my way of telling him that I won't be expanding on that, so he shouldn't bother asking. He's not telling me everything. I'll adopt a similar approach, if it's all the same to him.

He nods, understanding, widening his stance a little. "I like being respected, and sick as it sounds, I also like the fact that people are too frightened to cross me." He pauses, drilling into me with potent eyes full of sincerity. "But for the first time in a very long time, I like the thought of someone liking me. I love that you challenge me. I love that you're ballsy, though I know I won't love the reason why."

My breath hitches. He knows. He's figured it out. Maybe not every tiny detail, but he's latched onto the fact that I've been scared before, and he wants to put any doubt in my mind to rest. Any doubt that I think he could hurt me. It's admirable, but it's also a waste of words, because I'm not scared of him in that sense. I'm actually scared of becoming too attached to him. Of getting too used to feeling safe. Of becoming too dependent on his comfort. Depending on someone leaves you open to hurt.

"I realize there's a lot to know about you," I whisper. "And I know beyond doubt that I might not like some of it, but none of that wondering or worry is making me like you less. *That's* what scares me."

Theo's large chest visibly sinks on a deep breath. "Thank you for your honesty," he says, his hand going to his spiky jaw and stroking thoughtfully. "You're right. And I don't expect you to like everything there is to know about me. That would be asking too much. I only expect you to like *me*. I only expect you to appreciate the man I am to you."

I swallow, hating and loving what he's saying. Loving partly because my conclusions have pretty much been confirmed, and hating because the confirmation hasn't even dented my intrigue or attraction. It's only heightened it.

After a few seconds of silence, he strides over to me with what I think is determination. Or resolution. Or both? He gestures to my hand, and I offer it willingly, inhaling steadily as his touch meets mine, his fingers flexing gently. He watches us come together for a few beats. "Feels good, doesn't it?" he asks, glancing up at me, a little awed by the simple feeling of our skin touching.

I nod, wholeheartedly agreeing. Never before has a man's touch comforted me. His hand squeezes mine and he pulls me from the table, heading for the door. As he guides me from the dining room, my feet work fast to keep up with him, my heart going wild. We pass the waiter, who immediately steps back, out of our path.

"We're finished," Theo tells him, curt and short and without looking at him as he continues to lead me through the extensive suite. I focus on the warmth of his strong hand surrounding mine, fighting back unwelcome memories. Worryingly, it's very easy. Or is it a worry at all?

Theo opens another door and pulls me through, shutting it with more care than I expected. We're in a bedroom. A huge, lavish bedroom with a showpiece of a bed that's probably the biggest I've ever seen. Theo gently tugs my hand, takes me to the bed, and sits me on the end before dropping to his knees and holding my hands. It occurs to me that he's trying to ease me by being at equal eye level to me, and there's something a little submissive about him being on his knees at my feet. It's a measured move, but it's making me worry about what he's going to say. I swallow and brace myself.

"Since you've been honest with me, it feels only fair that I offer you the same courtesy. I'm going to tell you how it will be between us."

Butterflies explode in my tummy. "You'll *tell* me?"

He smiles, his thumbs drawing small circles on the backs of my hands. "I need something from you, Izzy."

My muscles twitch with the need to tense. "What?" Something about the way he's looking at me, unsure and hesitant, is telling me I might not like it.

Theo rests back on his haunches, his arms suspended between us as he keeps hold of my hands. "I need compliance. Total surrender." Dark, cobalt eyes sear my skin, his face becoming alive with want. "I will treat you like a queen and fuck you like a whore." My mouth drops open. He just said that? "And I promise you," he goes on, ignoring my shock, taking my hand and placing it on his chest, pushing it into the muscle, "you will never be in danger. You will never be afraid again."

It's beyond me, but I just disintegrated. He's told me he would fuck me like a whore, but he rounded all of that off with a promise. A promise I can't ignore but wish I could. "I'm afraid of you," I admit. "Afraid of how you make me feel."

"How do I make you feel?"

The word *safe* dances on the end of my tongue, but I swallow my confession, looking away. "Consumed." I'm not lying.

"I'm with you." He pushes my hand harder against his chest. "I can give you what you need, Izzy. And I'm hoping you will naturally give me what I need."

"Want," I correct mindlessly. "What you *want*."

His smile stretches, bright and gorgeous. "Trust me, Izzy. I *need* it." He gives a little tug of my hand, and I fall to his lap with a tiny gasp. He encases my whole face in his big palms, so tender, but equally possessive. "The first time I touched you, you had me. I'll never be able to explain how it felt. How it feels now." His eyes scan my face, his thumbs stroking gently over my cheeks. "My skin on yours, I crave it. But I need controlled environments."

"Why?" I ask, accepting his soft kiss on my lips.

"You need to trust me."

I don't ask for more than that. Just like he hasn't asked why I need to feel safe, or who has hurt me in my past. I trust him. "Okay," I agree. I feel like I'm dancing too close to the sun, and, bizarrely, I can't wait to be burned.

"Whatever you've run away from, Izzy, it can't touch you as long as I'm here."

I don't appreciate the reminder. "I said *okay*."

"I heard you."

"Then please just take me to bed." I'm done with talking. Wants and needs have been established, and now I just need Theo to own me. To quench the insatiable thirst he's unearthed. To give me something I've never had. Pleasure.

CHAPTER 7

I'm not just taking you to bed." Theo holds me under my armpits and hauls me up so I'm standing over him while he remains on the floor at my feet. He reaches forward, looking up at me, and curls his palm around my ankle. I jolt violently, fire shooting up my legs and detonating in my chest. Explosions already. I need to grab his shoulders, I need support, but as I lift my arms to reach for them, Theo's hands fly up and catch my wrists. He looks at my confused face as he gently takes my palms up to his shoulders for me. "Let me," he whispers, releasing my hands and allowing them to rest on his massive shoulders, closing his eyes as my touch meets his shirt.

The realization sucker-punches me in the gut. *Oh my God.* He doesn't like being touched. I think about the way the members of his staff shift from Theo's path when he's near, and I remember every time I've gone to touch him myself. He's caught me and controlled the touch. He's seen my intention and taken charge of it. Callum giving me a wide berth all those times had nothing to do with me. It's natural for Theo's driver/friend/bodyguard to give people space because he does it all the time for Theo. And the butler, Jefferson. He told me to keep my distance. He wasn't warning me to stay away. He was warning me not to touch Theo. All of Theo's stealthy, quick moves, the times someone has gone to touch him. He's expertly avoided them all.

I stare down at him, flummoxed. He needs controlled environments. Everything about Theo Kane since I met him has been controlled, and now I realize that will extend into the bedroom. He nods a little, seeing my comprehension, and his hands come back to my ankles, instantly replacing my shock with want. His touch doesn't only make me feel safe. It makes me ache.

He smiles up at me, then lowers his eyes to my feet. "Like I've already told you," he says quietly, "you had me the moment I touched you." Lifting one of my feet to his knee, he starts to unfasten my sandal, his fingers constantly skimming the sensitive flesh of my ankle bone, driving me wild. But I wait, knowing it'll be worth the agony. I had him. My touch. Our skin touching. A little part of me is intrigued, but a bigger part is relieved that he feels the same as me.

He releases my foot and drops my sandal, collecting my other foot and carefully removing that shoe, too. Once he's done, both his hands slide around the backs of my calves and he lifts on his knees, bringing him higher, sliding his hands as he goes. He's looking up at me, working his hands under my dress until he has a possessive hold of my arse. He squeezes, cocking his head a little, pulling me forward so his face is level with my breasts. Then he slowly drags my dress up until my bare flesh is exposed to his mouth. I still and close my eyes, knowing he's going to come face-to-face with my scars at any second. I'm mentally preparing my go-to answer that I use when I'm asked what happened, feeling his movements falter. He's seen them. Right now, while I'm hiding in my darkness, he's staring at the aftermath of my past.

I wait for him to ask about the marks on my skin, but a few moments later, he still hasn't. So I locate the courage I need to look down at him, finding him focused on my tummy. Staring. I breathe in shakily as he looks up at me, his face blank. Then he slowly drops his lips to the side of my belly button and licks around the area. My world doesn't just flip upside down. It spins. And it spins. And it spins and spins and spins. Yet I still see Theo's face. Clear as day, as bright as I'm sure it has ever been. My head falls back on my shoulders, my eyes closing in complete ecstasy, my gratitude fierce. The gentle swirl of his tongue is just the start of things to come. If this is fucking like a whore, then I'll sign up for a lifetime's worth.

"Izzy," Theo rumbles, my name sounding like an enticing plea as he kisses his way over my dress, up my throat to my chin as he stands. "We're worlds apart but so fucking close." He nibbles up to my lips. "Lift your arms."

I raise them, no thought or hesitation, and he pulls my dress up over my head. I go to reach down to his trousers to feel the hardness, bold and daring, or more like desperate. But he seizes my hand in a harsh grip, stilling me.

"I crave a controlled environment," he reminds me. "That means you make no movements without my say-so."

I groan, not liking the prospect of no free rein over his body. "Please," I try.

He shakes his head against my lips. "Trust me." Picking me up, he carries me to the bed. "Are you clean?" he asks, and I nod my head. "Are you protected?" I nod again, hoping he'll confirm what I need to ask in return. "Me too."

I study him as my head comes to rest on the soft pillow. His face is the softest I've seen it, his eyes the bluest, as he removes my bra and knickers painstakingly slowly, casting them aside. He swallows hard as he spends a few rapt moments taking me in.

Waiting as patiently as I can, fighting to keep my arms by my sides, I watch, breathless, as he starts to strip down. His shirt buttons are unfastened one by one, slowly revealing the chest I've imagined constantly. The tattoo I've only had a peek of is nowhere to be seen when the two sides of his shirt hang open, but I can see taut skin. Biting down on my bottom lip, I hold my breath and bend one leg, bringing the sole of my foot up and pushing it into the covers, squeezing my thighs together. Liquid fire surges into my core, my nipples pebbling. His eyes drift slowly from my breasts to my thighs, back and forth as he rolls his shoulders and shrugs off his shirt, letting it float down to the floor.

Awe slams into me, tangling my mind, and my held breath chokes me. "Oh my God," I whisper, trying to comprehend the sculpted lines of Theo's torso. Every muscle is sharp, to the point I'm sure I would cut myself if I were to trace one. Definition so clear, skin so tight, and swells of muscle so hard. My mouth dries as my eyes roam the planes of him in wonder, drifting down to his stomach and the perfect V that leads neatly to his groin. His trousers hang low, a sliver of the waistband of his boxer shorts peeking out. My sights fall onto his hip, where more ink spans the narrow area, and I cock my head a little, trying to fathom what I'm looking at. My eyes shoot up to his when I realize what it is. Praying hands. His face is straight, the muscles of his neck pulsing, and there, cascading down onto his shoulder, is another piece of art. Rosary beads. They drip down his skin, onto the top of his thick arm, and dangling from the bottom is a delicate cross. Theo is still, letting me take it all in, and when he slowly turns away from me, I suck in air. Spanning his wide shoulder blades and sinking down the center of his spine is a crucifix, encrusted and intricate. It's beautiful, yet almost haunting. The praying hands, the rosary beads, the crucifix. Is he that religious?

I shift on the bed a little as he comes back to face me, unbuttoning his trousers and pushing them down his thighs, taking his boxers with them, before stepping out. His cock springs free, stiff,

thick, and long, as stunning as the rest of him. I've never seen anything like him. He's the finest example of God's creation. There's
not one ounce of fat anywhere to be seen. He's solid, inconceivably
so. One of his thighs is probably thicker than my waist, his legs
long and powerful. He looks lethal but beautiful, hard but soft.
My body is in chaos, my nerves burning, all in response to what
I'm faced with. My want has gone through the roof and desperation is now crippling me. He looks like a warrior, raw and primal.
A fighter.

I look up to him, and he nods a little, as if he knows and
accepts what I'm thinking. And then he dips and collects something from the bedside and starts unraveling it in his hands,
coming closer to the bed. He gently claims one of my hands,
brings it up to the headboard, and starts weaving the silk material around my wrist, secure but not too tight, before connecting
it to the post of the bed and tying it, pulling my arm taut above
my head. I don't even fight. Don't protest or have a smidgen
of worry. He needs a controlled environment and he's going to
achieve that by rendering me incapable of movement. You can't
get more controlled than that. He repeats on the other side, all
the time gentle, all the time focused. I watch him in fascination,
every move he makes, every flick of his eyes to mine to check
that I'm okay, and every ripple of his chest as he bends. When
he moves down to my legs, I have to lift my head from the pillow a little. He takes my ankles and pulls my legs apart, and
I gasp, feeling need dripping between my thighs. His eyes are
glued there, his breathing noticeably changing.

Oh, God. I throw my head back on the pillow, tugging at the
straps holding my arms in place. "Theo," I whisper, feeling him
pull my leg, the softness of silk weaving around my ankle. My
legs, too? I'll be *totally* helpless. He ignores my desperate plea
and carries on, tying my other ankle to the opposite side. I'm

spread-eagle on the bed, held in place and at his mercy. In my darkness, I manage to silently consider the fact that I don't need to be strapped to a bed, helpless, to be at Theo's mercy. Just being close to him sees to that just fine.

"You look so beautiful," he rasps, tracing light circles around my ankle bone. I jerk on the bed, the straps pulling taut. His touch is like molten lava, the effect reaching my clit and burning. Theo gasps, and I snap my eyes open, finding him dragging his palm up my leg to my thigh. He stops just south of my entrance, staring at me. I pulse, drinking in air, my eyes wide and wanting. "This," he rumbles, edging closer and closer to my core. "This perfect wet pussy." He slips his finger through the moisture, and I yell, yanking at the straps. "It's mine." A thick finger pushes forward and sinks into me. Muscles I never knew I had squeeze tightly, and my head thrashes from side to side, hungry and panicked. But I save my breath. I don't beg, because I know it will get me nowhere. I need to calm down. I need to stop bucking on the bed. That will get me nowhere, too, but he's teasing me, working me up. Pleasure and pain. The pain is the waiting part.

Theo's finger, just one finger, fucks me beautifully, a big palm falling to my breast and squeezing gently. "Open your eyes, Izzy," he orders, releasing my boob and grabbing my jaw. My eyelids lift, immediately finding his face suspended over mine, lips parted. "I'm going to feast on your nipples, bite and lick, and you're going to keep still."

I shake my head, knowing he's demanding the impossible.

"Yes," he counters. "And if you're a good girl, if you keep quiet and still, I'll sink my cock into you and give you what you need."

"I can't take this," I mumble, feeling emotional and fraught, tugging at my restraints again. I was fine when he started tying me up. Thought I could handle it. I didn't anticipate my desperation spiraling to these torturous depths. It's unfamiliar ground.

"Yes, you can." Theo pulls his finger free and climbs on top of me, straddling my waist, but not resting all of his weight on me. I'd never take it. His hands placed on the insides of my arms serve as extra restraints, pinning me in place and forcing me into the mattress. He lifts a little, his thick arms braced as he looks down at me. The tip of his cock is skimming my stomach, the head leaking with his desire, smearing across my skin as he gently sways his tight hips.

He scans my face, deep in thought, humming as he does. His cheeks are shimmering with a light layer of sweat, his dark hair dampening at the roots. "It's torture, isn't it?" he says, flexing his hips deeply until his cock falls to my opening. I whimper my answer, unable to keep silent. He smiles a little. "From the moment I touched you, I've felt tortured. But it's the beautiful kind. Addictive. Mind-blowing. I need you to feel how I've felt since that night. How senseless with want I've felt, how frustrated that you kept resisting me." He grinds forward a very little bit, breaching my entrance with the tip of his arousal before withdrawing. I slam my lips together, my nostrils flaring. "I'm going to make you wait, Izzy."

"No," I yell, angered by his tactics.

His hand slaps over my mouth to silence me, his eyebrows arching in warning. "Yes," he confirms simply, leaning down and biting at my cheek. "Ready to go insane?"

"Theo, please, I beg you."

"I don't want you to beg me. I want you to feel my desperation. I want you to match it."

He drifts down until his mouth is level with my chest, his cock still poised at my entrance. Regret washes through me—regret for denying him, for pushing him away, and regret for surrendering to him now. I'm out of my depth.

Heat spreads across my right breast, delicious and warm, the pleasure brief before his mouth latches on and sucks hard. With Theo on top of me, it's impossible to move, but I try my very hardest, bucking and gritting my teeth. He swaps his lips for his teeth and bites down. Pain rips through me, but I suck back my scream, slamming my eyes closed and praying for mercy. The pressure of his bite is harsh, to the point my nerves go numb.

"Please, Theo, please, I'll do anything." My voice is ragged and distressed.

Swirling his tongue around my suffering nipple, he licks it back to life. "You taste so good." Another thrust of his groin and a quick, teasing dip of his cock into my wetness reminds me of what I'm begging for.

"Please," I gasp, hating the satisfaction he's getting from my begging. He smirks, victorious, and then lifts from my body and gets up off the bed. I watch, horrified, as his long legs eat up the distance between the bed and the door and he disappears through it. *What?* He's leaving me here? Making me wait? For how long? I lose my shit, flailing on the bed like a deranged woman. "Theo!" I yell, over and over, until my throat is sore and my lungs are burning from exhaustion. I could cry, my emotions getting the better of me. I've finally succumbed to him, given in to his allure and relentlessness, and now he's leaving me here after working me up into a pent-up mass of need? How? How is he doing this, not just to me, but to himself?

"Theo." His name is a despondent whisper as I relax my strung muscles and slump on the bed, willing my body to pipe down, to stop singing with craving. I'm exhausted but far from satisfied, tied to a bed in a Vegas hotel room while the man who has infiltrated my head and my life is out there doing . . . I look at the door. What is he doing?

Resting my head back, I close my eyes and try not to think of the fact that I actually feel like a whore, though he's yet to fuck me like one. Is this a game to him? It feels like it, because if he were as desperate as he claims, he'd currently be buried inside me and sating both our needs. I never imagined I'd beg for sex. I never imagined myself at the mercy of a man's power ever again. Yet there's something utterly wonderful about being at Theo's mercy. And his power over me is welcome.

I don't know how long I'm here, helpless and longing, but my exhaustion begins to get the better of me, and I start to drift in and out of consciousness. It could be an hour, maybe two. I don't know, but it feels like a year. My breathing is finally level and my heartbeat normal. I see only Theo in my darkness. I still feel an unfathomable craving hijacking me, even if it's been doused with a lot of madness. *Insane.* He said he'd send me insane, and he has.

The bed dips beside me, stirring me, and I flip my eyes open. Theo is straddling me again, looking down at me quietly. "How painful was it?" he asks. "How frustrating? How much do you want me all over you?"

"You've made your point," I croak, looking away defiantly.

"So you won't push me away again?"

"No," I spit, clenching my teeth.

"Good girl." He shuffles down the bed, getting his legs between mine. I want to remain moody and defiant, but when I feel his erection back where I want it to be, my body comes alive again, nerves screaming, like he's flipped a switch and cranked up the volume. I pull against the straps, this time steadily rather than jerkily, holding them taut and using them as leverage for my tight muscles. He's hovering there, holding himself up on his solid arms, tinkering on the edge of penetration. I've learned begging will get me nowhere, so though it kills me, I wait for him, my breaths shallow, my body twitching. The small bunch of nerves in my clit pound, drowning in the wetness of my desire.

I know the moment he's going to enter me because his neck

veins bulge in preparation. My back bows as he slowly and lazily plunges, stretching me wide, depriving me of breath. The discomfort has my hips shifting beneath him, trying to get accustomed to his length and girth. Oh, Jesus. I start to tremble. "More?" he asks, his voice like gravel, his hips pulsing, needing to push on further. I nod and he slides in that little bit more. Not all the way, but it's still painful. "More?" he asks again, circling a little now, trying to stretch me.

"Wait." I swallow, my eyes glued to his. And he does. He stills, watching me, as if he knows listening to me right now is important. It is. And he knows how grateful I am for his easy acceptance. I can see it in his gaze.

"Just tell me when."

I nod and breathe through the next roll of his hips. "All the way."

"You sure?"

I nod, so sure, and he glides forward measuredly with a loud curse, throwing his head back. I cry out in pain, and he freezes, fully submerged, panting. The need to close my legs overwhelms me, my ankles kicking against the restraints as I yell at the ceiling. I groan, overcome with the pressure of his size filling me.

"Fuck...me," Theo rasps, slowly drawing out. "Unreal." He drives forward again, yelling his pleasure. "Jesus, woman, you feel so good." He grinds deep into my womb.

I start to sweat, willing my body to accept him.

"Give yourself time to get used to me, Izzy," he says gently, pumping forward again, his drives steadily gaining pace. He drops to his elbows and lays a palm across my throat to stop me from moving my head. More restriction. My pain steadily works into discomfort, and then the discomfort into pleasure. It surprises me, and I'm suddenly alive with more want and more need. It no longer hurts. He's stretched me into acceptance.

He blinks and lifts, withdrawing slowly before surging forward. I grunt, my legs yanking against the straps. His reasons for
restraining me are becoming more obvious. My arms would be
everywhere, clawing at him, smacking him, pulling at his hair. It's
frustrating as hell, but I appreciate the need even if I don't appreciate the restraints. I let out a little moan of pleasure, and I get
pushed up the bed on his next plunge, pulling my legs straight.

He freezes, and I know he's going to let loose completely once
he's found his breath. "I can't hold back anymore. You ready?"

"Yes." He needs this, just like I needed the gentle break-in.

After only a couple of seconds and a long inhale, he locks eyes
with me, and I fear the worst. His fingers flex over my throat,
his other hand coming up to my hair and fisting it. His lips
straighten. His eyes go dark. His jaw pulses. And he lets rip.

My screams are long and constant as he smashes into me over
and again, deranged and chaotic. My eyes slam shut, my head
thrown back as I accept his power. It's like he's releasing years of
frustration, years of pent-up aggression. Our bodies begin to slide
on each hard hit, sweat drenching us, his palm slipping over my
throat. "You can take it, Izzy," he growls, never letting up, going
at me like a wild animal, fast and furiously, totally mercilessly.

I pull at the straps, shocked when the pressure of his cock filling
me drops into my groin and starts to swirl deliciously, my pleasure
taking on new heights. I find his eyes and find a knowingness.

"Here it is," he pants, keeping up his brutal momentum, slapping into me as he slides his palm to my cheek and strokes more
tenderly. "It's good, yes?"

"Yes." Oh good Lord, I'm coasting fast toward an orgasm that's
going to knock me unconscious. Seizing each twinge of pleasure
and holding on to it, I tense everywhere, wishing beyond all
wishes that I could feel him beyond penetration. Touch him.
Stroke and caress him. He grips my hair, keeping his eyes on mine,

and surprises me with a deep gyration of his hips. His chin drops to his chest. "Come on, Izzy," he encourages me. "I'm not going without you."

Urgency springs into my aching muscles. I concentrate as the pressure builds and builds, holding me in a permanent state of anticipation. It's coming. It's coming. It's . . .

"Fuck!" My body jacks off the bed, my neck cricking when I snap my head back, my eyes closing tightly as bolts of pleasure attack me. I'm surrounded by a white noise that dulls the sounds of Theo's barks of ecstasy, and the feel of him thickening inside of me turns my shouts of pleasure into long, drawn-out moans. Then I hear the faint sound of a groan as his cock starts to pulse, long and slow, warmth filling me deeply.

I go lax, exhausted, and Theo collapses onto me, his weight spread carefully all over my pulsating body.

An exquisite sense of calm ripples through me. And my climax carries me into unconsciousness.

Chapter 8

Numb. I feel numb, pins and needles assaulting my legs and arms. And I'm suffocating, being squeezed beneath something. My eyes spring open, my mind working quickly to remind me of where I am and who I'm with. *Theo*, I tell myself, immediately settling. His head is resting on my shoulder, the smell of clean sweat filling my nose. I can't breathe. "Theo," I whisper, looking up to see my arms still restrained. I contract my internal muscles, feeling his softness still buried inside me. "Theo, wake up." I scan the room for a clock. What time is it? Oh no. Jess. "Theo!"

He jumps a little, pushing me into the bed some more, and then slowly lifts a fraction. Sleepy eyes look down at me, blinking rapidly. "Hey," he croaks, appearing disoriented.

"You need to untie me." I pull at the silk straps, reminding him that I'm still his prisoner. "I need to call Jess. She was asleep when I left. I don't want her to worry."

"Where's your phone?" He begins to lift, and I start to panic. He's not going to release me?

"In my purse in the lounge," I tell him, sucking in air when he slips free of me, part of his release coming with it and coating my inner thighs. "But I can get it if you untie me."

He ignores me and wanders away, and I lift my head to watch, staring at his naked back incredulously. The artwork decorating his skin rolls as he stretches his arms up to the ceiling, the sight really quite something to behold. I flop back on my pillow and give a futile tug at my restraints. Great. How long does he plan on keeping me here?

He's back a few moments later, holding my phone. "Five missed calls," he says flatly. "Jess."

"Damn," I mutter, following his path to me. "Please untie me, Theo."

He shakes his head and gets on the bed, lying down and rolling onto his side to face me. "I had this repaired." Pointing at the screen, he raises a brow.

"I dropped it." Shrugging as best I can, I ignore the exasperated shake of his head. "Untie me, please."

"You don't need your hands to talk. What's your PIN?"

"What?"

"Do you want to call your friend?"

"Yes."

"Then tell me your PIN."

Closing my eyes, I breathe out. "One, eight, zero, six."

"Eighteenth of June." He puts the phone to my ear as I scowl, and I hear Jess's voice a second later.

"Izzy, where the bloody hell are you?" She sounds utterly pissed off.

I stall, looking at Theo, whose eyebrows are high, interested. I bet he's wondering what I'm going to tell her. Or how much. I can hardly share the fact that I'm tied to a huge bed in a huge suite at the Bellagio. She'll flip her lid. "I'm with Theo," I confess. I can tell her *that* much.

"I bloody knew it! I've been roaming the casino floor looking for you. What happened? Where are you?"

Guilt engulfs me. "I'll explain later," I tell her, not prepared to go into it while I'm being watched so carefully. "Where are you?"

"Kyle and Denny called. Suppose I can catch up with them now I know you're alive." Her scornful tone is warranted. "Come meet us. We need to discuss."

"Oka—" Theo starts to slowly shake his head at me, telling me that's the wrong answer. I give him a questioning look, and he takes the phone from my ear and moves in, bringing his lips close.

"We're not done until I say we're done," he whispers, dragging his lips across mine. I moan softly and inhale his manly scent.

"What am I supposed to say?"

"Tell her to have fun and you'll call once I've dropped you back at the hotel." He breaks away and returns the phone to my ear.

I struggle for breath so I can speak. "I'll call you when I'm finished," I wheeze. "Shouldn't be long."

"Jesus, Izzy. What are you playing at?"

"I'll call you," I reiterate, glancing at Theo. He nods approvingly and mouths, *Say goodbye.* "Speak later," I whisper.

"We will," Jess retorts heatedly. "Oh, and Izzy?"

"Yes?"

"Just how big was it?"

I flame bright red, and Theo chuckles, amused, jiggling the phone at my ear. "You can answer," he mouths, smug. I narrow my eyes at him. I highly doubt he would be so open if he had a scrawny dick.

"So-so," I reply.

Jess groans in disappointment, and Theo's eyes widen, shocked. He disconnects the call and dives on me, straddling my waist again. "Like that, is it?" He takes my nipple between his finger and thumb, rolling it threateningly.

I lock up and shake my head, feeling him squeeze down. "Theo."

"So-so, huh?" He tweaks, and I yelp.

"No more," I plead. Oh God, I can't take any more pain. Not now. I want the last thing I remember to be that ridiculously powerful explosion. "Please, no." I land a leveled glare on him, hoping beyond hope that it works.

He cocks his eyebrow.

I crumble, defeated.

And then he latches onto my nipple and bites down. Hard.

"Fuck!" I buck under him, enraged. "Theo, for fuck's sake, st—" I swallow my words when he starts to suck, at the same time driving his fingers into me. "Oh." I sink into the mattress, like putty in his hands. Or like putty in his mouth. Which is now kissing its way down my stomach, pecking and licking and nibbling as it goes, eventually arriving at the apex of my thighs. I look down, just as Theo removes his fingers and glances up. His lips quirk. And damn it, so do mine. I shouldn't be smiling. I should be raging mad.

"I'm going to suck your next orgasm out of you, Izzy."

I still.

"I'm hungry." He kisses the inside of my thigh, and I feel him smile against my flesh.

I clench my eyes shut as he licks along the sensitive crease of my bikini line. "Oh good God." My head is going to explode.

I'm sure I hear the sadistic bastard chuckle lightly. "I'll be whatever you want me to be. Your god, your prince, your knight, your king." He slams his mouth over my core and sucks ravenously.

I shout and pull my arms taut against the restraints, my wrists burning from the friction that I'm inflicting on myself. "Theo!"

"Keep shouting, Izzy."

My chest convulses with the rest of my body as he laps, sucks, and kisses me. "I'm going to come." I can feel that pressure descending again, making every torturous tactic he's adopted worthwhile.

"No, you're not." He pulls away, and my looming orgasm fades. I shout, lurching up off the bed like a madwoman. When I get free, I'm going to kill him! His mouth returns, licking between my folds, exploring hungrily, his hands grabbing my boobs and massaging just as urgently. My building climax resurrects, and I start rotating my hips to help it along, panting my way there. But then he pulls away again, and I whimper in despair.

"You want to come, sweetheart?" he asks, inching up the bed to find my face, squeezing my cheeks and forcing my eyes open.

My internal muscles are pulsing unbearably, begging for him. "You bastard," I breathe.

He smirks at me and kisses me hard on the lips. Despite myself, I open my mouth, my tongue darting out to find his. He pulls away as I groan, and pushes up on fists that are wedged into the mattress on either side of my head. Drifting back down my body, he spreads my thighs until they pull against the straps and can't go any farther. Then he's on me, and though I try not to fall victim to his evil tactics again, I find myself squirming, moaning, and closing my eyes in mind-blanking bliss.

It builds, and I burn up once more, the heights of my pleasure clear in the vibrations of my body. I can't control them. I'm at the mercy of Theo's mouth and my body's need for him. I've never felt so close to crazy and blissful at the same time, wondering which way he's going to send me. Because it's down to him. Theo decides.

Blood whooshes into my clit, preparing to explode.

And he pulls away again.

I sob, tears springing to my eyes. "Please," I beg quietly. "Please, please, please." I turn my face into my armpit and hide.

"Here you go, baby." He flicks his tongue across my clit,

pulling me back from the brink of desolation and pushing me to the edge of ecstasy. "Take it." He swirls slowly, and I detonate, my spine stretching violently, the straps cutting into my wrists and ankles. The pleasure rips through me unforgivingly, and just as I'm about to moan my way through it, Theo's lips meet mine, the pad of his thumb finding my clit and rubbing gently as I go at his mouth like I might never get to taste him again.

He applies pressure where I need it, my face nuzzling him away and burying in the crook of his neck, my muscles spasming as I come down from my high. The frustration and teasing just made it all the more intense and powerful when he finally granted me the pleasure. I sigh, happy. "Thank you."

He lifts his head and gazes down at me, brushing damp waves away from my forehead, silent for several long seconds before he speaks. "You're amazing," he says softly, grazing his fingertips over my cheek as it heats beneath his touch. And when his cobalt eyes land on mine, my world doesn't just turn upside down this time. It narrows into a tunnel, condensing everything, making what needs to be seen so very clear. Theo. Just him.

"Are you religious?" I ask quietly, flicking my eyes down to the rosary beads on his shoulder.

He glimpses down himself, as though he needs a reminder of the art decorating his body. "No."

"Then why all of the religious symbols?"

"God forgives everyone," he says thoughtfully. "Even if they haven't abided by his rules. They're there to remind me..." He pauses for a beat. "That I've broken his rules."

My mind begins to gallop as my next question hangs on my tongue. I deliberate asking, wondering what rules he's speaking of, but when his eyes harden, I suck back my question, though my curiosity is still rampant. I can tell by the look on his face that we won't be going there. So I go somewhere else instead. "Did you tie me down because you were worried about me touching you?"

Theo smiles as he reaches up to my bonds and slowly starts unraveling them. "I'm hypersensitive to most people around me, Izzy. You more so. Every move you make, I see it coming. But I'm worried that in bed with you, I won't have that advantage." He lets my arms drop, and I work some life back into them while he scoots down and takes care of my feet. When I'm free, I sit up, bringing my knees to my chin and curling my arms around them. He wraps the straps into perfect coils as he watches me on the bed. "Are you okay?"

I nod a little, even though I'm not. I can never touch him when we're intimate? I can't stroke him or caress his beautiful body? The loss suddenly hits me hard, and I glance away from the magnificent naked sight of Theo.

"Izzy?" he questions, troubled. "Tell me."

"I'm fine." I force a smile, brushing off his concern, and get up from the bed, set on finding my clothes and tracking Jess down. I never get to feel him? The more I think about it, the more devastated I am by that. He doesn't trust himself. Why? He knows it's me. He'll know where I am.

I make it two paces before my escape is halted by a large palm wrapped around my wrist. "Izzy, wait," he orders gently, pulling me back a little, though I keep my focus forward on the door. "I've told you I need a controlled environment," he reminds me gently, holding me in place.

"I know that."

"It's not through choice."

"I can never touch you in bed. When we're intimate. I want to be able to feel you." I let it all out and hear his sigh shortly after. He turns me to face him, lifting me from my feet with one arm around my lower back, using his other hand to take both of mine and place them on his shoulders one by one. Then he lies down on the bed, arranging me by his side. My brow remains creased the whole time, wondering what he's doing and why. It's all so very organized.

He draws light circles on my cheek. "If you ever want to lie in my bed with me, then you can."

"What if I move in my sleep? You'll be asleep yourself. You won't know."

"I won't be asleep. I've never been a big sleeper. I'll just lie with you. Watch you. And if you fidget or move, I'll be fully aware of it, trust me."

"You need to sleep." He's a machine.

"Sleep, when I could look at you all night? Easy decision, Izzy."

How could I not melt hearing that? But... "I've seen your staff," I begin, watching as he frowns, obviously wondering where I'm going with this. "They move out of your way, never come too close."

"They know me well."

"But I don't."

"What do you want to know?"

"Why'd you hunt me down?"

"Hunt?" He widens his eyes in feigned surprise. "You make me sound like an animal."

I laugh under my breath. He just took me like one. "Why me?"

He smiles mildly. "I have to brace myself for anyone's touch. Grit my teeth and hold my breath. It makes my skin crawl, but when you took my hand in the alley that night, my skin didn't crawl. It tingled."

"But you still don't like it."

"Oh, I love it, trust me. But I don't trust myself, Izzy. My reaction is ingrained too heavily into me. I can't help it."

"Reaction?"

He shrugs. "I don't like being touched."

I get the feeling he won't expand on that, so I fire another question. "Why?"

"Who are you afraid of?" he counters, evading my question and hitting me with his own.

I try my hardest not to tense. I fail terribly, my muscles aching in an instant under the pressure of his question. He's already figured out that someone hurt me. I can't venture into my painful past again. "Tell me," he demands, leveling an expectant gaze on me, his hand drifting down to my tummy and circling over my scars.

I shrink and shake my head, indicating that I'm not prepared to go there, just as I now know he won't be indulging me. "I need to go find Jess," I mumble. He doesn't push me, and I'm grateful. I can live without his secrets if he can live without mine.

Theo squeezes me a little before lifting me to my feet. "Then I will take you back." Releasing me, leaving me feeling a little lost, he steps back and indicates across the room to the bathroom. "Help yourself to a shower."

I smile my thanks and gather up my things before scooting across the soft carpet and shutting the door behind me. I drop my clothes to the floor and fall back against the door, covering my face with my hands. The needy ache overwhelming me feels suffocating. I haven't just dipped a toe into Theo's world. I've dived in headfirst.

CHAPTER 9

When I call Jess, she tells me they're in the Chandelier bar in the Cosmopolitan, a few hotels down the Strip. There's no need for Callum to drive me back, and I see both disappointment and worry on Theo's face when I tell him.

"It's an easy walk," I say as he escorts me to the elevator. "I'll be there in a few minutes."

"Vegas isn't a place where a young woman should be roaming around alone." He reaches for the call button and straightens out his jacket. "I'll walk you."

"You say it like I'm decades younger than you," I muse, gazing up at him when I feel him cock me a sideways look.

"Go on," he prompts, his lip curving. "Ask me."

"How old are you?"

"Thirty-one. You?"

I smile, delighted. "Twenty-seven." I return my focus forward and catch his small smile in the reflection of the mirrored doors. I return it until he shakes his head a little, looking down.

"Izzy White," he sighs, just as the doors open.

I look to Theo, not wanting to step in at the same time as him and collide with his big body. He nods for me to lead, which I do quickly, Theo following. The elevator stops at a few floors on the way down, more people boarding. As Theo moves to the back of the cart, I watch him, wondering what would happen if any one of these people were to catch him unexpectedly on the arm. I can see he's going out of his way to ensure that doesn't happen, his eyes wide and watching carefully.

When the doors open, he waits for everyone else to exit before stepping forward himself, but someone waiting outside the lift starts to enter. Theo moves speedily, leaning back to miss the flailing arm of the person rushing inside.

I look on, stunned. "That was some fast moving," I say, waiting for him to join me. His hand comes up between us, showing me his palm before he slowly takes it to my lower back and pushes me on.

"I have a lot of practice," he says quietly, for the first time making me wonder if one of Callum's many duties is to guard him from being touched. His bodyguard. It seems ludicrous, yet since Theo hasn't told me the consequence of an unexpected touch, I can't appreciate the level of seriousness.

We exit the hotel and wander down the long curved path past the famous fountain display, my instinct putting me on the inside of him so no one standing by the concrete barriers admiring the show can accidently knock him. He looks down at me and smiles, like he's privy to my intention.

"I can't believe you came all this way," I muse, settling into his side when he wraps an arm around my shoulders.

"And just to get my leg over, too."

I laugh loudly and look up at him, probably more dreamily than I mean to. "Business," I remind him.

"Oh, yeah. Business first and foremost, of course."

I shake my head to myself. I'm the business. "Well, I hope the *business* was worth your while."

"It was more than worth it," he says wryly, returning his attention forward and moving to the side when a tourist armed with a camera barrels toward us. Theo gets us on our way again once the path is clear. "But do me a favor," he adds.

"What?"

"Don't let my business wear that skimpy swimsuit again." He tosses me a disapproving look, and I laugh. He's a smart man. After seeing my stomach, he knows very well why I wore that particular swimsuit, though he's not letting his discovery divert his disapproval. I don't know why that makes me happy. "The answer is '*Yes, Theo*.'"

"Yes, Theo." I chuckle, feeling him nudge me playfully.

Our short walk to the Cosmopolitan is comfortably quiet and very fascinating. He weaves through the crowds expertly, keeping me close, not only ensuring no one brushes him, but no one touches me, either. When we reach the big glass doors, he opens them for me and places a cheeky palm on my arse when I pass him. I turn to face him once we're in the foyer, my way of telling him I'll be okay from here.

He stands a few feet before me, his hands in his pockets, his blue eyes regarding me carefully. "I'll be leaving early in the morning," he says quietly, almost regretfully. "So you can get back to your girlie holiday."

I nod acceptingly, though on the inside I can feel a void forming. "Okay."

"Call me," he says, though I don't mistake it as a polite request. I will be desperate to see him by the time I get home, anyway. As feared, he has a physical hold now, and I don't want him to let me go. I want to dive at him, bury myself in his huge chest and throw my arms around his neck, but I know I can't do that without invitation. And like he's read my mind, he removes his hands from his pockets and opens his arms to me. The magnetic force of him pulls me straight into his embrace without a moment's hesitation.

"Thank you for...dinner." I frown into his shoulder as I stand on tippy-toes to get my arms around his neck, feeling him smile against my ear.

"Thank you for bending to my will," he counters playfully, and I smile, too, lost in the comfort of his tight hug, his massive body completely blanketing mine. "Have fun, sweetheart." He taps my bottom, and I reluctantly pull free of him, losing the warmth the second we're no longer touching. I don't want to jump the gun, but I'm pretty sure Theo's behavior and the way he's looking at me are signs of the despondency I'm feeling myself. I honestly don't want him to go.

"I'll call you." I pivot on my heels and jog toward the escalators, not wanting to prolong the challenge of leaving him. I'm ripping the bandage off instead of peeling it away slowly. I take a cheeky peek over my shoulder just as I reach the top of the escalators, finding he's at the bottom still, watching me go. I smile and lift my hand and give him a small wave, and Theo mirrors it. Then Callum appears, coming to stand a few feet away from Theo. And I realize, he's probably been in the background the whole time.

I give Theo one last smile before turning away, taking a deep breath, and stepping off the escalator, reminding myself why I'm here. I find Jess at the bar with Kyle, though Denny is nowhere in sight. "Hey," I say, jumping onto a stool next to them.

"Izzy!" Jess sings, waving the barman over. "Oh my God, what happened?"

"Too much to go into now." I laugh.

"Cosmopolitan, please," Jess says to the barman before giving me her undivided attention again. "Tell. Now."

I look at Kyle, wary, and he laughs, indicating over his shoulder. "I need the men's room."

I smile, grateful for the privacy, though I doubt he'll be gone long enough for me to explain everything. "Thanks," I say as he wanders off, leaving me at the mercy of my friend's raging curiosity. "Shit, Jess," I breathe, slumping over the bar.

"Here, drink." She pushes a glass over to me, and I accept appreciatively, taking a long swig. "Holy shit, Izzy," Jess blurts, and I look out the corner of my eye to her, my glass still at my lips. I find her staring at my wrist, and I look down, cringing, knowing what I'm going to see. Red marks. Not too angry, but obvious. "What the hell?" She throws a horrified look at me.

"He . . . " I stall, wondering if I should share the reasons for Theo tying me up.

"He tied you up?" she asks, moving in closer, hungry for the dirt.

I nod and swig more. "Arms and legs."

"Eeeek!" she squeals. "And you liked it?"

I can see the hope in her. The desperation for me to have had sex for healthy reasons, which is really quite laughable given *how* I just had sex. But the truth is, I loved every moment. Even the teasing, torturing tactics Theo adopted. The pain that faded into pleasure. "It was pretty mind-blowing," I whisper, and she smiles, so bright.

"Did you find out more about him?"

I contemplate that for a moment. He didn't exactly tell me much, though I feel like I know him a lot better after a filthy fucking session. "He's thirty-one." I start with the simplest piece of information.

"What does he do for a living?"

"I don't know."

"You didn't ask?"

"No." I turn toward the bar. "We didn't really talk about that kind of stuff."

"Then what?"

"He's picked up on the fact that I've run from something."

"Did you tell him?"

"No. Just like he didn't tell me why he doesn't like being touched."

Jess's forehead creases in question. "He doesn't like being touched?"

"No."

"Why?"

I shrug. "I don't know. He needs controlled environments. He says he's hyperaware of me. Of my movements, more so than anyone else's."

"Wow," she breathes. "Does he have a phobia? Maybe sensitive skin or something?"

I shake my head, thinking hard. "He can touch me. He can touch anything. But nothing can touch him. But whenever I asked him about it, he closed up. Or countered with a question I really didn't want to answer."

"So you're both broken." She winces, her face apologetic. "I didn't mean it like it sounded."

I'm quick to reassure her. "I know."

Reaching over, she gives my arm a soft rub, and I smile in return. "Were you serious when you said his cock is so-so?"

I laugh. "He was listening. I didn't want to inflate his ego."

"So it's big?" she asks, excited. It's ridiculous. We should be more interested in the fact that Theo tied me up, and *why* he tied me up.

"Very," I confirm, unable to lie. "And he knows how to use it." I drift off in my mind, back to the bedroom of Theo's suite, seeing myself squirm and beg under his attention. The man is entirely irresistible.

Jess slumps back on her stool, taking her drink and sipping thoughtfully. "Wow, Izzy. Could it be serious?"

Her question gives me pause. "I don't know," I answer honestly. How serious could being completely and utterly consumed by someone be?

CHAPTER 10

I felt I owed it to Jess to give the rest of our holiday my all after disappearing on her. I owe it to myself, too. Theo turning up out of the blue knocked me off balance—more so than I already was with him just having a presence in my mind. But I can't deny how enamored I am by him. Completely hooked.

Over the past few days, we've sunbathed, drank, chatted constantly, and we went all out to visit as many of the hotels on the Strip as we could. Cocktails at Caesars Palace, dinner at the Aria, and a few spellbinding shows. It ate up the time, but it also distracted me from Theo. Finally, I can say that my first girlie holiday was everything it should be, and what I dreamed it would be. We haven't seen much of Denny, but Kyle has kept regular company with us. I can't be miffed about it, since Jess was so understanding about my unexpected situation. Besides, Kyle has been good fun. Extra good fun for Jess, judging by the smile on her face when they returned to the pool after sneaking off for an hour yesterday.

It's our last night in Vegas. As I gather up my purse and head to meet Jess, I contemplate the frame of mind she might be in. She went down to the lobby an hour ago to say goodbye to Kyle, who's heading home to Georgia. I find her at the bar, and when

I've parked my arse on a stool next to her and ordered my drink, I chance a peek at my friend, finding her grinning across the bar. I look over and see a tall blond bloke. "Missing him, I see," I quip, rubbing her shoulder comfortingly in the most sarcastic fashion.

"Who?" She looks at me seriously.

I straighten my lips and collect her drink, handing it to her. "Never mind."

She rolls her eyes and dives into her glass. "A summer fling, Izzy." She swings a determined look onto me. "It's our last night. Let's see Vegas out in style." Grabbing her glass, she downs the lot and eyes me in instruction to follow, which I do willingly. We both gasp and slam down our empties, then jump down from our stools. Linking arms with me, she marches us toward the casino floor.

* * *

We really are seeing Vegas out in style. I have no idea what I'm doing, but each time I kiss the dice, the guy next to me rolls what he apparently needs to win a stack of cash. So I keep kissing the dice while being plied with alcohol by the waitress tending the table.

"You're on fire, Izzy!" Jess declares, as everyone around the table laughs.

I shrug and kiss the dice once more when they're held under my nose, as Jess slides on up next to a South African man at the table.

Yeah, she's really missing Kyle. I, however, really do miss someone. I smile, unable to stop the warm, fuzzy feeling that the knowledge I'll be seeing him again brings. Walking away from him in the foyer of the Cosmopolitan was harder than it should have been. What will happen when I get home? The prospect excites and frightens me.

Everyone starts cheering again, knocking me from my thoughts, and I blink and look to my left, finding the man whose dice I've been kissing for the past hour is grinning at me. "I don't know where you came from, but you're not leaving this table."

"Actually, I need the ladies'," I say, placing my empty glass on a nearby ledge. "Give me two minutes." I dart off to the nearest restroom.

After washing my hands and refreshing my lipstick, I turn to make my way back onto the floor, bumping into Jess at the door. "Hey, you okay?" I ask as she scurries into a cubicle and shuts the door.

"Yeah, you made me need to pee, too."

I smile and decide to add a bit of blusher while I wait for her. I hear the chain flush and turn my attention to the entrance of the ladies' when someone walks in, recoiling when I find a man—the guy whose dice I've been kissing all night. "Um, the men's is on the other side." I laugh, but he does not. In fact, his jaw is rather tight.

"Get back to the table."

"Excuse me?" My blusher brush pauses midstroke of my cheek as he approaches, getting way too close.

"You said two minutes. You've been five." He looms over me hostilely. Is he playing a stupid intimidation game? For a second, it works, and my heartbeat annoyingly picks up. But I soon order it back down to steady. I lived on the knife's edge for too long. I refuse to let this arsehole intimidate me. I move to walk past him, ready to collect Jess and get out of here.

"Whoa, little lady." My path is blocked, and he takes my arm, holding it a little too firmly to be friendly, and my firm stance falters, wretched flashbacks threatening to come forward. God damn me. *Little lady?*

"Get your fucking hands off me," I seethe, determined not to let my vulnerability show. Never. Tugging my arm from his grip, I take a step back. "And get out of the damn ladies', you creep." An angry red mist starts to distort my vision, and I blink to clear it, just in time to see him catapult back and hit the deck. *What the hell?*

Callum appears, giving me the once-over, his jaw tight and twitching. "Are you okay?" he asks, dividing his attention between me and the man he's just floored.

I can only nod, my mouth dry and useless as Jess comes out of the cubicle, pulling her dress down, obviously keen to find out what's going on. I catch the man in the mirror pulling himself up, and it takes me a few slow seconds to register him reaching into his trouser pocket. He pulls out a flick knife, and the glimmer of the blade under the lights snaps me out of my inertness. "Callum!" I shout, watching as the blade glides through the air toward Theo's friend's chest. He dodges it and catches the man's arm, ramming it up his back, and the knife hits the floor with a loud clatter. And then there is a gun aimed at the man's temple. *A fucking gun. Of course he has a fucking gun.*

"Really?" Callum seethes, tossing the man back to the floor, keeping his gun trained on him. "You have five seconds to get the fuck out of here before I decorate this restroom with your brain." He sounds as calm as he looks.

"Oh my God," Jess breathes.

"One," Callum says calmly, prompting the man to scurry up from the floor, panic-stricken. "Two." He trips a few times on his way out of the restroom, constantly looking back. "Three," Callum says menacingly, lowering his gun to his side and watching as the man staggers and stumbles on his way. "Four." I can't be sure, but I'm pretty sure Callum's eyes are laughing. The man rounds the corner and disappears from sight before Callum gets to five.

The humor I detected in his warm brown eyes is gone the second they land on me and Jess. I shrivel on the spot under his disapproval, but quickly let my spine pull me up again when the shock of his appearance from nowhere finally sinks in.

I step forward, steady and strong. "You've been here the whole time, haven't you?" I ask, regarding him carefully. "Theo told you to keep an eye on me."

His face is deadpan. "You're welcome," he says flatly, indicating the exit.

I'm struck dumb, part awed, but mostly mad. "Welcome?" I blurt on a laugh. He has a nerve. "I can take care of myself."

"Looked like it."

My teeth clench as I collect Jess's arm and start leading her out of the restroom, pulling her back every time she looks behind. "He just saved our lives," she murmurs dreamily. "He's my Theo."

My shoulders drop. "One flash of a gun and you're anybody's," I grumble, dragging her on as Callum tails us through the casino. He even gets in the elevator with us, seeing us up to our room. How very kind of him.

Once I've let us in and Jess has had her fill of his ominous being for a few moments, I nod a polite thanks and shut the door, locking us safely inside our room.

Jess flops to the bed with a huge sigh, not nearly as shocked as she should be after seeing Callum pull out a gun. I drop my bag to the floor, undoing my dress and chucking it on my case.

"So romantic," she muses, looking over at me pulling on a T-shirt. "Theo actually had him watch over you. I can't believe it."

My friend seems to have misplaced the fact that it's also bordering on irrational. I crawl into bed and set my alarm for eight a.m., backing up the wake-up call we have scheduled from reception. "Not stalkerish at all," I mumble under my breath, turning onto my side and falling deep into thought. He had one of his men stay in Vegas to watch me. What's with that? I've only just come to terms with the fact he showed up here, and by *come to terms*, I mean been too utterly distracted by his attention to really think about how crazy it is. And now he's having me tailed?

I'm about to mentally start breaking it all down in an attempt to rationalize it when my phone starts ringing. I unplug it from the charger and have a mild panic attack when I see Theo's name flashing at me, threatening. Damn, I should have known Callum would be reporting back to him. Wait. Why am I panicking? He's the one behaving like some kind of deranged, obsessed stalker. It's him who needs putting in his place, not me. I sink into my pillow and answer. "Theo."

"Izzy," he breathes, evidently relieved, which just makes me sigh rather than launch into my intended rant.

I look across to Jess, finding her smiling excitedly, perched on the edge of her bed, intrigued by what's going to be said. I wave a dismissive hand at her, which she totally ignores, waving one right back. "Before you give me a lecture—"

"What on earth were you thinking?"

"It was just a bit of fun," I argue, but my tone is soft. Soothing. So much for putting him in his place. Instead, I'm finding myself naturally trying to ease his unwarranted worry. "I was kissing dice, that's all. He seemed like a nice bloke."

He definitely growls under his breath, and I thank the heavens that Theo wasn't at the casino. That guy would have been exterminated in a flash. "Do you know how hard I found it to leave you in Vegas?"

And now I'm smiling. God, he's like a sedative—a potent potion that is the cure for everything. "Enough to have Callum stay and spy on me."

"Not spy, sweetheart. Just to make sure you get home to me safely."

Oh, God. I flick my eyes to Jess, wondering if she's detecting the body-melt going on over here. Home to him. That sounds so right, even with the knowledge of guns and a little mild stalking. "I guess that means you're privy to my swimsuit-wearing crimes."

Theo laughs softly, the familiar, deep sound igniting a fire in my tummy, making me wish that he were here. Or I were there. Unreasonable as it is, I've missed him these past few days. Now I'm aching with the need to see him. "You guessed right," he says quietly. "We'll talk about punishments when you're home. Are you in bed?"

I turn onto my side, my head sinking into the pillow. "Yes. Talk to me until I fall asleep," I order on a yawn.

"Is Jess there?" His voice is suddenly rough.

That alone has my thighs clenching. "Yes."

"Then I guess that limits my scope for wearing you out."

Oh? I glance over my shoulder to see Jess disappear into the bathroom. "You could do that over the phone?" I sound coy, and he chuckles lightly.

"I feel like I could connect with you telepathically, Izzy. That's how in touch with you I feel."

God, he's on form tonight, saying all the right things. I sense he's not happy about the happenings on the casino floor, but I also sense that he's more relieved than mad. "Theo?" I say, looking up at the ceiling, wondering how I might word my next question.

"What?"

I hesitate for a brief moment before deciding there's only one way. I need to know. "What's going to happen when I get home?" It's been playing on my mind since he tied me to the bed and rained devotion all over me, albeit in his own little way. It didn't take any of my hunger for him away. If anything, it's multiplied it by a million. "Apart from you punishing me for my swimsuit-wearing crimes, I mean."

Theo laughs lightly but hesitates, and I see him in my mind's eye brushing the length of his index finger over his cupid's bow thoughtfully. "Us happens," he finally says, simple and straight to the point. Except I'm not sure what *us* is.

"What will *us* be?"

"In truth, I don't know." He sighs. "But I'm looking forward to figuring that out. If you're happy to come along for the ride. Are you happy to, Izzy? Do you want to explore what *us* could be?"

I'm sure I hear him breathe in, like he's holding his breath, waiting for my answer. But I can't be one hundred percent sure, because I sucked in my own breath at the same time. *Explore us.* I've had a glimpse into what I can expect, and though it defies what I know and stretches my imagination beyond what I thought I was capable of imagining, I'm certain I want to venture there again. Because it will be with Theo. "I do," I reply quietly, smiling when I hear his exhale. "I want to," I confirm.

"You won't regret it," Theo whispers. "I promise you."

"I believe you." I wholeheartedly do. If I could see him, I know he would be smiling. I love his smile. Softness on hardness. Light on dark.

"Good. Now get some sleep. I look forward to seeing you." He hangs up, and I drop the phone by my side, gazing toward the window. And I admit, no matter how crazy it may seem, I'm falling hard for the dark, menacing stranger.

CHAPTER 11

Holy shitballs," Jess cries as we break out of the airport into the cold air.

I shiver and pull my cardigan in, looking across the road to check how long the queue is at the taxi rank. But there's someone blocking my view. "Callum," I breathe. Of course he's here.

"Hey," Jess sings, muscling past me. She drops her case at Callum's feet and smiles up at him. "I never got to thank you for saving my life," she gushes, beginning to fidget when his expressionless face doesn't crack. "Um...so...yeah..." She coughs and frowns back at me, shrugging when I shake my head in dismay. "Thank you," she finishes, seeming to shrivel on the spot.

"I don't believe I saved your life," Callum mutters as Jess collects her bag and retreats, coming back to me for support.

"Cold," she mutters under her breath, slighted.

Callum stoops to pick up my bag before claiming Jess's from her grasp. She doesn't give it up easily. "I can manage," she snaps, snatching it back.

"Suit yourself." Callum brushes her stroppiness off without a shred of annoyance and wanders off toward the Mercedes parked a few meters away. I follow, glancing back at Jess lugging her case along behind her.

"What?" she asks, scowling.

"Want some help?"

"No."

I laugh and carry on my way, smiling my thanks when Callum opens the door for me. "I'm interested," I start, as I hold the top of the door, one foot in the car. "How does one get a gun through customs?" Callum smirks at me, but he doesn't answer. He just shrugs. So I go on and ask another question that's been playing on my mind. "What does Theo do for a living?"

His smirk now is gone, falling away fast. The cold, expressionless man is back. "He wants to tell you that himself."

I can't help my recoil, and I try to rub away the sick feeling in my stomach. He wants to tell me himself? That doesn't sound reassuring at all. "Why?"

Once again, Callum shrugs, not answering, choosing instead to march up to Jess and seize her case. My mind races, reminding me that there is so much I don't know about Theo Kane. And I'm quite sure I won't like it, just like Theo said himself.

"Hey, I was doing just fine," Jess fumes indignantly as she wrestles with Callum's hold of her case.

"Put a lid on it, woman."

I hang on the door, my eyes going back and forth between the pair of them, watching them fight over the luggage. Of course, Callum wins easily, leaving Jess scowling at him indignantly as he literally throws her case in the boot and slams it shut.

"Hey," she cries. "Be careful, you big oaf."

Callum tenses, his patience obviously wearing thin, his warm brown eyes flashing with frustration, his hand raking through his blond waves. He gives me an exasperated look, and I give him an apologetic one. "She's tired." I make Jess's excuse for her. "Grumpy."

"Should have left that scumbag to slap the insolence out of her," he gripes, turning toward Jess. "Get in."

"Don't tell me what to do."

I sigh, growing as exasperated as Theo's friend. She's being difficult just for the sake of it, not wanting to lose face. Callum strides over to her, taking her arm and leading her to the car, and she splutters and protests the whole way, kicking up a stink to the point people start looking. I slink into the car and shut the door, embarrassed, as she falls into the seat beside me.

"Arsehole," she spits, throwing herself back in the seat, huffing and puffing all over the car.

"You're such a princess."

She scoffs and arranges her bag on her lap. "He can be a gentleman when it suits him."

"You call holding a gun at someone's head gentlemanly?" Why isn't she shocked? I had a mini meltdown when I first encountered Theo's weapon.

Jess grins, nibbling her bottom lip. "I want him to hold a gun to *my* head." Her stare roots to the back of Callum, and I snigger on the inside, just catching Callum's eye in the rearview mirror. He looks a little bewildered, probably cursing Theo to hell and back for setting him up for this.

* * *

The drive from the airport is uneventful, though I sense tension past my own state of contemplation. *Us happens.* I smile to myself as we pull up outside our apartment, and Callum carries our cases into the hallway.

"Here." He hands me a black box, secured with a pretty red ribbon.

"What's this?" I ask, staring down at the embossed card as I toy with one of the lengths of ribbon. After a few moments, Callum hasn't answered, and I look up and see him getting in the car. Jess is quickly on my back, trying to get a peek of what's in my hand.

"Is it from him?" she asks, her eyes dancing with excitement. I'm not excited, more . . . apprehensive.

I move through to the kitchen, Jess hot on my heels, and take a seat at the table, placing the box before me. And I stare at it.

"Open it, then," Jess drops down into a chair, pushing the box toward me. "What are you waiting for?"

I start chewing my lip, sitting back. There's a tag on the corner, facing down so I can't see what's written there. I don't know why I'm so nervous. It's just a gift. But what could it be? I reach forward tentatively, like the box could bite me, and flick over the tag. I have to tilt my head to read the text.

Welcome home x

"Aww." Jess slaps a hand over her heart, coming over all dreamy. "For such a fuck-off big, scary thing, he's quite romantic."

I smile down at the box, curious and still very apprehensive. "What do you think it could be?" I ask, still avoiding diving in and ripping it open.

"Oh, wait," she says, and I look up to see her eyes closed, her fingers at her temples. And she's humming.

I reach over and slap her shoulder. "All right, smart arse."

"Open it." Jess pokes the box over to me again, and I load my lungs with air and start pulling the pretty bow free until it pools around the box. Flicking my eyes up to Jess, I smile when she encourages me on with an impatient look. I pull off the lid and peek inside, finding a note atop a pile of satin. I take the note and unfold it, reading the lines Theo has written.

I've missed you terribly.
Understand it?
Me either.
I hope you accept graciously.

Theo x

My damn heart melts in my chest as Jess plucks the note from my hand and gushes all over the table, oohing and ahhing, her hand back on her chest.

"Oh my goodness." She sighs, watching as I reach inside the box, smiling like crazy. "That face." She points at my reddening cheeks. "Jesus, Izzy, you're fucking glowing."

"We've just got off the plane from Vegas," I point out in a silly defense tactic that has my friend laughing her socks off. She has every right to. I'm well and truly buzzing with the knowledge that he's missed me, my veins warming as they pump blood to my pounding heart. I take out the satin-wrapped parcel, lay it on the table, and begin to pull each corner out until the sheet of luxury fabric is laid flat on the table, revealing...

"What the hell is that?" Jess asks, leaning in closely.

I'm damned if I know. Cocking my head, suddenly afraid to touch the unknown object, I try to fathom what it is exactly we're looking at. I figure out there's a cuff of some sort, lined with...

"Is that velvet?" Jess reaches forward and runs a finger around the inner circumference of the cuff, and it's then I notice a matching one, sitting neatly underneath.

"There's two."

"And there's some kind of gold bangle attached to each of them." She picks one up, and we both watch as she lifts it slowly.

Realization slams into me. "Oh..." I breathe, recoiling in my chair.

Understanding must dawn on Jess a split second later, because she gasps and drops the cuff to the table. "Oh my fucking God," she shrieks, standing up abruptly. "It's bondage gear."

"They're cuffs." I pick one up, playing with it thoughtfully. The leather of the cuff is soft, the velvet lining even softer, but the thick gold hoop attached to it is solid and hard. "He's worried he hurt me when he tied me up." I fall into a daze, continuing to study the pretty accessory, feeling it and slipping it over my wrist. I smile. "Perfect fit," I muse.

"Wow," Jess splutters, dropping back into her chair. "You're falling for a sadomasochist."

I giggle, despite myself. Her statement is grossly inaccurate. "He is not a sadomasochist."

She eyes me, her lips puckering. "But you *are* falling for him?"

I note my error and start to correct it, but Jess holds up her hand to shut me up before I can begin. "We'll get to that in a minute. I'm more concerned about this." She waggles a finger at the box.

I take the other cuff and place them together on the table, admiring them. "He isn't a sadomasochist," I reiterate, knowing I'm right. "He wants me to wear these so he can't hurt me." I look up to Jess. "He's worried I'll touch him and he won't be prepared for it during..." I let my words fade and let Jess draw the right conclusion. She nods, both in understanding *and* for me to continue. "Theo's senses are heightened to movements. Other people's movements. I think he's taught himself to be super aware over the years. He always catches my hands before I can touch him, and he takes control of my movement, putting them where I intended. He says he's hypersensitive to me and he's worried he won't have that advantage when we're in bed together."

"So you can't touch him when you're...you know...doing it."

"You're such a prude." I laugh.

"I'm not." Jess picks up one of the cuffs and studies it. "I'm just not into kinky stuff."

"It's not kinky. It's a necessity." I take my gift back and tuck it neatly into the box. "I can't touch him at all. At least, not without him expecting and controlling it."

She pouts to herself, her mind obviously racing. *Welcome to my world, Jess.* "I wonder what would happen?"

My hands falter, enough for her to notice and conclude that I'm as curious about that as she is. "I need to unpack." I leave Jess at the table and make my way through to my bedroom, flopping on the bed with my box. And as I stare up at the ceiling, I daydream. I daydream, hope, and pray that one day Theo will be comfortable enough to give me free rein over his body. Until then, I guess I should get used to being tied up.

CHAPTER 12

For once, I'm not complaining about the heat in the hospital. I haven't warmed up since I left Vegas. God, eight hours at work and my holiday already feels like eons ago, and the urge to tip a bucket of water over Jess's head this morning, when she smugly collected her coffee before going back to bed, was unbearably hard to resist. Her first shift back at work is the red-eye shift, the lucky cow. I, however, was up and out of the house by five thirty, more or less sobbing my way to work. I feel like I've been awake for years.

"Where's that sparkle in those gorgeous green eyes?" Mable asks as I unhook her catheter bag.

"In my bed," I quip. "How are you feeling? One to ten."

"Five," she answers immediately, hissing as she shifts on the bed. "Are you going to tell me about Dallas or not?"

"Vegas," I correct her, laughing. "Do you have a thing for cowboys, Mable?"

She gives me an impish grin. "A man who prefers to straddle a horse rather than me isn't top of my want list, dear."

I fold over with laughter, nearly dropping the bag full of pee. "You're a wicked old lady."

"Age won't take that away from me, young girl."

I look around at the rest of the patients in Mable's bay, all elderly, either sleeping or looking as miserable as you would expect someone who's stuck in a hospital to be. Mable is a refreshing change. "I'll miss you when you're gone," I say as one of the catering girls rounds the corner with the trolley.

"Well, until this damn hip starts playing ball, I ain't going nowhere, my love."

I do a quick mental rewind through all the updates I've had today. "Hey, did anyone collect you for your X-ray yet?"

"Not yet."

I look down at my watch. "It's a bit late now. Let me chase it up for you. Here's your supper."

"Oh, joy," she mutters, flipping a hand to her wheelie table. I push it toward her and watch with a smile as she grimaces at the tray.

"*Bon appétit*," I call, heading back to the nurses' station.

After disposing of Mable's pee and giving the empty bag to a health care assistant to hook back up, I take a seat at the computer and load Mable's file, then call the X-ray department. "Same old," I mutter when I get no answer, hanging up as Susan appears, looking a bit harassed, her round face red. "Everything okay?" I ask as she leans past me to collect a pen.

"Just a difficult visitor," she huffs. "It's not hard. Visiting times are two till four. I don't know what makes some people think the rules don't apply to them." She jots something down on a pad and tosses it back on the desk.

"Would you like me to have a word?" I ask, getting up from my chair. Susan isn't exactly the most diplomatic, and while most people respect her authority, the odd person questions it. Susan doesn't like being questioned.

She looks at me with a telling expression. "Do you think the ignorant swine will listen to you?"

"Worth a try, right?"

"Go on then." She nods down the ward. "Bay two, bed four."

"That's Percy's bed." The old boy was admitted after a massive heart attack, and on top of that, he's losing his marbles, bless him. And the raging bladder infection he has isn't helping.

"Yes, and Percy's son is a nasty little so-and-so."

I head for bay two and run into Rich, one of the hospital porters, as he rounds the corner with an empty wheelchair. "Hey."

He beams at me, his tall, lanky body bent over the wheelchair as he pushes it along. "You're back, and you look like shit."

Reaching up to my hair, I tuck it behind my ears. I'm too beat to care what I must look like. This shift has been like a baptism by fire. "It's great to be back," I chirp, full of feigned enthusiasm. "Who are you here for?"

He looks down at his clipboard. "Mable Loake. X-ray."

"Oh, great. I was just chasing that. She's bay four, bed one." I point down the ward. "But she's just eating her dinner."

"No problem." He wheels the chair off, grumbling something about having the day from hell. *Join the club*, I think, carrying on my way.

As soon as I round the corner, I spot a man in the chair beside Percy's bed, maybe midforties, and his scowl backs up Susan's gripe. We have a tricky customer. "Hi there, Percy," I chirp, focusing on my patient for now, approaching to find him poking at a chicken sandwich. He glances up at me blankly, and I immediately know that today is a bad day. "How are you feeling?" I ask, looking up to his drip, seeing another bag of antibiotics has been administered. He can't seem to kick this infection. I take a quick peek at the readings on his heart monitor, not liking his erratic heart rate, and take his temperature as I check his charts.

"How does he look like he's feeling?" his son pipes up, standing from his chair. "You feed him shit like this"—he takes the sandwich from his father's plate and throws it down with force—"and scratch your fucking head when he shows no signs of improvement."

"Sir, there's no need to swear," I say calmly and diplomatically, looking down at the thermometer to find that Percy's temperature is dangerously high. "Wow, Percy, that's shot up quickly."

"What do you expect with subquality care?"

I inwardly wince, gritting my teeth. "Your father is receiving the best care, sir. And visiting hours are now finished," I say tactfully, forcing a smile at him.

"Yes, so I've been told," he snaps. "I know how these places work. Throw out the relatives before you serve this crap so we don't see the shit you feed our loved ones." He flicks a big hand out and sends Percy's supper flying across the bed. It bounces off my thigh before it hits the floor, and I jump back, startled.

"Sir, please." I stoop and blindly collect up the remnants of his father's sandwich from the floor as I look at the monitor, noting the quickening of Percy's heart.

"And I bet that dirty sandwich finds its way from the floor back onto the plate."

"I'll order him a fresh one," I assure him, rising and coming face-to-face with the arrogant arsehole. I step back, not liking his big body looming over me, pushing me into a corner.

I'm safe in a hospital, I tell myself, over and over again, trying not to display the anxious vibes that have sprung up on me. "You need to move so I can tend to your father. His temperature is very high and his heart rate is very erratic." I fill my voice with all the authority I can muster, pushing my way past him to tend to Percy. "Percy?" I say, finding his eyes are closed. "Percy, can you hear me?" He's slipped into unconsciousness. "Percy?" I reach for the emergency call button, but my arm is grabbed, and I look back to find Percy's son snarling at me. I wrench my arm from his grip with a hiss of mild pain, now seething mad that he would hinder my attempts to care for his father. "Get your hands off me," I grate as I shove him aside and press the call button. I take Percy's wrist and check his pulse.

"What's going on?" his son asks.

"He's having another heart attack." Just as I say that, Percy's monitor alarms start going wild.

"Shit," I whisper, dashing off to get the defibrillator, hearing Percy's son shouting behind me, demanding to know what's going on. "Pam!" I yell, grabbing the cardiac arrest trolley and wheeling it back to Percy's room, Pam hot on my heels. "Percy's arrested," I say urgently, unraveling the leads on the machine as Pam cuts up the center of Percy's gown, exposing his chest.

"Tell me what's going on," his son demands, close by my side. I turn and bump into him, dropping the wires. God damn it, he's getting in my way. "Tell me!"

I'm fucking furious that he's stopping me from doing my job. *Be cool, Izzy.* I quickly collect up the wires and connect them before I turn to him, my eyes blazing, my jaw ticking madly. But I speak calmly. "Your father's heart needs a shock to reset it. You're in our way. Please move."

He snarls, but he doesn't retaliate, so I return to the monitor of the machine. "Clear," I shout, checking that Pam is away before I press the shock button. Percy jolts, and Pam immediately starts CPR. "Nothing," I mumble, looking up to see Percy's face, now as white as a sheet.

A burst of activity breaks out behind me, and we're joined by the cardiac arrest team. "Two rounds of compressions," I tell them as I step back, giving them room to take over CPR and the defibrillator. "Low pulse and one shock administered."

They take over and work on Percy calmly and swiftly while I fill them in on his vital signs, and Pam tries to coax his son from the room. The man is having none of it, shouting and hollering until I'm forced to call security to remove him. They arrive quickly, escorting Percy's son from the ward with his arm up his back as he continues to shout and holler. "I'll have you fired!" he yells, squirming to break free. "All of you!"

Adrenaline is racing through me as I wander out of the room, straightening out my dress and retying my hair. I meet Susan at the doorway, and she looks at me in question. "Heart attack," I mumble.

She sighs, linking arms with me and leading us away from the bay, leaving the arrest team to continue working on Percy. "Good work, Izzy," she says when we reach her office.

"I only went to ask his son to leave," I say, dropping into a chair at Susan's desk. "Welcome back, Izzy."

Susan smiles a little as she takes up a seat opposite me and pulls some papers from a tray. "He was fine when I checked on him. Temperature average, heart rate steady."

"His son was a total arsehole." I shake my head, as shocked by his behavior as I am by Percy's fast decline. "God, this has been the longest day ever."

Susan nods her agreement, looking down at her clock. "You can go home soon."

"One hour and counting," I say, just as Pam pokes her head around the door. The look on her face tells me everything, and my heart sinks. It's moments like this that sometimes make me forget why I love my job. "Thanks, Pam," I say on a sigh as I drag myself up from the chair. I give Susan a sad smile. "I need tea. Can I get you a cup?"

"Please." Susan points down at her desk. "I'll get this paperwork done while I'm here."

I nod and follow my feet to the hot drinks machine, making

two cups and stirring extra sugar into mine. And as I head back to Susan's office, Percy gets wheeled past, his old friendly face concealed by a white sheet. I lower my head in respect and say a silent prayer for Percy, feeling like a complete failure.

* * *

I drag my feet through the ward at the end of my shift, stopping to check on Mable before I leave. She's dozing, but a quick check of her consultant's notes tells me he isn't happy with the X-ray, her broken hip bone showing no signs of repairing without the need for last-resort surgery. It's just one more thing to feel glum about. I was so hoping she wouldn't have to have such an invasive operation.

I plod on my way, struggling to keep myself upright after my first long and mentally challenging shift. If I could have slept for a week this morning, then now I feel like I could hibernate for the winter. My bed is calling the loudest it ever has. Pulling the collar of my coat up and rearranging my bag on my shoulder, I round the corner onto the main corridor of the hospital, my already slow steps slowing further when I see Theo walking toward me. The sight of him resurrects me a little, and I come to a gradual stop, as does Theo, a few empty meters between us. He's suited in gray, his brown hair a sexy mess, his stubble short and covering his jaw evenly. His bright cobalt eyes dull a smidgen as he takes me in, a worried frown marring his perfect face. Jesus, I must look a fright. The last time he saw me I was dressed to the nines before he stripped me and made my world explode into a passion-induced haze. It's quite a contrast.

His thick thighs spread a little in his standing position, his head cocked to the side.

"Hey." I barely have the energy to even speak.

"Hey," he whispers, his lips pouting in thought. "You okay?"

"Tough shift," I tell him on a deep sigh. "You?"

"Let's not worry about me." He opens his arms, and I walk straight into them, keeping my hands in my pockets, despite knowing he'll be fully prepared for my touch should I wrap my arms around him. But I don't have the energy, no matter how happy I am to see him. His big arms encase me, holding me to his solid body, and it's without question the most comforting place I've ever been. His unique scent, the warmth of his body, and the feel of his lips on the back of my head. It's all so soothing. I don't even have the strength to wonder how he makes me feel so at home, when in reality I'm in the strangest place I've ever been. "Let me look after you tonight," he says above me, his big hand stroking over my hair. "I'll take you home to collect some things and you can stay with me."

"I'm hardly lively," I joke, his tenderness and the feel of him so welcome.

"I don't care." He pushes me from his chest and gazes down at me, a mild smile tugging at the corner of his mouth. "Just stay with me." The pad of his finger meets my cheekbone and grazes down to my chin, and I nod, a refusal not even entering my head. I can't think of anywhere I'd rather be. "Callum is waiting out front." Theo slides his arm around my shoulders and tucks me into his side, starting to walk us out of the hospital. His pace is slow and considerate, allowing me to take my time, my head resting on his shoulder.

When we reach the café near the entrance of the hospital, Theo points to the counter. "Drink?" he asks.

"I'd love a coffee." I don't want to fall asleep on him.

"I'll get you one. Go get in the car." He nods toward the doors before heading for the counter, and I smile as the lad serving instinctively steps back, his eyes widening at the size of the male approaching. Not for the first time, I wonder where that wariness is in me.

Wandering into the fresh air, I'm hit by the wind and shiver. I scan the cars for Callum, surprised to find him nowhere in sight. Wrapping my arms around my torso, I rush over to a concealed doorway for shelter from the biting wind, remaining close to the edge so I can spot Theo when he emerges from the hospital.

I send Jess a quick message to tell her I'm staying at Theo's, looking up when I notice a shadow in my downcast vision.

I step back, going from sleepy to alert in a heartbeat. Percy's son is scowling at me, his chest heaving violently. "He's dead, and it's your fault," he spits, grabbing the front of my coat and shoving me back into the door behind me. I yelp. "My father is dead because of your incompetence." He tugs me forward and slams me back again, knocking the wind from me.

"Get your hands off of me!" I shout, grappling at his grip on my coat and shoving him away. Survival instinct kicks in, as well as anger. The anger is hot, so hot it melts the panic. But he's lost his father. I need to remember that. No matter how much of an arsehole he is, I *must* remember that. I wrestle my bag onto my shoulder. "If you have a complaint, I suggest you contact the hospital. I was just doing my job."

He laughs, and it is one hundred percent sarcastic. "Your job?" Prodding me in the shoulder, he moves in, crowding me. "He was—" His eyes go like saucers, and he starts gasping for air, his hands reaching to his neck. It's only then that I see fingers wrapped around his throat, and he starts staggering back clumsily, choking, the color draining from his face. *Oh fuck.*

I force my feet to move forward, looking up over Percy's son's head, finding an expression of pure, frightening rage. Oh shit. "Theo!" I yell, following him as he drags the man around the corner and slams him into a wall. "Theo, stop."

He holds him against the bricks by his neck, looking murderous, and though I knew he has a nasty side, I don't think I truly appreciated *how* nasty. I dare not try to pull him away, aware that he's blinded by fury and won't be prepared for my touch. I'm helpless, standing to the side, seeing him squeeze tighter around Percy's son's throat as he pushes his face up close, his jaw ticking. "I don't know who the fuck you are—"

"He's the son of a patient," I blurt urgently, praying the information sinks past Theo's fog of anger. "Theo, stop!"

He doesn't stop, but instead slams him into the wall. "The sign you've seen, the one hanging on every wall of that hospital, the one stating that abuse toward staff will not be tolerated. Tell me you saw it." Theo leans in as Percy's son nods as best he can with a huge palm choking him. "Well, there's another sign, one you didn't see. It's an unwritten rule. Want to know what it says?"

Good God, a normal Theo is scary enough. An angry Theo is plain terrifying. For the first time since I've met him, he's making me anxious. What is he capable of? Percy's son nods again, terror pooling in his watery eyes, to the point I'm actually feeling sorry for him.

"That rule," Theo breathes across his face, "says if anyone lays a finger on my woman, the consequences will be grave. Want to know what the consequences are?"

Theo's taunting him, prolonging his pain *and* his fear. He's getting a kick out of it, relishing the sight of his victim's distress.

"Instant death," Theo whispers, keeping hold of him with one hand and reaching to his back with the other. He pulls out his gun and aims it square at the man's forehead, pulling back a lever that locks with a loud click.

Oh my God.

"Theo!" I shout, moving back, instinctively scanning the surrounding area for witnesses. There's no one; the place that Theo has dragged the man to is deserted, which I now realize was intentional. "Theo, please." I whirl around when I hear thundering footsteps behind me, finding Callum rounding the corner and bolting toward us. "Callum, stop him!"

He takes in the situation, his long legs slowing. "Theo, man, come on. Put the gun away," he says, moving in slowly and cautiously. "Deep breaths, my man. Deep breaths." Callum's voice is soft, soothing, and it seems to be breaking through Theo's haze of rage. "Be cool, Theo. Just be cool."

A few worrying seconds pass as I hold my breath, silently willing Theo to listen to Callum, before he eventually pulls the gun from Percy's son's forehead and lowers it to his side. But he still has him nailed to the wall with his spare hand, though he must have lessened his grip a little, because his prisoner starts gasping.

Air floods my lungs, too, and I look to Callum. He gives me a knowing nod, moving in with his hands held up, showing them to Theo. Only when Theo turns his eyes on his friend does Callum claim the man from his clutches, pulling him away and shoving him along the pavement, back toward the main entrance of the hospital. I watch as Callum releases Percy's son at the corner and straightens himself out, turning to face us. He doesn't come back over. Just waits on the corner.

I literally collapse with relief, falling against the wall, concentrating on regulating my shaky breaths. Tiredness has abandoned me, being replaced with shock. I'm caught between utter appreciation for Theo being here to protect me, something I've wished for my whole life, and absolute panic, not only because he seemed so out of control, the violence in him deadly, but because there is nothing to stop Percy's son from reporting me and my...what is Theo to me?

My thoughts frazzle as I gaze up at him, finding him looking composed and clear-eyed. Like the insanity switch has been flipped off. The madman has gone. I want to be angry. I don't want to wish he'd been around before now. Someone to protect me. Someone to threaten death on anyone who tried to hurt me. But I've seen enough violence to last me a lifetime. And in Theo, violence is clearly an instinct.

Emotion is creeping its way up my throat, and I swallow to try to keep it at bay. "Are you okay?" I ask mindlessly, with a lack of anything else coming to me, my voice a little ragged and broken.

Theo shakes his head to himself, his hand sliding onto his nape and stroking. "Shit." His voice is a little shaky. In fact, he *looks* shaken up, too. "I'm so sorry. I didn't mean to..." He glances behind him, blowing out a long breath. "I didn't want you to see that."

"I didn't want to see it, either," I tell him, and he looks at me, trying to read me. "I don't like violence."

"He was going to hurt you."

"It hurt more watching you behave like an animal."

Theo stares at me, and I don't look away. I remain resolute, steady, firm in my position, despite knowing he's trying to read between the lines. All of my barriers are up, and he won't get past them. And he must realize that, because he eventually relents, closing his eyes and looking up to the nighttime sky for a few moments before extending his hands toward me. "Please," he begs, and I walk toward him, his plea too hard to resist. I take his hands and let him feel for a few moments, his eyes dropping to mine. "My temper..." He fades off, swallowing hard. "It gets the better of me sometimes."

"Then don't let it." My tone is equal to his, soft and pleading. "I don't want to see you like that, Theo."

He nods, shame clear in his solemn expression. "I'm sorry." Pulling me into his chest, he lifts me to his body, and I go with ease. Because what else will I do? Reject him? "You feel so good against me," he whispers, pushing his face into my neck and inhaling, his bristle scratchy but comforting.

I silently agree and let him carry me back to the car, and I only release him once we arrive. Callum holds the door open for me, his lips straight as he nods sharply at me. And I wonder, how many times has he been forced to hold back his friend from doing some serious damage to anyone who might cross him? Or simply touch him? Lots, I expect.

And as Theo joins me in the back, claiming me and pulling me close, my mind starts to race. Has Callum ever been too late to stop him?

CHAPTER 13

We stopped briefly at my place to collect some clean clothes and my toiletries, and while I gathered my things, Theo mooched around my bedroom, sniffing out the cuffs he bought me on my nightstand and winking as he scooped them up and slipped them into his pocket. I didn't stop him.

As Callum takes us back to Theo's, I pay more attention to the drive this time, noting we head toward North London, our journey taking more than an hour with the rush hour traffic. By the time we pull up, it's pitch black and Theo's mansion is illuminated by hundreds of scattered lights around the property. The ornate lampposts lining the long driveway guide the way until we pull up through the thick carved concrete pillars.

Jefferson is the first person I see, followed by the same two big guys who were flanking the door the last time I was here. I don't miss the ample space Jefferson gives Theo to get out of the car, nor the fact that everyone keeps a safe distance from him.

Theo reaches in and takes my hand, helping me from the car, and Jefferson smiles brightly as he waits for us to move away before he closes the door and follows a few paces behind. "Your mother called," he informs Theo's back. "Said she couldn't reach you on your mobile."

I shoot a look up at Theo, but he doesn't entertain my curiosity. Theo's mother? My mind is quickly rampant with mental images of women, trying to imagine what she would look like. And what *is* she like? Smiley and loving like my mother was? Devoted and encouraging? Did she used to stroke Theo's back when he was a boy until he fell asleep, like my mum did? Did she make him eggs sunny-side up in perfect circles? Did she ever use her very last pound to buy him the latest issue of his favorite magazine? I smile sadly to myself, wishing her back. It was just me and Mum. We didn't have money, but we were rich with love. She adored me, and I adored her. We were a team. The terrible twosome, she used to call us. And then that wretched illness stole her away from me too soon. I swallow and blink back the memories, fond memories that are masked by the horrid final days before she finally gave up.

"I'll call her back later," Theo says, coming to a stop in the center of his huge, elaborate entrance hall. The sweeping staircase holds my attention for a moment, a flashback to my first time here capturing me in a daze for a fleeting second. Once again, the woman appears with a tray in her hand, except this time there are two glasses—the familiar tumbler with amber liquid, and a glass of white wine. Theo shrugs his big shoulders out of his jacket and takes the two paces needed to close the gap between them, handing her his coat before lifting the two glasses from the metal tray. He knocks back his drink and places the empty glass down. The lady nods and backs away before turning and leaving us.

Then the sound of the front doors closing fills the space, pulling me around. I find the two men who were flanking the entrance now flanking the exit. It's all so well rehearsed, the same routine as before.

"Izzy?" Theo's soft calling of my name turns me back around. He holds out the glass to me. "Drink?"

I accept, taking the glass by the stem. In all honesty, I'm too tired for wine. It could finish me off and have me falling asleep here where I stand. "Thank you." I force myself to take the tiniest of sips, not wanting to be rude.

Jefferson approaches, nodding politely to me before turning to Theo. "Can I get you anything else, sir?" he asks.

"I think I'm fine for the rest of the evening," Theo says, coming closer to me and slipping an arm around my waist. "Tell Callum I won't be at the Playground tonight."

"Yes, sir." Jefferson bows as he backs away. It's all so old-fashioned and formal. I feel like I'm in a modern-day Downton Abbey—butlers, serving staff, and all.

"Your home is run with military precision," I say as we take the stairs. I watch them carefully, each stripy step blending into the next. "Is your life one big controlled environment?"

"It's best for everyone," Theo says, simple as that, yet I'm guessing it isn't that simple at all, and I look up at him to gauge his expression. Even when his face is blank he's still a certain kind of prime stunning, the kind that I'm certain could never be matched, least of all topped. Right now, he's handsome but unreadable, yet his eyes are glossy and thoughtful.

"Better for everyone, or better for you?" I ask, slowly trying to work my way closer to the core of Theo.

He drops those deep blue eyes onto my curious form, a small smile tickling his full lips. "Primarily me, yes. But it's best all round. No mistakes can be made."

"Mistakes?"

"For someone who's so tired, you're firing questions rather sufficiently." He raises his eyebrows at me, and I look away, a little shyly. I'm assuming by *mistakes* he means unexpected touches. It's all quite strange, and if I hadn't touched Theo myself, I would think he had some kind of rare condition that would kill him if he came into contact with another human. I shrug off his observation as we reach the galleried landing, Theo leading us to the right.

"Where are we going?" I ask, admiring all the huge gold-framed portraits as we walk.

"To my private quarters."

Private quarters? "Sounds posh."

"It's peaceful and . . . private."

I conclude that to mean he doesn't need to be on his guard constantly, alert to any possible touch. "And what's the Playground?" I've heard that mentioned on more than one occasion.

We reach a set of heavily carved double doors, and I stop as Theo opens one, making way for me to enter. I look up at him when I get no answer. He seems a little tense. "I'll show you one day. Let's get to know each other better first."

My lips press into a straight line. "Better?"

He flicks his head in indication for me to enter, ignoring my question. "In before I strip you naked right here."

I nod mildly, thoughtfully, as I study him, concluding quite quickly that he's diverting me. He can have his way. For now. "Clever," I muse with a playful pout, wandering into Theo's private quarters, the doors opening up into a huge lounge area. Just like every other part of this mansion that I've seen, it's ostentatious and indulgent—the furniture large, the walls covered in huge paintings, and the carpet thick and luxurious. An oversize marble fireplace dominates the room, the flames dancing hypnotically. But despite the extravagance of the space, I'm comfortable and warm, not intimidated. It's exactly how I feel in Theo's presence.

I look back to find him watching me take it all in, standing quietly by the door. He strolls lazily over to me, coming to a stop behind me, and my entire body rolls with a shiver when he reaches past me and relieves me of my wineglass and places it on a nearby table that's decorated with a huge vase of stargazer lilies. "Let me take your coat," he whispers in my ear, placing his hands gently on my shoulders and pulling the material away. I swallow as he drags my mac off, keeping his mouth close enough so I can hear his shallow breaths.

I begin to feel anxiety take over, not because of where I am, who I'm with, or the potential of what's about to play out. No. None of that. Those thoughts set my blood on fire. What's not so welcome is the knowledge that I've just worked a tough twelve-hour shift and I could really do with a shower. "I've been at work all day," I say quietly, pushing the side of my face into his lips when he places them on my cheek. The feel of his bristle makes me hum, my eyes closing in bliss, every part of his front pushed into my back.

"Would you like a shower?" he asks, smiling against my flesh.

I feel my cheeks heat a little, embarrassed, and I nod against him, holding my hands by my sides. "Please."

"May I?" he asks, sliding his palms down my arms to my hands and holding each one firmly.

"May you what?" I pull away and gaze at him, his chin resting on my shoulder. His hard face is so soft and lovely.

"Shower with you."

My eyes with nothing to look at except Theo's wet, naked body? I can't promise I'll be able to keep my hands to myself. "Will I be restrained?" I ask. Does he need a controlled environment in the shower, too? Begrudgingly, I expect so. But I'm quietly hoping.

He turns me into him, bringing my hands up to his shoulders and lifting me from my feet. I inhale, my breasts pushing into his chest with every beat of my excited heart. "For me to truly enjoy it, then yes." He starts pacing leisurely across the room, taking us into a bedroom. *His* bedroom. I can sense the scale of the room, yet refuse to disconnect my gaze from his, falling deeper for the intentions shining through the blue. "I need to be relaxed."

I feel my heart sink a little, but try not to let it show as I dip my lips slowly, giving him plenty of time to prepare for my kiss. When I see his lips part, I close that final distance, breathing in as I slip my tongue into his mouth. He hums as he entwines his with mine, a deep sound full of pleasure and calm, and my fingers flex on his shoulders, itching to move up to his head and fist his hair. Yet my instinct is keeping them where they are. But then he nods, deepening our kiss, and I read his silent message, sliding my hands up his thick neck and into his hair. I feel him tense, hear him inhale. But he doesn't stop me. My body naturally moves closer to his, my mouth working slowly but deeply. His tongue is demanding and firm, his taste divine. It's exclusively Theo, and it's making me so drunk on him, his distinctive, gorgeous scent helping me along.

When he drops me to my feet, he pulls my hands away from his head, keeping our mouths working the slow, beautiful duel as he starts to unfasten the buttons of my uniform dress, his head tilting one way and then the other, pulling back here and there to peck and bite at my lips. I'm lost. So completely lost. My dress falls to the floor, and Theo's hands go straight to my back, unclasping my bra and pulling it away from my chest. My boobs ache, calling for him to acknowledge them, and I gasp into his mouth when he cups them briefly before clamping his thumbs and fingers around my hard nipples, rolling them.

"Your shirt," I murmur, desperate to get him naked but knowing I'm relying on him to give me what I want.

Theo registers my plea and releases my nipples, fetching my hands and placing them at the neck of his shirt. He's going to let me? I start blindly unbuttoning before he has a chance to change his mind, but I'm careful not to touch his chest. It's hard, but I manage, working my fingers to the bottom and dropping the tails of his shirt rather than pushing it off. I know my move is appreciated when he smiles against my mouth.

"Take it off," he orders gently, surprising me as he breaks our kiss and rests his forehead on mine. "I'm ready."

My hands are eager but gentle as I push his shirt off his shoulders, letting it fall to the floor. The rosary beads of his tattoo demand my admiration for a moment, and I tilt my head with a sigh as I look down to the praying hands on his hip. Odd, but beautiful on his body. I breathe in and tentatively reach for his face, resting my palms lightly on his jaw. He's looking at me with the most inconceivable amount of trust. It's a trust I'm not planning on breaking. Not ever. Our hungry breaths are meeting and mingling in the small space between our mouths, our eyes glued, my hands holding his face gently.

"Are you scared?" he asks me quietly, his voice a little shaky and rough. I know he isn't asking me if I'm scared of him.

"Terrified," I answer honestly, being sure never to lose his eyes. I press a soft kiss on the corner of his mouth. "I don't know what's happening."

"Me either." He kisses my lips and takes my hands down to his trousers, encouraging me to remove them, and I start to unfasten them while he kisses my neck. Need for him courses through me like wildfire, uncontrollable and unstoppable. "You're all I can think of when I'm awake," he says, flinching a little when I push his trousers and boxers down, my hand skimming the hardness of his erection. "You're all I see in my dreams." He steps out and slips his fingers in each side of my knickers, bending as he draws them down. I whimper as he licks his way back up my body until he's at my mouth, kissing me with reverent eagerness. "I crave your touch, and it's driving me wild because I can't let you have free rein over me." His tongue swirls around mine, and he hauls me up to his body. "I so, so want to let you have that."

"We'll work on it," I say to pacify him, showing him my hands and waiting for his nod before I link them around his neck.

Collecting the cuffs, he walks us toward the shower, a huge cornered-off area with a curved sheet of glass. He presses a button on the outside wall, and the small silver control lights up. A huge square plate suspended from the ceiling past the glass wall bursts with instant hot water, the drops splashing up the glass. He takes us in and places me on my feet, pushing me back against the oyster-shell tiles. "I've been desperate for this since I left you in Vegas," he rasps, claiming my wrists and turning me away from him.

I bite my lip as I let him cuff me, feeling softness as opposed to metal. He links the two single cuffs together by the thick gold bangles, securing me before he turns me back around and pushes me into the wall.

"Okay?" he asks, stepping away as I nod. He tilts his head back, letting the water pour over his face, and takes his hands through his hair, pushing it back, his mouth dropped open. A heavy beat starts between my thighs at the magnificent vision, his throat lengthening, water raining over the tautness onto his broad chest and tumbling down his thighs. My gaze stops at his groin and the sight of his pulsing arousal, my arms twitching against the restraints. I close my eyes, frantically searching my mind for strength.

Heat meets my stomach—heat beyond the water, and I convulse with a cry, my eyes snapping open. Looking down, I see the top of his head moving as he drags his lips from one side of my tummy to the other, and back again, over and over. His tongue traces the lines of my scars, and I slam my head against the wall, my breasts aching with need. He's here before me, worshipping me, his lips now working their way south to my most sensitive place, and I can't grab him, squeeze him, or feel him. I start to mumble nonsensical words to the ceiling as his tongue dips past my folds, skimming my clit, and his hands land on the insides of my thighs, pushing them apart to give him better access. I pant, I squirm, I cry out. And when he latches onto my swollen nub of nerves, I scream, hearing his own sounds of pleasure as he loses himself in the gratification of feasting on my arousal.

Ragged breaths overpower the sounds of the shower raining all over us, and my climax builds with an almost tormenting slowness as Theo sucks softly, laps slowly, and bites gently. I think I might cry because of the agonizing pleasure he's inflicting on me, and I cross the point of no return, tumbling over the edge of frustration and into the depths of ecstasy. I'm blinded by the sensations, crippled by the fulfillment, my hands naturally fighting with the restraints. "Theo," I gasp, riding the long waves of my climax, my body rolling, my internal walls convulsing.

His mouth stays exactly where it is, sucking me gently. "I've got you," he mumbles, kissing my clit tenderly, and then slowly circling it with the tip of his tongue. "I've got you." He slowly stands, his cock dragging across my skin as he rises to his full height while I heave against the tiles, soaking wet, my body singing with satisfaction. Theo studies me as my vision clears of the brain-blanking lust, taking his fingertip and drawing a perfect soft line down my cheek. "Stay there," he orders, breaking away and reaching for his cock. He starts to pump over his arousal with a loose fist, his back meeting the curved glass opposite me, and I fall instantly under the exquisite spell of Theo pleasuring himself. My skin tingles as I watch his hand glide effortlessly over his taut skin, the head visibly throbbing. My eyes want to savor every piece of the vision, as well as his body reacting to the pleasure. His chest expands, controlled at first but growing more and more erratic with every stroke, and the vein in his neck balloons. His throat rolls on each swallow, his eyes are heavy, low, and lustful. And his thighs are spread slightly, the huge muscles tensing and releasing. When his body suddenly jolts, I hold my breath, anticipating his release as much as Theo clearly is, his fist now pumping, his mouth open and gasping for breath. "Come here," he demands harshly. "Kiss me."

I push away from the wall in a flash and pace over to him, capturing his lips, my hands thankfully held securely behind my back by the cuffs. "Oh, Jesus," he chokes into my mouth, his tongue not smooth now, more clumsy and stabbing. He pulls away and rests his head against the glass, looking at me, his arm moving fast. I bite my lip and meet his stare, watching as his climax builds in his eyes. His pupils are dilated so much I can hardly see the blue, and now the tip of his cock is sitting on my stomach as he thrusts back and forth. The heat could burn a hole in my flesh. I don't think I'll ever witness such an erotic sight again. I'm not even touching him, yet the pleasure dancing through me is immense. And when he holds his breath and his teeth clench, I know it's time. I zero in on his eyes as he yells, his chest heaving, his hand slowing, and his fiery essence hits my stomach in long, surging spurts as Theo's body rolls against the glass. I've had no climax myself this time, but the gratification I'm rewarded with, just watching him fight his way through his pleasure, is more than enough.

He releases himself and slides down the glass to his arse, looking overcome, totally out of it. His head drops back, his eyes close, and he brings his knees up to rest his arms on.

I take myself to the floor, too, sitting on my knees opposite him. And I wait patiently for him to come back down to earth. It's a good few minutes before he shows signs of lucidity, time I'm happy to spend admiring him slumped on the floor before me.

I smile when he finally finds the energy he needs to open his eyes. "Morning," I whisper.

His beam nearly blinds me. "Morning?" he asks groggily, reaching for me and gently turning me around. He removes the cuffs and massages my wrists for a few blissful seconds, humming. His gesture is sweet but not needed. I'm in no pain, the padded cuffs seeing to that. I let him pull me onto his lap, his hands guiding mine around his neck. "It could be, sweetheart. I wouldn't know. Time melts away when I'm with you."

I settle on him, cuddling into his chest happily, feeling so appreciative. I don't think I have ever felt so utterly cherished.

Or safe.

CHAPTER 14

He washed me down in his shower, shampooed my hair and rinsed, working his strong fingers through my scalp. The act wasn't sexual. It was loving and caring, and it did nothing to stop my feelings from deepening. When Theo said he would treat me like a queen, he really meant it.

I have a fresh glass of wine in my hand as I roam around his bedroom, snuggled tightly in a soft robe, admiring the décor. I eye each post of his four-poster bed as my lips hover over the rim of my glass, and then take in the sumptuous bedding—all creams and golds and huge great big pillows. A dressing room off to the side is lined with rows of suits, and the bathroom is massive and drenched in lushness. Everything is over-the-top big. Like Theo.

I pad through to the lounge, working my way around the room, gazing up at the framed portraits as I sip my wine. After our shower, I feel alive and refreshed. Being here with Theo, immersed in his world, I forget my draining day. I hold the glass at my lips and frown at the painting currently before me, a pretty depiction of the Last Supper. It's another religious symbol, and Theo, apparently, isn't religious. In the reflection of the glass, I see the bright sparkle in my eyes bouncing back at me. It's a rare sight. I've never felt so happy, so relaxed and safe—shielded from my past and the world. Theo makes me so happy. He makes me feel valued. Untouchable. So special, and completely consumed.

I don't understand it, but I can't ignore it. Trying to reflect back on my life without Theo in it is impossible, because his presence now is so powerful, anything before is diluted by it. And that is so very appealing. He's chasing away the fear I fight to keep buried every day. He's soothing my hidden sadness. He's given me something I didn't realize I wanted.

Safety.

He feels like he could be my...I let my thoughts fade there, telling myself that I'm getting ahead of myself. Or am I? I consume his thoughts, invade his dreams, and he craves my touch. For a man who doesn't like to be touched, that's a profound confession. He's made me endless promises, told me I can trust him. I've never once doubted that. I trust him with my life. And I trust him with my heart.

I return to my earlier thought, the one I stopped myself from thinking. And though it scares me a little, I admit that he feels like he could be my cure. And I also admit that I'm falling for him.

I breathe in and laugh a little on my exhale. *You silly woman, Izzy.* I'm not falling. I've fallen. Hard. So damn hard. It's an incredible feeling. One of hope, peace, and happiness. Just like I imagined. It's also unstoppable, and that's terrifying. I've been in control of my emotions for so long. I've dictated the rules, managed my fears. Now, I'm at his mercy. My heart is at his mercy. My feelings are his to control.

I've fallen in love with a man who is feared by most but has shown me nothing but utter tenderness since we met. I've fallen in love with a man who pulled a gun on someone but was doing it to defend and protect me. I've fallen in love with a man who radiates violence, but I just know he would never be violent toward me. I've fallen in love with a man who can't bear to be touched but craves *my* touch. I've fallen in love with a man who has a natural, powerful urge to protect me. To look after me. Yet I don't really know him. Do I need to? Can I leave my heart open and exposed to a man who is so confounding? "Don't hurt me, Theo," I whisper to myself. "Don't let me down."

A noise behind me has me pivoting and finding him filling the doorway to his bedroom, a towel wrapped around his lean hips. My head tilts, and I fall into a daydream, running my gaze over every inch of him until I reach his smiling eyes. His face. Fierce but angelic. "I love you," I whisper to myself, so quietly I know he couldn't have heard me.

He gives me a questioning look, his smile fading a little. "Did you say something?"

I clutch my glass with both hands and shake my head. "No."

"Your lips moved."

"I was praying for resistance."

"Why?"

"Because I can't touch you, and when you're there like that, it's really hard, Theo. It's hard all of the time."

When I expect him to look smug, he surprises me and drops his eyes to the floor, ashamed. "I'm sorry."

"No." I rush to soothe him, trying to locate something in my head to counteract the playful statement that's injured him. "Don't be sorry. I wasn't thinking." I, too, drop my head, annoyed with myself. I don't ever want him to be sorry for being who he is. Because every single thing that makes him Theo Kane is why I'm standing here in his lounge making my silent confessions.

I hear a soft sigh, and then soon after see his bare feet in my downcast vision. "Here." He takes my glass from my hand and places it on a nearby table before claiming my hands. I look up through my lashes as he negotiates my arms around his shoulders, flattening my palms on his nape. The softness of his hair there calls for me to stroke and feel, so I flex my fingers gently until Theo releases. I exhale deeply and caress him tenderly as he shuts his eyes and hums. It's so strange that such a big, formidable man needs to be handled with such care. "That feels good," he murmurs dreamily, moving in and taking my hips. His heat radiates through the thick material of my robe and penetrates me to my soul.

Shifting one palm to my nape, he pushes my face into the crook of his neck, forcing me onto my tiptoes. I smile into his skin. Even our cuddles are carefully controlled.

"Come lie down on the bed with me." He lifts me from my feet and carries me into his bedroom, settling me gently on the colossal bed. "Comfy?" he asks with a crooked smile, sinking into the covers beside me, pulling at my hip to face him.

Comfy doesn't cut it. I could be floating on clouds. "So-so." I shrug, resting my head into the squishy pillow.

His smile is a vision, and we lie there for a while, facing each other, our noses just a few millimeters apart. I spend the time running continuous circuits of his face, reaching forward to feel the bristle of his jaw.

"Tell me who that man was," he says, breaking the silence.

"At the hospital?"

"Yes."

"I did tell you. He's the son of a patient."

"I thought you might have been lying."

"I wasn't," I reply, a little injured. I wonder for a moment if Theo thought Percy's son was someone else—like the man I've run from. Part of me wishes he were. Part of me wishes he'd found me, because I could guarantee he wouldn't come near me again after encountering Theo Kane.

A frown that vanishes from his brow as quickly as it appears leads me to believe I was right. "Then why did he attack you?"

"His father died today."

"He attacked you because his father died?"

"He was looking for someone to blame, as any grieving relative might do. It's happened before, though not to that extent. We get shouted at, accused of incompetence, but it's all part of the job." I shrug.

His eyes narrow a little. He doesn't understand. "You heal people."

"I try to help them get better, yes."

Theo falls quiet, seeming to think deeply about something. The sight is fascinating, the giant man quiet and contemplating. "Why did you decide to become a nurse?" His hand moves to my neck, to the place Frank left his claw marks.

I look out the corner of my eye to his hand touching my skin softly. "Because hospitals are safe places," I whisper mindlessly under the amazing feeling of his touch.

"Safe?" he questions. "Izzy, in the short time I've known you, an old man has tried to strangle you and a pissed-off relative tried to..." His words fade, and he shakes away his obvious dread.

"I was handling myself just fine," I argue softly, dragging the pad of my thumb across his bottom lip. My fear isn't of physical pain; I can handle pain. It's more psychological. The feeling of complete helplessness. Of being weak. Vulnerable. But I wouldn't expect Theo to understand. Neither do I want to tell him. So I say nothing more, because I don't know *what* to say. I'm not up for laying bare my nasty history. Besides, Theo is keeping the reasons for his phobia to himself. It might be childish, but I'm not comfortable with him having more on me than I have on him. Yet if this thing between us is serious, are we really going to hold back our secrets from each other? Can we do that? *Should* we do that? I breathe in deep, close my eyes, and re-member my mother's happy face. Her joy. Her spirit. But just as quickly, that lovely image vanishes, replaced by her sad, empty eyes. She would love to know there was someone in my life to look after me. She'd take comfort in that, I know it. How many times did I wonder if she was looking down on me, shouting at me for the decision I made? How many times did she turn in her grave when I . . . ?

I feel something take hold of my jaw, and I flinch, recoiling so Theo loses his hold on me. I snap my eyes open to remind my-self of where I am, then just as quickly scold myself for letting my mind wander. Theo pulls away, wary, regarding me carefully. "You've never done that before," he whispers, his brow becoming heavy. "You've never startled when I've touched you. Why now, Izzy? Where were your thoughts?"

I fall into my shell, not liking his probing questions or looks, and roll over, getting up from the bed. My instinct is to flee. Fight or flee. It's always been flee. Fighting never paid off. It just re-sulted in extreme physical scars to accompany the mental scars. Whether I've fled by shutting my mind down, blanking it all out, or by physically running, it was always flee.

I stride across the room to the bathroom, coming to a startled stop when Theo rounds me and fills the door, a palm braced on each side of the frame to block my way. I stare at his chest, my hands nervously twiddling the end of my robe's tie.

"Share with me," he says gently. "Please, Izzy."

I square my shoulders and look up at him, filling myself with fake resolve. "What about you? Will you share, too?"

"You don't need to hear of my crimes." Theo's tone suggests I really don't, and my fortitude wavers as I step away from him.

"And you don't need to hear of my tragedies," I counter with grit that I'm really not feeling. I would love to offload every tiny detail of my horrid past. To stop hiding it, to relieve the pressure of the secrets. To face it head-on and find some kind of complete closure. But I'm scared now, more than ever. He'll hate me as much as I hated myself, and I wouldn't blame him.

"Who are you?" Theo asks, keeping me in place with a steely gaze. "Why aren't you on social media?"

I suck in air. *What?* "You've looked me up? Why would you do that?"

"Don't tell me you haven't Googled me."

My hesitation is a sign of my guilt. "For what use it was, yes."

"What's your story, Izzy White?"

"What's yours, Theo Kane?" I retort.

He smiles a little in understanding and drops his hands from the doorframe, letting them hang by his side. I can see his chest pumping in time to the feel of mine. All this delving into my past, albeit unproductive for Theo, is challenging me. I've thought about it more since I met him than I have since running away. I don't want to think about it. *Ever.*

"I'm a man most are wary of," he says quietly, studying me closely as he speaks.

He must realize that he's telling me something I already know. "Why are they wary?"

"Because they're scared."

"To touch you," I say, and he nods. "Why can't they touch you?"

His jaw pulses a little, and I see with perfect clarity how much effort it's taking to tell me, which only leaves me increasingly worried. Even just talking about his phobia stokes his temper. "I don't like being touched when I'm not expecting it." Theo's chest visibly pulses as he gets a hold of himself. "I need warning to prepare myself. I've learned to read people, to predict their moves, but it's a constant challenge. It's exhausting, hence the control of my home." He pauses for a beat, letting me absorb it all. "Your touch sinks past my skin, Izzy. It warms me. With you, I barely need to think. My body responds to you. I don't know why, but it does."

"Except in bed."

"While I'm lost in you, I want only to be lost in you. I won't risk losing my focus when we're intimate. Like I've promised you before, I won't hurt you, not in *any* way." He gives my cheek a light brush with his palm, his smile fond as I nuzzle into his hand. "I hope you believe me."

"I do," I assure him, feeling a little overcome. "I've never doubted that part of you."

Dropping a kiss on my lips, he strokes over the curve of my arse. "Now, tell me about you," he mumbles against my mouth.

I withdraw fast, and it is complete instinct. "What?" I feel myself folding in once again.

"I've shared, now I want to know about you."

I stare at him, seeing the questions in his eyes. Yes, he's shared, but I'm certain there must be more to it than that. Like *why* he's like he is. But this has to be give and take, right? He's shared a little, and if I want this to work—and I so do—then I have to reciprocate, no matter how much it hurts. "My mother died of cancer when I was seventeen. She was all I had, and I..." I gulp, battling with my instinct to run before I can be forced to share something I really do not want to share. "We weren't rich. We only had each other, so I had nothing when she was gone. No home, no money. I needed money."

Theo is quiet for a second, and I just know it's because he's trying to hold back from asking the question that I really don't want him to ask. But, of course, he does, ignoring the pleading in my eyes. "So what did you do?"

I look down, so ashamed of myself. Not just for what I'm about to tell him, but for bending the truth. "I was a stripper, Theo. I took my clothes off for men." I wish that was all there was to tell. I so wish that was the end of my story.

I see him move away a little. Like I'm dirt. "A stripper," he murmurs, so quietly.

"I'm not proud."

"How old were you?"

I'm wincing again. "Seventeen." I hear a low growl. "It wasn't for long. I scraped some money together and got out." Another lie. "I hated not being able to ease my mother's pain when she was ill. It was natural for me to study medicine. So I left Manchester and came to London. I wanted to be a doctor, but I couldn't afford the fees. Nursing was the next best thing. It was as far as I could go on my own." That much is the truth. The rest of the horrid story will remain under lock and key. I look up to Theo, hating the undeniable shock on his face. Shock and disgust. It's exactly the reaction I expected, but was so hoping I wouldn't get. And now I hope he regrets probing me. "I'll leave." I back up, feeling filthy, humiliated, and empty once again.

Theo quickly comes to life, following my steps. "Stop walking, Izzy."

"Only if you stop looking at me like I'm dirt."

"Stop fucking walking."

I stop. Theo stops. And I blink, letting a fat teardrop tumble. "I don't like talking about it."

"Fucking hell," he breathes, raking a frustrated hand through his hair. "I'm shocked, that's all. You're so . . . normal."

Normal? If only he knew. I find my eyes dropping to the carpet again, unable to look him in the eye.

"Is that what you ran from?" he asks.

I nod, not allowing the blanket of guilt to suffocate me. Guilt for being selective with what I tell him. For bending the truth. His face when I told him what I did to scrape some money together is the one and only reason I need to keep the rest buried. "I needed a fresh start." I fear the worst when his gaze drops to my stomach, lingering over the sight of my scars. Then he looks up at me, too many more questions in his eyes. My teeth clench, warning him to leave it there, and he studies me so very closely for a few moments, his eyes trying to strip back a few more layers of my history. I won't let him. It's a staring deadlock for a few minutes, both of us unmoving and unwilling to say any more.

Then he breathes out, defeated. "Come here." He raises his arms for me, and I walk right into them, grateful and relieved he's not pressing me further, though I sense he's dying to. I bury my face in his shoulder, overcome by his acceptance. By the fact he's not disgusted by me. "I'm sorry about your mother," he says in a hushed whisper, and I hold him tighter. "What about your father?"

"I don't remember him. He died when I was two."

He breathes out in disbelief. "I'm sorry."

"Stop apologizing. I don't need your sympathy, Theo." I let him hug me, breathing calmly and deeply. He's the blanket of peace I need. "You're not repulsed?"

Theo withdraws, his chest contracting with a silent laugh, his eyes finding me, his head shaking in wonder. "Repulsed? God, no. You're amazing," he says, planting a light kiss on my lips. "You're a survivor. You saved yourself, and that's admirable. I'm just crushed you went through that on your own." He picks me up and carries me to the bed, putting us both back in the exact same positions as before. My eyes are heavy, but I fight to keep them open, my view too spectacular to give up. But then Theo tucks me into his shoulder, kisses my head, and rubs my back, and exhaustion finally beats me.

My eyes close.

But I still see him.

"And now you're saving me," he whispers quietly.

CHAPTER 15

I feel my sleepy smile falling from my face as I stretch, my drowsy mind registering the lack of warmth pressed up against me. My eyes spring open, finding the bed beside me empty. Pushing up onto my elbows, I blink as I gaze around Theo's bedroom, listening for any sounds of him nearby. It's silent. I look at the bedside clock. Three a.m.

"Theo?" I call, pushing to the edge of the bed, my feet sinking into the carpet. I finish my stretch, reaching up to the ceiling before turning on the lamp. Getting to my feet, I head to the bathroom. No Theo. I find my bag on a chair in the corner of his room and pull out some skinny jeans and an oversize white tee, throwing them on quickly and roughing up the waves of my hair. I venture into his extensive private quarters, but after peeking in every room, I still find no Theo. Where'd he go?

The house is silent as I gingerly take the stairs, my hand sliding down the golden banister as I look around, waiting for someone to appear. I make it all the way to Theo's office without seeing a soul and knock lightly on the door, getting no response, so I try the handle, finding it's locked.

Pouting to myself, I turn and ponder what to do. "Call him,"

I say to myself, jogging toward the stairs to go fetch my phone, but as my foot hits the bottom step, I hear something. I stop and crane my neck to see toward the back of the huge entrance hall, finding a single door slightly ajar. I wander over and push my way through to a long corridor with another door at the end. The walls are bare, the space stark, and the sound of music is muffled from beyond. It becomes louder as I approach, and I push through into another office, this one not as ostentatious as Theo's, but still very lovely. It's well equipped, far more functional as a working space, with computers, filing cabinets, and three desks. But no Theo.

Curiosity getting the better of me, I wander across the space and open yet another door, finding yet another corridor, this one far shorter than the last, with many doors leading off each side. A small part of my mind is telling me to turn back, to not venture farther. But a bigger part is urging me forward, promising me answers to questions I've asked myself a million times. And that's a little too hard to resist.

I follow the sound of music to the end and open the door. "Like a bloody maze," I say to myself as the music hits my ears hard.

My eyes go round, taking in the scene before me, my mouth slightly agape. "Oh my God," I mumble to myself, my stare nailed to a huge hexagonal cage. There are two men beyond the bars, bare-chested, bare-knuckled, sweaty. And covered in blood.

I wince when one guy slams the other to the floor and starts pounding his face like a madman, blood and sweat flying everywhere, my flinches coming thick and fast. My stomach turns as a crowd around the perimeter of the cage yell and cheer, thirsty for the violence, encouraging it. Then the noise drops when the guy pinned to the floor goes limp and stops trying to fight off his attacker, though the punches don't slow. If anything, they come faster and harder until I can no longer see the unconscious man's face through the blood coating him.

What the hell is this place?

I turn and find a round stage behind me, with a runway leading off toward the back. Tables are positioned around the perimeter, people drinking and socializing, and I find myself mindlessly walking toward the raised platform. "Oh God, no," I breathe, my heart just about ready to explode.

There are poles, and two half-naked women do what can only be described as acrobatics around them, flinging their bodies up and down the metal, getting into some insane positions, and all with skyscraper heels on. My eyes widen further when I note one of the women is Penny, the girl I found in the alley. She looks completely different, her body clear of marks, as she grinds her crotch against the pole. *What?*

I back up, ready to bolt, trying to wake myself up, because I have to be dreaming. I have to be. The cage, the stage, the dancers and violence. All my worst nightmares are here in this opulent club. The Playground.

I force my breathing to calm and start pacing back toward the door from which I came, but my steps slow as I register through my anxiety that Penny's face is glowing. She's...happy? Enjoying herself? She doesn't look like she's here under duress. And then I remember her words when I was tending to her, when I told her she was at Theo's.

Then I'm safe.

I rip my eyes away from her as she bends at the waist, thrusting her arse into a guy's face, though he remains in his seat, just watching. He doesn't touch her. Doesn't even try. I look around, seeing most of the people at the tables around the stage are men, though there are a few women, too, all impeccably dressed. It's a stark contrast to what I've experienced. Some of the crowd are watching Penny and her friend intently, but some are chatting and drinking. There's no heckling, no men throwing themselves onto the stage.

I see a well-appointed bar with sharp bartenders, as well as suited waiters delivering drinks on trays. My shaky being starts to settle a little, and I don't know why. Everything in here is a trigger to me.

I wander past the bar in a bit of a daze, trying to take it all in. It's bustling, the music loud but not ear-piercing or uncomfortable. People can talk easily without the need to shout.

My pace slows when I catch a glimpse of Theo across the room, and any last scrap of anxiety is chased away at the sight of him. He's seated in a booth that's cordoned off with gold posts linked together by thick crimson ropes. He's reclined, a glass in his grasp, but his face is tight, the lines of his handsome features sharp as he talks to a man sitting opposite him. He nods once and stands, offering the guy his hand. They shake and Theo leaves the area, drink in hand. His casual dress is perfectly sexy, just a simple navy shirt open at the collar and tucked into a pair of jeans that fit his long legs too well. I press my lips together, as well as my thighs, an untimely hot flush getting the better of me. As he strides toward the bar, everyone moves from his path, some nodding in respect. It is literally like the parting of the waves. I'm completely rapt.

And I just remain where I am, my shock at discovering this place being replaced by something that's dominated me since the moment I met Theo Kane. Wonder. Appreciation. I'm spellbound.

"Can I help you?" a voice hits me from the side, and I find a waiter giving me the once-over with confused eyes.

"Um..." I follow his stare down to my bare feet and wince. "No, thank you."

"Are you a member?" he asks.

"Not exactly." I laugh nervously.

"Oh." He smiles. "Dressing rooms are in the far right-hand corner of the club." He points and I look, seeing Penny disappear through a door. Oh, Jesus.

"I'm not a stripper." I swallow and search out Theo, pointing to him. "I'm with him."

"You're with Mr. Kane?" the waiter questions dubiously.

My hand comes to my hair and starts to smooth it over as I nod. "Yes."

"Right." He looks doubtful as he decides what to do with me, scanning the club for I don't know what.

"She's with Theo." A woman speaks up, pulling my attention to a nearby table. She smiles at me, sliding out of the booth with a few files in her hands. She's mature, maybe sixty or so, and very well dressed, sophisticated in a black trouser suit, her blond hair short with choppy layers. Her blood-red lips frame perfect teeth as she holds her smile, approaching me.

"Yes, madam." The waiter falls into gracious acceptance as he backs away.

"Get me my usual, Simon, please," she says. "For you, Izzy?"

My hand comes to my chest. I feel highly underdressed in the company of this strange, perfectly groomed woman. How does she know my name? "I'm fine, thank you."

"I insist." She looks to the waiter. "Something light. Maybe white."

He nods and leaves us, and the woman holds a hand out to me. I look down at her perfectly manicured fingertips, the color of her polish matching her lips, and she gives me a knowing smile when I return my gaze to hers. She comes closer, gently taking my arm. "Come have a seat with me." Leading me toward the booth, she gestures for me to sit, which I do, completely non-plussed. She's still smiling as she takes a seat opposite and places her files down.

"How do you know my name?" I ask, unable to stop myself from scanning the club, looking for Theo.

She offers me her hand across the table, and I eye it suspiciously for a few moments before accepting. "I'm Judy." She gives me a little wink. "Theo's mother."

I don't mean to pull my hand from hers, but it happens all the same, my surprise clear. "Oh..." I breathe, now seeing that the shade of her eyes is an exact replica of the deep spellbinding blue of Theo's.

"It's a pleasure to meet the girl who has been the unexpected object of my boy's affection."

I blush a million shades of red, burning up before her. He's told his mother about me? I die a little on the inside, wishing I wasn't currently looking such a state. "Forgive me for my appearance," I say, embarrassed, as I pull at my tee. "I didn't expect to find myself here." I blindly indicate around the room. I *really* didn't expect to find myself here. And the fact I'm still actually here and not high-tailing it is a miracle.

"You look delightfully adorable." She brushes my concern aside, a fondness in her eyes that I've only ever encountered in one other person in my life. I drop my gaze to the table as my mother's face creeps into my mind.

"Thank you," I murmur, aware of the sadness in my voice.

"Theo tells me you're a nurse."

I nod as Simon returns and places two wineglasses before us. "That's right." Looking up at her, I find the fondness remains as she takes me in, sipping on her red wine. "And now I know what Theo does." I gaze around the club again, specifically to the cage where two men are now dragging an unconscious body toward the exit. I have to look away, feeling my stomach turn in circles.

"I told him to tell you sooner rather than later." She looks over to the cage, too. "Does it bother you?"

"Yes," I answer honestly. "I'm not a fan of mindless violence." I dealt with it for too long. "Or..." I fade off and look to the stage, where two more women are flaunting their arses at the men seated around them. These two women are smiling, too. Enjoying themselves.

"I understand," Judy says, pulling my attention back her way. "Let me rephrase that. Does it bother you enough to say goodbye to my son?"

Her question takes me by surprise, and I just stare at her, recalling how shell-shocked Theo looked when I spilled a fraction of my history to him. It's no wonder. He must have wondered how on earth he would explain the Playground. Not to mention the cage of death over there. I look over, now seeing a man mopping up blood. Good Lord.

"Izzy?"

"I'm...a little thrown at the moment," I admit. Thrown in so many ways. I'm thrown about this place, but I'm even more thrown that I'm so calm. I point toward the stage. "The girl who was just stripping—"

"Penny?"

"Yes." I take my glass as I study Judy, wondering if the genuine beam of a moment ago is now painted on. It seems somehow forced. "It's good to see her well."

"She's working safely now. I guess that's a good thing."

She's working safely *now*. "Are all of the strippers ex-hookers?" I ask. Judy alluding to a safe working environment is cementing my early thoughts about Theo. He likes saving women. I just didn't ever anticipate that in saving them, he was setting them to work in his strip club. *His fucking strip club!*

Good God, I feel like I've fallen down a rabbit hole. Of all the men I could meet, a strip club owner? I frantically look around the bar again, hoping to catch sight of the man himself. If only to siphon off some calm from him. I need calm. My world is suddenly rocking again, and, oddly, the damn source of that rocking is the only thing that can stabilize it again. This is fucked up.

"Dancers, Izzy," Judy says, pulling my eyes back to her. "They're dancers, darling. Not strippers."

"Sorry, dancers." I smile apologetically. I wasn't a dancer. I was a puppet. Forced to do things no human should be forced to do. My young, naive self was so lost. So...hopeless. "So they're ex-hookers?"

"Not all, but many."

I take a little wine as I wonder what Theo has told his mother about me, but I force myself to say something else before I give in to the urge and ask her outright. "He doesn't like being touched."

Her look now is knowing, her forced smile drifting into more of a genuine, mild grin. "Except by you."

I feel a blush creep up on me. "I have to give him *some* warning." I evade her eyes, feeling like she could be reading my mind, which is currently filled with images of me restrained in a Las Vegas hotel suite and Theo driving me nuts with his tongue, his touch, his... I shake my mind clear.

"You don't *have* to, Izzy," she states matter-of-factly. "He sees you move before you've even thought to." She smiles again, getting up from the table. "His words, not mine."

He sure has told his mum a lot. Has he told her that I used to be a stripper? Not a dancer, but a stripper? "You two are close?" I ask for the sake of it.

"As close as can be without touching." She laughs, and my eyes widen a little. His own mother? "Yes." She reaches for my palm and holds it gently, almost reassuringly. "Even his own mother isn't so special that she can touch him without permission or invitation."

"Has he always been like that?"

For the first time, her smile falters. "No, darling. He hasn't." She looks up from the table, her smile returning. "Speak of the devil and he shall appear."

I turn and find Theo standing behind me, taking in the scene before him with an extremely worried expression. It's warranted, I guess. My confession, this place.

"Mum." He nods to Judy, giving her a questioning look.

"I found her wandering around." She waves a hand flippantly over her head.

"So you thought you'd capture her and grill her?" There's disdain in his voice, but Judy laughs it off and wanders over to her son, who towers above her petite frame. She stops a few feet in front of him, and Theo lifts his hand, keeping his eyes on me. I feel like an intruder, like he doesn't want me here, and I shift on the spot nervously.

Judy takes his hand and walks closer to him, letting him drop a kiss on her cheek. "I didn't grill her. I simply introduced myself."

"I would have liked to do that another time, and somewhere else," Theo replies, not sounding very happy at all, and I disintegrate under his imposing presence and displeased stare.

"What was I going to do?" Judy sighs tiredly. "Leave her looking lost?" She breaks away from Theo and collects her files. "I'm done for the evening," she says, slighted, but giving me a secret smile as she leaves us alone. "It was lovely to meet you, Izzy."

"You too." I force a smile as I watch her go, not wanting to look at Theo when he's obviously not happy to see me. So I resort to looking around the club again, except now most of the attention of the patrons is pointed in this direction, observing Theo and the inappropriately dressed, barefoot woman standing a few feet away from him. I think if I were in my underwear, I'd feel less conspicuous than I do right now. I begin to wilt under all the curious looks, faffing with the hem of my T-shirt as I glance back to Theo. His face is blank.

"Penny is certainly..." I falter momentarily, looking for the right words. "...back on her feet," I finish, wishing I could scurry out of here unnoticed. Or better still, wishing I hadn't let my ears lead me in here at all. How long would he have kept me in the dark about this place?

Theo's lips twitch, breaking into a wry smile. And for my sins, I smile, too. "Too shocked to give me a hug?" he asks.

"I think I need one."

"Come here." He jerks his head a little, an order, but doesn't extend a welcoming hand.

My feet move without me telling them to, taking me to him. It's natural, which is plain strange, because everything about this is very unnatural to me. Reaching for his shoulders, I slide my arms around him, and he holds me fiercely, making me meld into his embrace, my eyes closing, my surroundings forgotten.

"I was going to tell you," he says quietly. "But then you said what you said earlier, and I know you don't like violence, and... well, this place."

"This place," I agree, breathing in as I open my eyes. Everyone is still staring at us, including his mother, who has paused at the door. Embarrassed, I break away from Theo, feeling the heat rise in my face. "We have an audience."

Theo doesn't look, just slides his arm over my shoulder and pulls me into him, walking us across to the cordoned-off area where he was sitting when I stumbled in here. "I expect so." He's unperturbed, guiding me past the barrier and indicating for me to sit. "We should talk."

"How about back at your room? I'm hardly dressed for this place."

He smiles. "It's funny."

Funny? "What is?"

"You making your first appearance in my playground looking like you've just been fucked." He winks cheekily. "I like this look on you." He lowers into a chair and signals for a server. "Usual, and whatever Izzy would like."

"Just water for me, please."

"Really?" Theo asks, obviously taken aback.

"It's three a.m.," I point out. "I should be in bed. Why did you leave me?"

He regards me closely, sitting back in his chair. "I couldn't sleep. Was worried about how I might explain this place to my girlfriend when I know she hates violence, and I'm pretty damn sure she hates strip clubs."

This is where my head is at right now. A mess, really, because of all the things he just said, only one word resonates. "Girlfriend?"

His smile is faint, though I sense nerves. "Have things changed now you've seen my playground? Between us, I mean?" He reaches over the table for my hand and gives it a squeeze. "I hope the answer is no."

"And if it isn't?"

"I'll do anything to make sure it is."

"You own a strip club."

"Very observant of you."

"Is it *only* a strip club?" I bite my lip, nervous as shit, and when Theo's stare takes on an edge of danger, I realize I have just put my big fat foot in it.

"The girls are safe," he tells me, knowing that is what I need to hear. "They are paid handsomely. They keep their tips. If they don't want to dance, they don't. No one can touch them or approach them."

I nod in acceptance and take my water when the waiter presents me with the tray, naturally taking Theo's tumbler from it, too, and passing it across the table to him.

The waiter's eyebrows jump up, and Theo smiles as he accepts the drink from my grasp. "And the cage?" I ask.

"We hold events," he says, discomfort showing again. "Fights."

"Illegal fights." I state it as the fact I know it is. Theo Kane, my boyfriend, the man who has hijacked my heart, owns an illegal fight club, and on top of that, a damn strip club. What are the chances?

Theo nods his confirmation, bringing his glass to his lips. I have questions, so many questions.

"Are you wanted by the police?" It just falls out of my mouth, and it shocks me as much as it shocks Theo, his glass stopping midtilt. I look away, embarrassed, though it doesn't escape my notice that he hasn't rushed to reassure me.

"No, I am not wanted by the police."

I peek at him, feeling small and awkward. "Have you ever been locked up?"

"No."

I'm surprised. A man like Theo, his temper, his...business. "Okay, th—"

"I've done some terrible things, Izzy," he interrupts me, holding his breath once he's uttered his confession. I stare at him, waiting for more. It's only when he blinks and looks down that I realize I won't get it. *God forgives everyone.* "Just let me be Theo to you." He gazes up at me. "Can you do that?"

Can I? This place is like a vortex of triggers. A deep instinct is telling me to run, yet there's a new instinct, one I'm in more control of, telling me to stay. I look up at the stage. Penny is back. Still smiling. Still looking full of life and energy. I didn't smile. Never. "You know I don't like violence. And strip clubs aren't really my thing." I shrug, blasé. I'm not telling Theo anything he doesn't already know. He just doesn't know the sordid details. He shifts uncomfortably in his seat, looking worried as I go on. "But apparently you *are* my thing." The smile that crosses his lips, revealing his dimple to the fullest, is my favorite Theo smile. "You appeared out of nowhere in an alley on a dark night and stopped me being attacked. You followed me to Vegas and wooed me." I raise a warning eyebrow when his mouth opens to challenge me. *Business*. Give me a break. Theo closes his mouth and nods for me to continue. "You had Callum stay and watch me so I made it home to you safely. You pulled a gun on someone who got a little too physical with me." I try to appear unfazed, following up each negative with a positive. I'd already figured out that Theo danced on the wrong side of the law, I just didn't know how exactly. Now I do, and despite my hatred of violence and my equal abhorrence for strip clubs, I can't say it's changed the way I feel about Theo. Because with me, he is gentle. With me, he's warm. And though it's a little backward, I like how he makes me feel. In bed. Out of bed. It's almost as if I've relaxed since I've met him. My muscles don't feel constantly strung. My mind isn't overanxious. It's as if a huge burden has been lifted from my shoulders. Oddly, I love Theo's instinctual desire to keep me safe. And I think I love my newfound instinct to let him. "To me, you are simply Theo."

He puffs out an astonished breath. "You surprise me at every turn."

"I've surprised myself," I tell him. "There's another thing that has really stunned me, too," I continue, feeling my glass nervously.

"Good. I was beginning to think you were inhuman," Theo quips sarcastically. "Go on."

"Your mother. You've told her about me."

He rolls his eyes a little. It's the sweetest sign of exasperation. "She took a call from the florist to confirm the delivery of the flowers I sent you."

I grin. "And you're not the wine-and-dine type?"

Theo grins back, trying to raise warning eyebrows at me. "Seems for you I am." Big fat grins remain on our faces as our eyes stay glued across the table for an age, both of us finishing our drinks before one of us finally speaks. It's Theo. "How was she, anyway? My mother."

"Lovely," I say honestly, stifling a yawn.

"She's a good woman." Theo stands and collects me from the chair, pulling me into his side again. "Let me take you back."

"Will you stay with me?" I ask, feeling eyes follow us all the way to the door.

"Try to stop me." He looks back to one of the barmen. "This door should be locked." The fear on the poor guy's face is potent. "Make sure it doesn't happen again."

"So scary," I mutter as Theo guides me through, grinning up at him when he peeks down at me.

"The code on the lock is one five zero five, if ever you need it."

"Fifteenth of May," I muse, returning my attention forward. "Your birthday?" He nods and leads me down the corridor, through the office, and up the passage that leads back to his house.

"I assume people don't come through your house to get into the club," I say as we take the stairs.

"There's a separate entrance to the grounds and club on the other side of the property."

"And the police?" I ask, wondering how an illegal establishment of this size and obvious popularity stays off the radar.

"What about them?"

"Well, the illegal fights. Wouldn't they try to close you down if they knew?"

"Probably," Theo says flippantly, like it's of no consequence, shutting the bedroom door behind us.

"You're not worried about that?"

He pulls my T-shirt up over my head and then removes my jeans. "No."

"Why?"

"I have too much dirt on too many coppers," he says, pointing to the bed. "And Mother's married to one."

"No shit," I blurt.

"Yes shit." He laughs, removing his shirt.

I momentarily forget what has me so stunned, the sight of his chest sending me cross-eyed. I shake myself out of my little moment. "Your parents are divorced?"

"My father died."

I quietly note the pain that flashes across his face. "I'm sorry."

He doesn't acknowledge my offer of sympathy, instead nodding to the bed again. "Get in."

I follow his order obediently, slipping beneath the sheets as Theo strips down and throws his clothes on the nearby chair with mine. I get the feeling the conversation ends there, so I don't push him. I wouldn't want to talk too much about my mother, either. Sliding in beside me, he reaches for the lamp and flips the switch, and the room plummets into darkness. I wait for Theo to find me before I make a move, and when he does, I go happily into his arms, resting my head on his chest and closing my eyes, hearing his heart beat steady and strong.

"What do you mean, dirt on them?" I ask, my curiosity raging.

"What strip club did you work at?"

I still, scowling to myself. So this is how it's going to be? I ask him a question he doesn't want to answer, and he asks one that he knows I won't want to answer? Crafty. Clever. But isn't this terribly toxic? The secrets? You'd think, yet I find them comforting. Because we're both at peace simply being Izzy and Theo to each other, even if we know there's more to the story. But I want to forget. And so does Theo.

I turn my lips onto his skin and kiss his chest, ignoring the small part of my mind that's telling me my theory is stupid and naive. "Good night," I whisper, feeling his hand in my hair, rubbing soothing circles.

"Good night, sweetheart."

CHAPTER 16

Jess is slurping coffee in her dressing gown when I walk into the kitchen of our apartment early the next morning, her face a picture of curiosity. I skirt past her to get myself some caffeine. "Good night?" she asks casually, joining me by the kettle and resting her hip on the counter.

"Lovely, thank you." I choose to focus on the amazing latter parts of the night, rather than the shaky start outside the hospital when Theo had Percy's son in a choke hold, and then when I discovered what the Playground actually is. I pour and stir, keeping my eyes on the swirl of my coffee.

"You're glowing," she says, and I look at her out of the corner of my eye. She's failing to conceal her smirk. "How hard have you fallen?"

"Harder than I should." I take my mug and mirror her position—hip resting on the counter, my hands wrapped around my coffee.

"Why?"

I shrug, trying to be blasé. "I just get the feeling..." I let my words fade, thinking for a few moments. "I don't know. Like maybe I'm setting myself up to be hurt."

A mild smile breaks out over the rim of her mug. "Izzy, when you give your heart to someone, you're trusting them not to break it. You can't hold yourself back forever."

I nod lightly, knowing she's right. I can't let my past tarnish my future. But is this future too similar to my past? I shake my head to myself. Theo is *nothing* like him. God, why did I have to let my walls down to a man like Theo? Why not a normal, strait-laced, law-abiding guy with a regular job? They're silly questions, really; I don't even know why I'm bothering to ask myself them. I know exactly why. For a start, there's that feeling of being safe whenever he's near. That comfort is like a highly addictive drug, after being afraid for so long. But more than that, I feel like he's giving me parts of himself that no other is privileged to have. Even his mother. He's soft, gentle, kind, caring. He's a pile of contra-dictions, fascinatingly so. "I don't think he has any intention of breaking my heart." I just worry that he'll do it without intention.

"Do you trust him?"

"Implicitly." I don't hesitate. "He won't hurt me. I just fear the damage he can do to himself." Jess frowns, so I go on. "How he lives, what he does, the way he handles things. No one can live by the sword and never get cut." And if Theo gets cut, so do I. His pain will be mine.

She frowns. "Live by the sword?"

"His temper, his phobia." I bite the bullet. Besides, I can't ex-pect my friend to understand my muddle if she doesn't have all the information. "His strip club."

She nearly spits out her coffee, her mug hitting the counter hard. "What?"

I nod as I slurp my coffee, appearing as cool as I weirdly feel. "The Playground. It's a strip club. But not the kind that—"

Jess holds up her hand, stopping me from going on. "You don't need to go there, Izzy."

I'm grateful, but I'm keen to relay all the justifications I walked myself through last night. "He's good to the people who work there. They're happy." I shrug. "And Theo is still Theo." It's really that simple. "He treats me like a goddess." Makes me feel like one, too. I push away from the counter and head for the bathroom, hearing Jess in pursuit of me. "The Playground is also an illegal fight club," I tell her over my shoulder, rather blasé.

She gasps, nearly tripping over her own feet in shock. "You're joking, aren't you?"

"Nope." I place my coffee on the sink and strip down, jumping in the shower while Jess gets comfy on the toilet seat.

"And you found all this out last night?"

"Yes."

Her cheeks puff out, her face a picture of shock. "Bloody hell, if only Theo knew about—"

"He does know."

Her round eyes widen further. I really can't blame her, though I'm certain I dealt with all this a lot more rationally than Jess is doing. "He knows...?" She wants clarification, because there is *much* Theo could know about.

"He knows I used to be a stripper."

"You didn't used to be a stripper, Izzy. You used to be little more than a fucking slave." I flinch, and so does Jess. "Shit, I'm sorry."

"Don't be. You're right." I force a smile as the shower screen clouds before me, and I lose sight of her. "Though Theo doesn't know the gory details, okay? He doesn't need to."

"God, yes, of course."

"Thank you." I grab the shampoo, and as I wash my hair and body, I wait for more questions to come. But after a few minutes, I hear the bathroom door close. And I know she's worried.

* * *

"Izzy, a word in my office when you're done, please," Susan calls as I'm helping Mable get comfy. I look over my shoulder, seeing her collecting some medical files off the desk. It's near the end of my shift, and I've been on edge all day, worrying whether anything will come of the *incident* involving Percy's son last night.

"Two minutes," I say, my mind racing with apprehension.

"Sounds serious," Mable chimes in to my thoughts, patting the bedsheets around her lap.

I hum my agreement and pour her a drink of water, handing Mable some painkillers with the cup. "Still a five?" I ask.

"Four." She tips the small cup to her lips and swallows. "Tell me how that strapping man of yours is."

I return her wicked grin as I make a few notes on her charts. "Strapping."

"Off the shelf?"

"Maybe."

"Look at you being all coy." She chuckles, reaching for my arm and giving me a little poke. "But there's no hiding the spring in your step."

"I'm springing?"

"Oh yes. And glowing." She winks, looking highly pleased with herself. "I'm happy for you."

"Thanks." I give her hand a quick rub as Susan passes again and nods toward her office. I don't like her serious expression at all. "I'd better go."

"Okay, dear. I'm going to have a nap before *The Great British Bake Off* starts. Pass me the remote control, will you, my love?"

"Of course." I leave Mable after making sure she has everything she needs and make my way to Susan's office, unable to bat down my growing apprehension. "Everything okay?" I ask, finding her sitting at her desk.

"Izzy, please close the door and take a seat." Susan points to a chair, and my trepidation increases as I shut the door, knowing this *must* be serious. Susan's door is never closed unless it's serious.

"What's going on?" I ask as I lower into the chair.

She holds up something. "I was going to ask *you* that question."

I frown, eyeing the paper in her hand. "What's that?"

"A letter of complaint."

I shoot a look at her as she unfolds the sheet and scans the letter, pointing to the bottom. "From Percy Sugden's son. He turned up at Casualty late last night with extensive injuries. Broken jaw, broken arm, broken nose, to name just a few."

What? I wince, dread filling me. He had none of those injuries the last time I saw him. "Susan, I—"

"He told the police that you had an argument with him."

"He attacked me outside A&E," I clarify, more sternly than I intended. There was no arguing, not at all.

"He says you instigated a confrontation, but he tried to walk away."

I sit forward in my chair, astounded. "He cornered me in a doorway and threatened me."

She raises her eyebrow, returning her eyes to the paper and scanning the words. "He claims otherwise. He's said when he tried to remove himself from the situation, he was ambushed by two large men, one who he recognized as your boyfriend." She looks back up at me expectantly. But what is she expecting? For me to take responsibility for these lies?

I gape at her, stunned. He's twisting it. "Theo stepped in because Mr. Sugden was threatening me." My alarm is making my voice higher. "Theo pulled him away, and then he let him go." I neglect to mention the gun, since Susan hasn't. I realize I'm being selective here, but there's one thing that matters: Theo released Percy's son uninjured, even if he was shaken to the core. Good. He deserved to be.

"That's a different version of events to what Mr. Sugden has told the police." She sounds so high-handed, so unlike herself. This isn't my boss as I know her. And come to think of it, what she's dictating from that letter isn't how she knows me. Surely she doesn't believe this trash.

"He's lying," I grate, incensed. "There wasn't a scratch on Mr. Sugden when I last saw him, and Theo and Callum were with me for the rest of the night."

Susan sighs, dropping the paper to her desk. "I'm sorry, Izzy. With a complaint so serious, we have no choice but to suspend you pending further investigation."

"What? Susan, you saw that man. He's an arsehole. He's lying."

"Then how do you suggest he sustained those injuries?" she asks. "Broken limbs, Izzy. He hasn't tripped up a curb or walked into a door."

I close my eyes briefly and try to calm myself, feeling tears threatening to break free. What is happening here? "I don't know how he sustained those injuries, but I do know it has nothing to do with me *or* my boyfriend."

"Well, I have to treat every complaint according to protocol, Izzy. Mr. Sugden's behavior prior to his complaint will be noted in your defense, but someone gave him those injuries. He says you encouraged the beating."

I fall back in the chair, absolutely dumbfounded. "I encouraged it? What, like egged them on?"

Susan remains silent for a few moments, clearly thinking hard. I hope it's hard enough to see damn sense. "Izzy, it may not be my place to ask, but do you really know this man you're involved with?"

I stare at my boss, trying to form words in my head that don't include a flat *fuck off*. I've never once had any kind of complaint made against me since I qualified as a nurse. I've never had a confrontation with another member of staff, a patient, or a relative. Susan must know that this idiot's claim is out of character for me. I egged Theo on? What I actually did was plead with him to let the idiot go. I stopped Mr. Sugden from being pummeled to death.

I run through the horrid incident in my mind, from the moment Mr. Sugden cornered me to the moment Theo, Callum, and I got in the car. We were all together and...

My thought process grinds to a halt, ice gushing into my veins. In the car park. Callum forgot to pay for the parking and Theo went to validate the ticket. My eyes dart across the desk before me, trying to figure out if the few minutes he was gone would be enough to inflict so much damage on Percy's son.

I should laugh at myself for asking such a pathetic question. Theo would need only ten seconds with him to inflict serious damage. I have no doubt. I push out a deep breath, now questioning what *really* happened. It doesn't matter that Mr. Sugden is stretching the truth and twisting things. If Theo has knowingly jeopardized my job, I will lose my fucking shit.

I look up to Susan and find her lips pressed into a straight line. "I'm sorry, Izzy. I suggest you contact the union, and I expect the police will be in touch to question you." Her head tilts, sympathy engulfing her face. "You should leave now."

I get up, feeling numb, and walk away to collect my things. My head is a riot of thoughts as I go, questioning Theo's honor to respect my wishes. There's no doubt Mr. Sugden held me responsible for his father's death and wanted some kind of stupid vengeance, and Theo has given him the opportunity for the best vengeance ever. What better way than to get me fired? Ruin my career, and on top of that, have my boyfriend locked up.

I wander out of the hospital with my coat over my arm and my bag dragging along the ground. I'm in conflicting places, my mind a tattered mess. This was a lose-lose situation for me.

Had Theo not been there for me last night, I've no doubt Sugden would have clouted me one, *but* I wouldn't have been suspended from duty. Yet Theo *was* there, and yes, I'm unscathed, but I'm now facing the possibility of having my career fall down the drain as a result. Or Theo could have walked away like I thought he had, instead of sneakily going back to find Sugden and pulverize him. Then I'd be uninjured *and* still have a career. But Theo thought Percy's son was someone else. He thought I was lying to him.

With a loaded sigh, I drop to a bench outside the hospital and stare blankly at the ground. How could he do this? Years of training wasted. My sanctuary taken away from me. I have bills to pay. What am I going to do?

My phone rings, and I sluggishly pull it out of my coat pocket, finding Jess is calling me. She's on shift. Surely news couldn't have made it to the other side of the hospital already. "Hey?"

"Oh my God, Izzy. I just heard."

I sink into the hard wood of the bench. Seems it could. "Sugden's lying."

"What the hell happened?" She's whisper-shouting now, probably locked in a closet somewhere on the maternity unit.

"I think he was waiting for me after my shift last night. He cornered me and threatened me. You know, your usual end-of-shift wind-down. He didn't know Theo was with me."

"Seriously? Is the man blind? How did he miss him? He's a fucking giant."

"He was getting me a coffee. I went outside to wait for Callum." I glance around to check my privacy and lower my voice. "Theo had him held at gunpoint, Jess. Callum had to talk him down. But the gun hasn't been mentioned. Theo let him go, and the last I saw, Sugden was all in one piece."

"Oh, fucking hell," she breathes. "The last you saw?"

"Theo disappeared for a couple of minutes to validate the parking ticket." I close my eyes and cup my forehead in my palm, my head beginning to pound. "Callum was behind the wheel at the barrier, so Theo went." It's only now I realize Callum could have gone. If the car needed to be moved before he returned, surely Theo could have slid over to the driver's seat and done it.

"A couple of minutes? You think he could do that much damage so quickly?"

"I *know* he could."

"God, Izzy, I know it's not what you want to hear right now, but you can't blame Theo for losing his shit if Sugden attacked you."

"No, but I can blame him for losing my job."

She falls silent for several seconds, but I can hear her breathing. She can't argue with me. Because I'm right. She knows it, I know it, and I'll make damn sure Theo knows it when I see him. "What are you going to do?"

"I have no idea, Jess," I answer wearily, because I truly don't. My verbal pleas to Theo, calling him off Sugden, were words. Hearsay. Unprovable. Sugden's injuries are physical and visible, hard evidence if ever there was any. I'm screwed, and for the first time, I'm wondering who the hell I've *really* gotten myself involved with.

"Go home," Jess says. "And get a bottle of wine on the way. I'm off shift in a couple of hours."

"Okay." I exhale, hang up, and mentally calculate how many bottles of wine I can carry by myself. I'm going to need more than one.

What a fucking mess. My feet are heavy as I start my walk home, my mind weighed down, too, and as I reach the end of the road, I slow to a stop, seeing a familiar Bentley rounding the corner up ahead. My shoulders drop. I'm too tired to have an argument, and that's exactly what we're going to have. I follow the path of the big, posh car, slowly turning on the spot until I'm facing the road and it's pulling up in front of me. The door opens and Theo slides out, my eyes lifting to accommodate his height. He looks smart, his deadly body encased in a gray three-piece suit. Today, I can't appreciate the finely tuned man before me. Today, I can only wonder with increasing worry how damaged my career will be because of him. And, annoyingly—because I'm mad with him—whether Theo will be taken away from me. Arrested. Thrown in jail. As I said to Jess, you can't live by the sword and never get cut.

His deep blue eyes glimmer with delight until he clocks my expression, and then the brightness dulls, his dimple fades, and his forehead furrows. "Izzy?" He closes the door softly and takes a step toward me. "What's wrong, sweetheart?"

"Why didn't Callum go to pay for the ticket?" I ask, cutting straight to the point. If I don't start getting answers, I'm going to explode all over Theo.

His head turns to the side, but his eyes remain on me. "What?"

"Yesterday when you picked me up from work, after you held a man at gunpoint. Why didn't Callum go pay for the car park ticket?"

"Why are you asking such a trivial question?"

"Just answer me!" I yell, finding anger amid my exhaustion.

His jaw ticks. "Don't take that tone with me, Izzy."

"Why, what will you do?" I ask, stepping closer, bold and brave. I won't back down. Never. Besides, isn't my bravery one of the things Theo claims to love about me? Let's see how much he loves facing my wrath. "Pull a gun on me?"

Nostrils flaring, he takes one step back, putting the space he needs between us again. He doesn't like this. My rage. He doesn't know how to handle me. "I went because it was easier." He takes another step back. "Callum was driving. What the hell is wrong with you?"

"I've been suspended," I declare evenly.

His forehead wrinkles. "What?"

Taking a deep breath, I repeat myself, though I know he heard me just fine. "I've been suspended from my job because the man who you held at gunpoint last night has lodged a complaint, not just with the hospital, but with the police, too."

Theo laughs a little under his breath. He actually laughs. Lord, give me strength before I lose the plot. "He can't prove that I held a gun to his head."

"He hasn't mentioned the gun in his statement, and he doesn't need to. He doesn't have a gunshot wound," I tell him, my jaw aching from tenseness. "But he does have countless broken bones."

Theo recoils. "Say what?"

"How could you?" I ask, forcing my voice not to shake with the anger bubbling up. "I told you to leave him, but you still went right ahead and—"

He seizes me by the tops of my arms, and I jump, yet I don't break free from his hold. It's too firm. His face, tight with frustration, comes right up close to mine. "I never laid a finger on him."

"Liar," I spit back. "You conveniently left us in the car for a few minutes. Where did you go?"

"To pay for the parking."

"You sure?" I ask, wrenching myself free from Theo's hold with some serious effort. "Because Sugden's injuries suggest otherwise."

"What fucking injuries?"

"Broken jaw, nose, arm. He's reported it to the police, Theo. You'll be arrested, I'll lose my job, and probably be arrested, too, as a damn accomplice." I raise my hand in anger and panic, forgetting myself for a moment, and launch it at his shoulder. It's a stupid move, fueled only by hopelessness.

He catches my arm by the wrist without even looking, his eyes developing an edge of lunacy, and I withdraw my body, wary, my wrist still stuck in his viselike grip. His lip curls. "He's made a statement saying I kicked the shit out of him?"

I nod, not daring to speak. He looks homicidal.

His nostrils flare, and he releases my wrist, looking down at it when I start to rub away the slight pain from his squeeze. Gently this time, he reclaims my arm and takes over rubbing before bringing it to his mouth and kissing it sweetly, closing his eyes and breathing in a long, calming inhale. "I'm not fucking standing for this." He drops my arm and strides off down the road toward the hospital.

I stare at his back, letting the last few moments sink in. He's not standing for it? Then what does he think he can do? I look at his car on the roadside and dip to get Callum in my view when the window lowers. He's watching Theo walk off. "You'd better get in or any hope you have of keeping your job will be lost," Callum says, shaking his head. It's a sign of dread, and it has me straightening and finding Theo again. He's at the bottom of the street already, his long legs eating up the distance in no time.

"Izzy, get in the fucking car."

Callum's demand has me moving quickly, and I jump into the car in a panic. As soon as I've pulled the door closed, he speeds off down the road. Before I know it, he's swinging into the hospital grounds. The barrier takes an age to lift, to the point Callum starts cursing his impatience, and once he has just enough room, he puts his foot down, forcing a few pedestrians to jump from our path.

"For the record," Callum says as the Bentley skids to a stop, "he really was paying for parking. Wait there." He jumps out, shutting the door and breaking into a sprint across the car park toward the entrance. I watch him pelt away, my mind a haze, trying to catch up. He really was just paying for parking? Theo's not stand-ing for this? So, again, what's he going to do?

" 'Wait here'?" I say to myself, seeing Callum disappear through the doors of the hospital in pursuit of my rankled boyfriend. "I don't bloody think so." I let myself out of the car and chase after him. Not fast enough, though. I lose sight of Callum, getting caught up in a crowd of people at the hospital entrance. "Excuse me," I shout, fighting my way through, knocking people out of the way as I go.

By the time I make it to my ward, I'm out of breath and sweat-ing, my lungs burning. I pull to a slow jog near the entrance, trying to calm my breathing and my frantic state.

That's when I hear the commotion, and I flinch as the sound of Theo's voice thunders through the hospital, echoing off every wall. "You can't suspend her for something she didn't do," he yells. "I won't have it!"

"Sir, please. You can't come in here throwing your weight around." Susan's high-pitched shrill hits my ears, and I drop my head into my hands in dread. "Please leave, or I'll call security."

"Fucking call them," Theo bellows. "What kind of imbecile does she work for? You know Izzy. Her kindness and her passion for her job. You're going to let a depraved arsehole put her in-tegrity and her reputation into doubt?"

I follow the sound of his voice to Susan's office, seeing the door open and Susan backed into the corner, despite Theo being on the other side of her desk, albeit with his fists planted on the wooden surface, leaning over. Callum is hovering behind, silent and still.

"I have to follow protocol," Susan stammers, her gaze flicking to me at the door. I hope she can see the sincerity in my eyes, the alarm and remorse for Theo's threatening behavior. If she was concerned about my involvement with him before, then Theo has just confirmed why she should be. His presence is ominous. Intimidating.

"Theo," I say, approaching his heaving back. "Please, let's just go."

"No, Izzy. Not until someone around here starts acting on common sense rather than fucking protocol. It's a fucking joke." He lifts, straightening to his full height. "You know as well as I do that she would never confront someone, let alone a grieving person. Bollocks to protocol. Why the fuck aren't you fighting in her corner?"

"I know Izzy," Susan retorts. "I have no idea who *you* are, and you're most certainly not welcome here. It's time for you to leave."

"I didn't inflict those injuries," Theo growls, his stubbled jaw ticking. "I wanted to, believe me, and if Izzy hadn't stopped me, I promise you, he wouldn't have wound up in Casualty, he would have wound up in the fucking morgue."

I close my eyes and fold on the inside, silently begging him to stop. I love his protective instinct, have grown to crave it, but I'm slowly grasping the consequences. I'm so utterly torn.

A hive of activity breaks out behind me, and I swing around to find two hospital security guards. Oh shit, no. Callum moves fast, ever alert, grabbing one who launches himself toward Theo. He restrains the startled security guard quickly, thrusting him front-forward against the wall, his arm up his back. The man squeals in pain, and time seems to slow to a crawl, my attention whirling to Theo and then to the remaining security guard, the one who's lacking one big fucker holding him back.

I watch as the distance between him and Theo shrinks, the free security man's body seeming to fly through the air toward my boyfriend. I don't know what happens. Instinct? It must be. "No!" I jump in his path to stop him from reaching Theo, knowing the reprisals will be ugly.

"Izzy!" Theo yells, though the sound is muffled, because the large arm of the security guard just connected with the side of my head, and I cry out in shock as I'm sent flying across Susan's office, my body crashing into a nearby filing cabinet with a loud bang. I grunt, pain searing through me as I drop to the ground, stars dancing in my vision. Pain rips through my shoulder, and I grab it and squeeze as a blurry Theo appears in my sight, his hard face filled with concern. "Izzy, sweetheart." His hands find my cheeks and pull my head up, his eyes searching mine.

I blink, trying to clear my vision, trying to focus on Theo. But something beyond his wide shoulders distracts me from the worry in his eyes, and I look past him to find a pair of hands closing in. But I can't speak. My tongue is thick, refusing to engage and deliver the words of warning to Theo. The guard's hands meet Theo's shoulders, but before he gets a chance to yank him back, Theo's moving of his own accord. And he's moving fast. I only briefly catch the lethal look in his darkening eyes before he shoots to his feet and turns on the security guard. The startled man is on his back in a nanosecond, Theo's deadly grip wrapped around his throat. I have nothing—no energy, no fight, no will—to try to stop him. I'm useless, yet I appreciate in this moment that my career has just disappeared before my very eyes, disappeared in a haze of rage and violence.

"Theo, for fuck's sake." Callum once again puts his own life on the line to save another's, seizing Theo and wrenching him away before quickly getting out of reach. "Calm the fuck down."

Theo's wide, crazy eyes fall back onto me. They clear the moment he finds me. He dips and lifts me into his arms, and I do nothing to stop him. And I bury my face in his chest, not for comfort, but because I can't face the carnage that's been left in his wake. He takes a few long paces, his breathing labored, and comes to a stop, turning. I open my eyes and see Susan still tucked away in the corner, her face terrified. Guilt consumes me. I know he wouldn't harm her. But she doesn't.

"If you won't deal with this, then I will," Theo vows, before carrying me out of the office.

When I see the gathering of people outside—some staff, some patients—I resume hiding, sinking my face into Theo's chest and letting the tears roll. I've secretly wished for this my entire life. A man who would protect me, fight off the bad, and make me feel safe.

Now I have it.

And I'm worried it might be the worst thing that's ever happened to me.

CHAPTER 17

I don't recall much of the journey to Theo's, my mind in too much disarray. But I felt his heart strumming wildly under me when he climbed into the car with me attached to his chest, and I felt it calm slowly as he massaged my head and dropped constant kisses in my hair. I felt the corners Callum took in the car, and I felt us ease to a stop—at lights, junctions, and roundabouts—until we had stopped for the last time. My phone ringing is what rouses me from my despondent state, my numb mind coming to life and reminding me that I should be at home with wine and my best friend. Not here dealing with the aftermath of Theo's temper.

"Jess," I croak, forgetting myself for a moment and trying to break away from Theo's chest to find my mobile. He hisses, stiffening, and I freeze as he growls in warning.

"Fuck's sake, Izzy," he spits, his chest expanding on a deep, calming inhale. Right or wrong, this only angers me more.

"Then let me go," I snap as the door opens, courtesy of Jefferson.

"Miss White." He nods, standing back from the car to give Theo room to get out, his big arms holding me tightly against him, refusing to release me.

"My phone."

"Callum has it." Theo dismisses me, striding toward the house, and I look back over his shoulder, seeing Callum with my phone to his ear, following us. Only once we're inside his mansion does Theo set me on my feet, his hands holding me in place to ensure my stability. "Okay?" he asks, looking me over.

"Fine," I say curtly, turning to Callum and ignoring the routine delivery of a tumbler filled with scotch in exchange for Theo's jacket.

Callum's eyes fall to mine, my phone poised at his ear. "Would you like me to pick you up?" he asks, glancing away. I can only assume Jess's answer is quick, because Callum soon says, "I'm on my way," before hanging up and handing my phone to me. "Jess would like me to pick her up." He's straight-faced, giving nothing away.

I take my phone. "I got that." I turn back to Theo, who's placing his empty glass on the tray. He made quick work of that drink. Good for him. I'm about to make quick work of him. "We need to talk." I flash him a fierce stare. "Now." I don't want to sound cocky, but I'm pretty sure my big, strapping, formidable, hard-case boyfriend looks a little worried by the prospect.

"Do you want a drink?" he asks, looking past me to his housemaid.

"No."

"You need to eat," he tries, indicating the dining room across the hall. "I'll have the cook prepare you something."

"No, I want you in that office." I point past him, my jaw tight. "Now."

He peeks out the corner of his eye to me, nibbling his bottom lip. I'm definitely not imagining it. He's worried. Good. I hope he's considering the damage he's just caused.

As Theo continues to assess just how much of a pissed-off

female is before him, I glance around the hall, seeing Callum backing away, cautious, and Jefferson looking more stunned than a hooligan who's just been hit with a Taser. Theo doesn't take orders from anyone. People don't talk to him like this. Well, I do. I return my attention to Theo and step forward. He doesn't retreat. "Are we talking, or am I leaving?"

He closes his eyes in defeat, lifting his hand for me to take. I ignore it and storm past him, entering his regal office and planting myself in a chair opposite his desk. Two seconds later the door closes, and a few seconds after that, a very cautious-looking Theo appears, rounding his desk as he unfastens his tie.

I fight to regulate my breathing while I try to ignore the beauty of the man before me, his nervous temperament weirdly even more attractive than any of his other dispositions. He's hesitant, twitchy, and his face is a picture of uncertainty. He looks vulnerable. It's the most endearing thing I've ever seen.

He lowers to his chair slowly and places his tie on the desk. "How much trouble am I in?" He gives me a nervous smile that I shoot down with one filthy look. "Yikes. A lot, huh?"

"You've just dashed any hope I had of keeping my job."

He drops his gaze, hiding his ashamed face from me. It's ridiculous, but his remorse offers me some relief in my turmoil. At least he appreciates the shitstorm he's caused. At least he isn't being a pigheaded idiot. "You're being wronged. I can't allow that," he says feebly, vainly searching for a justification. "I spared Sugden the punishment he deserved—one I so wanted to give— because your happiness is important to me. Your job makes you happy."

"And then you wasted all that effort," I say, because I appreciate it was a *massive* effort for Theo to hold back from annihilating Sugden. "You charged into my boss's office and wreaked havoc."

He shoots forward in his chair, yet I remain in place, unperturbed by his fast move. "There was no havoc until the security guard touched me."

"You frightened Susan out of her skin."

"I was stating facts."

"You were shouting facts!" I yell, tossing a hand out and sending a pile of paperwork on his desk gusting into the air. It's either that or smack him one, and we all know I can't fucking do that. "It may have escaped your notice, big man," I hiss, standing and planting my palms on the wood of his desk, leaning over until he's forced to retreat in his chair, "but you're a fucking huge beast and most people are pretty fucking wary of you. When you start ranting and raving like you did, you're likely to scare them to death, Theo."

"He shouldn't have touched me," he murmurs, rolling his shoulders, like the sensation is still lingering. "I'm sorry."

His increasing sorrow cuts me deep. He doesn't regret throwing his weight around. He only regrets upsetting me. But one thing I know for sure is that he can't control himself if someone touches him when he's unprepared. He acts on an instinct I am yet to understand, but I know it's something he can't stop. He needs therapy. Help.

"You need to make me understand," I say, my quiet words immediately winning back his attention. Granted, his actions could be considered gallant, but it's hard to see past the damaging repercussions when I don't understand what makes this man tick.

"I don't like people touching me. What's so hard to understand?"

I shake my head with a sardonic laugh. I can see this conversation is going to get me nowhere, except a one-way ticket to Frustrationville. "I need a drink," I declare, pivoting and walking away. He doesn't come after me, probably because he knows damn well there's no one to take me home, and no way on earth I'll break free from his grounds without raising the alarms.

I head for the Playground, making my way down the corridor, through the office, and past the last hallway before using the code Theo gave me and letting myself into the club. This time the space is less busy, probably due to the early hour. Penny is the only dancer. She clocks me, offering a small, discreet wave, but frowns when I give her an obviously forced smile. I land at the bar, order a chardonnay, and the barman smiles at me knowingly as he pours, before sliding it across the bar and telling me to enjoy.

"I will," I grumble, savoring the cool, sweet liquid as it trickles down my throat.

"Tough day?" he asks as he polishes glasses and loads them onto the shelf. He's short and cute, his red hair spiky, his freckles dark.

"Putting it mildly."

He smiles and tosses his towel over his shoulder. "So, you're Mr. Kane's . . ." He fades off, putting some glasses in the washer. "Girlfriend?"

I study him as I take more wine. "Sorry, I didn't catch your name."

"Troy." He offers his hand across the bar, and I shake it. "Nice to meet you, Izzy."

I flash him a wry smile. "I see you already know *my* name."

He chuckles, pointing to my glass. "Top-up?" I nod, and he gets to it quickly. "Everyone knows *your* name. You're the only person who dares go near him without the worry of having your head ripped off." He shudders. "I'm sure you've seen him in action."

"Yes, he was just in action tonight at my place of work," I mutter, holding up my glass to Troy in a sarcastic toast. "I'm pretty sure he's just lost me my job."

"Oh, shit. It really has been a tough day." His sympathetic eyes suddenly dart past me, and he's gone in a shot, getting on with tidying the shelves of liquor. I look over my shoulder and see Theo standing on the other side of the club, watching. His hair is a mess, like he could have been raking his hand through it constantly, and his dark blue eyes are annoyed. I fully expect him to march over, but when another man approaches him, he yanks his eyes away from me and offers the guy his hand. It's the same man Theo was talking to when I stumbled in here last night. I follow their path as they walk over to the roped-off area again and Theo motions Troy to him with a hard stare and a flick of his hand.

"I'd better go," Troy says, claiming a tray from the pile stacked at the end of the bar and heading over to Theo and his guest.

"Yes," I mutter, returning my attention to my wine. "Because only the unwise refuse Theo Kane."

An hour later, I'm still wallowing in my wine when Jess appears across the Playground. She looks amazed as she soaks up the atmosphere, Callum hovering behind her. A small smile curves his lips when he dips and whispers something in her ear, making her shudder, her eyes darting toward me at the bar. She gives me a pained face as she hurries over, yet why so pained is yet to be determined. Something tells me that it's not my current state of affairs causing her aggrieved expression.

She lands on a stool next to me and drops her head into her hands. "He picked me up. He *physically* picked me up and carried me across a huge fucking puddle, and I swear, on the Lord Almighty above, I had an orgasm right there in his arms."

Laughter rumbles up from my toes and bursts right out of my mouth. "You're kidding?"

"It's not funny, Izzy. I was stiff as a board in his hold."

"Was *he* stiff?" I titter, my wine shaking as I bring it to my lips. She looks traumatized, and my laughter increases, my reflux threatening to send my wine everywhere except down my throat.

I struggle to swallow, flagging Troy when he appears behind the bar. "You'd better get my friend a drink. She's having a bit of a meltdown here."

"Please," she squeaks, waggling a finger at the hard stuff on the top shelf. "Anything."

Troy joins in my amusement and pours her a neat whiskey. "Get that down you."

"Thanks." She gulps it, gasps, and then throws herself around on the chair, clearing her throat. "What the hell is going on?"

My eyes bug at her. "You recovered from your little moment rather quickly."

She scoffs and moves in closer. "I'm sorry. I just needed to get that out. Callum said you're not talking to Theo."

"So you've had a conversation with him, then?"

She shudders again. "I could listen to him talk forever." Looking past me, I follow her eyes, seeing that Callum has joined Theo and the other man. "Such a hunk."

"But quiet," I muse.

"And moody," Jess adds. "It's so fucking sexy. And cold. But I still quite fancy him. It's annoying."

I roll my eyes, just catching Theo looking up at me. He still appears troubled, his face tight with irritation as he nods mildly to the guy talking to him. It all looks very serious. Who is he? And what are they talking about?

"So tell me." Jess breaks into my thoughts, pulling me back around on my stool. "Rumors are rife."

"What rumors?"

"At work. So far, you're fired, Theo kicked the ever-loving crap out of the security guard, and there's a warrant out for your arrest. Oh, and Susan was blindfolded and locked in a closet while Theo performed Chinese torture tactics to get her talking."

I gape at her. "What?"

Jess shrugs. "You know everyone likes to add their own little bit to enhance the drama."

Fucking hell. As if the drama needs enhancing. "This is what happened," I say, moving in, as does Jess. I spend the next half hour giving her a blow-by-blow account of everything, from the moment I arrived at Percy Sugden's bed and first encountered his son, to a few hours ago, when Theo lost the plot in Susan's office. "So suffice to say, I'm out of a job."

Jess looks bamboozled as I draw to a close, my wine freshly topped up again, courtesy of a very attentive Troy. I smile and raise my glass to him at the end of the bar. "Shit," Jess says simply.

"Yes," I agree. "And now I'm waiting for the police to track me down and question me."

"So if Theo or Callum didn't kick Sugden's arse, how did he wind up with broken bones?"

"Damned if I know. Maybe he upset someone else. I imagine it happens daily. He's a total arsehole."

"Well," she breathes, taking a casual swig of her drink as she gazes around the Playground. "I would say you could get a job here, but, you know, been there and done that."

I gape at her, and she winks, continuing to rain humor on my overall diabolical situation. I guess if I didn't laugh, I might cry. "You're fucking hilarious." I smack her knee and she smiles a little, placing an upturned hand on the bar for me to take, which I do, squeezing. "Thanks for coming."

"No sweat." She looks down at her work uniform. "Though I would have preferred not to be sporting the juices of various vaginas."

My nose wrinkles, clocking a few spots of faint blood on her front. "I'm sure Callum didn't notice."

Jess peeks up with a grin. "He did, actually. And he asked a bunch of questions like he was really interested in my day. At least he sounded it." She looks past me, pouting. "I can't figure him out. I know I irritate him, but the man pushes my buttons. Part of me wants to take that gun he carries and hold it to his head, and the other half wants *him* to hold it to *mine*."

"While—"

"He fucks my brain out."

"Jess!" I laugh, and she shrugs, nonchalant.

"Oh, who's this? She looks important."

I crane my neck and see Theo's mum wandering in from the main entrance, a stack of files under one arm and a gorgeous Chanel purse suspended from the other. The suit screams Chanel, too. The woman is the epitome of class. "That's Judy. Theo's mum." She heads straight for the group of three men in the cordoned-off area and gives the unknown man with Theo and Callum a kiss on the cheek in greeting. The stranger accepts with a huge smile, reaching up to caress her face. The lightbulb goes off. "That must be her husband," I say to myself, watching their exchange intently.

"Theo's dad?"

"No, he died." I observe as Judy gives Callum a kiss on the cheek, too, and then she holds her hand out to Theo, who drops his lips to the back in greeting. "Her second husband is a cop."

"You're kidding?" Jess says. "Her son carries a gun and runs an illegal club, and her husband is a police officer? Makes perfect sense."

I hum my agreement, casually sipping my wine as I continue to watch the group talking. "I think he might be a bent copper." It's the only explanation.

"I can see something I'd like to bend."

Callum looks up, like he could have heard Jess, and she quickly turns back to the bar, her face flaming. "Does he have superpowers?" she asks the marble counter. "Because every time I have a filthy thought about him, he looks at me. It freaks me out."

"Or maybe he's on the same wavelength."

"Oh, Jesus. I know I'm all bold and brash, but I wouldn't have a clue what to do with him if he was naked before me. Lick him, fuck him, or dribble on him."

"All?" I laugh, waving a hand at Troy, who tends to us quickly. "Thank you."

"You feeling any better?" he asks, indicating the bottle in his hand. It's empty.

"Much."

"Should I open a new one?"

I look to Jess, who is quick to hold up her glass. "Why not," she says. "I'm on a late shift tomorrow, and Izzy is unemployed. Let's get shit-faced."

"Cheers." I'm all for that.

CHAPTER 18

I'm not sure what time it is, but Jess and I have now worked our way through two bottles of wine. We're still propped on our stools, except now we're facing the club, leaning back on the bar. Theo is still at the table with Callum, Judy, and her husband, and by the looks of things, the meeting has come to an end. He stands, prompting everyone else to rise too, and turns to Callum as Judy and her husband leave the area, headed in our direction. She smiles as she approaches.

"Izzy," she says, extending her hand as she nears. I take it and she crowds me, holding one of my cheeks as she tenderly kisses the other. "How are you, my darling?"

Her concerned tone tells me she knows all about my day. "Jobless," I reply, trying not to slur.

She breaks away from me and takes my hand, looking at me with an understanding smile. It irritates me to high heaven. There's nothing to smile about. And she can't possibly understand. "He'll fix it. Don't you worry."

"How?" I ask, truly interested. There's nothing to be done, apart from rewinding time.

"Trust me." She flips me a little wink before turning to Jess. "You must be Jess?"

"Yes. I love your suit! And your bag. And your shoes," my friend gushes, smiling brightly. "You'll have to forgive me. I've been helping Izzy—"

"Get plastered?" Judy finishes, a wry smile on her face. "You're a good friend." She takes one of Jess's hands, too. "Enjoy yourselves, girls. I'm going home now."

Judy's husband joins us, nodding politely but sharply. "Ready?" he asks her.

"Yes, but first let me introduce you to Theo's Izzy." Judy pulls me down off the stool and more or less presents me to him, like she's showcasing something with pride. "Isn't she adorable? Izzy, this is my husband, Andy."

"Hi." I hold my hand out. "Nice to meet you, Andy." I'm sure I hear Judy sigh.

"Pleasure, Izzy." Andy smiles warmly. "I've heard a lot about you."

"All good, I hope." I chuckle like a fool, mentally kicking myself. Such a cliché thing to say.

"I'm sorry to hear about your current predicament," Andy says, not sounding very sorry at all.

Oh, great. Does everyone know? I refrain from blurting in my drunkenness that my predicament is the six-foot-five-inch son of his wife. "Thanks," I say tightly, lifting my drunken bones clumsily back onto my stool.

"Come on, Judy. I'm starving and I have a dozen reports to file."

"Yes, yes," she pacifies him, taking my cheeks in her palms and squeezing. Her face turns serious, and I find myself sitting back a little, wary of what she's going to say. "He can't help it, Izzy. Be patient with him." She kisses my cheek and then leaves us, not giving me the chance to respond. Not that I would know what to say. Maybe he needs to start helping it before *everything* goes to shit.

Jess looks all gooey-eyed, while I'm feeling torn between maintaining my grievance and forgiving Theo for royally fucking up my career.

"She's so lovely." Jess sighs. "So motherly and loving."

"Or a lioness," I muse, imagining Judy turning into quite the formidable one herself should anyone cross *her boy*, no matter how big, dangerous, and capable of looking after himself he is. Judy lifts her hand in goodbye to Theo and Callum as she goes, and they both nod as an applause erupts. She looks across the club to the stage, and I follow her stare, seeing Penny thrusting her crotch in a patron's face while his friends cheer her on. Judy's lip is curled in disdain, and I recoil, interested. Oh, she really doesn't like her. I barely have time to wonder why before Andy pulls his wife out of the club and I spot Theo and Callum wandering over, people clearing their path vigilantly.

Jess stiffens next to me. "Oh God, please don't let me speak. If I try to speak, kick me. I'm drunk. I'll only say something stupid and look like a twat."

The expression of disbelief I aim at her isn't noticed, because she's staring down into her glass. "You've already made yourself look like a twat when you were sober. At least now you'll have an excuse."

"Shut up. I can't read him," she hisses at her wine. "It's frustrating. Makes me behave out of the ordinary."

I snort, most unladylike. "Whatever. He's coming."

"Stop."

"He's looking at you."

"I hate you."

"With take-me-to-bed eyes."

Her head whips up, just as Theo and Callum come to a stop

before us. Callum's eyes aren't take-me-to-bed eyes at all. They're more like scrutinizing eyes. "Hi," Jess squeaks before throwing back more wine.

Callum watches, waiting until she's downed the lot. "I'll take you home," he says finally, and I grin, looking out the corner of my eye to see her increasing discomfort. I'm not sure what's wrong with her. Alcohol usually makes her bolder, but she's almost painfully awkward.

"Jess." I nudge her when she makes no attempt to show her face. "Callum is ready to take you home."

"Okay." She slides her glass onto the bar and jumps down, kissing me quickly before grabbing her bag and scurrying away. "Speak tomorrow."

Theo's looking at his friend with a slightly lifted eyebrow, but Callum just shrugs, trudging on his way to catch up with Jess. "Take the rest of the night off," Theo calls, a wicked smile on his face.

I fall apart on the bar stool, watching my friend alternate between staggers and determined strides, until Callum is forced to help her out before she veers completely off course and lands in the ladies'. "She's steaming," I say with a chuckle, grinning into my glass as I sip.

Theo appears in my peripheral vision, and I turn toward him with my glass at my lips, finding him leaning against the bar, watching me. And I remember: I'm not talking to him.

I drop to my drunken feet, then spend a few moments concentrating on finding the stability I need to walk away with my dignity still intact. After a considerable amount of time, I give up and start my zigzagging meander across the club. I don't need to worry about bumping into anyone. They're all being rather helpful and moving from my path. "Thank you," I say politely to one man. "Good night," I say to another. "Thanks." I smile at a lady, who grins as she shifts out of my way. I feel more conspicuous than I'd like, everyone obviously concluding I need the space. Either that or they're worried I might throw up on them.

As I make it to the door, I take a quick glimpse over my shoulder and find Theo mere feet behind me. I realize, even through the haze of alcohol, that all those helpful people weren't moving for my benefit at all. They weren't being helpful. They were being sensible.

I narrow my eyes on him as he reaches past me and punches in the code. Then he kindly motions for me to lead the way. I push my way through without thanks, letting it close behind me. There are no people in the corridor, but there are walls on both sides of me. I stop and focus forward, blinking my blurry vision clear as best I can. Then I stagger two steps to the right...and bounce. Then two steps to the left...and bounce. I roll my eyes to myself and continue to ping-pong my way toward the office, vaguely hearing a deep, rumbling chuckle from behind.

"This is your fault," I mutter. He doesn't speak. Probably can't from laughing too much. Wrestling with the door, I finally get it open and let myself in, turning and finding his laughing eyes before I slam it in his face. Then I bounce off every piece of furniture in the workspace before I make it to the other door. I resort to closing one eye to zero in on the handle, eventually finding it and performing the same childish actions as before. I turn and scowl at Theo, then slam the door in his face.

The never-ending corridor that leads back to his house sees me ricocheting off the walls all the way. By the time I make it to the end, the room is spinning, and I don't have the energy to be spiteful and slam any more doors in his face, so I stumble to the stairs and whimper when the stripes of the carpet become a wavy mess, making me sway on the spot. I'll never make it.

But I don't have to. My feet are swiped from beneath me and

I'm suddenly floating. Theo doesn't breathe a word of scorn, nor does he make fun of me. And like it's ingrained in me, I don't move a muscle now that he has me in his hold. He carries me up the horrid stairs and into his bedroom, laying me on the bed gently. And he strips me down, patiently and calmly as I drunkenly writhe atop the covers, just wanting to crawl under the sheets and say goodbye to today. When his hands are gone from my body, I snuggle down and exhale.

And a few moments later, I vaguely feel his fingertips trace across my tummy. "What happened to you, baby?" he whispers, placing his lips on my forehead.

"You really don't want to know," I slur, raising my arm into the air. He sighs, taking my wrist and laying it somewhere on his body. His chest, I think.

I sigh and drift off to sleep.

CHAPTER 19

My head is throbbing as I sheepishly peek out of Theo's bedroom door, listening for any sounds of life. I'm wearing the massive, luxuriously soft bathrobe that was left on the end of the bed for me, the oversize garment skimming my ankles as I wander through his private quarters in search of my bag. It's nowhere to be seen, but the faint ringing of my phone from within is sounding from somewhere.

As I'm scanning the lounge, Jefferson wanders in, looking amused as he holds up my bag. His old eyes are shining behind his round spectacles, his silver hair as neat as always. "Miss White," he says, taking in my disheveled form.

Embarrassed, I try to quickly give my tangled waves a finger comb. "Morning, Jefferson." I reach for my bag, but my phone stops ringing before I have a chance to search it out. "Is Theo still here?" I have no idea what time it is, but I could do with a few more hours of sleep. My head hurts. A lot.

"He's waiting for you in the dining room." He moves to the huge fireplace and collects an empty tumbler from the mantel. I imagine Theo standing there last night having a needed drink as he stared into the fire while I was snoring in his bed. "I'll walk down with you."

"Now?" I blurt, looking down at my less-than-presentable form.

"He insisted." Jefferson makes for the door, not looking back to check if I'm coming.

"Because one would be unwise to say no to Mr. Kane." I sigh, taking my phone from my bag and following Theo's butler. Not a word is spoken between us on the way down, and after Jefferson has walked me to the doors that lead into the dining room and I've smiled my thanks, he leaves me to gather some strength to enter.

A minute later, I'm still trying to find that strength. "Izzy?" Judy's voice is a welcome distraction from my annoying battle to open the door, and I turn to find her watching me from across the hall. "You okay?" she asks, smiling as she takes in the dressing gown I'm wrapped in. Theo's dressing gown.

"Yes." I smile, thumbing over my shoulder. "Theo is having breakfast." Memories of last night, of her constant reassurance that he will solve the problem he's created, all come trickling back. How? How will he solve it?

"Are you going to join him or stand there all day staring at the door?"

"I'm—" I'm cut off when a door slams across the way, and we both look to see Penny leaving Theo's office. She looks as sexy as ever, despite being quite formally dressed.

"Oh, hi," she says, frowning at my attire. I feel my cheeks heating, my hands pulling at the sides of the robe. I might be embarrassed, but I can still sense the change in atmosphere. Judy's shoulders visibly rise.

"Made yourself at home, I see," Theo's mother snipes, tossing Penny a filthy look.

I recoil on Penny's behalf, but Penny just rolls her eyes and gets on her way. "See you, Izzy," she calls, disappearing through the door to the Playground.

Judy scoffs and returns her attention to me, practically spitting nails. "Tart," she mutters.

Ouch. "You don't like her?"

"Not particularly, and I dislike the fact that Theo has given her somewhere to live even more."

"She's living here?" I ask, surprised.

"Hopefully not for long." Judy approaches me and faffs with my robe, forcing a smile onto her face. "Have you and Theo made up?"

"I was just—"

"Have patience," she says, reaching for the door and pushing it open, encouraging me in. "He's trying so hard, Izzy."

I deflate, thinking it a waste of time to argue with his mother, and enter the dining room to face Theo. I look down the length of the long table, finding him at the end, a newspaper in one hand, a cup of coffee in the other. I can only see his top half, but I note he's casual today, wearing a simple black crew-neck T-shirt. His hair is a damp mess, his stubble bristlier than usual.

He looks...completely and utterly breathtaking.

I stand awkwardly at the entrance, fiddling with the tie of the robe while he slowly places his cup down blindly, watching me.

"Morning." He eventually breaks the silence with his rough but soft greeting.

"Morning," I parrot, my mouth beginning to water when I catch a whiff of freshly brewed coffee. The atmosphere is difficult, neither of us forthcoming with conversation, and I think about Theo's mother telling me to be patient. Easier said than done when you're dealing with such complexity.

A loud sigh travels down the table toward me and Theo drops

his paper. "Please, Izzy, come and sit with me." He pulls out the chair next to him.

It's not only Theo's request that kicks my legs into action, it's the aroma of that coffee. I settle on the chair and nod when he holds up the coffeepot. "Where did you sleep last night?" I ask while he pours. There were no signs that he'd joined me in bed. The covers on the other side were untouched, and I couldn't smell him on the sheets. The thought of the state of me and Theo look-ing at my drunken, unconscious being in his bed makes me shrink in my chair as I bring my coffee cup to my lips.

"I didn't sleep." He sits back, one hand resting lightly on the edge of the table.

"At all?"

"At all," he confirms, and we fall silent again, the tension build-ing between us. There's obviously lots both of us want to say, but neither he nor I seems willing to lead.

So I natter pointlessly some more, just to fill the uncomfortable silence. "You must be tired."

"I was thinking," he says, ignoring my statement.

I nibble at the inside of my mouth as Theo regards me closely. "Do I want to know what about?" I ask, my apprehension obvious.

He smiles a little, turning his hand over on the table. Naturally, I place mine in his, and he brings my knuckles to his mouth and rests his lips there. "I've been thinking about how I can make it up to you."

"By getting me my job back," I say, though my statement is lacking the curtness I intended. Probably a result of my tired-ness and rotten hangover. "But I can't see that happening after you caused anarchy. The police were already involved. Now I imagine the NHS will be pressing charges, as well as Sugden."

He rests his elbows on the table, now holding my hand in both of his. "There are many things I can influence, Izzy."

My mind goes off on a tangent, trying to decipher what he means by *influence*. It takes only a few seconds of considering, even with a fuzzy head. I reflect back to last night—to Judy telling me that Theo would fix things. Theo was with Andy, Judy's husband. He works for the police. He knew about my predicament, and I'm guessing he knows every other detail of the whole horrid situation. The lightbulb in my head pings on. "The police won't be contacting me for a statement, will they?"

He keeps me in place with serious eyes, shaking his head a little.

So I go on, everything clear. "There will be no charges pressed against you, either, will there? Not by Sugden, Susan, or the hospital security staff."

Theo shakes his head again.

I flex my fingers until he releases my hand, sitting back in my chair. He's done some terrible things. He told me so himself. But he's never been in jail. "Why are you not worried about the police?"

"Because they can't touch me."

I breathe in. "Why?"

"I deliver them lowlife scumbags like the bastard who attacked you and Penny in that alley the night I found you. He was wanted for dealing."

"And in return, they won't touch you?"

"Correct."

"So you keep them sweet?"

"It isn't just for my benefit. I'm taking dangerous men off the streets."

"You're dangerous," I point out.

"Are you scared of me?"

My jaw naturally tightens. "No."

"Case in point."

I gawk at him. "How the hell is it case in point, Theo? I'm one of the only lunatics who *isn't* scared of you."

"And that's all that matters to me," he replies evenly, like that really is the end of it. "Your job is still yours, Izzy."

I stare at him in utter disbelief. Just like that? But even if all of this disappears, I could never return to work. "Don't you see, Theo?" I ask, fighting to keep my arse on the chair instead of getting up and storming off. "If I go back to my job, do you think things will be easy for me? Susan might have been forced or intimidated into dropping her complaint, but I won't be able to pretend it never happened, any more than she will be able to. The atmosphere will be unbearable." I swallow down my anger, fighting to maintain a calm tone. "You think you can use your power of persuasion and your connections to the police to make all this go away? It's not that simple, Theo." There's a very faint line on his forehead, evidence of a frown he's trying to hold back. It only confirms my fear. He really did think it's that simple. That I could dance back into work like nothing happened.

"It sounds simple to me," he argues, looking slighted, confirming my thoughts.

"Well, it's not." I stand abruptly, and he looks up at me in shock. I think he actually expected me to fall to my knees in gratitude. Kiss his feet and reward him for getting me back the job that *he* lost. The man is insane. "Your skin might be thick and impenetrable, Theo, but mine is not. I care what people think. I care that the people I respect and value as friends think my boyfriend is a fucking maniac." I breathe in deeply as Theo sits back in his chair, quiet and accepting of my outburst. "I care that people look at you and think that you're a bully and probably keep me in my place with your iron fist. Maybe literally." I just catch him wincing as I turn and walk away from him, the anger that was clogging up my throat now turning into emotion, the tears building, the despair becoming too much to shoulder.

"Izzy, wait." He rounds me, ensuring he doesn't touch me, and blocks the doorway. I take in his bare feet, the thread of his worn jeans dragging the carpet as he steps toward me. "I would never hurt you."

I look up at him, my eyes brimming. "Not physically, no. But you're hurting me here." I thump my hand over my chest. "The hospital was my haven, Theo. It was the one place in the world I felt safe, and you've taken it away from me." I quickly look down, realizing I've said too much, and close my eyes, hoping he doesn't push me.

"Izzy, look at me," he begs, his hand reaching for mine slowly. I don't withdraw or stop him, but instead let him tentatively brush across my skin before he takes hold of my hand. I look up at him, finding sorrow and despair to match mine. "I want to be your safe haven," he whispers, lifting my hand to his cheek, holding it there. The feel of his bristle across my palm is harsh but so soft. I don't want it to be, but it's soothing.

I'm losing my battle to keep my emotion at bay, and tears tumble down my cheeks as he gently takes me in his arms. I feel overwrought and helpless, yet safer than I've ever felt before. He's taken away my safe place and replaced it with another, but my new safe place is probably impenetrable. It's made of steel and reinforced with iron. It's real, and it can truly protect me. It's him.

I sob into Theo's chest, my head a riot of troubled thoughts. I can have my job and the security of the hospital, or I can have Theo and the security of him. Simply him. And as I cling to him, my tears soaking into his T-shirt, my small body jerking in his strong hold, I silently accept that no one can keep me safer than Theo can. But I have to work. I want to keep doing what I love.

He sighs into my hair as he cups the back of my head, pushing me more and more into his chest, as if wanting to meld us together. And he holds me for the longest time until my jerks have subsided, and my tears finally stop falling.

"I'm sorry," he says on a sigh. "So sorry. I'll make it right, I promise." He frees me from his arms and smiles sadly as he wipes under my eyes. "Forgive me?"

How can I not? How can I reject him when he's looking at me like this, with sincerity and hope in his tired eyes? I swallow and nod, breathing out. "You need to control your temper."

He nods, looking away and falling into thought. It's reassuring, because I can see he's silently agreeing with me. "Come." He plants the gentlest of kisses on my forehead and then slowly turns me in his arms, leading me out with his palms engulfing my shoulders.

"Where are we going?" I ask, reaching up and sliding my hands onto his. I feel heat close in at my ear, my shoulders rolling up, my eyes closing.

"My room," he says, so seductively, the super low tone going *super* low into my groin. I bite my lip as he pushes me on up the stairs, sparks of anticipation dancing across my skin. "We're about to have make-up sex for the first and last time. Are you naked under my robe?"

My mouth is suddenly parched, so I nod. He growls mildly, flexing his hands beneath mine, a silent instruction to move them. The moment I peel them away, one of Theo's palms slips down to my waist, taking the tie of the robe. He tugs until it loosens, still walking us up the stairs. When we've reached the top, I'm steered right, and he grips the soft material at my shoulders in his fists. "Keep walking," he instructs, and I force my sight forward, focusing on the door to Theo's private quarters ahead. Cool air finds my breasts first, teasing my nipples into hard bullets, then crawls across the rest of my naked front. I shiver, concentrating on keeping my slow pace as Theo looms behind me, following my steps and drawing the robe away from my body. I hear the light thud as the mass of fabric hits the carpet. He's dropped it, and while I know it will be found by Jefferson before Theo is done with me, I haven't the inclination to tell him to pick it up. His arm extends past me to reach for the door, and his lips meet my naked shoulder. I turn my face into him, letting my eyes flutter open as the heat of his mouth on my skin chases away the coolness engulfing me. I'm hot, lustful.

"Please don't tie me up," I beg quietly, letting him at my face, his teeth nibbling across my cheek to my lips. I want him to let me touch him, feel him, to hold him like he holds me.

My plea is ignored, his front pushing into my back. I walk forward, hearing the door close behind me, and then I'm swooped into his arms and carried into his bedroom. He lays me on the bed, placing my hands over my head. I look up and see the bedposts. Then back down to see the cuffs he bought me in his hands. I hold my breath, watching as he unfastens the leather bands one at a time, as he walks on his knees and settles his jean-clad arse on his calves, fixing the cuffs around my wrists.

"I want to touch you," I murmur, locking eyes with him, hoping he sees in their depths just how much.

He pauses, straightening a little, looking down at his chest briefly before back at me. "Then touch me," he replies, taking my hand and resting it on his pec.

I relish the feel of him, but it isn't what I meant. "While you're making love to me."

He smiles, understanding, but goes back to his job of securing me. "I hope in time, sweetheart." He fixes me up with both cuffs and collects two long lengths of satin from the drawer beside the bed. He loops a length of material through each chunky metal hoop and ties them to the bedposts, pulling them taut so my arms are stretched to full length. I breathe in deeply, my legs shifting, my breasts aching painfully with need. This time, he leaves my legs free and straddles my waist, still fully clothed. A palm lands on the mattress at each side of my head, his face coming close to mine. I pant, my heart hammering a needy beat as I search his eyes, finding need in him, too. But on top of that, desperation, hunger, and, most of all, devotion. It's shining from his eyes like shards of hopeful light.

He lets his mouth gently brush over mine, from side to side, back and forth, and I moan, lifting my head to catch his lips. But he pulls away, and I whimper, letting my head drop back to the bed. He draws a perfect line down the bridge of my nose and onto my mouth. "Don't think," he breathes, dragging his thumb across my bottom lip. "Don't speak." Then he replaces his thumb with a worshipful kiss. "Just *feel* how much I want you. Feel how much I need you. I'm just Theo, Izzy." Keeping his body suspended on one arm, he reaches down with his other, his fingers walking their way across my stomach, down, down, down . . .

My back arches off the bed, my arms burning from stretching so much. He slips his fingers between my thighs and spreads me wide, watching me falling to pieces as a result of one single touch. My pants come short and fast as I struggle to breathe through the agonizingly pleasurable feeling of his fingers gliding over my flesh, his touch softly circling my tiny bud of screaming nerves.

"Feel nice?" he asks, his own chest heaving. He keeps his hand between my legs, playing with me while I'm rigid, and pulls his T-shirt off with his other, grabbing the hem and ripping it upward. I close my eyes and pray for help. "Does it feel nice, Izzy?"

"Yes," I answer into my darkness, the vision of his torso so potent, I can still see it perfectly behind my closed lids. One finger slips inside me, and I gasp, turning my face into my armpit, searching for somewhere to hide. He's suddenly moving, the abrupt loss of his weight on my hips and his finger plunged deep startling me. My eyes flip open and see he's removed his jeans already. The thick smoothness of his cock has me licking my lips. He climbs on me, looks down, grasps himself, levels up, and enters me with ease, sliding through my welcoming wetness and hitting home on a satisfied exhale of ragged air. Beads of sweat form across his top lip, glistening between his whiskers as the weight of his stare holds me in place. Theo stills, submerged the deepest he could be. Those blue eyes are so reverent, to the point they could hypnotize me. His forearms cradle my head. "Wrap your legs around me," he orders. "Tightly."

He doesn't need to ask me twice. My free legs coil around his perfectly formed waist and lock down, my ankles linking and pushing into his lower back. One would think my position would hinder his movements. But no. He starts to gently rock, the friction minimal but the fullness consistent, his slow grinding, circling, and rubbing working me up into a fevered mess. He's being delicate with me. Looking at me with adoration. His strength feels so right held between my locked thighs. His confidence is here, so is his domination, but there's something missing.

"I'm not feeling like much of a whore right now," I say, my forehead resting against his, his movements consistent and meticulously executed.

"Don't worry, sweetheart. I'm not feeling like much of a hard bastard right now, either."

I smile and ravage his mouth, and he lets me maul him for a few pleasurable moments. My kiss becomes hungrier and my internal muscles pull at him constantly, trying to draw his release forward, too. I'm not going to last much longer. "Are you close?" I ask, not bothering to try to hide my hope. "Tell me you're close."

"You go, baby."

"No." I cut the build back, seeking out the crook of his neck and burying my face there.

"Go," he orders again, tactically switching the direction of his rotations and stirring a tremor of pleasure that cuts right through me. My muscles lock.

"No, Theo." My arms start to yank and pull, my impending orgasm defying my orders and steaming forward.

"Go," he breathes, sliding his palm to my nape and lifting my head, holding his mouth to mine. "Take it and remember through the haze how good it feels. Me inside you. My cock surrounded by your pussy. My body owning yours." He sweeps his tongue through my mouth. "Remember how much you mean to me."

The orgasm slams into me with epic force and bends my body, injecting strength that defies my small frame, jolting Theo up as I scream my way through it. I lose control of everything, my body racking violently as pleasure burns through my bloodstream.

My legs fall limp, my head to the side, and I gasp for breath as he circles his groin, maximizing the sensations and the length of my release. He molds the back of my neck until I'm drained dry and boneless under the weight of him. "Oh God." I shudder, the aftereffects showing no signs of freeing me from the wonder of my release. It just keeps coming and coming, putting my heart under strain and sending my mind spiraling.

"That sounded good," Theo muses with deep satisfaction, rolling his hips on and on.

"Stop," I breathe, my clitoris starting to zing sensitively. My stomach muscles feel shredded, my skin clammy.

"I'll never stop." He leans down and nuzzles my face. "Give me your mouth." I turn into him, letting my mouth fall open in welcome. The soft roll of his tongue around mine has me moaning and humming, the sounds pleading as well as gratifying. I can't get enough of him. "I'm going to free your hands," he whispers past my lips. "I'm going to turn you over, and you're going to hold on to the bed, okay?"

I nod, eager, though slightly nervous about the power that I'm about to accept into my body from behind. Teeth lightly bite my lip and pull away, and he reaches to my wrists in turn and unfastens the leather cuffs. A satisfied smile creases his cheeks when he checks my wrists, clearly finding no friction marks. I don't have the chance to see for myself. One swift move sees him flipping me over to my hands and knees. "Hold on," he orders, taking my hands to the gold bar spanning the bed.

I grip hard, feeling my hips being pulled back as he's poised behind me, spreading my legs with his knee. My head drops, my lungs expanding in preparation.

"Arch your back, Izzy," he says, drawing a perfect straight line down my spine to my bum, leaving a trail of fire in his wake. I groan, my back bending to his will.

"Now that make-up sex is done, are you ready to be fucked like a whore?"

I swallow hard, nodding into my darkness, just as his palm collides with my flesh. A yelp, part surprise and part pain, jerks my body back, and my bum crashes into his groin. I get another swift slap in return.

"Be still," he growls, his hand skimming the skin of my abused arse.

My hold on the bar tightens, blood whooshing in my ears. The folds of my entrance get separated, and when the tip of his cock slips across my slickness, I grit my teeth. "Your pussy." He slides in, his voice shaking. "Oh Jesus."

The muscles of my walls greedily draw him into me, my hips rocking to accommodate his sheer size. Strong fingers dig into my flesh and hold me still, and I hear him working to control his labored breathing. Any minute now, he's going to power into action.

I need to be prepared, so I join Theo and try to regulate my ragged breaths.

It's futile.

The first crash of his body against mine catapults me forward on a scream. And from there, he finds his pace quickly, and he keeps it, pounding on, yanking me back onto him repeatedly until I'm dizzy and my throat is sore from my variations of screams and cries, ecstasy and pain, despair and delight. My arms brace against the bed, and the sounds of two people fucking wildly fill the room, probably even the whole damn mansion, maybe reaching as far as the Playground. How the bed is sustaining us is beyond me. He goes on and on, yelling, slapping my arse, and reaching down to feel my breasts. I begin to wonder how much more I can take when I hear Theo suck in air and hold it. He's on his way. I can feel the thickening of his dick even through the chaotic thrusting of our bodies.

"Oh, fuck," he bellows, slamming on harder. My mind blanks of everything except the unexpected orgasm that smashes into me with equal force as Theo's body. The power of it takes me out, and I collapse to the bed, Theo following me down and grinding his hips in smooth, effective rotations.

The sheets are wet beneath me, my hair damp, and my skin burning. I was just fucked like a whore. And, strangely, I feel more precious than ever with my big man twitching on top of me, his skin slipping over mine as my cheek rests on the pillow and I stare across the bed. "See how much I want you?" he pants, biting at my shoulder.

I beam wide, happy beyond description, and his mouth pauses. I feel him smile against my skin before he abruptly flips me to my back and pins me to the bed, my arms high above my head. His chest hovering above me, shimmering with sweat and undulating with his erratic breathing, only stretches my smile more, making my face hurt. How? How does he do this to me? He blows a cool stream of air across my cheek, dislodging a lock of hair that's stuck there. Then he grins, arching a brow as he scans my flustered face.

The vision of raw masculinity floating over me is just...it's just...just...I sigh. I've run out of words. Theo Kane is like marshmallow coated with steel. He's a big softy in a hard exterior. He's a certain kind of cut handsome that I think only I can see. Because the hard lines of his gorgeous face don't affect me like they do others. I don't tremble in my boots or shake with dread in his presence. Instead, I quiver with want and vibrate with need.

My gentleman sinner. "I want you, too," I say, and he smiles, closing his eyes and placing the wet skin of his forehead against mine.

But he doesn't say anything. He doesn't need to. I can feel his appreciation, hear it in his calming breathing, and smell it in the thick scent of sex in the air. And I wonder...is he speaking in code? I've fallen for him, so fucking hard, but for the first time, I think about how Theo sees me. How he feels. Am I just a strange fascination to him, because he finds himself hyperaware of me and my touch? Because he craves it? Likes it? My heart sinks a little, because I wish for so much more from him. Then he drops the most tender of kisses on my lips and my heart lifts again. I'm being stupid. He's given me no reason to doubt his intentions. Even his psycho behavior speaks of a man who cares.

"Let's get ready. You can come with me today." He peels his body away from mine and gets up off the bed. I quickly prop myself up on my elbows so I can indulge in the delight of his naked back as he strides to the bathroom. I cross one leg over the other and ogle the striking definition, my gaze climbing up his thighs, over the perfect swell of his arse, up to his back. I tilt my head and get a few precious seconds to admire his tattoo before he disappears through the doorway. I collapse back to the bed and smile. "Where are we going?" I call, hearing the spray of the shower kick in.

"I have a few errands to run."

What errands does a man like Theo Kane run? "I need clothes."

"Then we'll stop by your place." He appears at the door with a razor in his hand, a cheeky grin spanning his face. "Do you think Callum strangled Jess or fucked her?"

I bolt upright on the bed and mentally run through last night. When it comes back to me, I throw wide, wary eyes at Theo. He nods, silently telling me that I remember right, before he returns to the bathroom. I'm up like a bullet. "Which is more likely?" I ask, joining him by the Jack and Jill sink.

He swishes the water around the bowl, looking at me in the reflection of the mirror. My unabashed curiosity is clear, and Theo seems to find it amusing. "Knowing Callum, probably both."

My expression morphs into horror as Theo chuckles, flipping the tap off. "Knowing Callum? What, does murdering someone while he fucks them turn him on?" I'm getting very worried for my friend. I've not been able to read Callum from the second I met him, but his capabilities are pretty clear. He's as dangerous as Theo, if a little more in control of himself.

"He's not very patient."

"I need to ring Jess." I leave Theo at the sink to go in search of my phone.

"Hold up, panicky pants." Theo catches my wrist and pulls me back. "He won't hurt her."

" 'Panicky pants'?" I've never heard such a hard nut use such a wussy phrase.

He heaves his exasperation and returns to the mirror. "It's you. I turn into a pansy-talking pussycat when you're around."

His admission stirs an unreasonable amount of satisfaction in my tummy, and I jump up onto the counter of the sink to watch him shave. I sit up straight, my hands in my lap. "Is he involved with someone?"

"Callum is involved with many someones." He squirts some shaving gel in his palm before smoothing it over the roughness of his stubble.

"Oh," I breathe. "Like dancers?"

"Like dancers," he confirms. "He's my friend, but he's not exactly chivalrous."

I snort on an unattractive laugh. "Sounds like someone *I* know."

Theo's hands slow over his stretched neck, his eyes lazily turning onto me. "Do I not treat you like a queen?"

"Yes, but you fuck me like a whore." I'm not complaining. However, Theo's reference to Callum's bed habits has me all curious, not only for my friend and the man who has caught her eye, but for me and the man who has my heart. Did Theo sleep with the dancers? Did he see them as easy access? His *bed companions*. I definitely can't imagine any of them turned down the pile of leanness before me.

"No," he says out of the blue.

"No what?"

"No, I haven't slept with any of the girls who work for me."

"Did you read my mind?"

"Yes." He turns back to the mirror and leans in, checking the coverage of shaving cream on his face. "Keep those racing thoughts of yours under control, sweetheart."

I bite at the inside of my cheek, watching as he collects his razor and swishes it in the water. Has he ever treated another woman like a queen?

"Only my mother," Theo says, and I look at him, startled.

"You're freaking me out."

"Good. You freak me out every second of the day."

I have a satisfied smile on my face again, but it falls a little when my encounter with his mother in the hall earlier pops up in my mind. "Penny..."

"Definitely not Penny."

"But you're looking after her."

"I'm helping her get back on her feet."

I could laugh, but I hold back. She's definitely back on her feet. In six-inch heels. With her legs wrapped around a pole. "Who is she?"

"I told you, the daughter of an old friend." His answer is full and final, and I sigh, but move on before I annoy him with more questions.

"You know, you say Callum isn't exactly chivalrous, but he carried Jess over a huge puddle last night."

"He did?"

"Yes."

"Probably planned on drowning her in it."

I roll my eyes dramatically, and he laughs, bringing the razor to his cheek. "Wait!" I shout, making him pause with the blade an inch from his skin. I show him my hand and reach forward, taking the razor. "Don't shave."

"Why?"

"Because I like this." I smooth a palm over the roughness beneath the cream.

"You want me to keep it?"

"Yes." I drop the razor and pull the plug from the sink, draining the water and rinsing my hand.

"Then I'll keep it." He picks me up and places me on my feet, walking me back to the shower.

"You need to get all the cream off," I point out, letting him manipulate my steps.

He grins and claims my arms, holding them still before he dips his head and starts rubbing his cheeks against mine, coating me in the masculine scent.

"Hey!" I yell, laughing as I use my face to try to wrestle him away. "Theo, that tickles!"

He growls, not relenting until he has me in the shower and the water washes the cream away from both of us. His clear face comes into view, his smile bright, and a palm comes down onto my arse. "Turn around, hands on the wall."

I'm looking at the tiles faster than my self-respect should allow.

CHAPTER 20

Well, would you look at that," Theo muses as we pull up outside my apartment. I stare ahead, to the Mercedes that belongs to Callum.

"He's here?" I look at Theo, and Theo looks at me.

"Looks like it. Unless he couldn't get her body in the boot, so he carried it down to the common to dump it." He gets out and slams the door, grinning as he rounds the car to my side.

"That's not funny," I say as he opens the door and helps me out. I dash to the front door, fumbling to find my key as I go. I don't get to insert it into the lock. I don't even get the chance to locate it in my bag. The door swings open, and I'm knocked back a few steps by the sight of a bare-chested Callum.

"Fucking hell," I breathe, part shocked, part...well, shocked. I'm *really* shocked. My jaw is lax as my eyes, level with his ripped chest, drift in and out of focus. In reality, he's no more cut than my big man, but I'm getting used to seeing Theo's chest. I didn't think anything remotely similar could exist. I was wrong. I blink as I shake some life back into me, looking up into Callum's sleepy eyes.

"What time is it?" he croaks, looking past me to Theo.

"Ten, you lazy bastard." Theo's front meets my back as Callum grumbles under his breath, turning and wandering down the hall, his trousers undone and hanging low, a hand raking through his ruffed-up blond waves. I grin to myself but jump when Theo's mouth meets my ear.

"Keep your eyes to yourself," he whispers, pushing me onward.

My face screws up in guilt. "Don't know what you're talking about." I follow Callum, looking for Jess as I go. Where is she? When I enter the lounge, I find Theo's friend shrugging on his shirt. "Where's Jess?" I ask him, craning my neck to look into the kitchen.

He peeks up at me without lifting his head, fastening his belt, but he doesn't speak. What's going on?

"So you stayed here last night?" Theo asks, dropping to the chair in the corner of the room. He looks stupidly too big and mean for the quirky floral piece.

Callum's lead gaze moves across the room, from me to Theo. "And?"

"All right, grouchy pants." Theo chuckles softly.

Callum's hard face creases into a frown. "'Grouchy pants'?"

"Don't worry," I jump in, dropping my bag. "I was 'panicky pants' this morning."

Theo scowls at me, and Callum grunts. "Woman's turning you into a fucking pussy."

"Speaking of pussy..." Theo sits back in the chair, working hard on keeping a casual persona. It's a piss take. He knows it, I know it, and Callum knows it, too.

"No," Callum grunts, short and sharp.

"Then why the fuck are you here?"

"Because I've never in my life seen a woman so drunk, and I figured it was dangerous."

"Because she wasn't sober enough to give you her consent?"

"Fuck you," Callum snaps, shoving his feet into his shoes as he points at me.

I recoil. "What the hell have I got to do with it?"

Callum smiles tightly. "She's your mate. You like her, and Theo likes you. Which means should anything happen to her, you'll wail, Theo will have to deal with it, and I will get earache as a result."

My eyebrows are high and surprised, and Theo bursts into a fit of laughter across the room. I look at him like he's lost his mind, because it sounds like he has. I've never heard him laugh so hard. "You're a twat, Callum Tyler." Theo chuckles around his insult. "A fucking twat."

Callum grabs his car keys. "Again, fuck you."

"When was the last time you got some?"

"Fuck you." He strides out of the room.

"A while, then?" Theo shouts to his back. "Why would that be, Callum? There are plenty of women willing to drop their knickers for you."

"Fuck you." The door slams, and Theo continues falling to pieces in the chair, rubbing at his eyes.

"What was all that about?" I ask.

He breathes some calm back into him, letting the odd chuckle slip here and there. "He likes her," he finally says.

I scoff, marching out of the room to find Jess. "Could have fooled me." I swing her bedroom door open and find her half dangling off her bed, dribbling into the pillow. "Jess." I shake her, dodging the flailing arm that swipes at me. "Jess, wake up."

"Go away."

"Callum just left. Did you know he stayed?"

She lunges upward like she could have been electrocuted, her wild hair covering most of her face. She brushes it away and finds me. "What?"

"Callum, he just left. He stayed?"

"I don't know, did he?" She scans the bed, her forehead heavy, clearly trying to rewind through her memories and find the information she needs. "Oh, no. Please, no."

"What?"

"I threw up." She heaves, like she could vomit again. "And I might have told him I had an orgasm when he carried me over that puddle."

"You didn't?" I'm as horrified as she is, praying she dreamed that part.

She fake-cries, falling to the mattress and burying her face. "I fucking did."

I shake my head at her in disappointment. But I'm laughing on the inside. My cool, together friend has been bamboozled by a man. I never thought I'd see the day. "You twat."

"I am. I'm a twat."

"I need to get changed. And you need to get all that alcohol out of your system before you start your shift tonight."

Her head shoots up, panicked, her blond hair sticking out here and there haphazardly. "He's gone?"

"Yep. And he hasn't had any for a while, despite there being plenty on offer." I waggle a suggestive eyebrow at her. "Just thought you should know."

She blows a raspberry and plumps the pillow under her head. "I guarantee he's heading straight back to the Playground to let off some steam with one of the strippers."

"Dancers," I correct.

"Do they put out?"

"Sounds like it, but I think he likes you."

"What makes you say that?" she asks. "The vomit on my chin?"

"And your fetching hairdo this morning," I say with a smile as Jess pats down her wild locks. "I'm heading out with Theo."

"How are things?"

I shrug. "Well, I won't be arrested, by all accounts, and my job is still mine if I want it. But I need to think about what I do next. I can't stroll back in there like nothing happened."

"And Theo?"

I back away from the bed. "The man has me dancing on the edge of frustration and complete heaven." Reaching the door, I take the handle, mirroring Jess's soft smile. "Catch you later."

I make my way to my room, and once I'm dressed and ready, I find Theo still looking out of place in the floral chintz chair, his phone to his ear. I pull on my leather jacket as he looks me up and down, clearly approving of the baggy shirt and ripped jeans I've thrown on. "Half hour?" he says into the phone and nods before hanging up and gazing at me thoughtfully.

"What?" I ask, beginning to fidget under his concentrated stare.

He gets up from the chair and comes over to collect me, leading me out of my apartment. "I was just trying to comprehend how much I adore you."

Good Lord, he's sure making up for his stupidity. Does *adore* equal *love*? I quickly bat those thoughts away. "Where are we going?"

"Somewhere." He helps me into the car, leaving me in a high state of curiosity. Where's *somewhere*?

* * *

Somewhere is a back street in Soho. Theo pulls his Bentley up to the curb, and I get out, looking around for any clue as to where we're heading. There's nothing obvious—no shops, restaurants, or bars. I throw my bag onto my shoulder and eye Theo as he pulls off his shades. His silence is beginning to get under my skin. A few long easy strides have him by my side, collecting me and pushing on down the street. I let him direct me until we arrive at some steps that lead down to a glossy black door, and I look for a sign that might tell me where we are. Nothing.

"This way," Theo says, taking the steps before me and reaching back for my hand. I accept and descend with him, constantly searching for clues as to where we are and what we might be doing. He presses a silver buzzer, and the door opens a few seconds later, revealing a man. *Jesus!* I recoil, alarmed. He's huge, and the whole left side of his face is covered in tribal art that creeps down his neck and disappears past the collar of his white T-shirt. Holy Lord, he looks frightening.

"Stan," Theo says, letting him move back before coaxing me inside. I don't realize that my grip of Theo's hand has tightened until he flexes his fingers, looking down at me with reassuring eyes. I smile a small smile, moving into his side, and he catches me and tucks me in.

"Kane." The tattooed giant presents his hand and waits for Theo to accept. "Good to see you, my friend." He smiles, wide and toothy, shaving off ninety percent of his scariness with the friendly gesture.

"This is Izzy, my girlfriend."

Stan turns that friendly smile on me. "Theo Kane's girlfriend, huh?" He waits for Theo to release his hand before offering it to me. "Now that's a title one should respect."

"'One' as in you, or 'one' as in me?" I ask, shaking his hand.

He laughs and makes off down the corridor, gesturing for us to follow. "Both, darling."

We cross the threshold into an open-plan space with bifold doors spanning the entire back wall, leading onto a small but well-kept garden. The huge area is sparsely furnished and divided into a kitchen, dining space, and lounge area. Theo pulls a chair out for me at a large white table, and I take a seat.

"Coffee?" Stan asks, bringing a coffeepot over to the table and settling with us. "Or something hard?" He flips Theo a grin.

"Coffee's fine," Theo replies, seeming to ignore Stan's vague joke.

"Maybe *I* need something harder." He holds up the coffeepot to me and I nod. Who is this guy and why are we here? And, more worryingly, why would either of them need the hard stuff? It's eleven in the morning, for goodness' sake.

Theo levels an almost impatient expression on Stan as he pours my coffee, and I wrap my palm around the mug when it's handed to me. Then I wait for either man to shed some light on what's going on.

"So." Stan sits back in his chair, his eyes crossing from me to Theo constantly. "How's life treating you?"

"You've not been at the Playground for a few months," Theo says, ignoring his question. "Is winning becoming boring?"

Stan laughs lightly. "There's only one man left to take on, and he won't fight me."

"You don't want him to," Theo retorts seriously, slight menace in his words. "You have talented hands. We wouldn't want to fuck them up."

Stan looks down at his hands with a smile. "Very true."

My head goes from side to side, trying to keep up with the conversation. "You're a fighter?" I ask Stan, seeing a perfect image in my mind's eye of him in the cage at the Playground.

"It's my other talent." He winks, and then nods toward Theo. "Your man here refuses to take me on."

"I don't want to tarnish your perfect record," Theo says, stroking the side of his mug.

"Or break my talented hands?" Stan laughs, showing them to Theo. "You're so thoughtful." An edge of sarcasm is there. "Are you telling me you've developed a conscience?"

"No, I'm reminding you that I don't fight anymore."

"Shame." Stan sighs. "I miss the bloodshed."

My eyes shoot to Theo, finding him shaking his head a little. He used to fight? Bloodshed? A long licking shiver travels down my spine, making me sit up in my chair. I can only imagine what damage he's capable of.

Theo looks across to me, sensing my reaction to this news, his hand falling to my knee and squeezing. "My days in the cage are behind me."

My mind is spinning off some very vivid images of Theo pulverizing many men. Who would be stupid enough to take him on? He's dangerous and capable of serious damage when he's in full control of himself. And when he's not . . . I shudder, dreading the thought. "I didn't know that you ever did," I reply quietly.

"Oh, he did." Stan chuckles. "Anyone stupid enough to challenge him."

"Like you," Theo counters. "But lucky for you, I'm retired."

"At thirty-one? You have years left in you."

"Yes, but the men who faced me in that cage didn't by the time I was done with them."

"True story," Stan agrees, looking off into the distance, like he's reminiscing. "Your moves, man. It was like watching a dance," he muses thoughtfully. "A beautiful dance."

Theo shifts in his chair, obviously uncomfortable. Of course Theo's moves were fluid and graceful. It's how he escaped being touched. Otherwise, I'm guessing the level of damage inflicted on his opponents would have been irreparable. Any man who entered the cage with Theo Kane was dancing with death, quite literally.

Theo squeezes my knee, catching my attention. I'm grateful for the respite from such sobering thoughts. "Stop thinking," he orders me gently. Then he looks over to Stan. "Can we get on with this?"

"Sure. Let's move to where the magic happens." Stan's chair scrapes the floor as he stands and claps his hands together, rubbing them. "Let me get my cuffs."

I rise from my chair with Theo's help. "Cuffs?" I ask, looking up at him as he guides me into the garden and down the path to the back of a separate building.

"Yes, cuffs."

The room we enter looks clinical, with a huge black chair in the center, a couple of stools, and white cupboards around the circumference. Framed art hangs on the walls, and a window on the far side shows a waiting area full of people flipping through folders. Stan pulls the blind and they all disappear.

"You're getting another tattoo?" It never occurred to me before now, when a pair of metal handcuffs are clanging in Stan's hands, to wonder how someone managed to ink Theo without having their head ripped off. "He's going to cuff you?"

"Damn straight I am." Stan laughs as Theo gets on the black chair. "I'm brave, but I'm not that brave."

Theo gives him a tired look, pulling his T-shirt up over his head and casting it aside. "Here," he says, pointing to his left pec.

"Over the heart." Stan inspects the taut skin of Theo's chest, slipping on some glasses. "Cute."

"Stop talking." Theo rests back in the chair, the insane muscles of his torso rippling as he goes, and raises his arms over his head, draping them over the back of the chair.

Stan holds the cuffs up to Theo and waits for a nod before rounding him and locking them over his wrists and through a metal bar on the back. "Okay?" he asks once he's done, standing back. A swift yank from Theo demonstrates the security of his arms. "Hey, don't break my chair."

"You'd rather I break your neck?" Theo retorts.

"Fair point." Stan pulls on some rubber gloves, snapping the latex around each wrist for effect. The sharp sound makes me flinch as I sit as quiet as a mouse in the corner, watching in fascination. Stan gets to work quietly, laying a piece of tracing paper over

Theo's pec, making his jaw quickly tense as Stan's eyes become noticeably very wary. "All right?" he asks.

"Just get on with it." Theo closes his eyes and breathes in, though I know he's not bracing himself for the pain that is soon to come. He's bracing himself for Stan's touch.

I inch forward on my chair, trying to see what Stan is outlining on Theo's skin, but it's impossible when Stan leans in, getting up close and personal with Theo's big chest. I scowl to myself, frustrated and intrigued by what tattoo he could be getting. More religious symbols? Maybe a prayer to match the praying hands, huge cross, and rosary beads. He said they're there to remind him that he's broken God's rules. It's a little backward, if you ask me, since Theo isn't showing any signs of changing that. I'm certain God wouldn't condone holding a man at gunpoint. Theo has done some terrible things. I swallow and sit back, my eyes on the man who has stolen my heart. Is that a crime? Is it bad that I've fallen for him? I ponder that over and over as Stan works, not even getting close to reaching a conclusion. Can something be terrible and wonderful at the same time?

Once Stan's finished tracing the outline, he sits back and indicates for Theo to look. And once Theo's given a sharp nod of approval, I'm once again trying to crane my neck and get a peek, to no avail. The high-pitched buzzing sound of the mechanical needle kicks in, and Stan slowly moves in to Theo's chest, pulling his already taut skin tauter. There's a flinch from Theo, accompanied by the clang of the cuffs against the metal bar on the back of the chair. It makes Stan recoil slightly, his hands coming away from Theo's chest as it expands on a deep inhale. The sharp buzzing stops.

"We good, man?" Stan asks, watching him closely.

I look to Theo, just as his eyes meet mine. His face is blank, but his rough jaw is tight, and in this moment, I realize he's sought me out to stabilize himself. His chest deflates slowly and his breathing falls into a smooth, easy flow. "We're good," he confirms, keeping his eyes on me as he rests the side of his face on the inside of his big arm.

I smile, relaxing a little in the knowledge that he's siphoning his calm from me. I'm soothing him. Will that become a consistent thing in our relationship? Can it be? I love the thought of being his peace. Of feeding him the calm he needs.

The buzzing kicks in again, and I keep my gaze glued to Theo's as Stan resumes work, at the same time thinking about helping him. I'm back to therapy. He needs therapy. Would he consider that? For me?

There's not one more flinch from Theo. Stan works easily while I maintain my connection with Theo, knowing it's helping him. I lose track of time, my focus stolen by the stallion of a man staring at me like I'm the only thing in this room. Because to him, I am.

"Done," Stan declares, rubbing a tissue over the area and sitting back, his head cocked to the side as he inspects his work. "Simple but effective, I guess." He places his tools on the table and takes a pot of Vaseline. "Happy?"

Theo looks down at his chest, lifting his head from the chair. "Perfect," he confirms.

Stan smears a dollop of petroleum jelly across the area and grabs a square piece of gauze. I'm rising from my chair mechanically, moving closer, eager to finally get a glimpse of the design Theo chose. But Stan has covered the area already.

I pout like a little girl. "When do I get to see?" I ask, not bothering to hide my disappointment. He brought me along to help him, and I don't even get to see it?

Stan moves back, pulling off his gloves as Theo rattles the cuffs, a silent order for me to free him. "Later," he tells me, and I scowl at him. He's restrained. I could peel away that tape and look, and there would be nothing he could do about it. I eye the large rectangular padding on his chest, nibbling my lip. "Don't even think about it, Izzy," Theo warns, jerking his hands again. "Come here."

My nose wrinkles in irritation as I obey, moving around the back of the chair. I show him my hands and wait for him to nod before I flip the lever on each handcuff, freeing him. He sits up, rubbing at his wrists and rolling some life back into his shoulders, while Stan raises the blind at the window, revealing the waiting room full of people again. I wander over and scan the area, seeing other rooms leading off the space, most with the doors open, showing people in chairs being inked. "Is this your shop?" I ask Stan over my shoulder.

"Certainly is." He joins me by the window. "The part out there is for your average Joes. I only work on private clients."

I nod, looking around at the variety of people sitting and waiting. Some look like hard-core ink fans, arms and legs covered, and others look like they don't know if they really want to be here. A young girl catches my eye, holding her friend's hand tightly as she points out a small heart in a folder being shown to her by a heavily pierced guy crouched before her. She looks terrified. Stan must see my line of sight, because he starts chuckling. "Addiction is the only danger," he says, and I look at him, his profile clear and free from ink until he turns toward me, revealing the other side of his face. "It's just for effect." He winks, and I laugh.

"It works." I return my attention to the waiting room beyond the glass, hearing the soft pound of Theo's stride approaching behind me. "I might get one," I muse, smiling to myself.

His chest meets my back and his mouth meets my ear. "I'll hold your hand," he whispers. "What would you have?"

I ponder that for a few moments, leaning back into him. "I don't know. Maybe something like Stan's."

Theo chuckles softly and Stan belts out a roar of a laugh. "I don't have a death wish, Izzy. You can source another artist if you plan on ruining that pretty face."

I grin from ear to ear...but the grin plummets when a lone man across the shop catches my eye. My blood runs cold, my body locking up against Theo.

No.

No, it can't be.

I blink, trying to breathe steadily, trying to clear my vision, which is being hampered by relentless flashbacks. When that doesn't work, I close my eyes. But that doesn't stop the visions, either. I look out the window again, and the sight of *him* robs me of breath. His face, sharp and pointy, hasn't changed one bit.

He's here.

Oh God.

I spin around without thinking, nearly meeting Theo's bare chest face-first, panic preventing me from playing it cool.

"What is it?" Theo's bent and in my face quickly, his worried eyes searching mine. I just stare at him, my face undoubtedly a picture of dread. "Izzy?"

I grab some reason amid my chaos, pushing back the memories that are ambushing me and bringing my nasty past into my present. "Nothing." I shake my head, praying the bastard doesn't look up from his phone and see me through the window, while simultaneously praying that Theo doesn't force me into explaining. "It's hot in here," I mumble, naturally skirting past Theo so I don't touch him. And not just because I *shouldn't* touch him. I don't want him to feel my trembles. "I just need some air." My pace is steady but shaky as I leave Theo and Stan behind, breaking out into the garden at the back. I shut the door to Stan's studio and drink in valuable air, struggling to calm my racing heart. "He didn't see me," I tell myself, blowing out air loudly. Damn it, why is he here? I'm hundreds of miles away from my past.

I stagger forward with a startled yelp when the door behind me opens abruptly, and Theo appears, looking no less concerned than when I scampered away. Pulling myself together is of paramount importance before I clue Theo in to what's got me all jumpy and anxious. I'll never be able to explain without going into the sordid details. Theo will lose it. I can't say that I wouldn't like to see the nasty bastard in pain, but I also don't want my past being dredged up. I don't want Theo to know what he did. It's shameful, disgusting. Unthinkable.

But amid the chaos of my mind, I manage to note something. My fear is more about having to tell Theo about my horrid past, rather than fear of what that man might do to me, how he might hurt me again. Because I'm stronger now, I know I am. And because with Theo by my side, he can't touch me. But Theo can touch *him*. And crush him. Possibly even kill him. Possibly?

"Hey," I squeak, swallowing and straightening my spine. I'm fooling myself. I'm spooked, and he knows it.

"What's going on?" His T-shirt is in his hand, and he's in no rush to put it on.

"Nothing's wrong." I divert my gaze from his magnificent chest, looking as guilty as I sound.

He growls. "Either tell me what's got you behaving like a frightened animal, or I'll go back in there and find out for myself."

Panic makes a feast of me, eating me up from the inside out as I face Theo. "I just want to go." I reach for him without warning, and he catches my hand, holding it tightly. It's comforting me, but it's also warning me.

His lips straighten and his neck muscles bulge from the strain of his clenched teeth. "Don't make me go back in there, Izzy."

My bottom lip begins to quiver, annoying tears brimming in my eyes. The sight of me in such a state obviously tips him over the edge, and he whirls around, fighting to get his T-shirt on as he steams back into Stan's private studio. "Theo!" I yell, rushing after him. "Theo, please!" I go to grab him, but my mind stops me, telling me that his growing rage will hinder his awareness of me. I break into a sprint and overtake him, slamming my back into the door that will take him into the waiting area, blocking his way. "Please," I gasp, shaking my head as I look across to Stan. He's observing quietly, probably wondering if Theo is about to destroy his shop in a temper.

"Talk to me, Izzy," Theo demands, placing a palm against the wood beside my head. "Now."

Closing my eyes, I search for the strength I need to unravel my tangled thoughts and figure out what to do for the best. "I'll tell you," I breathe, deciding the promise of information is the best way to coax Theo away.

I haven't seen *him* for nearly ten years, and if I'm lucky, I won't ever again. I just need to get Theo out of here before he makes my presence known to the bastard or I'm forced to explain. "Just not here and now." I open my eyes and let him see the pleading in them. "When we get back to your place, I'll tell you."

His nostrils flare, and he glances out the window. Theo knows there's someone in that room I'm distressed to see. He knows he wants to do that person damage, even before he knows why I'm so upset.

I wait, anxious, and after a few tense moments, Theo pushes off the door and seems to realign himself. He seems to. But I know him, and I know it's taking everything in him not to barge into the waiting room and hunt down what's spooked me. "Let's go." He turns and strides out, leaving me to follow, like if he delays his escape, he might change his mind and do serious damage.

"Good luck," Stan says on a sympathetic, nervous laugh.

"Thanks." My nerves are totally frayed as I follow my big, highly tense man back to the car, the silence agonizing. I settle in the passenger seat of Theo's Bentley and look straight ahead, avoiding the pulsing body next to mine.

He curses under his breath and starts the car, pulling out of the space with a roar of the engine and speeding off down the road. His mood only reinforces my decision to get him away from my past so there's no chance of it tarnishing my present. I want to pretend that part of me doesn't exist.

The drive back to Theo's home is long and difficult. He's wound up like a tight spring, and I fear the damage he could do if the resistance gives and he lets loose.

Jefferson looks surprised when he meets us under the canopied drive, but he lets Theo guide me past without a word. The housemaid isn't waiting in the entrance hall with his drink, ready to take his coat, and the two big dudes who always flank the door are missing. I'm led up the stairs, into his private quarters, and the door is virtually slammed behind us.

"Talk," he demands harshly, pointing to the couch in order for me to sit.

"I'm not telling you a thing," I retort, turning my back on a shocked face and walking away. Call me sly, call me bang out of line, I don't care. I'm not telling him, not only because I fear the repercussions when he hunts down the man who nearly destroyed me, but because I never want to think about it ever again. And I don't want Theo to know about my horrid past.

"Izzy!" Theo's booming voice causes me to flinch as I enter his bedroom, making me swing the door with more force than I intended to. It slams, making the walls shake as I run across to the bathroom, knowing he'll be coming after me. As I turn to shut the door, I just catch sight of his raging face. He looks every bit as frightening as most perceive him to be.

I flip the lock and stand back, waiting for the inevitable banging as I try to catch a breath. But there's no bang. Theo walks right on in, the force of his shoulder making the lock ping off in surrender, with no scream of protest. His heaving frame fills the doorway as I move back. I'm not scared. Not of him and his threatening, hulking presence. I'm scared that I'm going to be forced into sharing something I don't want to share. And I'm scared that he'll drop me like filth if he knows.

"You said you would tell me." He grinds the words out, pointing an accusing finger at me.

"I don't want to talk about it."

"Izzy, just tell me." His entire torso expands with his deep breath of patience. "Otherwise, I'm left imagining all kinds of shit, and I don't like any of it."

And that's just one more reason to keep my mouth shut. So I shake my head.

"Damn it, Izzy!" He marches toward me and seizes my arms, and I cower, my chin dropping to my chest, hiding my building tears. "Tell me what the fuck happened to you before I lose my fucking mind." He gives me a small shake, further emphasizing his frustration.

I can't help it—tears fall from my eyes, landing in big splashes on the bathroom floor. I'm angry I'm crying. Angry I'm giving my emotions to that scumbag. I'm angry he's affecting me like this.

Theo moves his hands to my neck and tilts my head back, forcing me to face him. His angry cobalt eyes take me in, softening by the second. "Shit," he curses, yanking me into him and giving me a bone-crushing cuddle. The sanctuary and comfort of his big chest overwhelms me, and all I can do is cling to him. Hold him. Remind myself that I have him. My feet leave the floor and my legs curl around his waist, searching for more security. I feel untouchable in his embrace. I fear nothing, except for how deeply Theo is penetrating my heart, working his way soul-deep into me.

But most of all, I fear how much I like him there. And how much I need him.

"I'm sorry," he murmurs into the soft, sensitive space beneath my earlobe. I cling tighter in response, constricting the muscles in my arms and legs. He drops to his knees, holding me in place, and starts to pull his face from the crook of my neck, kissing his way over my ear and onto my cheek. "I won't force you." Finding my lips, he kisses me reverently, fisting my hair possessively but gently. His shoulders are locked in my arms, keeping him as close as possible to me as I meet his tongue.

And we stay there, on the bathroom floor, lost in each other for several minutes, kissing, holding, and calming each other. It's peaceful, all stress and anxiety being gradually chased away.

"Look at me," he orders, moving a fingertip to my chin and breaking our kiss. When he has my eyes, he smiles sadly. It's a smile of defeat. It's a sad smile of realization, because he knows I'm never going to share my burden with him. "I care too much about you," he affirms, leaning in and kissing my cheek. "I just want to keep you safe. And it kills me when you're upset. But I won't push you if you don't want me to. I can forget my needs if it's what *you* need. Anything for you, Izzy. Am I making myself clear? You come first."

I nod, grateful and relieved, so needing to hear him say that. He's got a hold of his rage. He's realized what's important, and my past is not.

Theo stands, lifting me with him, and carries us to his bed. I only release him when he collects my arms from behind his neck, and I do it begrudgingly. I sit against the headboard as he settles on his knees before me. "Let me show you something," he says, pulling his T-shirt up over his head. The large piece of protective gauze virtually covers his entire pec, and it is one big pec.

I watch as he picks at the corner of the tape and starts to pull it away, revealing reddened skin, slick with greasy jelly. Then the scroll of letters begin to reveal themselves, from right to left, so I'm forced to read it backward. I tilt my head, sinking my teeth into my lip.

By the time Theo has peeled the bandage away entirely, I'm transfixed by what is before me, elegantly scrolled across his pec. I read it again and again, my fingertips resting on my lips, like they might prevent me from breathing out my surprise. Of course, they don't, and I release a loud, shaky breath. "Theo..." I trail off, unable to find any words beyond his name.

He moves forward on his knees and takes my hand from my mouth, placing it on his chest. My touch slips across his slick skin and over the gray letters. "Read it to me," he whispers, encouraging me to feel, holding my wrist in place as my fingers dance across the lengths of script. "Read it to me, Izzy."

I look up at him through my lashes, stunned by what he's done. "Why?" I ask. "Why did you do this?"

"Just read it."

I look back down to his chest, my hand now covering part of the text, and flex my fingers until he allows me to remove my touch. And I read to myself.

My love for her holds me prisoner.
Her faith leaves me in awe.
Her hope encourages mine.
And her touch reaches my soul.
She is my peace.
My cure.
My love.

I flick my eyes up to his face as I try to push back the growing lump. "What is this?"

"Read it to me. I want to hear you read it."

I don't need to look back down at his chest. Those seven lines are branded on my mind and heart. My soul. "My love for her holds me prisoner." I swallow, breathing through my task. "Her faith leaves me in awe." I close my eyes, my heart pulsing in my ears. "Her hope encourages mine," I whisper, forcing my lids to open. He nods, bringing my hand to his lips and kissing it softly. I look down to his pec, my bottom lip quivering uncontrollably as I force myself to go on. "And her touch reaches my soul." I clench my teeth together, the words becoming distorted through my tears.

He's suddenly moving, taking my hands in his and tugging me closer. "She is my peace," Theo continues for me. "My cure." He kisses the corner of my mouth, so very gently. "My love. Do you understand, Izzy?" he asks, searching my welling eyes. "Do you realize how I feel about you?"

I stare at him as he stares at me, unwavering.

He swallows. "Everything I do is because I am in love with you. Not because I'm a fucking madman. Not because I thrive on violence. It's because I fucking love you."

I'm shocked into silence and stillness. And I can't breathe.

"I don't want you to say anything," he whispers, collecting air. It's a good thing he's not expecting me to speak, because I'm incapable. I'm at a loss. Stunned. He clamps his eyes closed for the briefest of seconds, though I expect in the short space of time that they're hidden from me, he collects a lifetime's worth of courage. He sighs, like it's a burden, and I will my body to relax in his hold, but I'm too damn shocked. "I just feel like you should have some warning."

I find my voice, his choice of words helping me. "Warning?" Like it could be dangerous for Theo to love me?

"I don't think you'll find my love easy to accept," he murmurs sadly. "I think you'll find it overbearing and suffocating."

I hesitate for a beat. "Why?"

"Because my instinct is telling me to hide you from the world and devote my life to keeping you safe." He watches me, gauging my reaction. I hope he's not disappointed. I smile, and my body goes lax, and my heart skips a beat. Those words are golden, probably the most reassuring thing he could ever say to me.

"I've already accepted it," I tell him quietly, straight-faced and cool. "Because I've fallen in love with you, too." His eyes widen as I swallow down the ball of emotion growing in my throat.

"I told you I didn't expect you to say anything."

"You need to know." I move forward, showing him my hands. He nods, and I place them gently on his muscled torso. He sucks in air and holds it, and I look up at him, finding him watching my hands as they glide over the finely tuned planes of his chest. "I feel like you should have some warning." I mirror his words quietly, and his eyes shoot to mine. I hold them. "Because I don't think you'll find my love easy to accept." I say what I know to be true.

"Only because I don't deserve it," he whispers, resting his hands over mine. "You are a good person, Izzy." He dips and places his forehead on mine. "I am not."

I close my eyes and let that statement sink in. I know he lives on the wrong side of the law, and I also know that it won't discourage me from loving him. To me, he is simply Theo. To me, he is comfort and love. I lift my hands from his chest and let him guide them over his shoulders, and then I move in, clinging to him tightly. I move my face to his neck, kissing it softly, my way of telling him I don't care. Besides, I'm choosing to see Theo as a saint, not a sinner. He actually helps save lives. By using the scumbags as bargaining chips to his own advantage, he is, in fact, helping the women who fall victim to anger and beatings. How could I not support that?

"Izzy," he breathes wearily. "I'm wired to charge when I feel threatened. It's the way I'm built. It's who I am. And that instinct has only grown stronger since I met you."

I press my lips together and blink some clearness into my vision. Theo's instinct is to fight under threat. To eliminate the danger. I cup his stubbled cheek, and he closes his eyes, nuzzling into my touch. "I understand."

"I realize that the best thing I can do when you're upset or distressed is to get you away from the cause. Not add to it. It might just take me a while to train myself."

I smile sadly, fully comprehending how much it takes for him to not only admit it, but actually do it. "I need to keep you," I say, leaning in and resting my mouth on his. "I need to know you're not going to do something silly and give reason for someone to take you away from me."

"Oh Jesus, Izzy." He pushes his lips to mine and swallows me up in his kiss, holding me so tightly in his strong, safe arms. "I'm not worthy of your patience, your compassion, or your bravery to take me on."

I hush him and embrace him, and he falls to his back, taking me with him. Resting my cheek on his shoulder, I stare across the vast expanse of his chest, reading the words he's had emblazoned there. All of them are so profound, but one line I read over and over again.

My love for her love holds me prisoner.

I reach across to place my finger on the start of the words, smiling when Theo's hand catches mine before my touch meets his skin. I wait for him to lower my hand to his chest, and then I ghost across the script slowly. And I wonder, does Theo realize that his love makes me feel free? With Theo in my present, I know my past can't touch me.

CHAPTER 21

It's only been three days since I was asked to leave the hospital, and despite Theo keeping me busy, I feel like I'm slowly going out of my mind. I've had three days off before; it's not alien, but the knowledge that I can't return to work makes this stretch different. My job might be waiting for me, but I can't go back. Not after everything that has happened.

I've researched positions throughout many of the London hospitals, and while there are plenty of vacancies to apply for, and I'll apparently have a glowing reference from Susan, I'm stalling. I don't know why. I feel safe with Theo, but vulnerable without my job. I feel comforted by his presence in my life, but anxious about depending on him too much. It's all confusing and very conflicting.

As I suspected, the police haven't been in touch. I asked Jess to drop off a letter of resignation yesterday and a letter of apology to Susan. I don't expect it to make any difference, but I wanted her to know how sorry I am for what happened. I also asked Jess to check up on Mable. The dear old lady told her to tell me that the pain is still a five and her hip replacement went well. It brought a smile to my face.

I've also been reassured that Percy's son has been...how did

Theo put it? Taken care of. I balked when he told me that, and he saw it, smiling as he explained that there was no more damage for him to do, even if he wanted to. Apparently, the man caved under the pressure of Theo and Callum's ominous presence and confessed his injuries were the result of a run-in with some unsavory types he owed money to. I expect he had a gun held at his temple while he confessed.

Thankfully, Theo hasn't pressed me any more on my little episode at Stan's tattoo studio, and I chose not to mention it to Jess, either. Almost as if not talking about it means it never happened, which is just the way I want it.

As I wander into the kitchen, Jess looks up from her coffee, her eyebrows bunched. "It's seven in the morning, Izzy."

"I couldn't sleep." I set about making my own coffee.

"Did you apply for any of the positions I forwarded to you?" she asks as she taps away at her phone.

"No." Not one of the jobs I looked at yesterday morning compared to my previous position. I realize beggars can't be choosers, but still. I stop myself thinking that I shouldn't be in this position, because it has me momentarily cursing Theo to hell and back again.

"What about the nurse bank?"

"I'm thinking about it," I say to appease her, splashing milk into my mug. I turn, armed with my coffee, and give her a wry smile. "How's Callum? Any more puddle-induced orgasms?" I hide my grin behind the rim of my mug as I take a sip.

"You're fucking hilarious." She gets up and swills her mug under the tap. "I've not seen nor heard from him."

"Disappointed?" I ask as she slowly turns toward me, resting her weight on her hip.

"No. I die every time I think about the other night." Jess grabs her bag and heads for the door. "What are you up to today?" she calls over her shoulder.

There's only one thing I have planned for today, and I'm not sure whether I'm happy or worried about it. "I have a date with Theo's mother."

She skids to a stop and looks back at me. "Bonding?"

"I don't know." I shrug. When she called me yesterday, at first I thought maybe Theo had asked her to offer, if only to keep me busy for a few hours. Then I wondered if she genuinely wants to get to know me. Or bond, as Jess said. I've only been in the woman's company briefly, and on few occasions, but I like her. That's not to say I haven't detected the tough streak she has hidden under all that Chanel.

"Well, good luck." Jess interrupts my thoughts and carries on her way. "I get off at six. I'll call you." The door slams and I look around the quiet kitchen, cursing myself for not taking Theo up on his offer to stay with him last night. Because right now, instead of standing lonely in my empty apartment, I'd be snuggled into his side, warm and content.

As I make my way to the bathroom to shower, my phone rings, and Theo's name on the screen chases away my discontent. "It's like you know when I'm thinking about you," I answer, flipping the shower on.

"I do. It's all the time, right?" His voice is the answer to all my woes, and I smile as I strip down.

"Right. Where are you?"

"In my office. Bored. Wishing you were here. Do you miss me?"

I roll my eyes, but I can't lie. "Yes."

"Should have stayed last night," he grumbles. "And the night before."

"I can't stay at your place every night."

"Why?"

I dump my pajamas in the laundry basket and pull the clip from my hair. "Because I have my own place to stay at."

"That's not a reason. Tonight, you're staying here."

"What if I don't want to?"

"You do." I can hear the smile in his voice, and I laugh a little at his sureness.

"I have to go. I have things to do before I meet your mother."

"Oh yeah. Sorry about that." His apology tells me that this wasn't Theo's idea. I don't know if that makes me feel better or not. "She's excited. I've never had a girlfriend before."

"Never?" I don't know why I haven't thought about this. "Ever?"

"Never, ever."

I reach into the shower and feel the temperature of the water. "I don't know what to say."

"There's nothing to be said. Have fun with my mother. I'll see you later, okay?"

"Okay."

He hangs up before I do, but as I place my phone on the vanity, it rings again. Theo. On a frown, I answer. "Hello."

"I forgot to tell you something."

"What?"

"Izzy?" He draws my name out, thoughtfully. Low. Gravelly.

I'm suddenly apprehensive. "What?"

"I love you."

I deflate, laughing a little. "You had me worried."

"You should be. I'm going to eat you alive later." He hangs up again, and I'm left with that wonderful promise circling my mind as I shower.

* * *

I walk into the Langham Hotel just after five and head for the plush cocktail bar, spotting Judy across the bar sitting in the arched window seat as I enter.

"Izzy." She smiles as she stands, arms reaching, beckoning me into her embrace. "How are you, darling?"

I let her hug me. "I'm well, thank you, Judy."

"Very good." She breaks away, holding me at arm's length and smiling at me fondly, her rouge lips stretched wide, displaying beautiful teeth. She's really quite a stunning woman. "Come, sit."

We settle and the waitress approaches, handing me a piece of polished wood with a list of cocktails inscribed down the length of it. I smile my thanks and run my eyes down the list of luxury drinks.

"You should try this one." Judy glides a perfectly polished fingernail down my menu. "It's scrummy."

I read her recommendation. *You're So Gangsta*. I laugh, reading the hashtag next to it: *#FeelingLikeABoss*. I look up at her, and she winks on a small grin.

"I'm having Heaven Is for Sinners."

My gaze drops to the menu again, finding the quirky hashtag for Judy's choice. *#FeelingMischievous*. I smile, returning my attention to Theo's mother as I place the menu down. "Why do I sense an ulterior meaning to your suggestion of what I should have to drink?"

"I love the height of the pedestal my son has placed you on," she tells me, quite offhand, and with absolutely no bad feeling threaded through her statement. "It's even higher than the one he has me on." Judy gives me a coy smile, signaling the waitress and ordering our drinks.

When we're alone again, I decide not to dance around but to ask her outright what's playing on my mind. Because clearly something is. "Does that bother you?"

A small stretch of silence spreads across the table, not uncomfortable, but not particularly comfortable, either. She's considering my question. I've already figured out that Judy is a bit of a lioness when it comes to Theo. She was the only woman in his life until I appeared on the scene. Or exploded, more like.

I wait, nervous, for Theo's mum to give me her answer, not liking the thought of being in competition with her or vying for her son's attention. She sighs and reaches over the table, taking my hand. "Izzy, darling girl, I only want to see him happy. You make him happy."

"And if I upset him?" I ask, continuing with my strategy of being straight to the point.

"You already have, haven't you?" She points a knowing look at me, gripping my hand when I try to pull it free, a little shocked that he's obviously shared our little disagreement from the other day, when I refused to confide in him after my meltdown at Stan's tattoo studio. "I'm not condemning you," she says softly.

"Then what are you doing?"

"I'm trying to support you."

She is? That's strange, because I don't feel very supported at the moment. I feel more threatened. "How?"

She sighs, releasing my hand and moving back to give the waitress room to place our drinks on the table. I reach for the heavily engraved stem of my glass and slide it toward me, then lower my mouth to the short straw. I take a sip of the slushy cocktail but can't fully appreciate the delicious taste when I'm feeling so apprehensive.

"Izzy, I see the way he looks at you," Judy says. "The connection is so powerful, I can feel it myself." She touches the breast pocket of her suit jacket. "Right here." I look up at her, seeing nothing but genuine happiness in her gaze. "I've always held hope that he would one day let someone in, give someone a chance to love him like I do. But I doubted there was a woman out there strong enough to take him on. His club. His personality. His reputation." She pauses and regards me across the table. "His phobia."

"He'll get better at that," I say, feeling like I'm trying to reassure her. Is she questioning if I'm strong enough to handle Theo?

"I truly believe he will, Izzy. And you will never know how much comfort that gives me."

"I think I do," I reply quietly, glancing down at my glass. "Can I ask you something, Judy?"

"Anything."

I look up at her. "His phobia—"

"Except that." She cuts me off, a hand held up to support her stern words. "Ask me anything, but, like Theo, I never want to discuss that."

I try to force my increasing curiosity back, but her inflexible tone makes it difficult. What on earth happened? "Okay," I concede, not liking the sudden edge of sadness on her face.

"Like he hasn't pushed you, you shouldn't push him. It'll drive him away, Izzy. Please don't do that."

"Okay," I say again, feeling so very guilty. "I'm sorry. I didn't mean to upset you." She looks almost haunted as she delicately lifts her glass to her lips, staring into her drink and taking what looks like a needed sip. But there is just one more thing I *have* to ask. I keep thinking about it, but haven't plucked up the courage—or found the right time—to approach it with Theo. Maybe his mother would be best to discuss it with first. "Do you think Theo would benefit from therapy?"

She smiles, as if in amusement. "I think you are the only therapy Theo needs."

My shoulders drop, disappointed. And I wonder, is that why Judy is so accepting of me? Because she sees me as a potential cure for her son? Is that why she's trying so hard to make me feel welcome? God, does she realize how much pressure she's putting on me? I don't know, but I feel compelled to enlighten her in case she doesn't. She's so blinded by the promise of her son possibly being *fixed*, she's neglecting to consider the strain it might have on me. I'm determined, no doubt, but I'm also not delusional. I'm no professional. Theo needs professional help. "That's a lot of pressure to put on my shoulders, Judy." Will she change her opinion of me, be less friendly if I fail to cure her boy?

"No pressure, my darling. None at all. Because even if he's never cured, I can still see you bring light into his dark world. His happiness, his peace, is all that matters to me."

His peace. "So he's not tried therapy?" I say, trying to get an answer to my original question.

"Therapy requires talking. You may have noticed my son doesn't like doing that."

What she means is, he'll have to talk to a therapist, tell him his history so a treatment plan can be devised. Theo won't talk about his history. Therapy is never going to happen. So, what? It's down to me, then? All the responsibility to keep Theo calm and happy is on my shoulders?

"Now"—Judy's expression alters significantly, from sad to smiley—"tell me about your childhood, Izzy. Let's get to know each other."

Judy's choice of topic has the roles reversed. I look away, playing with the stem of my glass. "Not much to tell," I lie. "I grew up in Highbury, went to the King's College, and have worked at the Royal London since." More lies, and I grimace to myself, hearing how mechanical I sound. "Well, I *did* work at the Royal London." *Until your son went on a rampage through the ward I worked on.*

As I expected, Judy ignores my latter statement. "Why a nurse?" she asks, appearing not to pick up on my robotic reply.

"Because as much as I would've liked to be a doctor, I couldn't afford med school."

"Your parents? Couldn't they help with the financial burden?"

I hold my tongue for a second, but I don't say what I'm wondering, which is why she's asking when I'd bet my life on the fact that Theo has already told her that my parents died. "My father died when I was very little," I explain for the sake of it, deciding it's easier than questioning why she would ask me when she knows. "My mother died ten years ago."

Her face drops, as does her glass to the table. "Oh, Izzy, I'm so very sorry."

I feel my forehead become heavy with my frown. "Theo didn't tell you?"

"No." She shakes her head, then comes around to my side of the table and takes a seat next to me. I look at her, a little perplexed. "I'm sorry for asking. It must be very painful for you. What were you, seventeen when you lost your mother?" I nod, and she closes her eyes, plainly finding it hard to comprehend. "I lost mine when I was thirty. It was so hard, even as an adult, but you were just a girl." She opens her arms and offers me her comfort. Naturally, and surprisingly, I go with ease. "You're even stronger than I thought. No father and no mother at seventeen, and you found your way in the world. Became a nurse!" She pulls back and looks at me, all proud. Thrilled, even.

I won't tarnish the moment with the nastier pieces of the story, because for the first time ever, I'm being rained with praise—praise that I always knew my mother would have smothered me with if she could see me now. The fact that Theo's mother is the deliverer, and not my own mum, adds only a hint of sadness to my moment. "You're amazing, Izzy." She kisses my cheek and hands me my drink. "Like a boss." Clinking my glass, she winks, and I laugh, relaxing for the first time since I arrived. "Because make no mistake, darling girl. You are the boss where Theo is concerned. Of his heart."

Her words pierce my own heart and inject the biggest dose of happiness. I'm guessing now wouldn't be the time to tell her that her darling son once told me that he'll treat me like a queen and fuck me like a whore. "Thanks, Judy. For the chat and the drinks." I sound sincere, and really, I am, but there's that lasting curiosity brought about from an earlier point in our conversation. What happened to Theo? He told me he's wired to charge when he's touched. I don't believe him. I believe something happened that made him that way. And besides, Judy told me he's not always been this way. But do I really need the details? And would I risk pushing him away to find out?

"Is that your phone, darling?" Judy asks, bringing me back into the plush bar, my lips hovering over my straw. I reach for my bag and fish out my mobile, but it cuts off before I get to answer. "It's Theo," I say, dialing him back.

Judy laughs, a little exasperated. "He's probably checking to see if I've scared you off."

I smile, hearing his voicemail kick in. I start to leave a message as Judy collects her own bag, holding up her phone, which is ringing. Theo's name flashes at me, and I disconnect my call as Judy answers him. "Darling," she greets him brightly, but then her happy expression disappears, being replaced with one way too serious for my liking. "No," she breathes, looking at me. "Yes, she's with me."

My back straightens, my pulse quickening as Judy glances at me. I have no idea what the cause for her worry is, but all of her anxious vibes are feeding my own concern.

"I'm on my way." She stands, signaling for me to do the same. "Well of course I'm bringing her," she snaps, showing a rare display of annoyance before hanging up and grabbing her purse, tossing a fifty on the table.

"What's going on?" I ask, letting her lead me from the bar, out to the front of the hotel.

She doesn't answer me, waving for her driver instead.

"Judy!" I shout, panic getting the better of me. "What's happened?" The driver pulls up and she rushes to usher me into the car, then drops to the seat next to me. "There's been an incident at the Playground," she tells me. "Get us there as soon as possible, Gerard."

Her driver nods and zips out into the traffic quickly. But not as fast as my heart goes from zero to sixty. "What's happened? Is it Theo? Is he okay?" My mind gallops with possible causes for the rush and panic.

"He's fine."

Relief sails through my veins at an epic rate. "Then what?"

Judy rests her palm over her forehead, appearing to soothe a pounding head, and her phone rings again. She answers that instead of me, listening intently, nodding and seeming to become more and more troubled, maybe even angry. Whatever has happened, it's not good.

CHAPTER 22

Judy's driver enters Theo's property via a different gate under her instruction, pulling up in a car park that serves the Playground. Judy jumps out and runs up the path lined with neatly trimmed topiary trees to the entrance. I'm hot on her heels, searching for Theo as I pass through a reception area and enter the main club. The subdued atmosphere hits me like a brick. There's no music, no dancers on the stage, no fighters in the cage, and no clients. The staff are hovering around the bar, their hushed whispers urgent and fearful. One of them nudges the other as Judy marches through the club, and a domino effect of further nudges ensues until they are all quiet.

"Where?" Judy asks curtly.

"Dressing room," one of the dancers answers quickly. She's wrapped in a thin robe, looking shaken.

As I keep close to Judy's heels, the sound of Theo's thundering shouts sounds through the club, and Judy's pace quickens, as does mine. "How the fuck did this happen?" he roars.

I nearly collide with Judy's back when she comes to an abrupt halt at the dressing room door, and I take in the scene over her shoulder, struggling to comprehend the sight. Penny is lying on the floor, unconscious, her body half-naked under a blanket as Callum kneels beside her, stroking her hair back from her face.

"Oh my God," I exhale, catching Theo's attention. His shirt is half tucked into his trousers, his tie loose around his neck.

"Izzy." He rushes over, and Judy moves to give him clear access to me. My cheeks are cupped in his palms, his worried face nose-to-nose with mine. He places a long, lingering kiss on my lips, inhaling deeply. He's so relieved to see me, I can feel his hammering heart slow as he holds me close.

"What's happened?" I ask, breaking away from him and hurrying across the room to where Penny is lying on the floor. Callum looks up at me, a sad smile on his face. "Well?" I ask, beginning to get a little rattled. "Will someone tell me what's going on?" I kneel beside Penny and take her wrist, feeling for her pulse. It's there and it's strong, but she's out for the count.

"She was attacked," Theo explains, kneeling beside me. A flash of violence travels across his face as he speaks.

"What? Here?" No. No, that can't be. The dancers are safe here. Protected. Theo makes sure of it.

"Yes, here," he practically growls, looking insane with anger.

I feel Penny's forehead before pulling her eyes open one by one. Her pupils are big, wide as saucers. "She's been drugged."

"Fuck!" Theo thumps the floor before getting to his feet and stomping across the room, kicking a chair out of his way as he goes. I ignore him and concentrate on Penny, hearing Judy trying to talk him down.

I pull back the blanket and look for any evidence of force, spotting a scattering of fresh bruises on her thighs and her knickers dangling from one hip, ripped. I swallow repeatedly, forcing away so many terrible memories. Now isn't the time to have a meltdown. I need to be steady and together. Callum hisses and I look up, my lips straight. "Him?" I ask, referring to the scum that attacked us in the alley.

Callum shakes his head. "He's on remand."

"Then who?"

"I don't know."

I grit my teeth and return to Penny, covering her body. "We need to get her in a bed."

"I didn't want to move her until you got here," Callum explains. "I didn't know whether she was hurt." He slips his arms under her and lifts her from the floor, and I rise with him, keeping the blankets in place.

"She's hurt," I mumble, sticking to Callum's side as he leads the way back to the main house. I look at Theo as I pass, unable to soften my scowl. "But you can't see the most damaging injuries."

Theo winces, pain sharpening the lines of his face as he drops his head back and looks to the ceiling. I get no pleasure from the reaction my cold, hard fact draws from him. He said she was safe here. He was wrong.

I follow Callum through the house, and once he has Penny settled in the very same bed where I last tended to her a few weeks ago, I go to scrub my hands. Callum disappears and returns only a minute later, carrying a wealth of medical supplies. I move over to the bed and push the blanket back from her legs with my elbows. "You need to arrange for someone to get her some emergency contraceptive as a precaution." Lacking stirrups, I gently ease Penny's legs back. "Can you help, please?" I ask Callum, looking across to him. He's watching me spreading Penny's legs, a little horrified. "Callum?"

"Yes." He shakes himself back to life and hurries over. "Where do you want me?"

"Hold her legs back by the knees," I instruct, letting him replace my hands with his. "Like that."

"Got her," he confirms, looking up to Penny's face rather than what's staring *him* in the face. "What are you doing?" he asks.

"An internal exam to check for damage." I inspect the bruising around her inner thighs, a collection of small dots from fingers gripping harshly. "Bastard," I breathe, collecting a speculum from the table and pulling it from the protective wrapping. Grabbing the torch, I flip it on as I inch forward, trying to figure the best angle without the help of a proper examination chair. "Penny, I'm just going to take a peek at you. I won't hurt you, I promise. It just might be a little uncomfortable." I look up to her oblivious, sleeping face. She's dead to the world, so I get on with assessing her. "There's no semen," I say to myself. "He probably used a condom. A little blood, but nothing too major." I gently pull the speculum free and nod for Callum to release her legs. He's quick to cover Penny's dignity, arranging the blanket around her bottom half. I set down my instruments and pull off the gloves.

Like I've been trained, I check under her nails for any sign that she might have fought her attacker. There's nothing. "I should sit with her and keep an eye on her until she comes round." I take a seat in the chair next to the bed and settle in for the evening. It could be hours before she regains consciousness, but she mustn't be alone when she does.

Callum moves awkwardly toward the makeshift medical table and starts to collect my supplies, probably just trying to busy himself with nothing else to say. "Leave them," I tell him without taking my eyes off Penny. "I might need them again. And you should still get that emergency pill. I didn't see any signs of semen, but it's better to be safe." I hear a despondent sigh. It's a strange sound from such a big man.

"Izzy," he starts, the sound of his feet approaching. "No one—"

The door swings open, and I lift my head to find Theo looking no less stressed than when I left him downstairs with the after-math of my filthy look. "How is she?" he asks.

"Alive," I spit curtly.

"I'll leave you two to it." Callum is out of the room like a shot, wanting to avoid the wretched atmosphere. I watch his back disappear and the door close behind him, and then return my attention to Penny.

"Izzy, I never—" Theo starts.

"Don't," I cut him off, not looking at him. "Don't tell me how bad you feel, Theo. This place is supposed to be safe. She was supposed to be safe. The poor woman has been through enough."

"No one has ever crossed the line here, Izzy. No one has dared."

"Who dares now?" I ask, shifting my blank eyes across to him. "Who dares to come into Theo Kane's club and do this?" My hand shoots out toward an unconscious Penny.

"I won't rest until I find out." His nostrils flare, the danger I know he's capable of flashing in his cobalt eyes.

"The man in the alley," I begin.

"He's on remand."

"You can be sure of that?"

"Andy's checking."

"I'll take that as a no."

His big shoulders drop, and his gaze falls to the floor. Guilt is consuming him, yet I can't find the graciousness to even *try* to ease him. It doesn't matter that my attempts would be in vain. He blames himself, and with a lack of anyone else to blame at the moment, I can't help but blame him, too.

"She should be in a hospital," I mutter, knowing I'm wasting my breath. "And the police should be called."

"I can't draw attention to my club, Izzy. Andy's on my side, but there are powers above him."

"I know," I grate, his words only building my anger. "God forbid the police turn up. God forbid you're arrested and thrown in jail."

The noise that emanates from his direction is a combination of a growl and a sigh, followed by the sound of his feet thumping the floor as he comes to me. He's in my field of vision a second later, on his knees. "Don't shut me out," he pleads, taking my hand and placing it on his chest, a silent reminder of what's etched on his skin beneath his creased shirt. "I can stand a lot, repel it all, but I can't bear the thought of you hating me. Don't hate me, Izzy." His pain-filled face dents my anger a little, our stares holding. "I *will* get retribution. I won't let whoever did this to her get away with it."

"How?" I ask flatly. "Gunshot? Beating? Breaking a few bones?"

His blazing eyes tell me that's exactly what he has in mind, just as I feared. "Whoever it is needs to pay."

"And how the hell will that help Penny?" I shout.

He winces at the volume of my voice, closing his eyes and spending a few moments breathing some calm into his lungs. "I try to do the right thing," he says, an edge of pleading in his tone. Pleading for me to understand. "I hand scumbags over to the police rather than give them what they deserve."

"You hand them over to the police as bait, Theo. Give the police what they want to keep them off your back." I look away from him and rest back in the chair. "Don't tell me it's completely selfless."

His exhale is loud and tired. "Izzy, baby, come to bed with me. Let me hold you."

"I need to watch Penny. She might wake and be sick or disoriented. She shouldn't be alone."

"Then I'll have one of the girls come and sit with her."

"Do they have any medical knowledge?" I ask, looking at him.

"Do they know how to monitor pulse rates and recognize the signs of deterioration?"

Theo looks across to Penny, his jaw pulsing. "No."

"Then I'm not about to hand over her care to a stripper just because *you* need a cuddle." The spite in me comes steaming to the surface, unstoppable and full of the hatred I'm feeling. "I'll stay here." I pull my hand from his and shift in my chair, turning as far away from him as I can.

He's stung. It's apparent in the slight withdrawal of his big body and the hurt inhale. There's silence for a few moments, but I can practically hear his mind racing. And then he lets his thoughts spill. "Why do I get the feeling that there's more to your anger than what's happened to Penny, Izzy?"

"Don't." I refuse to look at him, as if hiding my eyes can keep the secrets of my past from him. "Don't turn this around."

"Right," he breathes, his voice shaky as he rises to his feet. "I get it. Keep your secrets."

"As you keep yours."

Theo curses under his breath, walking away from me, defeated. Not stopping him from leaving takes everything out of me. I don't relish the sight or sound of him in despair, and, really, it's my own despair that's fueling it. My reasons for being angry. My past dictating how I handle this. But Theo's a big man. He can look after himself, as demonstrated on more than one occasion. Penny can't. She needs me.

When the door to the bedroom shuts softly, I glance across the room. In my mind's eye I can see him on the other side, probably forcing his fist back from smashing a hole in the wall. And then I close my eyes, and I see me. I'm unconscious like Penny.

* * *

Hours pass. I'm up and down from the chair like a yo-yo, checking Penny's pulse, blood pressure, and temperature at least every twenty minutes. I don't need to do it so often, but if I remain unmoving in the chair then I'm likely to doze off. I wonder constantly if I'm missing something—something important. She's not come round, her temperature hasn't changed, and her pupils are still dilated.

At eleven o'clock, I check her over again, beginning to doubt my judgment and diagnoses. I pull her eyelid up, looking closely into her eye. I'm so focused on my task, searching for more signs, I jump a foot off the bed when she jerks.

"I'm going to throw up," she chokes, rolling over to the side of the bed and heaving uncontrollably. "Oh God."

I dash for the bowl and round the bed, making it just in time for her to spill her guts. Wisps of her hair dangle down, skimming the contents of the bowl, and I pull them back with my spare hand, holding her hair out of her face as she continues to throw up, her retches loud, the stench wicked. But while it's unpleasant, I can't help but be grateful. She's with it, and evacuating any crap from her stomach is a good thing.

It's a long five minutes until she stops, and I lower the bowl to the floor before properly securing her hair with a tie. "Better?" I ask as she heaves herself back onto the pillow, her brow shimmering with sweat.

She turns slightly dazed eyes on me, her expression blank. "You must feel like my private doctor."

I smile, my ease growing. She recognizes me. "Actually, I'm a nurse." I start tucking her back under the covers. "How are you feeling?"

"My head's pounding." She places a palm across her brow. "Did I get steaming drunk and not remember?"

I bite my lip, wondering how best to break it to her. I take some painkillers from the side table, handing them to her with a glass of water. "I think you were drugged, Penny." There's no easy way. It is what it is, and she has to know.

Her face falls into thought; the mental battle she's having to try to recollect is almost painful to see. "Drugged," she murmurs, looking down at the two pills in her hand. "I don't remember."

"Take them," I insist, applying a little pressure to the underside of her hand for her to lift the pills to her mouth.

"Are they safe?" She gives me the eye as she tips them in and swallows them down with some water.

I'm biting my lip, liking her joke, but wondering if she's fully grasped the gravity of what I've told her. "Penny, do you remember anything?"

"I remember getting a glass of water." She looks past me, squinting. "And I remember heading for the dressing room to get ready for my set."

"And then?"

"Nothing." She smiles faintly at me, gripping her glass of water with both hands, resting it on her tummy. "But I'm guessing that's a good thing, right?"

I place a hand on her arm and squeeze. After everything she's been through, this woman, who's barely even an adult, is still so strong. "I've arranged for you to take the morning-after pill. It's just a precaution."

"Thank you." Already her eyelids are becoming heavy.

"You should sleep. I'll go tell Theo that we talked. He'll be anxious to hear you are okay." I back up toward the door, and she sighs, sinking into her pillow, her eyes closing.

"Thank you for looking after me again, Izzy." Her words get quieter toward the end, her grogginess and exhaustion carrying her quickly back into sleep.

I watch her for a few moments before I slip out, closing the door gently behind me. "Jefferson!" I jump, nearly colliding with him as I turn.

"Miss White." He smiles, though it's tinged with worry.

"What are you doing here at this hour?"

"I didn't want to leave until I'd checked up on the young girl. How is she?"

"She's okay ... I mean fine. ... Well, she woke but drifted off to sleep again." I thumb behind me to the door. "Someone should sit with her. I was on my way to tell Theo that she came round."

"Ah, Mr. Kane has left the grounds."

I feel my forehead become heavy. Where would he go at this time of night, other than the Playground? Left the grounds? "Where's he gone?"

"I don't make it a habit to question his movements, Miss White. I simply serve him." He moves past me to the door. "I'll arrange for someone to come up and sit with the girl."

"Jefferson," I call, making him stop midstride into the room.

"Yes, Miss White?" He doesn't turn around, and I sense it's because he knows I'm going to ask him something he won't answer.

"How long have you been Theo's butler?"

I can't see his face, but I expect he's smiling. "I've served Mr. Kane since he was a babe in arms, though he was rather less demanding of me then."

"So you knew his father?" The interest in my voice is so obvious, I could kick my own arse. I should be ashamed of myself for trying to get Theo's secrets from his staff, especially when I've cut off Theo so curtly. But, damn it, I can't shake off the curiosity.

This time, Jefferson does turn around. "Why, of course I knew his father. This was his house before it was Theo's."

"And the club, was that his, too?"

"Yes, and the country estate on the south side of the city, where Theo's mother now resides."

"And Theo's father made all of his fortunes to buy these magnificent properties through running a strip club and organizing illegal prize fights?"

Jefferson smiles, backing into Penny's room. "Good night, Miss White."

"Good night, Jefferson." He shuts the door and leaves me contemplating what I should do with myself. Theo's out. I can't face Judy, or anyone else for that matter. So I head for Theo's private quarters, pulling my phone from my bag on the way to call Jess. "Shit," I curse, discovering a dead battery.

Recalling a charging station on the sideboard in the lounge, I head straight there and hook up my phone, then go to get changed. I enter Theo's dressing room and pull down a shirt to sleep in, quickly changing into it and tugging my hair back as I make my way to his bathroom. I wash my face, brush my teeth, and head back to my phone. Five percent. It's enough. I pull it free and fire it up, the notifications of a few missed calls from Jess popping up when it comes to life. I dial her and slump onto the couch.

"Finally," she blurts down the line. "I've been trying to call you."

"My phone died," I explain. "Sorry. Things have been—"

"Yes, I heard."

I look down at my phone. "You did? How?"

"Callum turned up a few hours ago."

My spine uncurls quickly, bringing me up into a pretty prim seated position. "What for?" I'm thinking of too many potential reasons why Callum would go to see Jess.

"The morning-after pill."

But not that. "Huh?"

"He explained the situation. Figured me being a midwife, I'd have what you'd instructed him to source. I told him I deliver babies, not prevent them."

I can't help it, I laugh. "Bless him."

"The man is a fucking mystery, Izzy." She sounds exhausted by it all. "He left on a grunt and that was that."

"He left?"

"Yes! I was standing there in a T-shirt and knickers, and he fucking left. I give up."

"Was there—"

"God, yes. I could have exploded, and very nearly did when he wiped a bit of toothpaste from the corner of my mouth."

"And he left."

"He fucking left."

"Ouch."

"Tell me about it. He looks at me like he wants to ravage me and talks to me like he wants to strangle me. I'm done. It's exhausting trying to figure him out." She blows out a tired puff of air. "But forget about my frustrating shenanigans with Mr. Cold. What the fuck is going on?"

"She's come round, and she doesn't remember anything."

"Wow. I bet Theo's pissed off."

I nod my agreement, though I'd use a far stronger word than that. "Slightly."

"The poor girl. Who the hell would have the balls to walk into Theo's club and do that? They must have a death wish."

I look across the room to the door, pondering Jess's statement. A death wish. "Indeed," I say quietly, thoughtfully. Theo's impenetrable club has been penetrated. The Playground isn't untouchable. Theo isn't untouchable. The irony of my silent thought doesn't escape me. The untouchable man isn't untouchable. My conclusion just makes me worry all the more, because how long can Theo go under the radar? How long before he's cut by the sword? "What shift are you on tomorrow?" I ask on a sigh.

"Early. I should really get to bed."

"I'll call you tomorrow." I hang up and tap the side of my phone on my cheek, unable to shake off my thoughts. Untouchable. And I wonder, as Theo lets down his defenses to me, is he exposing himself in other aspects of his lifestyle? Instead of his strength, am I really a weakness?

CHAPTER 23

There's that moment between sleep and consciousness—the moment when you're waking up, you're warm and cozy in your bed, and your brain is empty of everything, except the delicious stretch you're building up to or the sigh of contentment as you snuggle back down, drifting off into the peaceful quiet of sleep. It's the moment before you've had the opportunity to remind yourself of who you are and what's happening in your life. And then it all registers, drip by drip, and you spend a few moments, your eyes closed, keeping the darkness, hoping that it's a dream and you're still in it. But you're not. Your eyes open and the drips are replaced with a gush of reminders.

As I stare up at the ceiling, I remember that I'm jobless and absolutely nuts over a man who should be totally unlovable. Except he's not. Far from it. At least, for me. My head begins to ache, and my heart weighs down in my chest. Is it wrong to love Theo so deeply, to stay and fight for it when I fear it could ruin me? And worse still, ruin him. To push him over the line he so delicately balances on. He told me he felt I needed a warning that he's fallen in love with me. He gave me that warning too late. I'm in now. And I fear there is no getting out.

My head drops to the side and my despondency multiplies at the sight of the empty space where Theo should be. Not content with seeing the vacant place in his bed where he should be, I reach across and feel his absence, stroking the cold sheets next to me as I turn onto my side. The notion that I might never get to wake up and lay beside him, just watching him in his slumber, brings tears of desolation to my eyes. It's ironic that of all the things burdening me at the moment, the lack of his closeness is the worst.

I should have gone home last night. Then I would have one less thing to be miserable about this morning—namely, Theo not joining me in bed. He didn't come to me, cuddle me, comfort me. It's not very fair for me to be slighted, since I gave him every reason to believe that I held him accountable for Penny's attack. And it's not very fair that I blamed him in the first place. I could see his remorse, as plain as the nose on my face. He won't rest until whoever's responsible is dealt with. But that simply adds to my growing list of concerns. How far can he push his apparent immunity with the police before everything catches up with him and he's thrown into prison? Taken away from me?

Sighing heavily, I slide out of bed and slip one of Theo's shirts on, fastening the buttons as I make my way to the lounge in search of him. Something tells me not to hold out too much hope of finding him, that he'll probably be going out of his way to avoid my spiteful tongue again. I glance at the clock on the mantelpiece above the fireplace. Nine a.m. My heart sinks. He either didn't come back at all last night, or he's left already.

I turn on my heels to go take a shower, trying to find the will I need to get on with my day. But I take no more than two paces, the couch across the room catching my eye. Or not so much the couch, but the sight of a long, seminaked body stretched the length of it. His arm is curled around the back of his head, his face turned into his bicep, and his other palm rests lightly on his stomach, rising and falling steadily with his calm breathing.

The black material of his boxer shorts is pulled taut across his thighs, and his face has a thousand lines of torment etched across it, even as he sleeps. Though he's still unfathomably handsome. He's a picture. Like the finest piece of art that has you staring in fascination, a million words of wonder tickling your lips. Or like something so gorgeous that you feel compelled to share with others, because everyone should experience the sight of it at least once. Once is enough to leave a lasting image imprinted on anyone's mind. But I won't share. I'll keep this vision to myself. Selfishly, I want Theo Kane to be my own personal exhibit.

And on top of his visual appeal, I want him as my own personal refuge. I could never walk away from him, not only because I need that refuge, have come to crave it. But because I love him with every fiber of my lost being. And he loves me. Without love, we are nothing. Without him, I feel like nothing. I'm just a woman content with hiding in the shadows of life. Or in the shadows of a place that she's told herself was safe. I allowed my inner demons to dictate where I went and what I did. And it's only since I met Theo that I've successfully fought their hold. I need to make peace with him. It hurts too much just knowing that the world shaking around us is beginning to penetrate our serenity. I can't allow it.

I take the few paces over to the sofa where he's lying and drop to my knees, fighting my desire to touch him. In time, I tell myself. He's worth enduring the wait for that ultimate prize.

"Theo?" I whisper, being careful not to get too close in case my voice rouses him too suddenly and he startles. "Theo, wake up."

I smile when he murmurs softly, his face turning out from his bicep, his eyes still closed. He's in that place between sleep and consciousness, that place where I've just been. A frown is marring his forehead, deep lines stretching from one side to the other. I want him to see me when he opens his eyes, see that I'm here and I want to put things right.

"Theo, wake up." I hold my breath when his lids start to flicker. I need him to see me, register me, and brace himself for my touch. His eyes don't slowly draw open. They spring open, making me withdraw a tad. Then he blinks a few times, rubbing deeply into the sockets before finding me again. I smile, resting back on my haunches and placing my hands in my lap.

"I thought I was dreaming." His voice is gruff and thick with sleep. "What's up?"

"Why are you out here?" I ask, looking down the length of his body. "Why didn't you come to bed?"

He clears his throat and pushes himself up, swinging his long legs off the side of the couch and relaxing against the back cushion. "I needed to sleep." He rests his head back and stares up at the ceiling. "I didn't want to wake you."

"Or risk clobbering me if I tried to cuddle you."

His head remains back, but his eyes lower and a few beats of silence fall. "I never want to hurt you," he says, meaning so much more than physically.

I nod as I lift my hand and reach for him. "I'm sorry for blaming you. I know it's not your fault. It's just—"

He catches my hand and places it back on my lap, rejecting me. "You had every right." His palms push into the couch and he lifts, rising to tower above me. "It was my fault." He moves carefully past me so as not to touch me and heads for his bedroom, leaving me on my knees, watching him walk away. Pain slices off a sliver of my heart.

"But Penny's okay," I call to his back as I scramble to my feet. I don't like his detachment or the guilt emanating from every pore of his body. I was so determined that he should feel it last night.

I took comfort in the signs of it. Now…now I'm scared by it. I let my personal hang-ups consume me and dictate how I handled it, and I so regret it. "Theo, it's not your fault. I was mad. I didn't mean—"

"It's all my fault, Izzy," he interrupts me flatly, not bothering to turn around. The continued snub, combined with his robotic words, has me in pursuit, moving fast to catch up with him before he makes it to the bathroom and shuts me out.

I manage to consider in the fleeting time it takes me to reach him what I'll do when I get there. Grab him? Intercept him? I don't get the chance to make my choice. He swings around and seizes the tops of my arms, jolting me to a stop. My breath catches at the back of my throat, and I snap my mouth closed as he brings his face close to mine. It's tight with lines of frustration, yet his eyes are softly searching mine. I wait for him to speak, to say anything that will settle my growing apprehension. I feel like he's purposely distancing himself from me.

It's a long few seconds before he talks, and when he finds his words, my fear soars. "I'll be busy most of the day."

I swallow hard, searching his eyes. They're clear, but I sense a deadly tinge, and I don't like it in the least. "Doing what?"

He drops me and steps back. "I have some business to tend to." Another step back.

"Tell me."

"You don't need to know."

Anger simmers in my gut, quickly turning into boiling rage. He expects me to accept that? "Tell me!"

"No." He backs away, unperturbed by my fury.

His dismissiveness astounds me, and before I can stop to tell myself it's a bad move, my hand flies out, aiming for his big shoulder. He moves like a gazelle, fast and gracefully, catching my flailing limb with ease. He saw it coming before I did. His palm encircles my wrist, holding it exactly where he stopped it, a few inches from his shoulder. I gasp and yank myself free. "Do you know who attacked Penny?" I ask.

There's a momentary flick of his eyes away from mine before he answers. "No."

"Don't lie to me." I hiss the words, moving closer to him, getting up in his face. "It's him, isn't it? That arsehole who attacked her in the alleyway. Who attacked me, too!"

"He got out on bail." Theo pretty much spits the words, disgust drenching them.

I inhale, shocked, moving back and dropping my gaze to the floor. It darts around our bare feet. "They let him out?" I don't believe this. Theo handed him over to the police, rather than break his legs, and they let him out, free to terrorize Penny again, and God knows how many other women? It's horrifying. "How did he get in the club?"

"I don't know." Just the way he says it tells me he's absolutely raging. Has he realized, like I have, that he's not untouchable?

"What are you going to do?" I look up at him, now worrying about his intentions.

"Hurt him." He doesn't hold back, doesn't bother to try to pull the wool over my eyes. I can see the intent on his face, the thirst to draw blood from the worthless lowlife. The power behind his words matches the physical power I know he has. "I'm going out with Callum."

"No." I shake my head, moving toward him. "Theo, please, no."

"You don't think he deserves it?" His question gives me pause. There's something in his blue eyes making me read between the lines. His question feels tactical. He's gone low, and I'm not sure I can blame him.

"I know what you're capable of, Theo." I push on, desperate for him to understand my plight. "You'll be locked up. You'll be taken away from me."

"That's not going to happen."

"It might! You thought you could hand him over to the police and they'd do their job. They failed, Theo. Not you." His face twists in agony. It kills me, because I know my words aren't sinking in. I lift my arm and let him see it, his eyes following my hand to his chest to where his new tattoo is still reddened and shiny from Vaseline. "Please, promise me you won't do anything stupid."

He studies my hand resting on his skin, taking a deep breath. "Promises are nothing but words that evaporate the moment they're spoken." Looking up at me, his face is completely blank. But the tinge of deadliness in his eyes is more apparent. "They disappear. They mean nothing." He turns and walks away to the bathroom, leaving me shell-shocked, my palm warm from the lingering aftermath of our physical connection.

It's ironic. I've welcomed Theo's protective instinct, craved it. His safety and security. His ability to keep danger at bay. Now that instinct means I might lose him.

I can't lose him.

He sees nothing but a need for revenge. Right now, he's not seeing me. My need. My pain. Anger bubbles up from my toes, fear engulfing me. "You stupid, selfish pig!" I yell. "What about us?" I snatch my jeans from the nearby chair and yank them on before grabbing up my bag and heading for the door. I slam it behind me and work on slamming a lid on my mind as well.

* * *

My day is spent doing anything to stop myself from thinking. I went home, showered and readied myself, then headed out with a list of things to do. It took me longer to write the list than it'll probably take me to actually do it all. I say *all*. All two things. The supermarket is my first stop. I stock up on everything, and I take my time doing it, roaming up and down every aisle, whether I need dog food or baking supplies or not. I pick the longest check-out queue, and I decline the offer of help to pack my bag. I don't grab a coffee from the Starbucks in the supermarket; I walk the five streets to another one instead. And I don't use the nearby Boots to finally get my photographs from Vegas developed; I walk a few miles to the next one.

As I sit on a stool in the booth, my phone linked via a USB cable to the machine, I flick through the images of my first girlie holiday in my twenty-seven years. I smile, selecting and printing as I go, reliving the time that feels like years ago through the images. After collecting my prints, I think of something else to add to my dwindling list of things to do. I need a frame. But not from this shop. Collecting my bags, I go in search of a home store.

* * *

Hours later, I'm on the floor in my lounge trimming photographs and arranging them in a huge frame made up of a dozen smaller ones. When I'm done, I'm surrounded by offcuts of photographs, and each of the frames contains a picture of either me, Jess, or both of us. I prop it up on the couch and stand back, scanning every image. Jess was my only family. Now, I have Theo. He should be in these photographs. But there are none in existence of Theo and me. I should fix that.

I hear the front door close and look up to find Jess wandering in, followed closely by Callum. My eyebrows jump up in surprise, then lower just as quickly when Jess approaches, dropping her bag to the floor.

"Hey, you okay?" she asks.

I sense a concern that can only mean Theo has given Callum the lowdown, and Callum has relayed it all to my friend. I squat and begin gathering up my mess. "What do you want?" I ask, flicking Callum a condemning look. "Did he send you?"

Callum frowns, his eyes flicking to Jess. "He's not with you? I thought he was."

My hands falter, and I shoot up. "He said he was going out with you," I blurt, immediately panicked.

"Does it look like it?" His frown turns into worry. Deep worry. "Fuck."

"I left him hours ago." I'm unable to control the growing trepidation. "So where is he?"

"What's happened? Between you two?" Callum asks, pulling his phone from his trouser pocket and looking at the screen.

"We had a disagreement. Haven't you spoken to him?" I ask as Jess hovers behind Callum, the silent, pensive observer.

"Not since yesterday. And now his phone's off. What did you argue about?"

"He told me Penny's attacker was released on bail." My voice rises a few octaves, and Callum's wide eyes are the cause. "Oh my God," I whisper. "You didn't know."

"No, I didn't fucking know."

Callum's news takes my panic to another level. "Theo said he was going to hurt him. I asked him to promise that he wouldn't, but he refused. He said he was going out with you. I left." My eyes drop and dart. "I thought you knew. I thought you'd be with him. You're always there when he needs to see to business." Always there to stop him tipping over the edge.

Callum's mouth twists, his eyes closing to gather patience. "Go get in the car." His worry, and now my own, too, is the only reason I don't protest. Without Callum by his side, who knows what Theo will do. He won't just hurt the man he's hunting down. Jesus, he'll be up for murder.

* * *

Callum is obviously uptight on the drive to Theo's, not that I expect small talk from him, but any talk would be welcomed. The silence is leaving the empty space free for me to fill with thoughts of dread.

When we pull up under the canopied driveway, Jefferson is waiting and looking as worried as Callum. "Miss White," he says, sweeping his arm out, giving me the space I don't need when Theo's not with me.

I smile my thanks as Callum joins me, and we move into the large, empty entrance hall. "Make yourself comfortable," he says. "I have some things to see to in the Playground."

I slow to a stop, watching Callum carry on his way, pulling the door open to the corridor that leads through to Theo's club. "What? I'm supposed to just hang around sick with worry, waiting for him to come home?"

He stops, the door handle in his grasp, and turns toward me. "Yes," he says simply. A stoic face is the last I see before Callum disappears through the door.

"Great," I mutter, pulling my phone from my bag and dialing Theo. It goes straight to voicemail, and I close my eyes, bringing the phone to my lips while praying that without Callum, he hasn't found who he was looking for. Why would he go alone? Why?

"Would you like a drink?" Jefferson asks, startling me from my thoughts. "Or perhaps something to eat?" His hands join in front of him, waiting for my answer.

"I'm fine, thank you, Jefferson."

"Very well." He bows his head and backs away, and then I'm alone in the great big house with nothing to do but wait and worry.

"Izzy, darling." Judy comes out of Theo's office, seemingly

relieved to see me. She hurries over, extending her arms and taking me in a hug. "Where's Theo? Is he here? In the club?" She breaks away, looking to me for an answer.

I shake my head, and her red lips purse. "I haven't seen him since this morning," I explain. "We had a . . . disagreement."

Her head tilts a fraction, making the perfect layers of her hair fall out of place. "About what?"

"Penny."

Her pursed red lips twist in disdain. "What about her?"

I sigh, building myself up to explain all over again. Why am I the only person who knows all this? "Her attacker. He got released on bail." She withdraws, a mixture of confusion and sheer aggravation splattering her lovely face. "I thought Callum would be with Theo," I go on, rushing my words to get them all out, and maybe even to defend myself. I shouldn't have let him go.

"Damn it," she hisses, stalking away, pacing up and down, thoughtful. "That little slut will be the death of him." She starts playing with her hands, her heels clicking on the floor as she walks back and forth.

My head retracts on my shoulders, her harshness cutting through me. "What do you mean, she'll be the death of him?"

An over-the-top smile is plastered on her face in the blink of an eye. It's an insult. "Nothing, darling. The girl is a troublemaker. That's all." She comes forward to claim me again, but I move away, wary, making her pull to a guilty stop.

"Judy, don't treat me like I'm stupid," I warn her, facing Theo's formidable mother head-on. "Theo told me she's the daughter of a friend who died."

She laughs, short and sharp. It's cold and it's heartless. "If only," she snipes.

"Theo lied to me?" I ask quietly, feeling hurt and confused. "Why would he lie?" My imagination goes into overdrive, reeling off the possibilities. What woman would be worthy of such protection from Theo? An ex-lover? Girlfriend? "Judy, tell me who she is." I'm slowly going out of my mind, my breathing becoming strained and erratic.

Her eyes close and she inhales deeply, defeat coming out in an extended puff of air. "His sister."

I recoil, shocked. "What? Your daughter?"

"No," she refutes viciously. "She's the bastard child of my dead husband and his whore of a mistress." Judy staggers back, her head whipping from side to side. She's checking that the coast is clear, making sure there's no one listening.

"A love child?" I whisper, beginning to piece it all together.

"Love?" Judy laughs, the sound tinged with a hurt I'm unable to comprehend. "She's the product of a fling, that's all. Nothing more."

My round eyes take in the desolate woman before me. "You hate her." I state it as the fact it is. There's venom pouring from Judy's Chanel suit, poisoning the air.

She drops into a decorative chair, the conversation already taking its toll. "Theo has some unreasonable sense of responsibility toward her." She waves her hand in the air. "I've long given up trying to dissuade him of his misplaced obligation."

"Where's her mother?" I ask, since she's mentioned responsibility.

She snorts her repulsion. "Gone the moment my dear husband's will was read and she learned she wasn't getting a penny from his estate. She disappeared. Left Penny to fend for herself as a child."

"That's awful."

"That's life, sweetheart." She rolls her eyes in the most heartless way. I'm stunned by her coldness.

"Penny didn't ask to be brought into this world illegitimately," I point out. "This isn't her fault. Why do you hate her so much?"

"Because, my dear," she says on a sigh, "my husband treated his bastard daughter better than he treated *my* boy. *Our* boy." She falls into thought, smiling a little. "Our sweet, placid little Theo."

I can't pull back my frown. Sweet and placid? Never would I describe Theo as sweet and placid. Not now, anyway. But judging by Judy's soft, reflective expression, there was once a time when those words could be applied to the formidable, deadly man. She's full to the brim with resentment and bitterness. I'm partway between compassion and disdain for her.

"Theo wasn't always so . . ." She thinks for a few seconds, looking at me. "Unapproachable. He was an adorable child, with no traits of his ruthless father in him. I loved that. I loved that he was nothing like my husband. But, of course, my husband hated it. Theo frustrated him. He saw his son as a pushover. He wanted an heir to take over his empire." She throws her arms into the air in the general direction of the luxury surrounding us. "He was a bully. Told Theo daily how much of a disappointment he was and how his bastard little sister had bigger balls than him. He wanted a boy as merciless as he was to continue his legacy, and Theo wasn't showing any signs of being that boy." Her hands land in her lap with a light thud. "But he got his wish in the end, even if the callous bastard isn't here to appreciate it. Theo is more formidable than his father ever was, *and* more respected." Judy swallows. "And feared." She looks at me. "Just how Bernard wanted him to be. Hollow. Cold. Merciless. But there's one thing my Theo has that his father didn't. Something more precious than money or status symbols or respect." She stands and comes over to me, regarding me as I shift from foot to foot, uncomfortable, trying to take in the endless bombshells. She takes my cheeks, holding me in place. "My boy has a heart, Izzy. And you possess it."

I choke up, not liking the conclusion I'm drawing. "His father made him feel unwanted?" I question.

I see tears form in her eyes, and she nods. "Trust me, darling. Where his father lacked, I made up for it."

"I'm sorry." I drop my head, sadness consuming me. And yet despite what he went through, he still shows compassion toward his half sister. Chose to take care of her instead of disowning her. "You can't condemn him for wanting to help her."

"No, but I can condemn *her* for continuing to make his life difficult. For getting him locked up, because that's what will happen. He's gone out there to hunt down whoever attacked her because he feels some misplaced sense of responsibility."

I glance up at her. "He'd do the same for me," I state, knowing it to be true. "Would you hate me, too?"

Judy smiles, understanding. "Theo's responsibility toward you isn't misplaced, dear girl."

I open my mouth to argue, but quickly suck back my words. It'll be pointless. Judy is scorned, and no matter how much I or anyone else tries to convince her otherwise, she'll never see through her haze of resentment. Theo is her child. Penny is not.

"Come." She slides an arm around my shoulder and turns me toward the stairs. "Go lie down. I'll see what I can find out from Andy."

Judy leads me to Theo's private space, my body not my own, my mind trying to process the revelations about Penny, Theo, and their father, my worry for Theo rapidly growing. She opens the door for me. Encourages me inside. And then leaves me with a soft smile. And I let her. I put up no resistance, and I soon find myself frowning at the closed door, the silence loud. She expects me to kill time in here while they try to find him? Expects me to do nothing?

I pull up Theo's name and dial him, pacing the room while I mentally demand that he answer, but I get his voicemail again. "Damn it, Theo," I yell, marching to the door and swinging it open. I'll find Andy myself. Get answers myself.

I make my way through Theo's private quarters, my strides even, my legs strong, my determination unwavering. As I round the landing, something at the bottom of the stairs catches my eye and makes me pause. "Theo." I exhale his name, trying to assess his condition quickly. He looks . . . perfect. His clothes are straight, uncreased, and there are no signs of any dishevelment. I hate myself for it, but I check for blood, too. There's nothing. No sign, hint, or scrap of evidence that he's been teaching any lessons or breaking any limbs. Though his face is tired. Drained. He looks like he could sleep for a year.

"Hey." He stuffs his hands deep into his pockets, looking up at me on the landing.

"Where have you been?" I ask, feeling my way around to the top of the stairs, not daring to release the rail for fear of crumpling in relief. "Everyone has been worried." I take one step down.

"Looking for someone," he says straight up, his despondency telling me that he didn't find them.

I bite my teeth together, nervous to say what I'm about to say. "I know who Penny is."

He shows no surprise. He doesn't even blink. "My father was all she had. Her mother wasn't interested in her, just my father's money and status. When Dad died, all she had left was me. It's been a constant battle to keep her on the straight and narrow."

"I admire you for helping her," I say quietly, needing him to know that. Judy would probably have something to say about it, but I don't care. He deserves some praise, despite my not agreeing with what he set out to do today. But he's back, and he didn't find who he was looking for. I can talk some sense into him. I know I can.

"Don't admire me, Izzy." Theo shakes his head and looks down at his feet. "There's nothing to admire."

My shoulders drop, despair gripping me. "Don't try to stop me," I warn.

He smiles mildly, looking up as he takes a step toward the stairs. "Admiration is more than I deserve. I don't deserve you, either."

"Why?" I ask, annoyed. "Why don't you deserve me? Because you were forced to endure your father's disdain? Because you weren't the son he wanted?" I realize I've said too much when his eyes blaze.

"Because I've become a man I don't want to be," he grates.

"Then. Don't. Be. Him," I say slowly, my fists clenching by my sides. Isn't it that simple?

"It's too late. The damage is done."

Damage? I step back, not liking his resoluteness. "What damage?"

"Me, Izzy," he says, shaking his head. "I'm damaged, and you, you gorgeous, *normal* woman, somehow love me." His voice breaks. "I don't understand it."

The sight of him looking so confused and overwhelmed rips me in two. Positively kills me. "You don't need to understand it. I love you. That's it."

"But this doesn't make any sense to me."

If there were a wall nearby, I would be throwing my fist at it. But there isn't, so I take the stairs, closing the space between us. My face pleads with him the whole way, willing him to accept me. To accept my love. And when his arms lift slowly, I pretty much throw myself into them and cling on to him with all my might. The joining of our bodies seems to center my off-kilter world, and for now, there is nothing wrong, no worries or troubles, just us.

"I'm sorry," he mumbles into my neck, nuzzling deeply. "I'm sorry for making you worry."

"I'm sorry, too."

"For what?" He starts to take the stairs, palming my bum and pulling it up so I wrap my legs around his waist.

"For storming out on you. For not stopping you from leaving. Why didn't you take Callum?"

"Because I didn't want him to hold me back."

It's just as I thought. I can't even appreciate that I know him so well. "And now?" I ask, pulling away from his neck when he reaches the top of the stairs. "What now?" He didn't find who he was looking for. I can't bear the thought of him going AWOL on me again. The worry. The stress.

He carries me into his bedroom and lowers me to the bed, stroking back the hair from my face and looking down at me, a hint of a smile on his face. "Now, I love you."

I hold my breath when his hand travels over my breast, down to the hem of my T-shirt. "I know you love me," I whisper, my spine bending into his touch.

"I need to show you how much."

"I know how much."

He shakes his head, telling me I'm wrong. "Trust me, Izzy. You have no idea." He pulls me up to a sitting position and lifts my T-shirt over my head. My nipples harden, ready and waiting for his devotion, as he unhooks my bra and pulls it down my arms. His head lowers, and he kisses each nipple in turn delicately, looking up at me with a small smile. I fall back onto my elbows, bliss replacing the lingering fear that's swiftly been chased away by his return.

He licks delicately, and I sigh, my eyes tightly shut, my head falling limp on my neck. The rush of tingles invading me is too much to bear, and I start squirming on the bed, mumbling incoherent prayers to the ceiling.

"She's beginning to see," he whispers against my breast, kissing his way up the center of my chest to my neck. He buries his face there, ravishing my flesh with a keen, greedy tongue.

"Theo." I pant, dropping from my elbows to my back, forcing

my hands to remain by my sides. He's going to have to restrain me soon. I can't be held accountable for my hands, which are twitching, desperate to go on a feeling frenzy.

He nips at my neck and breaks away, pulling my jeans and knickers down my legs as he goes. He stands to the side of the bed and reaches for his tie. It gets yanked loose, his expression straight but hungry.

"Tie me up," I demand, beginning to panic. I'm desperate, so happy to have him back. It's making my control slip.

He pouts, shaking his head. "Not today."

My buzzing form stills as he strips down, exposing his body in slow, torturous phases. His chest first, then his arms as he lets his shirt tumble to the floor. Then his thighs, drawing his trousers slowly down. Then his boxers, freeing his cock, the head visibly dripping with need. "Please," I beg, turning my head and looking away.

His hand quickly seizes my jaw and turns my face back toward him. "I want your undivided attention; do you hear me?"

"You need to tie me up," I insist, slamming my fists into the mattress beside me in a temper. It's either that or grab him. I can't do that. I know I can't do that.

"I do *not* need to tie you up." He collects my hand and smacks it into his chest, releasing a mild exhale. The force behind his words doesn't make me feel any better. He was telling himself. Not me. "This is yours. You touch it, feel it, kiss it. You do what the fucking hell you want with it."

My wide eyes drop to my flattened palm on the center of his chest. "Theo, don't be a hero," I say, wondering what on earth has gotten into him.

"I'm no hero, Izzy. I'm a damaged man." He begins to move my hand around in slow, precise circles, his muscles tensing beneath my touch. "But you can fix me." He drops to his knees on the bed, holding my hand in place. "I need you, Izzy. Please." He lowers and claims my lips softly, the feel of his warm, wet mouth relaxing me, wiping my mind of all protests. I keep my hand where it is, but I don't move it. Not even when he spreads his body all over me, sliding his hand up my arm and linking his fingers with mine, squeezing reassurance into me.

His body on top of me forces me to move my hand from his chest, but it goes straight to the bed, and Theo circles his groin, pushing his cock into my thigh. I jolt beneath him, the hardness against my soft flesh feeling so good. So right. But my free hands feel so wrong. I'm not used to it. I thought I'd be unable to contain myself, would be feeling every exposed piece of him, but now that I have the opportunity, I'm too frightened. I try hard to focus on Theo, his mouth on mine, his tongue exploring softly. His body against me, his heat mixing with mine, his hard muscles pushing into my soft curves. My need for it all is there, but it's being distorted by caution and a fear that I don't have when I'm restrained.

"Touch me," he demands. "Feel me. Izzy. Fix me." He pushes his forehead to mine, looking down at me with so much hope, I almost shatter under the pressure of it. Releasing my hand gently, he keeps his eyes on mine, leaving me with two free hands that he wants so badly on him. So steeling myself for the worst, I reluctantly bring my palms to his lower back, watching him carefully, keeping an eye out for any signs. He's expecting my touch. This isn't the problem. The problem is when he's going to be swallowed up in me, distracted from everything except the pleasure he's getting. I flex my fingers.

He doesn't flinch. Instead, he smiles proudly and swoops in with a hungrier kiss, passionate and demanding. I'm absolutely lost in it from the second our lips connect, my hands going straight for his hair and gripping hard. He groans, he shifts, rubbing himself into me, and then his hips lift and he falls to my opening. I bite his lip, keeping it in my grip as he pulls away to look into my eyes. He exhales, swivels his hips, and plunges deeply into me with a groan. My muscles lock, and I cry out, my spine bowing, my head tossed back in ecstasy. He's deep, so deep, stretching me beyond comprehension. "Breathe, Izzy," he orders gently, stilling, giving me time to get used to him. "Okay?"

I nod, bullying my lungs into compliance. "Okay." I unlock my muscles and melt back into the bed, flexing my hips a little in acceptance.

He hisses. His head drops. "Damn, woman, you feel too good to be true." An expert spin of his hips drives him deep, knocking my breathing to shit again. I move my hands to his shoulders and grab him. He flinches. He definitely flinches. But he continues to rock into me, his body hard, tense, and heavy. I purr, meeting every one of his advances, digging my nails into the damp skin of his shoulders. He begins to moan, his pace quickening. I can't help but think he's trying to get this done with as quickly as possible, like he's in agony and ecstasy and he's struggling with the conflicting feelings . . . which I know he is. I slide my hands down to his arse and grab it hard. He jumps, so much he nearly slips free of me.

No. This stops now.

"I'm not doing this." I wriggle under him, removing my hold, being sure not to touch him. "Theo, get off."

He moves like lightning, pulling out abruptly. It makes me wince and close my legs as I watch him pushing himself up onto his knees. I sit up, brushing my hair from my face. "I can do it," he insists. His stomach is creased with taut ripples that have nothing to do with the lack of fat on him. He's strung like a threatened animal.

"You're not ready." I'm speaking the truth, and he knows it. If he dares—

"You always say you're not scared of me." A hand rakes through his hair. "Prove it." He's getting himself in a state, putting himself under unnecessary pressure. "Let me show you I can do it."

I don't know if it's the stress of today, or just the stress of this moment, but I fly off the handle. "I'm not scared of you!" I shout, and he retreats, shocked. "You could hit me, Theo. Smack me or punch me full force in the face. And I'll get over it. I'll heal and forgive. Because I know it's not your fault." I hit my forehead with my balled fist, so fucking frustrated. He's quiet, shocked into silence by my outburst. I've never seen him looking so utterly hopeless. I breathe in some calm and swallow. "But you will never forgive yourself if you turn on me. Please, don't put yourself in that situation when you don't have to. It'll come in time."

He looks away, ashamed, and I hate myself for making him feel like that. "I don't want you to give up on me."

I press my lips together, feeling a bulge of emotion creeping up my throat. "I'll never give up on you." I walk forward on my knees and hold my hands out to him. He takes them, looking at me through glassy eyes. "I love you," I whisper, encouraging him to instigate the positioning of me on his lap. And he sighs when I wrap my arms around his shoulders. "I can do *this*," I mumble into his neck, squeezing him to reinforce my point. "I can hold you." Then I kiss his neck—once, twice, three times. "And this. It's enough for me." I'm not lying. I'm talking sincerely and whole-heartedly. I hope that one day we can have more, but my decision to be with him isn't riding on it. I love him too much.

"It doesn't seem fair." He cups my cheek, his eyes running over my dark waves. "I get to have free rein over you, and you don't me."

I smile sadly. "I will one day, but until then, don't ever lose your hyperawareness of me."

"There's no way." He kisses me and falls back to the bed, holding me tightly in his arms—the place I love the most.

"We'll fix this," I vow. "One day."

"And I'll love you *every* day." He kisses the top of my head and pulls me into him. "Protect you, worship you, treat you like a queen and—"

"Fuck me like a whore." I smile into his chest. "I don't want to rain on your parade, but it's kinda lost its impact."

He chuckles softly, nudging me. "I never said it for impact. I said it because I meant it."

"Good." I raise my finger in the air and wait for him to claim it and place it on his chest. Then I start tracing the lines of the script on his pec, slowly, peacefully...and happily. We lie in silence for an age, my thoughts no longer twisting my brain, but more untangling it. I'm thinking realistically and sensibly. It's the only way to approach this. To approach Theo. His vulnerability is a comfort, but it's also a burden. A heavy one that I'm willing to shoulder, because he loves me so deeply. He wants to be better for me. Any man who wants to change so desperately is worth the devotion. Theo is worth every bit of my devotion and more. "You could try something for me," I say tentatively, biting my lip nervously.

"Anything."

I have a feeling he might regret that. I look up at him, nervous. "Therapy."

Though his face remains straight, I feel his body stiffen beneath me. "Okay," he says on a mere wisp of breath, surprising me. "As long as you come with me."

"You want me to come?"

He nods, and my mind spirals. If I go with him, that means I'll hear everything he tells the therapist. "Yes," he says quietly, clearly reading my mind. I should be happy. I should be grateful. But I'm not. Because I sense Theo expects the same openness from me in return. I lay my head on his chest, escaping his gaze, and let myself wonder if I could do that. Tell him everything. The throb of my heart gives me my answer. No. Never. Quiet falls again, and I stare at the wall, hypnotized by the feel of his hand stroking circles across my back. But then Theo's mobile sounds, piercing our peace, and he groans. "I should get that. I told Callum I'd join him in the Playground half an hour ago." He lifts, bringing me with him. "I'll be an hour, tops." He manipulates my body on the bed and starts to tuck me in all tight and cozy before dropping a kiss on my forehead. "Go to sleep."

I snuggle down, happy to lie here and snooze while he's gone. "Promise me you won't get on the couch if I'm asleep when you get back," I mumble tiredly.

"I promise." He gets up and quickly dresses.

"But promises are only words that evaporate in the air the moment they're spoken," I quip, containing my smile when he pauses mid-pull-up of his trousers.

He slowly turns and gazes at me with eyes so clear. "Not anymore."

CHAPTER 24

When I wake, I'm in that place again, the one between sleep and consciousness, yet now my contentment carries over from my dream world into my real world. I smile and sit up, blinking into the hazy light. The clock says it's eleven o'clock, a whole three hours since Theo left me in bed. What happened to him being an hour? My phone glows from the nightstand and I reach for it, seeing a text from Theo.

Call me if you wake up. x

I pull up his number and go to dial, but a sound from outside his bedroom stops me. Shuffling to the side of the bed, I quickly throw on some jeans and an oversize T-shirt and head out to the lounge. I find it empty. Frowning, I hurry to the door and pull it open, jumping a little when I nearly walk into Penny.

She gives me a small smile. "Sorry, I didn't mean to wake you."

"It's fine," I say, taking her in. She looks good. Good for a woman who's been violated so awfully. "Are you okay?"

"I have a cracking headache." She reaches up to her head and holds the side. "Do you have any painkillers?"

"In my purse." I back up and grab my bag, retrieving the pills from my inside pocket. "When was the last time you took some?"

"Just before I fell asleep. About four."

I hand them over, satisfied there's been a long enough time since her last dose. "Here."

"Thank you." She holds them up with a small smile and wanders back to her room as I slip my feet into some shoes and follow her.

"I'm here if you need anything, Penny," I say to her back. "Even just to talk."

She nods, taking the handle of the door, looking back at me with a smile I know is appreciative. "Thank you. Really."

I wave off her gratitude with a dismissive hand. "Did Callum give you the pill I asked him to get?"

Another nod. "I took it straightaway. Is Theo okay?" Her question has me pausing a beat.

"Yes," I answer reassuringly. "He's fine."

"That's good." She shifts awkwardly, pushing the door open, and I ponder telling her what I know. Does she care? "I know you know," she says before I get the chance to decide.

I smile mildly, if a little awkwardly. "It makes sense now."

"I don't deserve him, really. I've given him the runaround for years. He just wanted to make me feel wanted."

"You *are* wanted."

"I know," she admits, sounding thoughtful. "I'm lucky to have him. And he's lucky to have you." She pushes her way into the room and closes the door, and I stare at it for a moment. I'm lucky to have him, too.

Tucking my phone into my back pocket, I head down the stairs to Theo, now eager to find him, not just to see him but to show him how lucky I feel. Does he realize?

After I've passed through the corridors and the office without seeing a soul, I break into the club, finding it bustling, music pumping, dancers dancing and...fighters fighting. The crowd of men around the arena is dense, all of them cheering on the two well-formed males in the enclosure. Sweat is flying as they swing at each other, both connecting on every hit. I grimace, looking over to the stage, where the dancers are pretty much seducing the poles for no one, everyone in the club more interested in the blood-bath happening in the cage.

I scan the space, looking for Theo, but find Jess instead, sitting at the bar. "Hey," I say as I pull a stool over and join her. "What are you doing here?"

"Thought I'd come see you."

"Except I wasn't here, and you didn't call me to tell me *you* were." My smile is teasing, and she completely ignores it.

"Callum picked me up."

"Nice of him," I reply flippantly, signaling to the barman for a drink. "Where's Theo?"

"With his mother."

"Thought so." I accept my drink when it slides toward me. I bet she's dishing out a thorough telling-off. I can't help but feel sorry for my deadly boyfriend.

"They're like rottweilers," Jess muses, looking across to the cage with a shudder. I don't look, certain I don't want to see the carnage. But I find myself swiveling on my stool on instinct when a roar of cheering breaks out, seeing one man going down in a hazy spray of blood and sweat. He hits the deck with a deafening thud, and Jess grabs my arm as I cringe and quickly turn away from the massacre.

"Everything okay?" she asks a little tentatively, sympathy emblazoned across her face.

I smile my reassurance. "Everything's fine."

Jess frowns, and my glass pauses at my lips. "Then why did Theo look like he was about to kill someone when he got here?"

"What?"

"When he arrived, he looked possessed. Two of the security guys were talking to him."

I lower my glass, rewinding back a few hours to when Theo left me in his bed. His phone was ringing. Who was calling him, and what did they tell him? "What's going on?" I say quietly, slowly lowering my glass to the table.

"Judy asked the same question, as did Callum and Andy." She turns and points toward the dressing room. "They all went that way."

I'm off my stool before she's finished, making a beeline for the dancers' dressing room. I don't want to think what I'm thinking, but Theo's apparent rage is making those thoughts unstoppable. His security men were talking to him when he arrived. Were they the ones who called him? Did they advise Theo where to find Penny's attacker?

My mind spirals. The hollering and heckling of the crowds around the fight fade, my surroundings blurred as I make my way across the club, pushing through people, around tables, and rounding the stage. I have one purpose: Find Theo and get an explanation for his apparent fury. Stop him from breaking his promise to me. It's only now I realize he didn't actually promise me he'd let it go. Was he appeasing me? Telling me what I wanted to hear? God, I'm so stupid for believing Theo could let it slide. My pace quickens, and I skirt my way through a cluster of men, apologizing when I bounce off the arm of one of them, too focused on where I'm headed rather than actually getting there. "Sorry," I blurt, looking up at him.

Familiar eyes meet mine.

My lungs shrink.

I stagger back and bounce off the chest of another man behind me. "Hey, careful, love." He steadies me, and I shake him off, watching as the man's face before me—an evil face—turns from showing shock to delight.

The man who ruined me, who brutally beat me, hasn't changed a bit. Trystan. His unkempt hair is still hanging over his ears, and his face is still worn in, a sign that he's still drinking too much. Nausea overwhelms me. He doesn't fit in here. His black silk shirt looks cheap and old, and his black trousers ill-fitted. He looks like a man who's trying to make an effort to fit in and hasn't quite gotten it right. What's he doing here?

"Well, isn't this a surprise." He sneers, taking my arm tightly. "I've missed you." The sound of his voice feels like a needle piercing my eardrum, pain searing my head. "You're below a classy joint like this. Trying to go up in the world, huh?"

I'm paralyzed, the ground coming up and swallowing me whole, giving me no escape from my wretched past. My frozen form just makes it easy for him to seize me, and he starts to drag me through the club, my feet tripping over themselves as I try to pry his clawed fingers from my wrist. I wait for someone to stop him, to intervene, but everyone is too rapt by the violence happening beyond the bars of the cage. I fight in vain to break free, but he's too strong. I'm going nowhere.

I look back, seeing the distance between me and the dressing rooms growing. Then I look for Jess where I left her at the bar. She's talking to the barman, only just visible through the crowds. "Jess!" I yell, but my voice doesn't even dent the noise of the club.

I yelp as I'm yanked with a painful jolt to my shoulder toward the door. I can't let him get me out there. I can't let him get me on my own, can't go back to those dark days. I spot two men at the entrance, and hope fills me. They'll see me. I'm about to call to them, to get their attention, when I hear Trystan curse. I'm shoved into a hidden alcove in the lobby area, his hand over my mouth, the stench of cheap cologne invading my sense of smell. The scent is familiar, and it's overpowering me, encouraging the unbearable flashbacks. Sneering, he pulls his hand back, and I close my eyes,

cowering, waiting for the blow. The sound of his palm connecting with my face explodes in my head, and my cheek bursts into
flames, the sting radiating through me, the pain familiar. Tormenting images bombard my mind, taking me back ten years to a
time I've fought to forget.

An attack of memories forces my eyes open, and I come face-to-
face with him. Eyes closed, eyes open. In this moment, there is no
escape. His hand cups me over my jeans, and I whimper. Then he
grabs my breast. "They've grown."

I choke on my sob, vibrating against his body pushed close to
mine, shaking my head frantically. He smiles. It stirs the repulsion in my stomach, makes me gag into his palm. "Tell me, have
you learned any new moves?" Letting my eyes close again, I do
what I haven't had to do for so many years. Detach myself. Blank
my mind and feelings. And, Theo's face is suddenly all I see in my
darkness. His hard, cut, angry, handsome face. I breathe in as I feel
Trystan's hand moving its way down to my inner thigh. Polluted.
I'll be polluted again. It'll take me years to cleanse myself, to feel
clean and normal again.

No.

I won't be that girl again. I *can't* be that girl again.

I don't know how, but I find strength in my fear, my knee coming up and meeting his groin with force. I wrench myself free,
shoving him away, and run as fast as my legs will carry me back
into the main club.

Two of Theo's security men are thundering toward me, both of
their eyes taking me in as they approach. I hurry past them, my
face down so they can't see my spooked expression, and then aimlessly fight through the crowds, seeing the ladies' bathroom up
ahead. I push my way in and slam the door behind me, immediately regretting coming this way. He'll come after me. I'll be
trapped in here. I stare at the door, waiting, my heartbeats pound-

ing in my ears. I chance a quick glance at the mirror, seeing a girl I thought I'd never see again. A scared girl, pale, with wary eyes and a shaky body. Marks on her face. Marks...everywhere. My hands go into my hair and grip harshly, my breathing getting more fraught and panicked. No. No, I mustn't let myself go to those places of terror again. He doesn't have that power over me anymore. My body disagrees, trembling terribly, my heart hurting from the vicious pounding. *Think. Think. Think.*

I reach for my back pocket and grab my phone, fumbling and dropping it to the tile floor. And as I bend to grab it, the door swings open, and I let out a muffled cry, closing my eyes and stumbling back, bracing myself for him.

"Izzy?" Judy's anxious call dents my meltdown just enough to make me open my eyes to check I'm not hearing things. My arse hits the bank of sinks behind me just as her face falls into focus, and the relief it brings—to see it's actually her and not Trystan—makes my legs buckle. I crumple to the floor in a heap of shaking limbs, unable to speak.

"Lord have mercy, what is it?" The sound of her heels rushing over echoes around the restroom, the knees of her Chanel trousers meeting the floor before me. "Izzy, oh my goodness, you're burning up." She feels my forehead. "And you're sweating." She dives for one of the folded face cloths that are stacked by the sink above me and runs it under a cold tap, bringing the cool material to my face and patting away worriedly. I hiss when the burn of my cheekbone flames under the cloth. God damn, the pain.

Judy looks over her shoulder when the door opens again, as do I, my shakes intensifying. Jess takes in the scene, eyes wide. "What's happened?"

"I don't know," Judy says, returning her attention to me. "I found her in here. I think she's having a panic attack."

"Izzy?" Jess says as she hurries over, her medical instinct taking over. "Izzy, can you hear me?" She grabs my wrist and feels. "Jesus, your pulse is through the roof. And what the hell happened to your face?"

"Get Theo," Judy orders harshly. "He's gone to the office. Second door on the left out of here."

Bile burns up my throat, and I scramble free from Judy's fussing hands and throw my head over the sink, retching painfully. "No," I plead as Jess heads for the door. "I'm fine." Theo is going to demand to know what's wrong. I can't tell him. It'll be a murder scene out there.

I feel a palm rubbing at my back and hear faint, soothing words from Judy. My head is blitzed with tormenting memories—the bruises, the bastard's hand sailing through the air and connecting with my face. His hand on my leg. The knife held at my throat while he warned me not to move. And then the cuts to my stomach when I was stupid enough to, making him fight with me, the knife flailing uncontrolled. I retch again, seeing Jess by the door in the reflection of the mirror. I shake my head as best I can, silently telling her not to get Theo.

"Go!" Judy yells. Jess looks at me, torn. But she doesn't get the chance to obey Judy's demand.

The sound of the door hitting the wall alerts me to Theo's presence, followed by a string of explicit language. He's crowding me a second later, his arms wrapped around my waist, his body bending over mine where I'm braced against the sink. He jolts behind me in time to my continued heaves.

"I found her in here," Judy explains. "In a mess, sweating, shaking."

"Izzy," Theo says softly, pulling my hair back. "What's the matter, baby? Talk to me."

I can only shake my head, trying to get a hold of myself as my mind works hard, fighting to build an explanation for my epic meltdown.

"Take your time," he whispers, his palm splayed on my stomach, his front pushed into my back. "Breathe."

It takes minutes for me to gain some kind of composure, but when I look up to the mirror, I see that my face is still drained of color. My watery green eyes meet Theo's fretful blue ones. And his worry transforms into rage when he catches the mark on my cheek. "I'm sorry," I mumble, fumbling for the tap to splash my face. "I suddenly felt unwell. I tripped in my rush to get to the bathroom."

His hand lands on mine over the tap, stopping me from turning it on, and I look up at him in the reflection of the mirror, feeling his whole body lock up against mine. "Leave us," he says over his shoulder, his lips hardly moving, his eyes holding me captive.

I detect Judy and Jess moving out of the bathroom as dread fills me. My excuse was lame. It was an insult, and Theo looks thoroughly insulted. When I hear the door close, I swallow, watching as his cobalt eyes become darker and darker, fury filling them. He begins to slowly rotate my body until I'm facing him, my head lowering to avoid his wrath.

What can I say? What will he do? Maybe if I keep him here long enough, the bastard who broke me will be gone by the time Theo gets out of the restroom. Firm fingers seize my jaw and lift. The sharp edges of his handsome face are as scary as can be. "Tell me why you're in this state. And tell me what the fuck happened to your face."

My eyes flood, and I glance away, evading the building rage. "I feel—"

"As God as my witness, Izzy, I will rip my club to shreds until I find an answer."

I shrink, wholeheartedly believing him. "Please," I beg, for no purpose other than stalling him. He's going out there whether I tell him or not, and I don't doubt for a moment that he'll hunt down what's got me in such a state.

He pulls my face up, his lips straight with impatience. "The man in the tacky black shirt," he says. "I've seen him before. At Stan's tattoo shop, in the waiting room. Who is he?"

I lose my breath, giving myself away. "He's no one."

"Don't lie to me, Izzy. I had Stan give him a free pass to the Playground."

"You invited him here?" I gasp. "You exposed me to him knowingly?" I can't devote one second to the fact that I have completely failed in my attempt to keep Theo in the dark. I'm too shocked.

"My men have been watching him since he arrived. I needed to know if it was him who got you all anxious that day at Stan's. Now I do."

"Watching him?" I question in disbelief. "He just dragged me through your club and cuffed my face!"

His jaw ticks wildly, and I know his men will pay for their failure. "Who is he?" Theo asks, more calmly than I know he's feeling. "Tell me who the fuck he is."

"Trystan," I choke, looking away. "He was a client at the strip club I..."

He sucks in air and drops me from his hold, stepping back. His body is vibrating, and I know this is just the beginning of his rage. Just the sparks before the explosion. "What did he do to you?"

My eyes close, air burning my empty lungs. I feel defeated. "He..." My words are lost on a sob.

Theo reaches and touches my cheek, and I flinch, not because it hurts, but because I can feel his burning anger. "Tell me."

"He raped me," I reply quietly, the words weak and loaded with shame.

Sparks of anger bounce around the room. "No," Theo whispers. "No, no, no."

I nod, feeling so hopeless, weak, and dirty. I see in my mind's eye the way he looked at me; I feel the soft touches that turned into hard punches when I dared flinch. The knife he had no control of. I fought his intentions. And I have scars on my stomach to prove it. "He used to watch me every day at the club. Then one night he followed me after work. I woke up in a hospital."

I hear Theo's inhale. Virtually hear his mind working fast to grasp everything. "The police?"

"The doctor called them."

"And?"

"And I didn't talk. Refused the internal examination." His face bunches, like he doesn't get it. Doesn't understand why I wouldn't talk and accept help. "I was a stripper, Theo. The club was nothing like the Playground. The clients were nothing like yours. I was ashamed of myself enough, without having others judge me and tell me that I asked for it. I just needed to get away. I needed to put it behind me and move on, not be dragged through questioning and interrogations." I take a breath to finish. "And I didn't have someone like you to protect me, either."

He swallows, and it's a hard swallow. "The hospital was your safe place. And when I lost you your job, I took that away from you."

"You didn't know." I register his increasingly quaking form. "Theo." I move forward, ready to reason with him, to stop him from doing what he's already planning in his mind. But he steps away from me, out of reach. He doesn't trust himself. His control is being hampered by rage. And in this moment, something dawns on me. Something I hate. "Where is Trystan now?" I question. Theo's men were watching him. They were on the way to the lobby when I passed them.

"Being held by security." He doesn't hold back. "And now after what you've told me, what he did to you, he's a fucking dead man." He stalks out, too fast for me to gather myself and make a grab for him.

And I stand there for a moment, staring at the door closing behind him. *He's a fucking dead man.* "Theo!" I come to life, racing after him. "Theo, no!" I yell, my distress crippling.

He starts pulling off his suit jacket as he prowls through his club, throwing it into a booth as he passes. Callum catches it out of pure reflex. "What the fuck?" he asks, scrambling out of his seat, leaving Jess looking bewildered.

"What's going on?" Judy asks, approaching, her eyes on her son's back. People are scurrying out of Theo's path as he strides through the club, murder etched across his face.

I carry on after him. "He's here."

"What?" Callum shouts, grabbing me and pulling me to a stop. "Who's here?"

"Trystan," I blurt mindlessly, trying to push him away so I can go after Theo.

Callum doesn't let me. He holds me in place with one punishing hand wrapped around my upper arm, his face coming close, tight with unease. "Who's Trystan, Izzy? And what the fuck did he do to you?"

I swallow, my lips quivering, not prepared to say the words.

I don't need to. "Fuck," Callum hisses, dropping me and running through the club in pursuit of his friend.

"What's going on?" Judy whispers, reaching for my arm as she watches Callum go. Turning toward me, she holds me in place with a fierce look. "Izzy, tell me."

"I was raped," I whisper, my throat clogged with apprehension so raw. Judy's eyes widen. "And he's here." In desperation, I pull free of Judy's grip and go after Callum, coming to a screeching stop by the cage, where he's standing beside Theo, looking past the bars.

Trystan is inside, being held by Theo's two men. I become a statue, my feet stuck to the floor, my heart slowing.

"Theo, don't do this," Callum pleads, keeping his eyes on a bewildered-looking Trystan.

Theo says nothing, joining his hands in front of his groin, getting comfortable in his standing position. I don't like this. He's suddenly too calm as he stares at the bastard who destroyed me. Long, painful seconds pass, as I wait with bated breath, silently begging Callum to talk sense into Theo.

"Theo, walk away." Callum turns to his friend. "For Izzy, just walk the fuck away."

"Never." He reaches for the front of his shirt and pulls it open, not bothering with the task of unbuttoning it, and the material falls from his torso like a burning flag. Then he stalks off. And my heart plummets.

"Callum, do something." I grab his arm, shaking him. Theo enters the cage and indicates for his men to leave, locking the metal door behind them. I nearly collapse at the sight of my man in the cage, in only his jeans, muscles pulsing, fists clenching. His torso is rolling, and he's cracking his neck, his lip curled. I glance around the club, noting everyone looking wary, but I also sense sick excitement, the crowds closing in around the edges.

I remember how Stan said he missed the bloodshed, and like a fucked-up kind of spiritual summoning, I see Stan in the crowd, grinning up at the cage, his tattooed face looking more menacing than ever. He helped set this up. He gave Trystan the pass to the Playground. He got him here. Theo's fury when he came down to the club earlier was because his men told him Trystan was here. It makes sense now.

I jolt forward when someone collides with my back, and I

turn to find Judy holding on to Andy's arm, looking up at the cage. "Andy, you have to stop him," she pleads, turning to him, begging.

"How, Judy?" her husband asks. "How do you suggest I do that?"

"I don't know," she shouts. She's so upset, the cool woman becoming deranged with worry.

My dazed face turns slowly back toward Theo, and then across to Trystan. "What's this?" Trystan asks warily.

"We're gonna fight," Theo growls.

"I don't think so." Trystan laughs nervously. It's the first time I've ever seen him looking threatened.

"I do," Theo says, wandering over to him, rolling his big shoulders. "I promise I won't kill you," he vows menacingly, yet everything inside me tells me he just made a promise that's evaporated into thin air. "Recognize that woman?" Theo asks, pointing toward me. Judy takes my hand as everyone turns to face me. "That's *my* girl," Theo says quietly. "My *fucking* girl!" His roar is deafening, his body suddenly quaking before he gathers himself and breathes in deeply, his huge chest expanding as his fists clench in preparation.

I shrink, looking for somewhere to hide when Trystan looks across to me, realization dawning on his nasty face. He sneers. "You set me up?"

Theo shrugs casually. "I'll give you first punch," he says, turning away from him. "I'm a fair fighter."

The whole place erupts into chaos, but Theo...Theo just smiles—a smile full of evil and intent. Trystan is about to experience pain like nothing else. I know it the moment Theo's eyes meet mine before he closes them.

"Oh my God," Judy gasps. "No, you stupid man!" She turns to Andy, clenching at the front of his shirt and hiding her face. I look up to her husband, finding him staring with haunted eyes over my shoulder at Theo. His arm wraps around Judy's back, comforting her. "I can skim over unlawful fights, Judy. Keep the police away," he murmurs. "But I'll never get away with hiding murder." His eyes close, like a million bad memories are attacking him. "Not again."

My blank face stares at the couple, my mind trying to process what's been said. *Murder. Not again.* Oh my God. "Judy!" I yell, pulling her from Andy's hold, forcing her to face me. There are tears streaming down her perfectly made-up face.

"He...he..." she snivels, and I search her eyes, frantic for more than that.

I shake her, my desperation getting the better of me. "What, Judy? Tell me, please."

Checking around us, she moves in close, her voice dropping. "His father. He used to punch Theo when he wasn't looking, said it would build the resilience and awareness. Said it would toughen him up." Her words fade, and she looks across to the cage, flinching. "It went on for years." My fear heightens. "Until Theo killed him."

I jump back like I've been electrocuted. "No." Ice spreads like wildfire through my veins, and I whirl around, just as Trystan launches himself at Theo's back.

Cheers explode.

Carnage breaks out.

And Theo turns into the killing machine I know now he really is.

His whole body engages, his muscles, his mind, his fists, and he swings around, cracking Trystan on the jaw with a rock-solid punch, sending him sailing through the air with a bloodcurdling yell. I see a broken jaw before I see a few teeth spray into the air. Trystan lands on his back with a thud, the crowd cheering like a bunch of bloodthirsty sickos. It's ugly. Yet Theo's animalistic movements are almost artistic in their unfolding. There's nothing uncontrolled about them. Nothing unplanned or wild. I can see the look of intent on his face. He knows exactly what he's doing, and that is far more frightening than the frenzied actions of the uncontrolled man that I've witnessed before. He has a plan. From the moment I lost my composure in that tattoo studio and refused to feed his need for an explanation, he was on a mission. I should have known he'd get to the bottom of it.

And now he's going to kill it.

My bottom lip begins to tremble, the outcome of this mess set in stone, history wrote before it's written. There's nothing anyone can do to save Trystan. He's trapped in that cage with a monster who won't stop until he's finished. I fear Theo will never be finished. He killed his own father. Turned on him. Punished him for hurting him. Trystan really is a dead man.

I turn at the sound of a quiet sob, Judy's sob, and find Andy looking full of dread as he tries to comfort his wife. Judy's eyes turn to mine, filled with tears. "There was only so long he would take his father's torment before he snapped," she says, sniffling over her words. "I don't blame my boy. His dad got what was coming to him. He was a cruel, cruel man."

The irony of it all doesn't escape me, even in the midst of destruction. Theo's father longed for his son to be his formidable successor. Went to extreme lengths to ensure it happened. And became a victim of the brutality he forced into Theo. The reason for Theo's handicap is shining like a bright diamond before me, cut and freshly polished. Theo never wanted to be this way. It's his father's doing, and a part of me—an unreasonable part, because it has to be unreasonable—can't help but feel like his father got what he deserved.

Looking blankly across to the ring, I watch as holy, painful hell is rained all over Trystan. Punishing blows to the face, hard smashes of his body to the floor, and endless kicks to his stomach. And the whole time, there's a disturbing half smile on Theo's face. He's avoided being locked up before now, gotten away with murder. This will end his freedom. All these people watching. He'll be slammed into jail for life. And I will lose him.

When Trystan starts coughing up blood, my legs find life, and I run to the edge of the cage, gripping the metal until my knuckles are white, screaming for Theo to stop. He doesn't need to kill him. He doesn't need to be locked up for murder. He's done enough. "Theo!" I scream his name, over and over, ignoring the dryness of my throat.

He stills, looming over Trystan's battered body with his fist drawn back, ready to drop another damaging blow. Not that Trystan would feel it now. He's unconscious, limp and lifeless on the floor. Theo turns around, his eyes wild, and I tighten my grip around the bars, bringing my face as close as I can.

"Stop," I beg quietly, though he would never be able to hear above the roaring crowd, so I rely on the pleading in my eyes. "Please."

He straightens, looking around at the masses of people in his club, delirious with excitement. Because Theo is in the cage. He's the ultimate fighter. Undefeated. An animal. Deadly. His big chest swells, sweat pouring from him. And after a few nervous moments, he drops his eyes back down to Trystan, his lip curling. Then he turns and stalks out of the cage, slamming the metal door behind him. A path clears, people jumping out of his way before running to the foot of the enclosure to see just how much damage Theo's done. I can see from here. Trystan is lying motionless in a pool of blood, not even the sound of the crowd stirring him. But he's breathing. I push away from the bars and whirl around, searching for Theo. I catch sight of him disappearing through the door toward the office and make urgent tracks, going after him.

"Izzy, no." Judy intercepts me, fighting to keep me in place. "Leave him, sweetheart. Let him cool off."

"No." I wrestle her away, escaping just before Andy makes a grab for me. I need to see him. Calm him. I run through the club like a woman possessed, people moving from my path.

I stumble into the office, my feet skidding to a stop. Theo is on the other side, his forehead resting on the door that will take him back through to his house. I wait, forcing my breathing to quiet. He eventually lifts his head and yanks the door open, steaming through. I'm in quick pursuit. I can't be certain that he's even aware I'm here, but it doesn't stop me. I need to make sure he doesn't do anything stupid. Or anything *more* stupid. He shouldn't be alone.

We're at his private quarters fast, Theo a good ten paces in front of me, and when he pushes his way in, I just catch the door before it shuts in my face. He heads straight for the fireplace, resting his hand on the edge, dropping his head and breathing deeply. He's trying to calm himself. His back is rippling dangerously, dripping with sweat. I approach with caution, keeping a keen eye on his every move. "Theo," I reach for his shoulder, instinct guiding me, telling me to comfort him in his darkness. "Theo, it's me." My fingers lightly brush over his burning skin.

He moves too fast for me to react.

The impact to my face is explosive. The pain indescribable.

Though I don't have to suffer it for long.

My world goes black.

CHAPTER 25

The pain. Jesus, the pain. My face feels like it's in flames as I blink, trying to gather my bearings. Fussing hands and panic-stricken voices are a blur of motion and sound while I try to figure out where I am.

"Izzy, open your eyes." The voice is stressed, and I try to zoom in on the silhouette of a body bent over me, groaning as I lift my hand to my face, the throbbing getting worse. My eye socket is tender, and I wince. "Leave it." A hand takes mine and pushes it back to the floor gently. Callum's face comes into focus, but only in my right eye, horrified lines marring his usual good looks. My neck cracks painfully when I turn my head to establish who else is on the floor with me.

"Sweetheart." Judy's red lipstick has completely worn away, leaving her straight lips stained and lusterless. Her dread-filled eyes flick to my left eye, and she flinches, quickly looking away. "I told you to let him calm down, sweetheart. Why didn't you leave him to calm down?"

"Oh, Izzy," Jess whispers, despairing and shocked.

I battle through the unbearable pain to try to locate any recollections, my brain hurting with the effort. But once I find the memories, there's no stopping them from thundering forward, re-lentlessly reminding me of why I'm on my back on the floor with Judy, Jess, and Callum fussing around me.

"No." I shake my head, hissing with the pain. In my darkness, I can see Theo's back, stalking through the corridors to his apart-ment. I see his face, riddled with a rage too potent to comprehend. The movements of his body as they made easy work of Trystan in that cage, and the minuscule effort it took for him to inflict so much damage. And then back here, when I tried to calm him. Why did I follow him? Why did I think I could pull him from his destructiveness? The vision of my hand moving slowly toward his shoulder spikes a whimper of despair, my mind screaming for me to stop. How I wish I could go back and stop my stupid self from touching him. And, finally, the top half of his body as it swung around, and his big hand as it collided with my face. It all hap-pened too quickly.

"I'm sorry," I sob, curling into a ball, making myself small. "I thought I could help."

Soothing hushes sound close to my ear, and I feel the smooth-ness of Callum's cheek against mine as he cradles me on his lap, holding me tightly. I can feel his heartbeat against my arm that's squished against him, his head shaking above mine.

"Where is he?" I snivel, pushing myself from Callum's arms. Theo will be devastated. I need to see him. I look around the room, panicked as I try to get to my feet. "I need to find him."

Callum helps me up, keeping hold of my arm. I wish I didn't need the support, but I do. My head starts to spin, and I stagger a few steps back into him, struggling to focus. "Easy," he breathes, steadying me. "You need to lie down."

"I'm fine," I insist, willing some life into my legs so I can go in search of Theo. I glance up, brushing my hair from my face.

And I see him.

He looks shell-shocked, whitewashed, a shadow of a man as he stands across the room in silence looking on. My mouth dries, taking away any chance I have of speaking, of calling to him, so I force my hand up, stretching for him, silently begging for him to come to me. He doesn't.

Instead, he starts backing away, his head shaking, his eyes locked on mine. "I did that," he mumbles mindlessly, his shoulder catching the doorframe and jolting him. But he keeps moving away.

"Theo," I call, seeing his intention too clearly.

"I hurt you." His eyes widen, like realization keeps dawning, his shocked mind opening up to the horror. "I hurt my love." His gaze drops, and I wrestle with Callum to free me, but his grip is too firm, too secure.

"Let go of me!" I scream, seeing Judy move in and stand in front of me, blocking my path to her son. She's facing me, her hands joining Callum's and holding me in place. "Stop!" I cry, my eyes bursting with desperate tears. "Please, let me go to him." The tears roll and through the blur of my vision, I see Theo turn, his back getting farther and farther away. "Please," I sob, frantically fighting my way out of their holds.

"Izzy, no!"

I break free and rush forward, a little disoriented. "Theo, wait." He stalks on, his pace increasing as he makes his way through his house. "Theo!" I chase after him, my weak, hurting body slowing me, and I yell, willing my limbs to cooperate.

When I make it back to the club, the space is empty and quiet, everyone gone, and I spot Theo, still shirtless, his torso smeared in blood and sweat. I come to a gradual stop when I register where he's heading. The cage.

"No." I look past the bars, seeing Trystan being helped out of the enclosure by two of Theo's men. The fact that he's conscious—

alive, even—doesn't relieve my worry. "Theo," I yell, and he stops, but he doesn't turn back. He just stands motionless for a few moments, rolling his shoulders, his head dropped. Then it slowly lifts, and I know he's found Trystan. He approaches, takes him from the two men, and virtually throws him back into the cage. He doesn't shut the door behind him this time. Looking up at me, his eyes rooted to my swollen eye, I know what he's thinking. He blames Trystan for it. He blames himself, but he also blames Trystan. Our eyes meet. I shake my head, silently begging him not to do it. Though, deep down, I know I am begging in vain.

Theo moves his eyes from mine to his feet, where his prey is sprawled, staring up at him, frightened. And in a lightning-fast move, Theo roars and throws his fist down into Trystan's throat with so much power, his neck visibly crushes, obliterating his windpipe and his ability to breathe.

Instant death.

My body bends at the waist, and I throw up at my feet, choking and heaving uncontrollably. "Izzy." Arms grab me, Judy pulling me up and into her arms, holding me upright on my shaky legs.

I look over her shoulder and catch Theo watching me. He's still. In a trance.

Then he walks calmly out of the cage, and I know exactly what will happen next. He's leaving. He's finished Trystan off to make sure he can't hurt me again. To make sure that when Theo's gone, I'm in no danger.

He strides out of the club, and his back disappears as I slowly crumple in Judy's arms. I've failed. I haven't fixed him. I've ruined him beyond repair, and the reality is all too painful.

Because he's gone.

And I know I will never see him again.

CHAPTER 26

The hours turn into days. The days turn into weeks. Dark and gloomy weeks. Empty weeks. Because Theo's gone. He left me hurt and broken, though I know my desolation won't touch the level of misery he will be feeling.

Wherever he may be.

Not a minute passes when I don't think of him. When I don't wonder where he is. I call his phone every day, hoping today might be the day it rings. Four weeks later and it still hasn't. Judy and Callum spent the first week of his absence searching everywhere they could think of. His bank accounts and cards showed nothing. Still don't. Andy did what he could, looked in all the obvious and nonobvious places, and turned up nothing. No missing persons report could be filed. Theo left of his own accord. And Andy quite rightly pointed out that if someone doesn't want to be found, then they won't be. If anyone can relate to that, then I can. Each day I've become less hopeful. Now I'm barely surviving.

He killed a man. Battered him to death in that cage. Andy sat me down and asked me if there is anyone who would miss Trystan. How would I know? I haven't seen him for ten years. If there was anyone in his life now, like me back then, I'm guessing they wouldn't miss the malevolent arsehole. I don't know what they did with his body. Or if it will ever be discovered. Not that it matters. You can't lock a man up for murder if he can't be found.

The only thing keeping me going at the moment is work. I managed to get myself on the nurse bank, and I've worked as often as I can, dreading my days off. Today is my day off. I've wandered to the nearest coffeehouse and sat in the window, watching the rain fall, the water sliding down the glass, distorting my view. Not that I'm looking. More staring blankly through the obstacles—the people, the buildings, the rain—at nothing.

When the chair next to me scrapes, a sign of someone pulling it out, I glance up and Judy smiles down at me, nodding at the table. I say nothing, returning my attention to the window, my hand wrapped around my takeout coffee cup where it rests on the table. She sits, sighs, and places her hand on mine.

"How did you find me?" I ask for the sake of it.

"Really, Izzy? If you're not at home, you're either here or at work." I look at her, and she shrugs. "And Jess called me."

"I'm fine."

"You are not fine. You're still not eating properly, you look pale, and I'm pretty sure you're anemic." A bottle of iron tablets is placed on the table before me. "I want you to take these."

I stare at the bottle, wondering when it became Judy's job to mother me. Then I inwardly scold myself for having such a hurtful thought. Anyway, it's not like I have anyone else to do the job. These past four desolate weeks have made me constantly wonder what I did in a previous life to deserve such a rough time.

I take the pills and slip them into my bag, hopefully pacifying her. I'm not anemic. I'm grieving. "Thank you," I murmur, turning back to the window.

"Oh, Izzy." She sighs. "Sweetheart."

"What?" I ask. "Are you going to tell me to move on? To forget about him?"

"I—"

"Are you going to?"

Total despair invades her smooth features. "I don't know what to say anymore."

I push my chair away and stand, swiping up my coffee, needing to escape before I burden her with more tears. But they come too fast, streaming down my face relentlessly, prompting Judy to shoot up from her chair and embrace me. "I'm sorry," I whimper pitifully into the expensive threads of her suit jacket. She must be sick of the sight of me, but she still insists on keeping our contact. I'm an emotional drain to her, a broken waif. Why is she insisting on burdening herself with me?

"Sweetheart, I just know Theo wouldn't want you to have your life on hold for him."

"Then he should come back to me so I can carry on with it. With him. Where is he, Judy?" My voice breaks, and my shoulders start jerking wildly. "Why isn't he coming back to me?"

"I don't know," she admits on a sigh. But I do, and it's killing me. I knew he'd never forgive himself if he ever hurt me. It was the very reason I halted his intention to take me without the restraints that kept me safe that one time he so desperately needed to show me how much he loved me. That he could do it. Stopping him was a wise move. What I did after he'd bludgeoned Trystan wasn't. And I'll never forgive myself for putting him in that situation. For exposing him. For pushing him to murder.

But what's worrying me the most is what Theo will do to himself, whether he'll punish himself. Reluctantly, I accept that this is his punishment. Depriving himself of me. And at the same time, he's punishing me, too. If I could only see him or talk to him, I could tell him that. I'm a mess, broken.

My heart is showing no signs of healing. The crack is getting wider each day he's absent. I'm slowly dying on the inside, and I fear nothing will bring me back to life except him. But my cure, my hope, doesn't want to be found.

* * *

I'm always so grateful when it's busy on shift. The days when my feet don't touch the ground because I'm flat-out hectic and I'm not given the chance to stop for a moment to breathe, let alone think. If I'm lucky, I'm so tired by the end that I can only focus on getting myself home and collapsing into bed.

Today is one of those days. In fact, today has been the busiest shift in my entire career, and I've gone three hours over my official quitting time. That's also a blessing these days. The unexpected arrival of patients, the bed manager asking for beds that we haven't got, patients having unexpected relapses. I've welcomed the chaos.

As I drag my coat on and scoop up my bag, I pass the nurses' station and call my goodbye, hearing the sounds of stressed conversations. I mildly smile on the inside. They have the whole night to get through. I wrap my scarf around my neck as I walk, checking my phone for the call or message that I know won't be there. It's habit, a part of my everyday life now. So is the disappointment when I see nothing from Theo.

I push my way through the endless double doors, working my way toward A&E and the closest exit. It's Saturday night, so I'm not surprised when I find a mess of rushed doctors, stressed nurses, and many patients in the wards, most of them drunk. Holding my bag on my shoulder, I weave through the scatterings of people, peeking in the bays as I go. Drunk. Drunk. Vomiting. Drunk.

I pass the reception area, where a huddle of people are waiting to be seen, checked in, or given information, and break through the doors into the cold evening air. Despite the no-smoking policy on the hospital grounds, there are dozens of people puffing away just outside the door, rather than walking the twenty meters that will technically take them off the property. I cough my way through the plumes of nicotine-infested air, my nose wrinkling, and cut across the walkway toward the main street.

I pick up my pace, but notice some paramedics up ahead offloading a bed from their ambulance, looking urgent and rushed. I slow my stride to let them pass. The drunken man tailing me, however, doesn't, and staggers right in front of the bed, causing the wheels to catch his ankles and knock him to his arse, as well as jar the bed to a halt. My hand covers my mouth, and the paramedics start shouting their annoyance at the drunken idiot for hindering them. The paramedic leading the bed is doing so with one hand, his other holding up a drip. His face flames red. "Move, you fool," he yells, trying to get the bed around the squirming body of the drunk on the ground.

I rush over to get the inebriated idiot out of their way. "Sir, you need to get up," I say, hooking my arms under his armpits and straining to lift his deadweight. My nose is invaded with the putrid stench of stale alcohol and weeks' worth of bad personal hygiene. "He won't budge," I huff, losing my hold. He falls back to the ground like a sack of potatoes, rolling and flailing around. I look to the paramedics, the unconscious patient on the bed catching my eye.

Time stops.

My heart stops.

The world stops spinning.

I stagger back and my body slams into the wall behind me, my lungs exploding from the impact. "Theo," I whisper, my shocked eyes trying to fathom the picture of the broken man before me. Blood. There's blood everywhere. "Oh my God," I breathe, my body caught between taking me to him and keeping far, *far* back,

frightened to get closer and see the full extent of the unsightli-
ness—his skin sallow and gray, his cheeks gaunt, and his stubble
now a beard. I hardly recognize him.

Instinct takes over, and I run to the bed.

"Miss, please." The paramedic intervenes, pulling me away.
"Do you know him? Can you tell us his name?"

"He's my boyfriend," I choke, scanning his face for any sign
of life. There's none. He's motionless. Looks dead. "His name is
Theo. Theo Kane." I shrug off the paramedic and shoot forward,
looking Theo up and down, seeing his chest naked beneath the
thin blankets. More blood. "What's happened to him?" My heart
breaks in two, the sight of my big, strong man so utterly broken
putting too much strain on the crack that's caused me agony since
he left.

The two paramedics negotiate the bed around the drunken man,
leaving him on the ground. "He was found by the docks. Unconscious, unresponsive, low pulse rate. He's not in a good way, darling."

They burst through the doors of the emergency care unit, and a
flood of nurses hurry toward us, obviously awaiting Theo's arrival.
The paramedic sends one out to the drunken man, and I barely
stop myself from shouting my outrage. Theo needs every nurse he
can get. They begin work on him immediately as the paramedics
carry on wheeling him down the corridor, reeling off everything
from his name to his blood pressure, from where they found him
to his injuries.

I'm in a daze of nothingness, running alongside the bed, listening and watching the madness unfold. I hear the word *critical*. I
hear them tell the nurses that he has a suspected punctured lung
resulting from broken ribs. But what's holding most of my attention is the sudden sight of Theo's body jerking. It appears to be
in spasm, constantly twitching on the bed. Yet when I look to his
face, nothing.

All my nursing instincts go out the window. I'm not calm, I'm not collected, and I'm not thinking straight. If these medical professionals weren't here, I wouldn't know what to do. My heart is beating so fast it's a vibration in my chest, my ears pounding with the pressure of blood pumping around my body.

Theo's wheeled into a cubicle and I'm stopped at the threshold, the nurse pushing me back a little to leave room for the many people working on him. It takes everything in me to obey. To give them space and not lunge forward and seize Theo in my arms. Watching as a nurse tries to insert a cannula into his arm pains me. His twitching body keeps knocking her off target, and she repeatedly stabs at his flesh, never hitting the vein she needs.

Pads are slapped onto his torso and wires clipped into place, leading to a heart monitor. The second it comes to life, my own heart nearly slows to a stop. His heart rate is completely irregular. He's unconscious, but his body continues to jerk. No matter how hard I search my medical brain for a reason for these symptoms, I'm coming up blank. Is he having a seizure? Then all hands are off him, just for a split second, but in that split second his body stills. And I realize why when hands return to working on him and his erratic twitching begins again.

He doesn't like them touching him. The comprehension gives me a tiny glimmer of hope. His body is trying to react, but he hasn't the strength. He's aware. He knows what's happening but can't stop it. And neither can I, because if I get these people off him, he'll die. His head is pulled back and a breathing tube fed down his throat. I wince at another sign of preparation. They think he could go into arrest at any moment.

I silently beg them to work faster, to give his heart the shock it needs to reset and find an organized beat before it stops completely. One of the nurses pulls the pads out, ready to give that shock.

But then it happens. He flatlines, and the pads get tossed aside by the nurse with a small curse. It's too late for pads now. The alarms go mad, the shrill, warning ring of the heart monitor piercing my ears so much I'm forced to cover them with my palms until the monitor is quickly turned off. I can't watch. But I can't leave, either. I feel like I'm in limbo, depending on these people to save him. I look at the screen of the machinery and see the flat line. I can feel my heart slowly stopping, too. "No," I mumble, my eyes bursting with devastated tears. "No, Theo, no." I back up, feeling everything inside me beginning to give up completely.

Everyone starts scurrying around the bed, the urgency of the nurses cranking up to the highest level. A cardiac team appears, pushing me aside, and Theo's quickly hooked up to various monitors. I'm frozen, just watching him slip away from me. He's not jerking anymore. Hands are all over him and he's not moving. A broken sob bursts past my lips, my hand coming up to cover my mouth as I back away. The calm talking of the nurses becomes distant, the movements slow. A male nurse is pumping frantically at Theo's chest while another rushes to get a drip into Theo's arm. Looking at the heart monitor again sends tremors down my spine. Still no beat. CPR isn't working "Oh my God," I whisper, my world crumbling beneath my feet.

"I need someone to take over," the nurse pumping at Theo's chest says, so calmly, sweat dripping from his forehead.

Another nurse jumps in and relieves him, and Theo's body starts jerking again, but now it's because of the constant compressions being delivered.

I look at the monitor again. Nothing.

The nurses throw constant worried looks at each other, the atmosphere becoming more and more tense. Some drugs are pumped into him as they continue to work frantically but calmly, attempting to establish why his heart has stopped. I watch as the pharmacist prepares the next combination of drugs, anything to try to encourage the electrical activity of his heart. It's a process of elimination, a race to find out why his heart has stopped before it's too late.

"Switch," the nurse performing CPR calls, moving aside to let her colleague take over again. She looks up at the clock. She breathes in. She flicks a despairing expression to the nurse who's just accepted the next round of drugs from the pharmacist. He administers them and stands back, his face grave.

They're going to give up soon. I can sense the defeat. I peek at the monitor. And again there's no change in the flat line. "Come on, big man," the nurse grates, sweating as he relentlessly pushes into Theo's chest.

"One more?" the other nurse asks her colleague as she looks at him. I hold my breath.

"One more," he agrees, removing his hands and letting her take over again.

Everyone looks at the screen, waiting for that line to start jumping.

But it doesn't. It remains a continuous green glow, like still water. The straightest, most perfect line you could imagine. The nurses are glancing at each other again, all of them thinking the same thing, but no one wanting to be the one to call a halt on their work. And then one of them nods his head and the other pulls her hands away from Theo's chest. That's it. They've given up. I shake my head as agony tears through my body like acid, burning away any hope that may have remained. "Please," I beg.

"I'm sorry, miss." A hand rests on my shoulder, and I look blankly up to the paramedic who brought Theo in. "We did all we could."

My head turns back to the bed as they all move away. My big man is now free from feeling hands, his body still, his face peaceful. I breathe in an unsteady breath, my lips trembling, my eyes pooling, as I tread carefully toward him, as quiet as can be, like I'm scared I might wake him. My teeth are chattering. My eyes pouring with tears. And my heart just died along with him.

My grief pours from my eyes in fast, fat drops, dripping all over his face as I lean over him, getting as close as I can, losing it completely. I cry like I've never cried before, in loud, body-jerking sobs. "Where were you?" I weep, my breath hitching over my words. "Where were you all this time, Theo? Why didn't you come back to me?" My forehead meets his shoulder, the pain, the devastation, hitting my heart like a bullet, causing the crack to branch off like breaking glass, ensuring it's completely broken.

Destroyed.

Dead.

I can feel grief gripping me, holding me prisoner in its clutches, and I know it will never let me go. He's gone. I've lost him. I'm fast slipping into darkness, my body physically rolling in pain.

Rolling.

My body is rolling. It undulated, and it wasn't my relentless sobbing that made it do so. I still, swallowing down my next sob, waiting for it to happen again. But it doesn't. I pull away from Theo's lifeless form, scrubbing at my eyes and looking across at the heart monitor. The line is still flat, and a doctor has started to disconnect the wires. "Wait," I murmur. I see him look over the bed to me out of the corner of my eye, but I keep my eyes trained on that screen, waiting, hoping, praying.

"Miss?"

"Just wait," I say, the seconds ticking by slowly. Nothing happens. No signs of life. I grit my teeth, willing movement of the line, even just a little flicker. "Come on," I breathe, grabbing Theo's hand. He jerks, and I jump back in fright. "Try again," I shout, urgency coursing through my veins. "You have to try again."

"Miss, he's gone," the nurse says gently, his hands paused on the wires.

"He moved."

"That's not unusual."

"He moved," I yell, squeezing Theo's hand, mentally encouraging another one.

"Miss, we know about spinal reflexes. It happens often after a passing."

"It wasn't a spinal reflex," I yell frantically, turning to one of the nurses who was giving Theo chest compressions. "He moved because I touched him. All of his movements when you brought him in were because you were all touching him. He doesn't like being touched." I release Theo's hand and rush over to the nurse, grabbing the front of his uniform. I'm aware this could be considered assaulting a staff member, but I don't care if they throw me in jail for ten years. He moved. "Please, try again," I demand, my deranged behavior sending the room quiet. "Please, I beg you. He's still got life in him."

The nurse flicks his eyes over to his colleague, then to Theo on the bed as I wait what seems like a lifetime for him to give in to my demand. Yes or no, Theo will be getting more CPR. I'll do it myself if I have to. Seconds tick by, and I give up waiting for him to decide whether he's going to try. I run across to do it myself, my hands looking so small against Theo's chest as I start pumping. I'm out of breath after a few seconds, my strength pitiful as I sob through my weak attempts.

"Move," the nurse says, pushing his way past me. "We need some weight behind the compressions."

So much air leaves my lungs, they hurt. He glances at the monitor as he puts his hands into position, and I can see the doubt in his eyes. But he starts pumping anyway, his jaw tight. He's exhausted; there's a sheen of sweat coating his face. He doesn't ask for someone to take over. He carries on, small grunts escaping with each compression. "Come on," he whispers. The gray skin of Theo's face and the blackness of his sockets seem to darken before my eyes as I wait, a lump that feels like a tennis ball settling in my throat. All three of us stare at the flat line, seeing no change, and I start to build my plea for another round of compressions. For more drugs. Anything. My joined hands come up to my face, praying.

And then it happens. What I've prayed for actually happens.

The line jumps.

My hands fall away from my face, my eyes burning, refusing to blink in case I miss it.

Another jump. "Oh my God," I breathe, tripping over my feet to get to the bed. My dark world gets an injection of life. Another jump. I grab Theo's hand, stroking at his sallow cheeks. "Theo."

"Fucking hell," the nurse breathes, and I look to him, my eyes welling. He looks like a ghost. "I can't believe it." He staggers back, scrubbing his hands down his face.

"I told you," I say, trying not to get too far ahead of myself. I just knew it. I knew he was strong. There's a burst of activity behind me, and I look back to see most of the staff have returned, all of them taking in the scene before looking at the heart monitor. I follow their stares and see a regular, strengthening beat. I cough over a sob, sniveling as I place my palm over his heart and his tattoo, and feel the beats, too.

Urgency springs into the nurses and they all crowd around, pulling machinery from here and there, and trollies loaded with medical equipment. When one grabs Theo's arm, he jerks violently, and she curses, dropping the needle she's trying to get into the back of his hand. She'll never get that line in. "He doesn't like being touched," I say, watching her throw the needle in a medical waste bin and grab another from a new, sterilized packet. She looks at my hand on Theo's chest. "Except by me," I add, my elation lifting more. He's unconscious, yet he still knows it's me. His movements when I touched him before weren't just because I was touching him. He was speaking to me when he couldn't talk. "I'm a nurse," I explain, removing one hand from Theo and indicating down my front to my uniform. "I work here. I can do that."

She peeks up at me before going back to Theo's hand and trying again. "Thanks, but I've got it." He jerks again, and she curses, tossing yet another wasted needle into the yellow bin after she's picked it up from the floor.

I gather myself, trying not to lose my patience, and circle the bed, collecting a needle. "We haven't got time for your overgrown ego," I mutter, grabbing some gloves and pulling them on quickly. I take Theo's arm, and he doesn't even flinch. I slide the needle into the back of his hand, hitting the spot the first time. Blood gushes into the capped vial, and I breathe out, holding my hand out for the plaster. "Thank you," I say, placing it over the cannula and resting his arm by his side. "When you connect the line, don't touch him." I make my way around the bed again, to another nurse, who has just pulled in a trolley loaded with everything she needs to take his vitals.

She smiles at me, though it's tinged with sadness. "The doctor's on her way. I'm sure you don't need them to tell you that there's a high chance of brain damage."

I return her small smile, turning to Theo. "He's going to be fine," I say, because there's no doubt in my mind that he will be. He knows I'm here. He felt my touch. He fought harder for me. He's going to be fine.

The nurse moves in and peels his eyelid back, holding her light up. And as I knew he would, he moves, hampering her. She huffs and tries again, getting the same result. "He's a fidget, isn't he?"

I smile and take over her duties, assessing and noting all of

Theo's vitals without interference from any of the on-duty staff, nor from Theo. He remains unmoving. He's still out cold. But I know he's with me.

* * *

Leaving the staff to organize Theo's scans, X-rays, and transfer to ICU, I wander out of the cubicle in a bit of a daze, my adrenaline fading. I feel wiped out. Pressing my back up against the wall outside the resuscitation unit, I look up to the bright, tubular lights and take a moment to gather myself. To try to comprehend what has just happened. But despite my overwhelming relief and happiness, I still break down. Rivers of tears pour down my cheeks as I try to process it all. It's going to take some time. I was meant to work those unusually long three hours over my shift. I was meant to exit the hospital via Casualty. I was meant to be there when the ambulance arrived with Theo's dying body.

The sounds of protest hit me from the side, and I look down the corridor, seeing a team of nurses fighting with the drunken man who forced me to step in, to approach the bed Theo was being carried in on so I could help clear the paramedics' path. I would never have gotten close enough to the bed to see Theo had that drunk not bowled aimlessly in front of them. That inebriated man was supposed to be there. He was supposed to cause havoc.

I breathe out, feeling my back mold to the wall behind me as my phone rings, and I rummage through my bag, sniffing back my tears, until I lay my hands on it, seeing Callum is calling. I frown. He hasn't been in touch since I picked up my stuff from Theo's place two weeks ago. The glow of his name knocks some purpose into me. "Callum," I say in greeting, pushing my back off the wall and peeking around the corner to Theo's bed. I can barely see him for medical machinery.

"Someone has seen Theo," he blurts urgently. "Down by the docks, entering a less-than-reputable fight club."

My mouth opens to tell him I've found Theo, but no words come. My mind is too busy absorbing what I've been told and what it means. A fight club?

"Izzy, there's only one reason he'd go there," Callum goes on. "A fighter. He hates Theo. He's been trying to get him in the cage for years." Callum is puffing over his words, and I conclude it's because he's running.

"Why does he hate Theo?"

"Because Theo beat his brother into a coma," he says gravely, and I inhale. "It was years ago. I'm heading down there now. I just wanted you to be prepared for the worst."

Prepared for the worst? I peek around the corner again, seeing wires, machinery, and Theo's battered body. I'm *looking* at the worst. He went to fight someone? I close my eyes, hating what I know to be true. He was punishing himself. He allowed himself to be beaten. Penance.

"Izzy, are you hearing me?" Callum's impatient voice wakes me from my thoughts, pulling me back into the hospital where Theo is lying, barely alive, and where his friend is on the phone telling me he might have found him.

I shake myself to life, turning away from Theo and walking down the corridor. "Callum, I'm with Theo."

"What?"

"At the hospital. Theo was brought in as an emergency. He was found by the docks half-dead."

There's silence, no more puffing or sounds of exertion. Just a long, lingering, shocked silence.

"Callum? Are you there?"

"Half-dead?" he finally whispers.

I can feel my voice is going to tremble if I speak, so I wait a few moments before I do, swallowing repeatedly while I find the strength I need to give Callum the details without falling apart. "It's bad, Callum," I explain. Another swallow. "Broken ribs, punctured lung. His injuries are extensive. And internal bleeding is suspected. He arrested." I close my eyes and try not to relive the horror of that moment. "They got him back, but he's in a coma. He's been stabilized and is being sent for X-rays and scans before being transferred to ICU."

"Jesus," he gasps. "What the fuck?"

"Punishment," I tell him flatly, seeing no point withholding what I know. "He was punishing himself."

Callum doesn't bother countering my claim. He knows, too. "The stupid bastard." There's emotion in his voice that I can appreciate and empathize with. "You're there on your own?"

"I didn't get a moment to call." I feel terrible now, but the thought didn't even enter my head. "It was all a bit... frantic. Then when they got a heartbeat back, he kept moving every time a nurse tried to get a line in. I had to do it all myself."

He laughs lightly in understanding. "Unbelievable."

I smile. It really is. "He knew I was here, Callum. He was gone, but he knew I was here."

"I have no doubt, Izzy," he replies softly. "I have no doubt. I'm on my way."

"Call Judy," I blurt, thinking I'd better brace myself for more tears. Judy's going to see the condition of her son and lose sight of the fact that he's actually been found.

"I'll pick her up on the way." He disconnects, and I hold the phone to my chest, preparing myself to call Jess and go over it all again.

CHAPTER 27

I knew I wouldn't be allowed in the X-ray and scan rooms, but I still followed the porters as they pushed Theo's bed through the corridors of the hospital, a nurse tagging along with his files. I waited outside while he was x-rayed and scanned, and then I followed them up to ICU, where nurses were awaiting his arrival.

After I've sent Callum a message telling him where to find us, I sit in the corner of the private room and watch as they hook all the machinery back up, the nurse from Triage doing handover to the ward sister. I smile when she advises them of Theo's moving habit, and the sister laughs, like the nurse currently handing over the paperwork is joking. She can laugh now. He's unconscious and unable to attack. She wouldn't be laughing if he were fit, healthy, and awake with his palms wrapped around her throat.

I look to the door at the sound of an urgent voice from outside the room and jump up, finding Jess is at the desk asking where I am. "Hey," I call.

She pivots around, lots of air leaving her mouth. "Izzy!" She runs to the room and throws her arms around me. "I've been so worried. What's happened to him?"

The firmness of her hug is blissful. So needed. "I think he put himself in a fight to lose."

"Why would he do that?" She releases me and guides me over to a chair, letting me sit. She must feel my exhaustion. Approaching Theo quietly, being sure not to get in the nurse's way, she hovers over the bed, shaking her head in despair at the sight of him.

"Guilt," I breathe. Resting back, I prop my elbow on the chair's arm and let my head use it for support.

"He looks terrible." She states the obvious, probably not knowing what else to say. "What have the doctors said?"

"It's touch-and-go. They've x-rayed and scanned him. We're waiting for the results."

The door bursts open, and Judy appears, deranged with worry. "Oh my goodness, Theo." She throws herself across the room to the bed, and Callum follows, his steps hesitating as he gets his first glimpse of his friend. A haunted look passes across his face, followed quickly by one of rage. He stops in the middle of the room and stares, taking in the mess that is Theo's body.

Judy's hand clamps over her mouth in shock before reaching and retracting a few times, her red lips quivering. "Look at him," she murmurs, devastated. "What did that bastard do to him?"

"Nothing Theo didn't ask him to," Callum says, pointing to Theo's wrists. "He restrained himself."

I'm up from my chair in an instant, moving closer to get a better look. He's right. Theo's wrists are a horrid sight of welts and lacerations, evidence of being bound. I neglected to notice them among the endless other injuries. "Why?" I ask without thinking. Of course I know why, but my mind is struggling to comprehend the extent of Theo's actions.

"The stupid bastard made it easy to beat him. He needed to stop his ability to react when he was touched."

I decide here and now that as soon as Theo is back to health,

I'm going to kick his arse. I grit my teeth and turn to Judy, her sobs showing no signs of receding. "He's going to be okay," I tell her, taking her hands and doing what she's been doing for me since Theo left.

"How can he be?" she asks, looking at his mangled body and wincing. "All of this damage."

I slip my hand into hers and squeeze. "I'll fix him," I assure her. "I promise." I've never made a more sincere vow. I've already decided that I'm quitting my job. Theo's recovery is going to be long and grueling, and I plan on being there every step of the way. I won't leave his side. Not ever again.

"Are you thirsty?" Jess asks. She looks mildly uncomfortable. She wants something to do, to be busy and useful.

"Tea would be good," I reply, guiding Judy away from the bed and sitting her in the chair. "Get Judy one, too, please."

"Got it." Jess heads for the door, and Callum follows.

"I'll help." He doesn't acknowledge Jess's startled face as they go, leaving me alone with Judy.

I pull a chair over to join her, her hands fiddling in her lap, her eyes never leaving her son. But my arse doesn't make it to the seat, because a mild gurgling sound splinters the quiet, making me bolt back upright, Judy joining me a second later. Theo moans painfully and tries to move, pulling at the wires attached to him.

"Theo." I take his hand and constrict my hold, my palm going to his sticky forehead and brushing back his long hair. "Theo, can you hear me?" I turn back to Judy. "Get the doctor." I could press the call button, but she needs something to do, and Theo isn't in immediate medical danger. He's just agitated. She's gone like a rocket, and I return to Theo's squirming form. "You need to keep still. You have broken ribs."

The moans come and come, his eyes now clenched shut rather

than resting closed. "Too much," he mumbles, those two simple words making me so fucking happy.

"You're hooked up to morphine," I explain. "You need something else?"

"Izzy." His head thrashes a few times, his movements becoming dangerously erratic. "Izzy."

"Theo, I'm here."

His eyes snap open, wide and wild, the blue so dull and lifeless. "Where? Where is she?"

"Theo, look at me."

It's a horrible long few seconds before he does, but when our eyes meet, he sees me, and he knows me. "Izzy," he sighs, relaxing into the bed. There's a slight flex of his hand in mine. "You're going to fix me." He states it as a fact, and I smile and move my face in closer, letting it settle in the crook of his neck.

I try not to think about how much more there is to fix now. "I'm going to fix you." I kiss his neck and relish the comfort I get from feeling his body warming.

He uses too much effort to lift his arm so he can feel my hair, hissing a few times on the way. His fingers weave through the strands gently, his movements a little jerky, though the sensation is still so comforting. "You saved my life," he whispers.

I smile my understanding, closing my eyes and enjoying our closeness as I thank every god in history for sparing him. He isn't talking about saving his life today. He's talking about from the moment we touched.

Chapter 28

He's so slow. Almost like an old man as he hobbles in short bursts before he's exhausted and has to take a rest. I'm on the couch in his lounge pretending to read, but I'm peeking discreetly over the top of my book, keeping an eye on him as he makes his way back from the bathroom. He stops at the sideboard and rests his hand on top, taking a break. It's only been four weeks. The doctor has said it's time to start getting up and moving around, but just a little to start. That was a week ago, and I can see a tiny bit of progress each day.

Those small steps are never enough for Theo, though. He was on his back for three weeks, and had two operations—one to repair a severed artery that was causing the internal bleeding, and one to crack his shoulder into place. He's expecting too much of himself.

I haven't pressed for the sordid details of his stupid stunt. He told me he was at his wits' end, needed someone to beat the guilt out of him. I still can't bend my mind around such self-hatred. Callum, however, wanted details.

I couldn't listen, so I left the room with Jess, deciding I'd rather hear what's going on between her and Callum. Apparently, nothing, and she seems accepting of that. They have an understanding, so I'm told. Personally, I think they're both delusional idiots, but, selfishly, I have no intention to help them along to realization. Theo is my priority. Just Theo. My old man. He's been through the wringer, and the toll it's taken on him is all too clear. His muscles have shrunk, he's a little pasty, and he can barely move without running out of breath. But he still looks at me with that familiar adoration in his eyes. He still reads my mind and my moves. And that dimple I love so much is making appearances more and more each day. He's still my peace, and I'm happier now than ever. Our secrets are no longer holding us back or dictating the path of our love.

I quickly flick my eyes back to my book when his head slowly lifts in my direction. "I know you're watching me," he mumbles, starting toward me again. "Bet you're wondering what you've let yourself in for." He lowers to the couch by my feet and lets out a long, exhausted breath.

I snap my book shut and toss it on the floor. "It's going to take time, Theo," I remind him for the millionth time. "You were technically dead." I poke his bare thigh with my toe, smiling when he looks down at my pink polished toes thoughtfully.

Claiming my foot, he lifts it onto his thigh, doing a terrible job of hiding the effort it's taking him, and starts massaging. "Tell me again."

"What?"

"The story of how you saved my life." He smiles across the couch, his eyes glossy with life. "It's my favorite story."

"I didn't save your life. The man giving CPR saved your life."

"Because you threatened him." He grins a little, proud and smug. "I wish I could have seen your sass being thrown around that room."

I roll my eyes, but I can smile about it now. "I knew you were still with me."

"I could hear you." He lets his head rest on the back of the couch, looking at me as he massages my foot. "It was weird."

"I bet your level of weirdness didn't match my level of fear."

His lips press together a little, thoughtful, his eyes dropping to his working hands on my foot. "I'm sorry."

"For scaring me?"

"Of course for that, but more for leaving you." He glances up at my face. Theo didn't get to see the blackening of my eye or how it became so swollen, it shut completely. I'm glad. It would have only taken his guilt to another level, if that's possible. Which I don't think it is.

As the silence lingers, I steel myself to ask what I've been afraid to ask since I found him again. I don't want to know how or why he ended up at the fight club on the docks. *That* I don't think I could hear. Seeing the result is something I'll never wipe from my memory. But what about the time prior to that? I haven't asked. I've waited weeks for Theo to find the strength he needs to share what happened after that horrible day, but he hasn't, and despite promising myself I wouldn't push him to talk about a time I know pains him, I've gotten to a point where I feel that he must. Like therapy, I guess. He can't move on until he's relieved of the burden, and neither can I. It's the last piece of the puzzle I need.

"Where did you go?" I whisper, barely loud enough to be heard. The purposely low volume of my voice is maybe an indication that I actually don't want to know.

But Theo hears, sighing and gripping my ankle, giving it a little tug. "Come here. I want to hold you."

"Do you need to hold me?" I ask, turning my body around and shuffling down the couch, placing my head on his lap.

"I always need to hold you." I know his reply to be true, but it doesn't fill me with reassurance at this particular moment in time. Arranging my legs just so, he strokes up my thigh onto my tummy and circles his palm there for a few moments, and then so terribly slowly and tactfully, over my breast. My breath hitches. And he smiles at his hand knowingly. "That's good," he murmurs, glancing at my frowning face. He flicks my nipple gently. "You're still turned on by me, even when I look like this."

I squirm with a girlish giggle when he flexes his hips up, pushing a surprisingly hard cock into my temple where it rests on his lap. I could just turn my head, tug down his shorts, and . . .

"Stop it." My hand flies out and stills his on my boob. "You're too weak." That's something I never thought I'd say.

He makes an over-the-top display of his exasperation, his head falling back with a groan. "You're pumping me with painkillers when all I need is to fuck you good and proper. That will sort me out."

I laugh a little. "You can hardly move."

"Then you'll have to do all the work," he tells me matter-of-factly, dropping his eyes but not his head. "For once."

I throw him an indignant look. "It's hard to do anything when you're restrained."

"So that's your excuse?" He quirks a playful eyebrow, and I narrow unamused eyes on him. I know what he's doing. He's goading me, trying to force me into proving him wrong.

"Maybe next week."

Another huff of displeasure. "My balls are going to explode. They need release."

Shuffling onto my side, I get comfy, placing praying hands under the side of my head on his lap. "You were going to tell me where you were." I get us back on track, and the lust that was building in his cobalt eyes vanishes, like it was never there. "Tell me," I push softly.

He smiles a little, though it's a nervous smile. "You'll think I'm crazy."

"I already think you're crazy." I reach up and stroke his bearded face. Now I'm super curious.

"There's a village a few miles from here. We lived there before Dad bought this place and renovated it. It was quiet. A simple life."

His childhood home? "But Judy looked there. She told me so." It was one of the last places she searched, since she was sure Theo would never want to be reminded of his childhood before everything changed.

"I know." Theo shrugs sheepishly.

I balk. "You hid from her?"

"I was a mess. I didn't want her to see me like that."

I bite my tongue, knowing it'll be pointless to argue over this. What's done is done. He looks around the room, falling into thought. "I liked it there. I went to school, played in the field, and went to Sunday school like a good little Catholic boy." He smiles. "Father Byron made me recite the Lord's Prayer whenever he saw me—in the shop, on the street, playing with my friends. Wouldn't let me go on my way until I'd reeled it off perfectly. No mistakes. He said God was proud of his children, especially those who knew his prayer." Looking down at me, he tilts his head a little, combing through my hair with his fingers. My lips twist, feeling sorrowful. He's speaking fondly. Because this is the nice part of his tale. There's more to come, some of which I know and don't like, and some of which I don't know. And I know I'm not going to like those parts, either.

"Things changed when we moved away," he goes on, lost in a reverie, now talking freely and easily. "Dad needed to be closer to business and took the fight club out of an old derelict factory and put it here. He was raking it in. Thriving on the money and the power." He laughs lightly, when I believe he should be laughing coldly. "He *really* thrived on the power. My carefree childhood was lost the second he moved us out of the village. He'd never paid much attention to me, but suddenly I had lots of attention. And it wasn't good attention. He used to cuff me around the head as he passed and tell me I should be prepared for the unexpected. Said I was a wuss. A poor excuse for a male. As soon as I was old enough, he threw me in the cage. I was sixteen. Just a skinny kid."

"No..." I inhale my shock, disgusted.

"I took a few too many poundings. I had no choice but to toughen up or be used as a punching bag every weekend. He carried on hitting me, and I carried on cowering."

I bury my face in his lap, wanting to hide from the horrors. Wuss? Poor excuse for a male? Now his father's words are laughable. Theo is the most prime example of masculinity. A perfect specimen. A warrior. Because it was survival. It makes me sick to think his bastard father would be proud of him.

"Your mom?"

He looks at me, and I get it. He beat Judy, too. Theo nods, seeing where my mind is. "He had handy fists. I trained myself to always be prepared for his backhands or unexpected jabs. I was constantly on my guard. Then one day I won my first fight. Dad lost a shitload of money and went mad. No one thought I'd win. He called another fight immediately with a notorious fighter. I won that one, too. I started earning Dad a lot more money. I was a cash cow. Isn't it ridiculous that I was happy because for once he seemed proud of me?" He shakes his head, dismayed. "Then one day I refused to fight. I was tired. Exhausted. He got mad and ordered his men to drag me into the cage. I battered them all and left, and Dad followed me. I didn't realize, and when I got into his office to go back to the house, he punched me in the back." Theo winces, and I squeeze his hand in support. "It was fucking hard. I wasn't expecting it. I—"

My gut tells me to stop him, so I do. I lift my hand and place it over his mouth, preventing him from finishing. I get it. I don't need to hear the rest. "Enough."

Theo has other ideas. "I lashed out," he mumbles against my hand before pulling it away. "Every punch he'd ever given me and Mum, I returned tenfold in that mad few minutes until he was unconscious. But I kept going. I couldn't stop. Didn't want to. I wasn't going back to those days again. Not ever. So I made sure I finished the job." He drops his gaze, ashamed. "Mum found us." Theo's jaw rolls. "From that day on, every time someone touched me, I jumped. I reacted. I had flashbacks and saw my father cuffing me, trying to groom me into a fighter. People were wary of me. It became instinctual to react, like a defense mechanism that I couldn't hold back." His face twists in agony, his eyes closing. "But honestly, I liked it. If people feared me, they didn't come close. They didn't dare touch me." Blue pools full of awe gaze at me. "But *you* did. *You* dared."

I can feel his pain. It's potent, penetrating me to my bones. "I knew you weren't a bad guy." He was forced to be this way. He can't help it. But under the iron body and hard face is a soft, loving heart. I have that heart. It's mine. "Were there no questions asked about your father? From the police?"

Theo shakes his head. "Andy covered for me. Or probably more for my mother. I knew she'd been involved with him for some time. After Penny's mother died, Dad's punches seemed to get harder. Andy hated him. One call to him from my mother had everything dealt with. Dad had a lot of enemies. It wasn't hard."

My mind goes to another crime Andy has taken care of. Trystan. It's been months since he *disappeared*, and not one person has come forward to report him missing. I had Andy check the records back in Manchester, too. Nothing. And he assured me, not for the first time, that Trystan's body will never be found. Once again, he's covered for Theo. And I'll never be able to thank him enough.

Lifting my finger, I trace over the beads of the rosary cascading down his shoulder. "You got these as a reminder."

Theo hums, relaxing under my touch. "I believed in God as a boy. Once I stopped going to Sunday school, bad things happened. My life wasn't good anymore. I still said the Lord's Prayer every day, but I don't think it was enough for him."

"You went back to the village you grew up in," I say, bringing the conversation round a full three-sixty. "That's where you were."

He nods mildly. "I went to church every morning. And I confessed my sins every evening. And still the guilt was there. It was too late for me. I'd abandoned him for too long." He blinks and laughs a little under his breath. "So I went to the club. I wanted to feel pain so intense I could feel nothing else. It didn't work."

I cave on the inside for him. His desperation, his pain, his crippling guilt. Nothing in the world could make me feel any sorrier. Pushing myself up, I straddle his lap and give him my hands to take to his shoulders. I hold on to them tightly, purposefully, as he regards me carefully. And I stare at him, determined. "I love you," I say, quickly placing my finger over his lips when they part. "If God thought it was too late for you, I wouldn't be here. He wouldn't have sent me to you." I take his hand and place it on my tummy, deciding that now is the time. I've held off for weeks, mainly to wrap my own mind around it, but also because I was worried about the gravity of it all. Babies are unpredictable. They have flailing limbs and they grow into toddlers that like to climb all over you.

Theo looks down at my tummy with a frown, and I go on, pulling in air to help me. "If God thought it was too late for you, he wouldn't give you a new life to take care of."

His eyebrows pinch in the middle. "What?"

"I'm pregnant," I say, plain and clear, as I push his hand into my tummy. Theo's eyes become progressively wider, his mouth dropping open, and I hold my breath, sitting back and waiting for it to sink in. While he stares at my stomach, I watch, fascinated, as his expression changes a hundred times, through countless emotions. There's wonder, there's shock, there's definitely happiness, and a million others, but the most acute of them all, the one I have considered the most and prepared myself for, is the fear.

"Izzy, you need to get off me." Theo pushes his back into the couch, distancing himself from me. "Please, you need to get up."

I do what I'm told quickly and jump up from his lap, and Theo follows slowly after with a few uncomfortable hisses, starting to half stalk, half hobble around the lounge. "But I haven't touched you in months." His hands come up to his hair and have a little tug. "Months, Izzy."

"Nine weeks, if you want specifics." I perch on the edge of the couch, my nervous hands wedged between my knees. I knew he would be shocked, but is he suggesting something here? "Theo, I hope you're not thinking what I think you're thinking."

"I don't know what the fucking hell I'm thinking." He swings around aggressively, and he pays for the sharp movement, hissing and clenching his ribs. "Damn." He starts breathing deeply, straightening back up. "Izzy, I thought you were on the pill."

"I am. Was." I correct myself.

"Then how?"

"I don't know. Maybe you have acid sperm." For the love of all things holy. It's happened. It's no good going over the hows and whys of it all. It won't change anything. I sag, trying not to let my budding frustration get the better of me. "Come and sit down," I order, patting the seat next to me.

"No, thanks." He begins with the half stalk, half hobble again, going up and down the room, stopping every now and then, opening his mouth to speak, then shutting it again and commencing half stalk, half hobble. He's making me dizzy.

"I know what you're scared of," I say, finally pulling his irritating circuit of the room to a stop. He looks at me in question, though he doesn't ask. "But you don't need to be," I assure him. "It's going to be fine."

"Izzy, I'm far from cured. That reflex is ingrained in me." His hopelessness is rife, and his doubt is strong. "Look what I did to you." He sighs, bringing his palms to his temples and dragging them down his beard. "I'll be a terrible father. The worst."

Resentment ignites in my gut and bubbles up to the surface, exploding. "Don't say that." I jump up and point at him, so fucking mad.

"Isn't it true?" he asks. "You'll never trust me with your baby. You'll be on the edge of your seat every moment of the day, and I'll be worse."

"*Our* baby," I correct him. "It's *our* damn baby, not mine. And I have a plan," I declare. I've thought about it so much—about therapy, shrinks, and counselors, all of which are lined up to help Theo with his surprisingly easy acceptance. But I had another idea last week when I was watching the Miami Open. I'm willing to try anything. I hold my finger up in indication for him to wait, dashing off to the bedroom and collecting my plan. I'm back in seconds, tipping the contents of the bag out at my feet, a hopeful smile on my face.

Theo looks at the floor, then to me, baffled. "We're going to play tennis?"

I can't roll my eyes. I guess the balls would suggest it. "No, I'm going to throw them at you."

He looks at me like I've totally lost my mind, and I've questioned a few times whether I have. I dip and collect a ball before pulling my arm back and lobbing it across the room without warning, aiming for his chest. His hand comes up and catches it with ease. "So you want to play catch?"

"You're not supposed to catch it." I take another ball and toss it with as much might as I can. And he catches it. "Theo!"

He laughs. "Izzy, if I don't catch it, it'll hit me."

"Exactly." I clap my hands, delighted.

"Why the hell would I let that happen?"

"Because after time, you'll get used to it. Unexpected touches, I mean. I'll throw balls at you all the time, and you'll learn to ignore them. I've been reading about exposure therapy, and I think it could really help you." I collect another ball and chuck it at his chest, and despite his two hands each holding a ball, he still catches the damn thing.

I growl, and his mouth forms a little O. "Oops." He drops all three balls at his feet. "Might take me a while to get the hang of this."

"At the very least, can we talk to your counselor about it at your next appointment?"

"What, about you throwing tennis balls at me for the next . . ." He drifts to a stop, thinking. "Seven months? Hoping I'll get used to it and not kill our child if he or she happens to touch me?"

I recoil, hurt. "You don't have to be so brutal."

"You've really been studying a lot about this, haven't you?"

I look away, a little embarrassed.

"Izzy?"

"Hmmm?" I don't look up.

"I love you."

I smile at the floor, slowly raising my head to find he's matching my gleam. "I love you, too."

"That's good, because I'd be fucked right off if I was doing this crazy shit for anything less than your love."

"So you'll try?"

"Anything."

I let out a squeal of joy and run at him, giving him plenty of time to prepare for my attack. "Thank you." I crash into him and immediately apologize for it. I've been chucking balls at him and all, and he's not even fully recovered yet.

He hushes me and tolerates his discomfort. "How many tennis balls did you buy?"

"A few...hundred."

He laughs and lifts me from my feet, ignoring my protests.

"Theo, put me down."

"Be quiet." His progress to the bed is slow, and my face remains tight with concern the whole way, but he's determined, and his smile through the obvious pain he's in is a joy to see. "There," he says, placing me on the end and nodding to the top of the bed. I start to shuffle up blindly, following his order, my keen eyes concentrating on his hands, which are slowly pushing his shorts down his thighs.

"You're in no condition," I murmur, my voice full of lust, my hands reaching to the hem of my T-shirt without thought and lifting it up over my head. Then I remove my bra. My statement is pointless, said through a silly sense of responsibility rather than objection. My blood is heating rapidly, rushing through my veins. My body is calling for him. My nipples are tingling sweetly. My eyes are heavy, my lips parted. I push my jeans down my legs and wriggle to get them off.

If he withdraws his offer, I might lose my mind. It's been months. *Months* since I've felt him. Months since he's fucked me blind. Months since we've connected, and now he's looking at me like he's looking at me, his blue eyes lazy and a slither of his tongue flashing across his wet lips. And that body. That big, strong body. He's not at full strength, the mass of bulk noticeably lacking, but he's still a mountain. He's still gorgeously perfect, and he still looks like a force to be reckoned with. None of this should matter. Deep down, I know I shouldn't be encouraging this, but I so need him inside me, dowsing the flames within.

Theo clicks his fingers, snapping me from my admiration. "It seems..." he whispers, resting his knee on the end of the bed, followed by his hand, and then his other knee and his other hand. He crawls slowly up, taking my ankle and pulling me down to him. My squeal of happiness muffles his hiss of pain. He has me caged beneath him, his torso resting on the forearm of his good arm. He smiles down at me. I smile back, pulling in air and holding it as he brings his face close to mine. "It seems that *you* are the one who is in no condition." He glances down the small gap between our fronts, his smile growing. "So I'll have to be gentle with you."

Dropping a chaste kiss on my chin, he scoots down my body and caresses my tummy with his tongue, licking around my belly button in sure, careful rotations. I smile on the inside, aware that he's using my condition as an excuse for his own need to be careful with himself. I can't take it away from him. My body goes lax, my mind clears, and I hum in contentment, bringing my hands up to the headboard and holding on to the bars.

"That's good." I sigh, feeling his finger hook into the side of my knickers and draw them down, his lips following their path and kissing their way down my legs.

"So good," he agrees, working his way up, teasing around my inner thighs. "Smells good, too." His tongue meets my slick opening and laps straight up the middle. My grip on the bars tightens, my body arching gradually as I moan. "God, I'd forgotten how sweet you taste." Gentle kisses are rained over every tiny piece of me, and I start to writhe on the bed, squirming and groaning and yanking at the bars above me.

"Theo," I pant, my clitoris kicking consistently. "Theo, please." Sitting himself up, he reaches to the bedside table and pulls the drawer open, taking out the cuffs, and I watch closely as he gestures for my hands.

He takes ages, his sore body moving slowly as he restrains me, and when he finishes, he spreads himself all over me, nudging my legs apart with his knee. "Where you should be," he whispers, lifting his hips and falling to my opening, slowly pushing his way inside me.

"Oh . . . my . . . God." I surrender to the feeling and melt into the mattress, the gradual sensation of him filling me, taking me off into a blissful state of appreciation. He gives me time, lets me gradually become accustomed to his girth again, circling and easing his way to filling me completely. Our eyes are glued together, his mouth nearly touching mine. The love and need passing between us is potent. So powerful. So needed.

"Okay?" he whispers.

"Perfect," I reply, absorbing his first plunge on an inhale. "You?"

"Better than perfect." His forehead meets mine, slippery across my skin. "You're a miracle cure, sweetheart."

He starts a tender rock into me, his grinding slow and his momentum steady. Pleasure is licking up and down my spine, my body rolling in waves to match Theo's moves flawlessly. The friction is divine. The pressure delicious. Having him taking me so worshipfully and lovingly is needed. My *condition* has nothing to do with his pace and handling of me. And I can't help thinking that Theo's condition doesn't, either, though it's an obvious handicap. This is a reunion, not just of our more fragile bodies, but of our souls, too. It's slow, it's careful, and it's devoted. He's refusing to break our eye contact as he works us both into a calm fever. He's growing within me, and the pressure is building in my core. He nods at me, pushing his lips to mine and kissing me achingly slowly, taking us both to the pinnacle of pleasure. My world goes hazy as my climax ripples through me, and Theo starts to groan, increasing the pressure of his mouth on mine when he joins me. Our wet bodies rub and slip, hardening in unison as we strive together to maintain our kiss.

And the flow of pleasure subsides only when Theo's body softens, his rolling tongue leading the way and slowing to a stop. "Wow," he whispers against my lips, brushing from side to side.

I sigh my reply, feeling utterly replete. "Are you hurting?"

"I've never felt more alive." His eyes close and his face disappears into my neck. "Thank you."

"What for?"

"For not giving up hope. For never deserting me, even when I wasn't here." He kisses his way up my cheek to my nose, pulling back a fraction to be sure he has my eyes. I wish I could stop them from welling up, but it's a battle I would never win if I tried, so I don't bother trying. He smiles, taking a fingertip and gently wiping under my eye. "You're stronger than me, Izzy."

I frown, not grasping how he's come to that conclusion. He's a beast. "But—"

Lips press to mine quickly, quieting me. "Let me finish," he mumbles, biting my bottom lip in light warning. "I'm not talking about physical strength; I'd crush you."

"Please don't," I beg jokingly, encouraging a beam of epic proportions to break out, his dimple raging. His dark blue eyes shimmer beautifully.

"I'm man enough to admit that I'm nothing without you. I'm man enough to admit that I'm so frightened that I'll hurt you again." He flicks his eyes up to my restraints, misery replacing the happiness of a moment ago. "I'll get past this," he vows. "There *will* be a day when you can have free rein over me." His eyes come down to mine, pleading with me unnecessarily. "For you and our baby, I can do it."

"I believe you." I wish now more than ever that I could throw my arms around his shoulders. "Release me," I order, pulling at the cuffs. He obeys my command, working quickly, and a few moments later, I'm wrapped around him tightly, squeezing my love and faith into him. I know he can do this. We'll figure it out together.

"I have a gift for you," he tells me, forcing me away from him. Leaving me hugely curious, he gets up from the bed and slowly walks naked across the room to the dresser. He pulls out a file and wanders back over, holding it up. "Though you've kind of ruined my surprise a little with your bombshell." He nods at my tummy.

I regard him carefully as he presents me with the file, and I take it tentatively. "What's this?"

He sits on the edge of the bed. "You've been looking after me," he says, and I frown some more because I have no idea what relevance that has to this file. "You quit your job, and I wish I could say that I didn't want you to do that, but I can't. I wanted you here with me, and I wanted you to look after me." He shrugs. "It's selfish, but I wouldn't change it."

"Neither would I," I reply, still not getting what this is all about. "I wanted to look after you." The fact that he can't bear anyone touching him, and I know how to handle his delicate condition, is beside the point. I would have done it regardless.

His lips quirk. "See? My very own Florence Nightingale."

I laugh out loud. "I'm a nurse. Just a nurse."

"Be quiet and open the file."

I eye him suspiciously, pouting as I follow his order. "What is it?" I ask, pulling out the first sheet. I scan the paper. "An application form?" I ask, confusion rampant in my tone. It's complete, too, with all my details filling the spaces. Then I nearly choke when I notice the heading on the sheet. My eyes shoot to his. "Theo?"

"It's your application to study medicine."

"What?"

"You've been accepted. The fees are paid, and all your papers are in there. You let go of your dream to be a doctor. I want you to have it back. It's the one thing I can do for you. You don't have to worry about financial support. I'll support you. I want you to have your dream."

"My dream is you." My lip begins to tremble, and I drop the sheet, my quivering hands not helping. I can't believe he's done this.

He takes my hands and squeezes. "You already have me. I want you to have this, too. As well as me." He rests his hand on my tummy. "And this. As soon as you're ready, I want you to pursue it. I want you to be a doctor. It's just one more reason for me to be in awe of you. One more reason on top of the hundreds there are already to love you and be proud of you."

I place my hand over his and press it against me, emotion racking my body. "And what about this?" Becoming a doctor takes years of study, stress, and hard work. And be a mum?

His eyes drop to our hands. And he smiles. He smiles so widely and so brightly, I'm nearly knocked off the bed. "I never imagined myself as a stay-at-home dad."

A happiness so rich spirals through me. "You'll be a stay-at-home dad?" I ask, imagining him now, my big, scary man...with a baby strapped to his colossal chest in one of those carrier things. The mental image delights me more than I can describe. It also turns me on.

"Yes," he answers simply, nodding to himself in agreement.

My smile must be breaking records in the brightest category. Theo looks at me, sureness and determination plastered all over his handsome face. He reads my thoughts, opening his arms, and I dive into them. Hiding his pain with a laugh of pure elation, he holds me the tightest he ever has. He's determined to fix himself. Not that I would dream of telling him, but I couldn't care less if I was never able to touch him freely. If it was just me and him, I'd find a way to manage it. I'd find a way to accept it. Because I already touch him in a different way, and it's far more meaningful than any physical touch. Our connection is earth-shattering even when I'm tied up and unable to reciprocate in that one small area of our relationship.

Because I touch his soul.

Every moment of the day, I touch him there. It's deep. *So* deep. I have his love, which means everything and more. But it's not going to be just us. There's going to be a third person, so I will do whatever it takes to help Theo. Yet though my resolve is fierce, it isn't a scratch on the purpose I can feel penetrating me from the force of his cuddle.

He'll do this, I have no doubt. Our baby has touched him already. In the deepest part of Theo, our growing baby's hand is resting next to mine on its daddy's soul.

EPILOGUE

THEO

I'm a smart man. I'm knowledgeable, and I like to think that I can turn my hand to most things. Not much in life has me scratching my head and considering seeking advice, but this thing right here has me stumped. I pull at the various straps, my mind aching. The instructions make no sense. The pads and clips are all over the fucking place.

"This is going to keep my baby safe?" I ask myself, tossing the contraption aside and collapsing back in the chair in complete exasperation. My ears prick up when I hear a muffled noise emanate from the baby monitor, and I look across to the table where it sits, seeing a few lights flash at me.

I don't hang around to wait for a follow-up sign that my girl is awake. I'm up from the chair like lightning and rushing to the nursery. The sound of her gurgling brings an instant smile to my face. As I pace over to the crib, my grin stretches wider, my eyes catching a glimpse of her blankets rising and falling where she's wriggling around. And the moment her face is in my vision, sparks of happiness overwhelm me. Her stunning green eyes find me in a heartbeat, and she stills for a second, taking me in. Then she smiles, a gummy, adorable smile, her little limbs starting to thrash excitedly. God, she's the most beautiful little thing I've ever seen.

"Hey, princess." My hands are in the crib and scooping her out fast, my palms spanning her entire midriff and then some. She continues to kick in my hold as I sink my face into her neck and breathe her into me. She smells fucking divine. "Hmmm," I hum, squeezing her, relishing the pure gorgeousness of her baby skin and smell. "I could eat you," I say, meaning it. She laughs the laugh that has her inhaling and holding her breath. I fucking love that laugh.

Freeing her from my bearded face, I hold her up in front of me. "How'd you sleep?" I ask, laughing when her grabby hands shoot for my face and start smacking and pulling. "Good?"

Her answer is a breathy baby squeal.

"Come on." I bring her to my chest and hold her there with one palm across her back, grabbing her blanket with the other. "You can help Daddy figure out this carry thing."

I stride out of the nursery and into the lounge, taking a seat on the couch and sitting her on my knee. She starts bucking and bouncing, shouting for the big square of pink fluff that I'm holding in front of her. I give her the blanket and pull the tangled mess of straps over. "Easy-to-follow instructions, it said."

I'm mindful that Lola will be shouting for some milk soon, so I sit her in the corner of the couch and surround her with pillows, getting her all comfy and secure, before I drop to my knees on the floor and spread out the material and straps for one last attempt.

After five minutes of crisscrossing, pulling, and tying, I think I might be halfway there. "Looking good, Lola," I say, collecting her from the couch and laying her in the middle of the contraption. She beams up at me, legs kicking out and all. "You're laughing at me, aren't you?" I guide each of her legs through what I'm assuming are leg holes, and I frown when I find an odd strap dangling down, holding it up as I try to figure out what this one does.

Lola's laughs suddenly change into impatient shouts. Damn, she's hungry. I look at my watch and note it's already fifteen minutes past her feeding time. "Okay, okay." The door behind me opens, and I look back to find Callum striding in. "Hey," I say, returning my attention to my princess. His heavy boots approach until he's standing above us, looking down at the mess of baby and straps before me. Lola's eyes light up, and the hungry shouts transform into chuckles again, the sight of Uncle Callum making her momentarily forget that she's starving.

"Evening, princess." Callum dips and chucks her cheek, smiling brightly at my daughter. "What's Daddy doing to you?"

"Trying to get this stupid thing together." I drop the strap in frustration. The other one we have, the one that's kept Lola close to my chest for the past ten months and that she's outgrown, wasn't this complicated.

"What is it?" Callum eyes the contraption with pinched brows.

"A baby carrier."

"It is?"

"Supposedly," I mutter, feeding Lola's chubby legs back out through the holes and scooping her up. "We don't like this one, do we, princess?" I kiss her cheek and stand.

Callum claims the pile of straps and joins me, turning it one way, then the other. "I think I've got it." He holds it up and gestures for me to give him an arm, so I shift Lola across my chest. "There," he says once I've fed my arm through the hole. "Other," he orders, prompting me to swap Lola to my other side.

Her little hand catapults toward my cheek and grabs on, yanking at my beard. "Ouch!"

"You need to shave that mess off," Callum grunts.

"Izzy won't let me."

"Pussy," he grumbles, and I smile, my eyes clenching shut as Lola continues to abuse my face. Giving Callum my other arm, I feel him pulling at the straps on my back, muttering under his breath. "Did you buy an XXXL?"

"One size fits all," I toss over my shoulder.

"Except Theo Kane."

"Fu—" I just suck back my intended curse. "Shut up. Is it secure?"

Callum yanks at the straps, jerking me back a little. "Safe as houses." He rounds me and puts his arms out for me to pass him Lola. "Come see Uncle Callum," he coos, losing everything masculine about him. I shouldn't pass comment. Since Izzy bulldozed into my life, my masculinity has diminished a little every day. Then Lola arrived and any testosterone that was remaining disintegrated at the mere sight of her.

"You sound like a girl," I say for the sake of it as I pass her over, ignoring his high eyebrows. "Be careful with her."

"Fuck off." It's a lame attempt to win some manliness back. He lifts Lola and blows a raspberry on her romper-covered belly, and she chuckles. I scowl, taking my palms to her ears and covering them, glaring at Callum. "Sorry." He shrugs and returns his attention to my laughing daughter, while I look down to the contraption that's now strapped to my chest. I pull out a pad of material, concluding it's where Lola should slot in. She's suddenly dangling before me, Callum holding her out.

"In here?" I point to the most obvious place and Callum nods, bringing Lola forward and aiming her legs for the holes. "No, she faces outward," I tell him. "So she can see around."

Callum turns her in his arms with a roll of his eyes and starts again. I take her tiny ankles and help guide them down until she's slotted into position. Then she begins to shout again, clearly losing her patience with the two oafs scratching their heads over a simple baby carrier.

"Okay, princess," I soothe, jiggling her a little, ensuring she's safe while Callum finds two Velcro straps and fixes them in place. "Comfy?" I ask her, dropping my lips to the back of her head and inhaling. "Damn, I'll never get enough of that smell." It's like a potent injection of life into me each time I take a hit. Lifting my head, I find Callum grinning at me. "What?"

"Nothing." He reaches for Lola's head and strokes over her fine covering of soft dark hair. "She's growing by the day."

I look down proudly, feeling her comforting weight on my chest. "She has her daddy's appetite."

"I just hope she doesn't inherit her daddy's build."

I toss him a dirty look. "She's Izzy through and through." I'm smiling again when Lola starts kicking her little legs against me, each hit enhancing the feel of contentment residing deep inside me. I had nothing to fear where touching is concerned. Not with my daughter. She pulls and grabs at me and it doesn't faze me in the slightest. It feels right, somehow. Natural.

From the moment she arrived, things changed. She was like an instant cure. A miracle. She's my little miracle. My handicap vanished like it was never there, and the weight that disappeared from my shoulders with it was almost too overpowering to bear. People can touch me, and for the first time since that awful day when I turned on my father, I don't react. Not even when I'm not expecting it. My brain is always switched on, and Lola is always at the forefront of it. My only handicap now is my crippling love for her.

With a smile of wonder, I drop one more kiss onto the back of her head and she shouts, thrashing again, reminding me that she's hungry.

A hand lands on my upper arm, and I look up to find Callum regarding me with a tiny smile on his face. He knows what I'm thinking. He appreciates the wonder that has me taking stock most days. After I've returned his smile, he drops his hold and clears his throat, locating his lost testosterone. "Come on, you giant pussy." He turns and strides to the door, yanking it open and disappearing through it. I clear my throat, too, striding after him . . . with Lola strapped to my chest.

As I descend the stairs to the entrance hall, Jefferson appears, holding a tray with Lola's bottle sitting in the center. "And how is the lady of the house this evening?" he asks, his eyes glittering behind his round specs at the sight of my daughter. On cue, Lola starts bucking against my front, her hands bunching and flexing as Jefferson nears with her milk. "Ooh, someone's hungry," he chuckles, stopping before me and offering me the tray. I take the bottle and shake it, flipping the lid off and squirting a bit on my wrist while Lola gets more vocal. "Perfect temperature," Jefferson informs me. I know it will be, but habit prevents me from taking his word for it.

"Thanks, Jefferson." I turn and follow Callum to the corridor that leads to the Playground. I pick up my pace when Lola's cries of hunger become more piercing, landing in the office quickly and hurrying to get her out of the straps on my chest. "Okay, princess," I soothe, hating the sound of her distressed sobs. Finding my chair, I cradle her in my arms and take the bottle to her mouth. She latches on and drinks ravenously, going soft and still in my arms. I breathe out and relax as Callum takes a seat opposite me. "What have you got to tell me?"

"Your mother's been upsetting Penny again." He rolls his eyes, following my lead.

"What about this time?" Penny took charge of the girls more than a year ago, and my mother wasn't best pleased. It's like managing two bitching schoolgirls, for fuck's sake.

"I don't know. If Penny says it's black, Judy says it's white."

"I'll have a word." I sigh, quickly checking Lola in my arms. Her little chubby hands are holding the bottle over mine, her eyes fixed on me. "What about the fight schedule?" I ask, ripping my eyes away from her. It's always a challenge.

"All set, the first being Friday." Callum chucks a file on the desk and opens the sleeve, revealing the betting stats for the anticipated clash between a local boy and one of the top fighters here at the club. "Shit," I blurt, and immediately scold myself for it, looking down at Lola. She's oblivious, of course. "They're some seriously hefty figures."

"It's split. Either way, we're profiting here. Penny's drafted the dancing schedule and wants your approval."

Lola starts coughing and I whip the bottle out of her mouth, setting it on the desk and sitting her up on my lap. "How many dancers has she got lined up?" I start gently patting Lola's back, feeling her little belly inflated under my other palm.

"Eight."

"Eight?" I question. "It's usually six."

"It'll be a profitable night for the girls. Penny wanted them to share the potential tips."

"Because they don't earn enough already?" I laugh, just as Lola lets out an almighty belch and literally deflates in my hold.

"Fucking hell," Callum blurts. I shoot him a look, and he immediately apologizes for his bad language. "Sorry. But, damn, Theo. How did that noise even come from such a tiny thing?"

"She's a greedy girl." I smile, so fucking proud. But I have to admit, for such a small, adorable thing, she produces some pretty horrific noises. And don't get me started on what she evacuates from her body. On that thought, her little face turns bright red and she strains. I sit back, wary, as she stares at me. Then the rippling sounds of an exploding bottom echo around my office.

"Good God," Callum mumbles, prompting me to look up at him. "Are you gonna tell me she's her mother through and through again?"

I laugh under my breath as Lola goes floppy in my hands. "That's my girl." I look up when the door of my office swings open and my sister appears, a piece of paper in her hand. She looks all business...until she clocks who's sitting on my lap. "Baby girl!" She tosses the paper she's holding on my desk and seizes Lola from my arms. "Come to Auntie Penny."

I glare at my sister, annoyed. "Be careful with her," I mutter, my arms feeling lost without my daughter in them.

"Oh, be quiet," she retorts, not losing her smile. It's so good to see her looking so well. She's finally pulled herself around, started caring for herself. I was stunned when she asked me for a change in position at the Playground. Stunned but happy. And, of course, more than willing to do whatever I could to help. And it made sense, since I signed over half of this place to her. My time here is coming to an end. Penny's settled into managing the girls perfectly, her experience in the job giving her an advantage. She understands them. Between her, Mum, and Callum, this place will be fine.

I grab the paper for something to occupy myself with, scanning the lineup of dancers for Friday. It all looks fine. That's ten seconds killed. I throw it down on my desk and search for something else to do, struggling to find anything. Everything is always in tip-top order these days—Mum, Penny, and Callum running things smoothly, freeing me up to take care of my girl. I wouldn't have it any other way. Lola and I have been busy overseeing the new build in the village where I grew up. Only a few more weeks and I'll be moving my girls out of here to the tranquil green pastures of the countryside. I have my future perfectly mapped out for the first time in my life. A quaint village school, my childhood church, a garden that stretches for acres with no neighbors within a mile radius. Perfect. I smile, falling into a daydream. A daydream that soon won't be a dream at all.

I watch as Penny fusses over Lola, walking around the room bouncing my baby in her arms. "What's going on with you and Judy?" I ask, desperate to put that one last grievance to rest.

Penny gives me a tired look. "She needs reminding that the girls are my responsibility. Her job is the finance side of things. Tell her to keep her nose out."

"Why can't you get along?" I ask, for the millionth time. My life would be truly complete if the two of them would stop with the cat snipes.

"Because, dear brother, I am the bastard child of our dear bastard father." She tucks Lola onto her side and gives me a knowing look. "She hates me."

I sigh, exasperated. My sister has a thick skin, and I'm thankful. Not many would stick around to face the daily wrath of my mother. "I'll speak to her."

"Again?" Penny asks, a curve to her lips. She's right. It'll make no difference. "Don't sweat it. I can handle her. We have a love-hate thing going on. Keeps us both on our toes." She winks at me, and I smile in return. I know they tolerate each other for me. It could be worse, I suppose. Penny's nose suddenly wrinkles, and she looks at her niece suspiciously. "I think someone's filled her nappy."

"Her changing bag's over there." I point across the office, with no faith my hint will be taken.

"That's nice," Penny quips. "You're an expert these days."

She heads over to give me back what's mine, but is interrupted halfway when Mum comes bowling in. My arms hang suspended in the air.

"Ah, there she is!" Mum hurries over to Penny. "Give her here." She claims her granddaughter and smothers her chubby face with kisses.

My arms drop heavily. "Like pass the fucking parcel," I mutter.

"Ewww!" Mum holds Lola at arm's length, mirroring Penny's turned-up nose of a minute ago. Lola isn't fazed. She laughs and kicks enthusiastically in Mum's arms. "Stinky girl! Yes you are!"

Penny swipes up her dance schedule and strolls out. "Her changing bag is over there," she calls over her shoulder.

Mum doesn't reply, but hurries over to the corner and collects up Lola's bag. "I'll see to her," she says, taking my girl away.

"Bring her straight back," I yell as the door slams behind her. And I feel lost again. I glance down at my watch, counting the minutes until I can collect Izzy.

"Want to come and check out the new cage?" Callum asks, sensing I need something to keep me busy until Mum brings Lola back.

I'm up from my chair quickly, giving my answer. We wander through to the club together, finding a few girls practicing routines on the stage. "I don't miss it, you know," I muse, taking in the space. I only venture into the Playground when I need to, and I really don't need to these days.

"Well, that's because you have better things to occupy yourself with." Callum leads the way over to the new cage, which is sitting prominently on the other side of the club. The metal is shiny, the floor spotless. Not for long. Sweat and blood will soon take care of that. "How's the house coming along?"

The mention of our new haven in the countryside lifts me. "Great. We should be set to move in a few weeks."

"And you're ready for a life in the middle of nowhere?" Callum asks, glancing across at me.

I only have to think about my happy childhood in the village to know I'm doing the right thing. "This is no place to bring up a child."

Callum opens the door of the cage and gestures for me to enter, and I step up and wander into the middle, gazing around. "Nice," I muse, and Callum laughs.

"What?"

His chuckles continue as he looks at me standing in the middle of the cage, his finger pointing to my torso. "You're such a mean motherfucker."

I look down with a frown, reminded that my chest is still wrapped in a baby carrier. I join him in his amusement, the irony not escaping me. "Hey, how's Jess?"

"Annoying," he answers curtly. "As always."

I laugh, deep and low, making for the exit. There's another love-hate relationship. The two have never gotten things on. It's frustrating for everyone who shares company with them. The chemistry is as strong today as it was when they met, but both refuse to act on it. I have no clue why. "Tell me—"

His hand comes up quickly and silences me. "I've already told you, I don't know whether I want to fuck her or strangle her most. It's taking me a while to figure it out."

"Both?"

He turns and walks away from me, tired of the conversation again. "She rubs me up the wrong way."

"You and Jess are Lola's godparents. You have an obligation to get along."

He scoffs and pushes his way out of the cage. "I get along with her just fine." He turns and holds the door open for me. "As long as I don't look at her."

I smirk at him as I exit, taking another quick peek at my watch. Six o'clock. Time to go pick up Izzy. "I'll catch you later." I make my way back to the house in search of my girl, my pace quickening the closer I get. I can feel her in my bones.

I spot Mum bouncing Lola on her hip as Jefferson fusses over my daughter. I swear, the girl has turned the whole house into an institute of pussies. Lola must sniff me out, because her little head darts toward me as I make my way over, ready to claim what's mine. She beams at me, so pleased to see me again. "Come to Daddy." I take her from Mum's hold. "Time to pick Mummy up."

Jefferson holds out her pink blanket and coat. "There's a chill in the air tonight."

"Seat?" I ask, being immediately presented with Lola's car seat by Mum. Crouching, I settle Lola in the chair and strap her in.

"I don't know how you think you're going to manage when you move out," Mum muses, placing Lola's blanket over her lap and tucking her in. I flick her a tired look out of the corner of my eye. It's a statement she makes daily. She knows I'll manage just fine. She's just sulking because she won't have constant access to Lola when she's at work.

"We'll be okay."

"And it's not healthy having her permanently strapped to your chest. She'll start to get separation anxiety." She reaches for the carrier still attached to me and tugs a little. "Are you going to take this off?"

"No." I take the handle of Lola's seat and rise. I don't know if I'll get it back on again. "See you later." I wander out and find my car waiting, the passenger door open, ready for me to load Lola in. She's secure on the front seat in a few easy seconds, and after kissing her forehead, I make my way round and jump in.

* * *

"Shall we wait here, or shall we go find her?" I ask Lola when we pull up outside the college. She starts thrashing in her seat, arms and legs kicking out, and I nod in agreement. "Good choice."

I jump out and round the car, unclipping her from her seat and feeding her legs through the holes on her carrier, which is still attached to my front. Once she's safely in position, we go on our way, the invisible pull leading me to Izzy getting stronger the farther into the college we go. Lola's little hands are wrapped around each of my index fingers, squeezing, her excitement growing.

Every person who passes us as we weave through the corridors to the lecture hall has dopey eyes, all of them cooing and sighing when they see us. My chest swells with a pride so rich, it makes me wonder how I got by without this unbelievable sense of contentment in my life. I feel so complete. So fulfilled and lucky. I smile in return at all of them, but I don't stop for them to swoon all over my little girl. I march on my way, eager to find my other girl.

We reach the lecture hall, and I deflate a little when I see the door still closed. A quick check of my watch tells me we're five minutes early. Unable to resist, I peek through the glass of the door, spotting her immediately among the dozens of medical students. She's relaxed back in her chair, a pad on her lap, a pen held at her mouth, chewing as she listens closely. My heart does a little gallop and an inappropriately timed surge of heat rushes south.

"Damn, your mummy is a vision." I sigh, and Lola shouts her agreement. "Shhh," I hush. "We need to be quiet. She's not done." Lola squeals her objection, bouncing on my front. I laugh under my breath and watch Izzy concentrating on the guy up front pointing to pictures of balls and lines on the board. Genes and blood cells, I think Izzy told me, or some complex stuff like that. She seemed to know exactly what she was talking about. I, however, didn't have the foggiest idea what all the medical jargon that spilled from her mouth meant. Though I did pay attention and expressed my interest.

"Your mummy is clever, too," I tell Lola. "Beautiful and clever." I rest my shoulder on the doorframe, having to dip my head a little to maintain my view of her. Izzy's fingers repeatedly go to her hair and push it back over her ears, the mid-length dark waves refusing to stay put. I look down at the back of my baby girl's head and drop a kiss there. "You have your mummy's hair." I laugh, probably too loudly, when Lola blows a huge wet raspberry.

"Shhh, you'll get us in trouble." I look up, and right on cue, Izzy looks over her shoulder and spots us through the glass. Her face, fresh and free of makeup, glows the moment she claps eyes on us.

I grab Lola's hand and hold it up, directing her little wave. "Say 'Hi, Mummy,'" I whisper, making Izzy chuckle. She throws a quick, discreet wave in return and turns back to the lecturer.

It's a long five minutes before everyone in the room finally stands and starts collecting up their books and bags, and Izzy is the first to break free from the crowds, hurrying to the door. I move back, and she bursts into the corridor, dropping her bag to the floor and going straight for my chest to claim Lola. Our daughter is squirming like a worm against me, so excited to see her.

"Oh my God, I've missed you today." She unhooks Lola with ease and lifts her from the carrier on my chest, hauling her in for a squeeze, closing her eyes in contentment. I look down at the contraption strapped to my chest, wondering how the fuck she figured it out so quickly. "New toy?" she asks, and I look up to find her grinning at the baby carrier.

I wave a dismissive hand, my heart turning to mush as I watch the reunion of my girls, my brain forcing my body to remain where it is until they're done. I need a cuddle, too. Izzy removes her face from Lola's neck and smiles up at me. "I'm certain you only come to collect me because you love the attention Lola gets you." She moves in and reaches up on her tippy-toes, pushing her lips to my scruffy cheek.

I scoff half-heartedly and slip an arm around her waist, pulling her in. "Rubbish," I lie. She has me nailed. For most of my adult life, people have given me a wide berth. And I liked it. I loved the fact that most were too wary to come near. Funny how having a baby strapped to your chest solves that. "Are you ready?" I ask, relinquishing my hold, but only because I know the sooner I get them home, the happier I'll be and the more devoted time I can spend with them. Izzy nods, and I dip to collect her bag, as always, staggered by the weight of it loaded with medical textbooks. Tucking her into my side, I start to walk them out to the car.

"My boobs are going to burst," she grumbles, shifting a little to ease the pressure.

I wince in sympathy, knowing how much she suffers. She's called me a few times in tears, her aching breasts heightening her emotion, saying she wasn't sure if she could continue studying. I talked her down calmly and quickly before she did something she would regret. Like quit the course. "Good day?" I ask, trying to distract her from her sore boobs.

"Long," she replies, seeming a little unenthusiastic to share any more than that. I understand, so I don't push for more, just cuddle her into my side harder, being careful of the boobs. She's expressed her desire to shut down from studies the moment she's free from the college and back with her family. The thought prompts a smile. Family. I have my love, and I have my daughter. The good to counteract all the badness of my life. The pure to overshadow the tainted. The peace to drown my demons.

* * *

As is routine now, Izzy bathes Lola once we're home before getting her ready for bed and curling up on the couch for her bedtime feed. And as is routine for me, I sit at the opposite end silently watching the beautiful sight of my daughter suckling from Izzy's breast. There are not many things these days that give me greater peace or pleasure than the vision of my two girls connected so intimately. Izzy's head is resting back, her eyes closed lightly, and Lola is drifting in and out of sleep, her mouth stopping and starting with tired sucks.

Once I'm certain that Lola's had her fill and her suckling stops and doesn't restart, I edge up from the couch and move quietly toward them. Izzy's eyes flip open when I gently gather Lola from her arms, her sleepy smile appreciative. She covers herself and sighs, leaving me to lay our daughter down for the night.

I don't remove my wonder-filled eyes from Lola's angelic face, navigating my way to the nursery without needing to look up. Gently laying her down, I tuck her in tightly and spend a few moments watching her sleeping, once again silently trying to come to terms with the fact that she is mine. "Goodnight, princess," I whisper, dipping low to kiss her baby skin.

Making my way back to the lounge, I head for Izzy. She must hear my footsteps, because her head turns on her dainty neck to find me, her take-me-to-bed eyes hitting me with force. My cock lunges behind my jeans, virtually stripping me of breath. I say nothing and scoop her up from the couch. Her arms go around my neck and cling on as I pace toward our bedroom and lay her gently on the bed. "Time for you to unwind," I declare, pulling my T-shirt up over my head and tossing it aside. Her eyes drink me in, her exhaustion disappearing and being replaced with a longing I appreciate every day. My body's reaction to her is as strong now as it was the moment I found her. Blood rushes to my cock and pounds its presence, and I groan in response, slipping my thumbs into the waistband of my jeans and drawing them slowly down. Her panting breaths become shallower with every inch of myself I reveal, until her eyes are glossy with lust. "Take your clothes off, Izzy," I order, stepping out of my jeans and kicking them to the side.

Her eyes drag over my torso, up to my eyes, a sliver of her wet tongue gliding across her bottom lip. Pushing herself to her knees, she holds my eyes while she slowly, purposely slowly, unbuttons the front of her blouse. The physical battle I'm having to stop myself from lurching forward and ripping it open is painful. There's no bra underneath. That gets discarded the moment she's through the door, and though the reason for her relieving herself of the material that keeps her swollen breasts secure during the day is pure relief, for me, it's like a red flag to a bull. It enhances the torture of having to wait for this time at the end of our day for us to reunite. It's plain...fucking...agony, made just about bearable by the knowledge and reason that my daughter needs Izzy more than I do. Only just, but she does.

Waiting with bated breath for Izzy to put me out of my misery, I gulp down some restraint, and she smiles, knowing the willpower it's taking me. Then she slides her blouse off one shoulder, giving me a painful peek of one swollen breast. Beads of sweat form on my brow, my hands twitching at my sides. "Stop messing with me, Izzy," I warn, stepping forward. Her lips curve and she drops the shoulder on the other side. I let out an audible moan, talking some reason into my desperate bones. I mustn't grab them. Gently does it with the boobs.

"Tell me," she whispers, ridding her arms of the shirt and slowly pushing her jeans down her legs. Tossing them across the room, she reclines to her back and opens her legs, pushing her fingers into the tops of her knickers. "Are you going to fuck me like a whore?"

I smirk, reaching forward and grabbing her knickers, yanking them down her legs. She squeals and squirms, laughing, as I wrench her knees apart to make room for me. I settle between her legs, holding her arms above her head, but I'm sure not to rest too much of my weight on her tender breasts, though I make damn sure my cock is pushing into her core. Her breath hitches at the contact, so I circle before lifting my hips and letting my solid dick fall to her opening. The slickness of her combined with the dripping head of my erection has her shouting despairingly. "How the tables have turned," I whisper, leaning down and biting her lip, pulling the swollen flesh through my teeth.

"Let go of my hands," she begs, fighting against my hold.

"No." I swivel and drive deeply into her, our connection sending my world into a spin.

"Theo!" Her hips thrust upward, meeting mine, sending me oh so fucking deep. "Release me."

I smile through my paralysis and force my hands to surrender her wrists, giving her what she wants.

And, most significantly, what I *need*.

Her touch.

Slipping over my skin, grabbing viciously, and forcing my body closer to hers. The feel of her all over me is out of this world.

The hands of the woman who touched me and refused to let go.

The hands of the woman who cured me.

Acknowledgments

As ever, a million thank-yous to everyone who makes each book I write possible. I feel like I'm running out of ways to express my gratitude, but I hope you all know by now how much each and every one of you means to me. And a special mention to my real-life man, Jamie. I know I'm impossible when I'm lost in my fictional worlds, but I always come back to you. Thank you for not only supporting me but also validating my dreams. And for loving and protecting me so fiercely.

About the Author

Jodi Ellen Malpas was born and raised in the Midlands town of Northampton, England, where she lives with her two boys and a beagle. She is a self-professed daydreamer, a Converse and mojito addict, and has a terrible weak spot for alpha males. Writing powerful love stories and creating addictive characters has become her passion—a passion she now shares with her devoted readers.

Her novels have hit bestseller lists for the *New York Times*, *USA Today*, *Sunday Times*, and various other international publications, and can be read in more than twenty-four languages around the world.

You can learn more at:
   JodiEllenMalpas.co.uk
   Twitter @JodiEllenMalpas
   Facebook.com/JodiEllenMalpas

Can't get enough of Jodi Ellen Malpas?
Don't miss her other books!

THIS MAN SERIES

ONE NIGHT TRILOGY

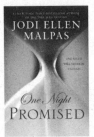
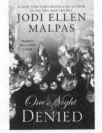
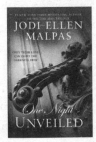

STANDALONES